Intimate Nightmares

Krymzen Hall

Black Lacquer/Silk Linen Publishing

Texas

ISBN: 978-0-692-16143-2

Black Lacquer/Silk Linen Publishing: Texas

Visit: Krymzenhall.com

Printed in the United States of America

Author's Note

We are born into either fortune or misfortune, depending on the view we see as we age. I am of the misfortunate type and no, my view on that hasn't changed. I don't look back on my childhood with any sense of nostalgia, or longing to relive it for just a day or two, as I'm sure many people do. In fact, if I had my choice, I'd erase that part of me (or set it on fire) and begin life at twenty-one-ish, fresh, with the clarity and maturity of a functional adult, the clarity that took decades to find.

Even though I learned a lot through a challenging young life, I don't see my childhood as a learning experience. I see it as one sustained, incredibly long bad dream.

I got lucky. I turned into a wonderful adult, one who cares, one who hates hate, one who knows right from wrong, and one who would do anything for just *about* anybody (hey, I'm kind, not stupid). It's utterly remarkable how somebody can leave behind a dysfunctional, dreadful life in early adulthood and turn into a remarkable person.

Not everybody makes it out.

After I had left home, though, it took years, much therapy, and supportive people to truly heal. Truth be told, some things stay with me, and, the most I can do, is forgive myself, ask others to forgive me, and move on the same way God has forgiven me and expects me to move on to do His will. This doesn't mean I forget. I'll never forget.

I bet it's the same way with you, and this is the best advice I can give.

True, things could have been worse for me. But my hell is my hell, and I have the right to own it—and to loathe it.

To this day, I sometimes wonder what life would have been like for me if I had been of the fortunate births. And I do ask God why I wasn't. I suppose this book and all I bring to it is why.

I did a lot of bad shit when young, the product of an incomplete frontal lobe and whole lot of poverty, coupled with parents who had no business being parents. Don't get me wrong, I loved them, and they did the best they could with their limitations. But, those limitations came in abundance. Mental illness has the tendency to do that to people. It leaves the offspring living in guilt and shame, until we find a way to forgive ourselves for our sins.

The sad part is that, not only do we live with our own poor childhood choices, we live with the mistakes and malice of other people, adults in particular, who'd bestowed their own dysfunctions upon us.

I could sit here and turn this note into a book of its own. And maybe one day I will. For now, why don't we get to why I think I'm here:

This is not a story about me per se. It is embellished for fictional purposes. Sure, as all authors do, I took in all of my lessons, my experiences, my bumps, and my bruises, coupled with what I feel is God-given, remarkable talent, and created something far from fiction for many people. One thing about a good novel: The story may be an imitation of an existence, or a figment of an author's imagination, but the emotions evoked from a great work, and the changes it brings to a reader's life, are far from phony.

If it can be dreamt, it can be lived. It is inside this notion, inside the faith readers grasp near the end of the journey, that determines the worth of the story. Upon completion, I pray I have left you with hope. Writing this wasn't easy—guess no writer classifies their work as such. But daybreak always follows nightfall, and you'll need to remember this to get through the darkness in parts of this journey so you can reach the light.

Through countless revisions, edits, critiques, and the passage of time, *Intimate Nightmares* is what it is today. The content has changed over the last decade. Never in my life have I killed so many people and then brought those same people back from the dead. The permission to invent is what makes the world of writing, including its offspring, *Intimate Nightmares*, such a marvelous place to visit.

I sit here, fourteen years later, with the finished story. It was important for me to show the richness in love, the deep intimacy and openness that comes from intense passion between two people fortunate enough to find a depth few think exists.

Just as the story breeds beauty, so do the cities surrounding it. Baltimore and San Antonio, two places dear to me, are not lost on the reader, although certain elements of these pretty places have been altered for dramatic effect.

For Linda...

"Even if she be not harmed, her heart may fail her in so much and so many horrors; and hereafter she may suffer—both in waking, from her nerves, and in sleep, from her dreams."

-Bram Stoker, *Dracula*

Prologue

"What did you do after you vomited, Agent Jackson?"

"Went back inside and did my job, Doc. What do you think?"

"Did you feel weak?"

"Weak?"

"Less of an agent because you couldn't stomach the scene."

"Seriously? Less of an agent?"

"Yes. Seriously."

"At first. Happy?"

"None of this is happy..."

"No shit."

"...but snapping at me only keeps you here longer."

"Whatever."

"What did you mean by, *at first?*"

"I felt weak until I saw the rest of them."

"Them?"

"Colleagues...I have never seen so many grown men cry at the same time."

"What did you do when you went back inside?"

"Confiscated the drugs, the money...tried not to look at the blood or the bodies."

"They were children, chained. Understandable. Do you think you can get past this and do your job?"

"I have a family to feed. I don't have a choice."

"That's not an answer, Agent Jackson."

"It's all I got."

Chapter 1

What did you do after you vomited, Agent Jackson?

"Nate, you with us?"

"Yeah, man, I'm good."

Supervisory Special Agent Nathaniel "Nate" Jackson, Jr., quickly refocused, and then glared at the juvenile delinquents as he walked the line, up and down, getting close enough to the kids to scrape the skin off their personal space. He hashed and rehashed the rules of the Scared Straight program as if daring the kids to make a wrong move. So far, all the boys were waiting patiently next their mothers. Good, he thought, no drama. Nate had a plane to catch, a wife to woo, and no time for nonsense.

His six-three, 240-pound body standing 90 percent lean, towered over the kids as he moved like an intricate design of well-laid, solid parts cut to fit a well-oiled machine. His partner, Dave Rayburn, was behind him, a white version of Nate's light-skinned, interracial self, although less thick and a lot more country and with a lot more hair. They were both dressed business casual, with Nate in a light-blue, long-sleeved shirt and navy-blue tie and Dave in his signature tweed blazer over a white T-shirt and Lee jeans.

Nate cut his eyes to a kid near the front of the line. "You will not lean, young man."

3

"And if I lean?"

His mother nudged him to behave.

"Then *I* lean," Nate said.

"How metaphorical of you."

His mother nudged him again.

"Pardon me?" Nate asked, not looking for a pardon.

The kid didn't respond.

Nate led him out of line. "What's your name?"

"Jeremy. My crew calls me J-Bug."

"My name's Agent Jackson, and my crew calls me Agent Jackson."

Jeremy's lack of eye contact indicated Nate's power of intimidation. "I don't give a damn," he said.

"You should. Spell metaphorical."

"Or what? You gonna hit me?"

"Nope."

"Why not? You think you a real man walking all up in here. My pops said real men hit they kids, keeps them in line. Keeps them scared. You got kids?"

"Yep."

"They good?"

"Yep."

"You hit them?"

"Nope."

"My pops would call you a pussy-ass bitch."

Nate never flustered. "What do you think about that?"

Jeremy appeared to study Nate's body as if it would cave in on him. "I stopped thinking a long time ago, Agent Jackson. Guess that's why I'm here."

"A real man doesn't hit his kids, Jeremy. And a real man doesn't lead out of fear. Look around. Your peers don't listen to me because they *fear* me. They listen because they *respect* me. There's a difference. I'm tough, but I care. And they know that."

Jeremy was silent for a moment before he responded. "You sound smart."

"I hold my own."

"Bet."

"I can talk to your dad. When I'm done, he'll never hit you again."

"He dead. Got shot up in the street last month. Tried to sell some watered-down shit."

Nate looked over to his partner, and shook his head at what these kids endured daily.

"It's all good, Agent Jackson," Jeremy said. "The struggle is real, but I'll make it." He nodded back toward his mother. "Moms is strong."

Nate looked at Jeremy's mother. "No doubt." Then he looked at Jeremy. "Jeremy, can you do something for me?"

"You seem cool. I guess so."

"You gotta do it every day."

"What's up?"

"I want you to look in the mirror and say, 'I'm going to college.' Can you do that?"

"Agent Jackson, my ass ain't goin' to no college."

"Yes, you are. What do you like to do?"

"Music."

"You sound like my son."

Jeremy cracked a smile. "There's nothing like it."

"And there's nothing truer on this earth than what you tell yourself about yourself."

"Damn, that's some deep shit."

"Think about it." Nate pulled one of his business cards from his pocket and handed it to Jeremy. "Call me if you need anything."

Jeremy nodded and grabbed the card. "I got you."

"One last thing."

"Sup?"

"You didn't spell metaphorical."

"Why you bringin' up old shit, Agent Jackson? That was two minutes ago."

Nate couldn't help but chuckle, but he tried to stay disciplined and set a good example. "Spell the word or you will write all the definitions to all the words on the first three pages of the dictionary."

"Seriously, man?"

"Agent. Yep."

"Why?"

"Because one time I told my father he was superficially angry. If I had to do it, so do you."

"That's cold."

"I can make it freeze too. If you don't do it, another month in lockup. Your choice."

Jeremy looked back at his mother.

"Don't look at her. She can't help you. Look at *me*."

Jeremy looked at him.

"Well?" Nate asked.

A few seconds passed. "Fine. But I get a free pass on penmanship."

"Oh, that's a nonissue. You're gonna do it on a computer."

"You're killing me, Agent Jackson."

Neither of them could help but laugh. "Finish it, and we'll talk about those college apps."

Jeremy shook his head with a confidence he hadn't seemed to have when he'd walked in. "Bet."

Nate directed him back to the line. He received the "ready" from the prison staff and the gated door opened. Nate and Dave escorted the kids down some of the most dangerous cellblocks in Baltimore County, Maryland.

The inmates screamed, cursed, threatened, preached, and rattled cages until the students were either crying or running for the door. Nate stood back with Dave and watched the effects of the program his employer, the Baltimore Field Office of the Drug Enforcement Administration, had agreed to sponsor at his relentless requests.

Nate, Dave, and the kids walked into the cafeteria area, where some of the inmates were roaming free to snarl at the frightened children. Other inmates pounded tables, spat in faces, and yelled into stirring echoes. But they didn't touch the juveniles, even though they came dangerously close.

When the session ended, most of the kids had gotten the message, and yet a few stayed the same little assholes they were when they'd entered. But Nate had adjusted to it. He knew some kids he would never reach.

Jeremy was talking to his mother at the entrance, shook up, it seemed, and on the verge of tears. For some reason, this kid resonated with Nate. "How you feel, Jeremy?"

Nate expected a thank you, but got much more. Jeremy hugged him just below the sternum. Nate didn't know how to react. He'd received praise in the past, but never like this. Reciprocation was the only thing Nate could think to do, so he hugged Jeremy in return as Jeremy's mother thanked him repeatedly. "We need more men like you, Agent Jackson."

Dave whispered in his ear. "Maybe this program *does* make a difference."

Nate and Dave said their goodbyes to the prison staff and the parents. They were about to get into Dave's truck when a black SUV rolled up beside them, windows tinted, wheels shiny, paint glossy, giving off the illusion that the life of an honest man paled in comparison to that of a callous kingpin. The driver's-side window lowered, and a man in the passenger seat leaned across the driver to speak. "What's up, Jackson?"

"Jesus Christ, is nothing off-limits to you, Reese?" Nate asked. "You're recruiting at a goddamned Scared Straight program?"

Johnny Reese was no corner pusher. He was big time. A drug lord who, in the eyes of his followers, had built a legacy more powerful than the luxury vehicle he rode in. "You can't be here all the time to save my future child labor from this life, Jackson. I'll try back tomorrow."

"I catch you recruiting my kids, I'll pull your spleen out through your throat."

"Touchy. Tell your wife I said hello."

"You little bitch." Nate lunged.

"Can I get some help here?" Dave shouted.

It took five prison guards to stop Nate from reaching inside the SUV. He got one arm free twice, and he slipped the other one past his team once. He almost pushed through. Then he remembered his location, remembered that the eyes of many young men were watching him. Nate calmed down. "It may not be today, or tomorrow, but I will take your ass down, Reese."

7

"Good day, feds." Reese and his crew sped off.

"This is exactly why I work in Baltimore and live in San Antonio." Nate looked in the direction of the SUV.

"Don't let him rile you, Jack," Dave said, using the nickname he'd given Nate years ago when they'd met in Knoxville. It was a play on Quarterback Jack, Nate's nickname in his days on the college field. "He doesn't know your family."

"That's not the point, G."

Another agent had given Dave the nickname *Graffiti* because of Dave's tremendous skill at art. Nate shortened the nickname because, well, he could.

"C'mon, let's go," Dave said. "You have an anniversary to celebrate, right?"

"Ten years."

"And you still gonna hit it, right?"

Nate found some humor in his friend's efforts. He chuckled. "Hell yeah."

"Then let's get you to that plane so you can tap that ass."

Dave drove them back to the Baltimore field office. Nate changed from his business casual attire into comfortable traveling clothes, which consisted of long gym shorts and a white T-shirt with cut-off sleeves that read: *Yes, I have a special needs child. Problem?* Then he turned the Spurs baseball cap backward and put it on. A good luck ritual he never failed to do.

The last stop was Agent Fenton Greene's office. He was Nate's boss, the ASAC, Assistant Special Agent in Charge. A white man with years of Baltimore in his blood and a lifetime of pain in his memory, pushing sixty with a full pension.

His office was large enough to encompass a conference table, two desks, a television, and a wet bar. Picturing the politics his boss had to play on a daily basis made Nate cringe every time he entered the office.

"Shut the door," Agent Greene said.

Dave shut the door and remained standing.

Nate pulled out a chair and casually sat down with his forearms on his thighs. "Boss, this can't wait?"

"They're in," Agent Greene said, referring to two undercovers. "Johnny Reese bought the whole goddamned thing."

"Outstanding," Dave said.

"How long?" Nate asked.

"Two years is the target."

"Damn, that's a long time to be undercover and play nice with Johnny Reese," Nate said.

"From what I heard, you can't do it for five minutes." Agent Greene looked back and forth at both of them. "You two are the best I've seen. But if we're gonna pull this off, you can't fly off half-cocked at every comment."

"My bad. He mentioned my family and I lost it."

"Rayburn, wait outside."

Dave left with no argument.

"Jackson, your need to protect people makes you an asset, but it also makes you dangerous as hell, and if not controlled, makes you a target. Your volatile ass isn't good to anyone dead. Got it?"

Nate acknowledged his boss with a nod. "Yeah, I got it."

"You came on board and tore through Baltimore. Your rise to power in the DEA is unprecedented."

"But?"

"It comes with a price because you're so young. What are you, thirty?"

"Thirty-one."

"How many times do you say excuse me?"

"Excuse me?"

"Funny. Think about it."

Nate couldn't decipher the lesson.

"Never," Agent Greene said.

"Never?"

"You never say it because people move out of your way every time you walk down the damn hall."

"Never registered."

"You're the best in the business, Jackson, but it means nothing if you can't help other people become the best they can be. People look up to you. Make sure you model what you want them to see."

"I'll do my best."

"You'll get there. Just remember, no matter how good you think you are, there is always somebody else thinking the same thing. The prize goes to the wisest, not the strongest. This DEA at-risk program was your idea. Make sure it stays a *good* idea."

"I hear you. Can I go catch my plane now? If I miss this flight, I *will* be dead. The whole idea here is to stay married."

"You're in your thirties, married ten years. Say that when you're in your late fifties and sittin' at thirty-five...dismissed."

"See you soon." Nate opened the door. "You ready, G?"

"Oh shit, I forgot I'm taking you to the airport. Man, I had a lunch date with Agent Greene's daughter."

"Get out before I kill you dead, Rayburn, and hang your head on my wall."

Nate stepped out and started to shut the door.

"Jackson, Rayburn, one more thing."

The guys peeked into the office. "What's up?" Nate asked.

"There's another anniversary approaching. You guys gonna be alright?"

Nate looked at Dave, knowing that it had been almost five years since the feds had caught the Federal Street Strangler, the devil himself who'd kept girls chained in his basement for years. It had been a joint operation conducted alongside the FBI.

"We're cool," Dave said.

"I hardly think about it." Nate lied as if he hadn't relived it in the mandated counseling session earlier today.

He left with Dave.

Dave sped to the airport faster than the law they'd sworn to protect allowed.

~~~

Delta Airlines would like to announce the arrival of flight four-eight-nine-seven with service from Baltimore Washington International Airport.

Arianna Jackson stepped closer, realizing it had taken twenty-eight years to figure out who she wanted to be when she grew up. A corporate woman, running a business while staying in love, anxious to celebrate ten years with an immaculate man, flawed to some, perfect to her.

She stepped again. Moving any closer would have allowed the perpetual, downward movement of the escalator to swallow her stiletto.

Arianna straightened her burgundy suit, smoothed out her strawberry-blonde hair, and quickly doused her lips with a lipstick the same shade of pink as her camisole. She checked her face in the reverse view of her cellphone's camera—the mascara, perfect, the blush, just right on her Caucasian skin. The champagne eye-color perfectly highlighted her brown eyes without overpowering their natural hypnotic effects on her husband. Ten years with this man. She had to look perfect.

An array of travelers were trickling down, from the Texans coming home to the students ready to make good use of San Antonio for spring break. No husband yet. The notion seemed to be true: The one person you wanted to exit the plane was always the last one off.

All of him, wearing his backwards baseball cap (which let everyone behind him understand he was a Spurs fan), appeared on high. He placed his carry-on over his shoulder and checked his phone. A hooded sweatshirt draped his arm. The temperature difference between Baltimore and San Antonio usually fell somewhere between thirty degrees, give or take the sunshine on either end.

If the black gym shorts and white T-shirt with cut-off sleeves weren't enough to let Arianna know Nate was tired, the ankle socks and Nike slippers he had on were clear indicators that all he wanted to do was sleep.

She waved. He smiled and shook his head in a way that let Arianna know he'd expected her to do *something* to remind him of how much she loved celebrations.

The escalator closed in on the ground. "If somebody had told me my beautiful wife was gonna be waiting for a brotha with a"—Nate looked up—"big-ass metallic balloon I'd have said..."

"Said what?"

"She better be."

They embraced.

"Hey, you," she said.

"Hey, baby. Happy Anniversary."

Arianna tried to get some air. Nate wouldn't let go.

"Nathan, are you alright?"

He grabbed either side of her face while still holding his phone. "I am now." He kissed her, then slid his hands from her face down her neck and across her shoulders. Arianna reached up and draped her hands across his back. The balloon rose to the ceiling.

Let's go, baby girl." Nate's hand swallowed hers. He walked in front as they passed Baggage Claim. Arianna relished having a man confident in his own skin. He parted the crowd—to her—like Moses, leading Arianna through the people waiting to claim their suitcases. There was no need for him to stop because he had plenty of stuff stored at the DEA Field Office in Baltimore. Whatever else he'd need he would bring in a carry-on or buy it there.

"We're not far," Arianna said as they crossed through Ground Transportation heading to Short Term Parking. Rarely had she parked and escorted him out. But ten years called for more personal service.

They approached her white Jeep Grand Cherokee.

Before pulling off, she asked, "You sure you're alright?"

"I missed you." Nate scooped her by the neck and pulled her to him. He slipped his tongue into her mouth, and they kissed until they were out of breath. Nate pulled away. "Let's go before we jump in the backseat, get caught, and I lose my badge."

"Ten years and you *still* do it."

"What?"

"Mesmerize me. Doesn't matter *how* I look or what I do. It's in everything you say."

"Because you make everything so effortless." Nate checked his phone as if he hadn't just made Arianna's day. "Hey, by the way, did you pick up that grease remover stuff for the garage?"

Arianna shook her head at his oblivious compliment. *He did it again. Damn, I love this man.* "Uh, yeah."

"Good." Nate tilted back his seat. "Ani?"

"What?"

"Next time you pick me up from the airport, wear that skirt because it does shit to me."

Arianna smiled and drove off, thinking of their anniversary. "Are we still gonna celebrate this weekend?"

He smiled. "Sure."

The month of March felt flawless in San Antonio. Just beyond the cold and not close enough to buckle under the high heat. Sunshine shone more than clouds, but normally there was enough rain to help nature along and give the air a clean smell. Nights could get nippy, but overall, they were perfect for the intimate walks Nate and Arianna often took around their upscale, Stone Oak neighborhood.

Arianna pulled into the cul-de-sac and parked in front of their home. The two-story, red brick house paired attractively with the oak tree Nate had planted when they'd moved in. It was surrounded by a bed of red and white mums edged in brick. Waist-high shrubbery lined the perimeter of the house. With no leaf out of place, the bushes looked like perfect squares with smooth, round edges.

Arianna waved to her housewife neighbor, Gloria, watering her lawn with curlers in her hair. Gloria often brought over treats for the kids. Arianna kept cordial, Nate less so; the kids just wanted the candy.

Nate led. By the time Arianna had locked the door and made it upstairs, Nate was lying on his stomach, the pillow smashed against the headboard. Apparently he'd dived into the bed.

13

Arianna contemplated returning to work. A stack of resumes was waiting for her review for her open secretarial position. Calls needed returning. Budgets needed tightening and tweaking. Her Articles of Incorporation needed reviewing.

The shots were hers to call. She kissed Nate on the cheek and whispered, "Get some rest, baby."

"Nuh uh." Nate's words filtered through the rasp in his voice. He grabbed her hand. "Not today."

"I thought you were asleep."

"Not without you."

Arianna smiled. *Ten years. Why not?* She called Taesha Skye, her close friend and certified public and promiscuous accountant. "I'll be in the office tomorrow morning, girl."

"Good, because I might not be in at all. Jerome's taking me out."

"Funny. What happened to that Marco guy?"

"Married."

"Oh...Kent?"

"Issues."

"I see...Rob?"

"Too clingy."

"Um, okay...Hugh?"

"Too good for my own good."

"Ritchie?"

"Next weekend."

"Daniel?"

"Girl, Tuesday, now hang up and go have fun. Not everybody has a Nate."

"I'm sorry."

"I'm not. I like my life. I'll see you in the morning for real. I have a surprise for you for your anniversary. Ten's a big deal."

"Really? What?"

"Bye, Arianna."

"What is it?"

"BYE."

Arianna ended her call and pondered which store her impending gift card belonged to. Then she looked at Nate. *Not everybody has a Nate. She's right about that.*

She took off her clothes and put on one of Nate's T-shirts, then climbed into bed and rolled onto her side. He put his arm around her and pulled her to him.

Arianna nestled closer, knowing there were worse places to be trapped, including ones that didn't smell as good as Armani Code.

Nate rolled on top of her, eclipsing her tiny, five-five, one-hundred-and-fifteen-pound body. "Put me to sleep, Mrs. Jackson," he whispered in her ear.

Chapter 2

When Arianna woke up, Nate wasn't in the bed.

The sun was leaving its last pieces of light. Dusk brought with it full driveways with tail-end commuters pulling in. Stone Oak was located just outside the outer loop leading into the city. Most homeowners living in the area had corporate jobs downtown, and traffic often caused commutes to extend beyond the daylight. The tough rides home made Arianna grateful for such a strong support system, good friends, and a good husband.

She got out of bed and slipped on some jeans. The house was dim and quiet. "Nathan?"

Arianna walked out into the hall, didn't see her kids or Nate. She whispered to herself. "Where's my family?" Then she received a text. *Have you checked your closet yet?*

The outfit wasn't hard to find. Until a minute ago, Arianna'd had no idea she owned a teal cocktail dress, size four, silky, and sleeveless. Stockings were draped around the hanger and the diamond earrings dangled on the hanger's hook.

She responded to the text. *Oh my God, I love it, Nathan. Where are the kids?*

Behind you.

Arianna turned around and saw her family. Her children, Darius, nine, and Tre, two, were standing there with Nate. She saw macaroni fall off the picture Tre was holding. He was grinning ear to ear. "Mommy." He walked up to her. Arianna tied his tiny tennis shoes before grabbing his macaroni masterpiece.

"It's the best heart I've ever seen, like ever, ever, ever, Tre."

"Ani," Nate whispered. "It's a crocodile."

"Crocodile?"

He shook his head. "Crocodile."

Arianna looked back at Tre. "It's a...bomb-ass crocodile, Son." She hugged him so tightly she almost smothered his tiny body and caused more macaroni to fall off the picture and onto the floor. She heard Nate giggle at her attempt to redeem herself.

He nodded to Darius. "This one wrote you a rap."

"Oh, really now. Let me hear it."

Darius read his rhyme. "Mom, it's been ten years. And since you guys made us, Dad drinks too many beers." He looked at her. "That's all I got."

She angled her neck and smiled, looking at her rapper. "That was Grammy material right there."

"Wait until I finish it. I'll have Dad on crack."

"Hey, now," Nate said. "Not funny."

Darius looked at him. "Sorry. Can I go now?"

Nate nodded in Arianna's direction.

Darius hugged his mama and whispered in her ear. "I told him to get a red dress. But you know how hard-headed he is and doesn't listen to anybody. Is he looking at me?"

Arianna giggled. "Yep."

Darius walked close to Nate, avoiding his dirty look, but hugging him before he departed. "Such an awesome dad."

"I know. Get out, D, if you wanna live."

"Of course."

Tre tugged on the end of Nate's shorts. "Daddy, what's cracked-ed?"

"Your brother's head if he says anything else stupid."

17

"Nathan."

Tre ran out of the room. "Watch your head, bro-bro."

Nate shut the door. "Those boys love them some you."

"When did you guys do all this?"

"Here and there, bits and pieces. We're guys."

"Did you sleep at all?"

"Enough."

"Where are we going? It's a school night."

"*We*, you and me, are going out. The kids are going with Pam and Marcus to eat some incredibly good pizza."

"We're not eating some incredibly good pizza?"

"Well, I could make a very crude joke and say I'm eating something much better tonight, but I won't."

"And why not?"

"Because it's not a joke." Nate grabbed either side of her face and pressed his lips to hers.

He kissed Arianna until she felt almost smothered in his touch. "You gonna save something for tonight, Nathan?"

He backed up and chuckled. "I never run out."

They heard a horn. Nate looked out the window and checked the clock. "About damn time."

Arianna looked outside. Rolling up to the curb was a brand new red Expedition laden with temporary tags and more bells than a Christmas tree. Pamela Carter, Arianna's best-friend, seemed unable to wait for the vehicle to make a complete stop before hopping out. She was dressed in the same color suit as the truck, as if it were fate. Detective Marcus Carter of the San Antonio Police Department, in the driver's seat, told a different story. He got out still dressed in his work attire as well, a slightly wrinkled beige shirt minus his tie and the smile Pam displayed. He looked tired, his eyes heavy, his dark skin appearing dry, with faint streaks of white on his face, the effects of past sweat. His hair needed a good brushing to smooth out the waves. His taller stature slumped.

Their twelve-year-old-daughter, Gwen, stayed inside the vehicle and texted, oblivious to the world around her.

"They got it," Arianna said, referring to the new vehicle.

"That bitch is bad too. Let's go."

They walked downstairs.

Arianna opened the front door. "Marcus doesn't seem happy, Nathan."

"Just be cool. He's under a lot of pressure."

"Should we be putting the boys on them?"

"His idea. Says he needs it."

They walked outside.

"I like your hair." Arianna played with the loose curls of Pam's short bob before glancing at the truck. "They took the offer, huh?"

"Yeah," Pam said. "Took some doing. I thought Marcus was gonna punch the salesman in the face."

Marcus grumbled. "He would have had it coming. Trying to give me a ridiculous interest rate with my high-ass credit score. Bitch, please."

Arianna looked at Nate as he walked over to Marcus. She slyly widened her eyes. Nate subtly waved his hand. He'd handle it. "Pop the hood, man."

Pam and Arianna walked closer to the rear of the truck and began talking about the color and the interior. Nobody could deny it was a sweet SUV.

"You guys deserve this, Pam," Arianna said.

"It's hard to get totally excited, though," Pam replied, "when you're worried about your husband."

"What happened?" Arianna studied her best-friend's mocha-colored face and saw the pain. They stood almost eye-to-eye, with Pam about an inch taller.

"He had a *bad* day. He has so much on his shoulders and I feel completely helpless. He came home distraught over a dead-end lead Houston had gotten on his mom. I begged him to talk and he almost exploded. Told me to get in the car because the dealership was waiting on us. All this, and you know he's still dealing with Zach's death."

Zach Sanchez was Marcus's late partner, killed in the line of duty.

"I'm sorry, Pam. I wish we could do something."

"I don't know how long he can go on without finding his mom's body. Zach was a huge support in keeping him focused on the job. Now he's gone too. And new trucks can only do so much."

"Her case is what, two decades old?"

"A little more, I think. They'll probably never find her."

"There's always hope. He can cling to that."

"And Zach? Where's the hope in that?"

"That's tough, I know. Sometimes Nathan leaves late at night, comes back empty. I know exactly where's he's been."

"What do we do, Arianna? Sit back and watch them drown in grief?"

"We love them through it, Pam. That's it."

Pam sighed and looked into the truck. She smiled at Gwen. "That phone."

Arianna chuckled. "I know." Then she noticed Pam's sadness for her husband in her brimming eyes. "Hey look, don't worry about the kids tonight."

"Are you kidding? And miss Marcus trying to teach Tre his phonetics?"

They laughed as Marcus shut the hood. He gave Pam a distant smile, and she returned his half-hearted favor, but at least it was something.

Nate hollered for the kids. Darius raced down the sidewalk and jumped into the backseat. Everybody knew Gwen wasn't amused. "Oh my God, like scoot over, Darius."

Tre trotted slowly. The adults stared at him like he was the child star on the red carpet. "I-I geh peessa."

"Yes, you get pizza, big guy," Marcus said. "Where are your letters?"

Tre covered his mouth in a toddler's forgetful panic, and ran back into the house, bringing back his plastic letters. He walked up to his mommy and put his hands out. Arianna picked him up. "Kisses."

She saw Nate looking at her like she was the only mother in the world and the only freak in the sheets. Arianna knew he was going to tear her up tonight, and she had no problem with it. She gave Tre one last kiss and strapped him in.

"Alright, man," Marcus said to Nate. "Let me take my ass home and shower."

"You sure about this, Marcus?" Arianna asked. "You look really tired."

"I'm good," Marcus replied. Then he looked at Tre. "You ready to roll, dude?"

"Yeah!"

"See, he's cool, Ani," Nate said.

"Your ass just wants to get laid," Marcus said, then he stepped inside the truck. Nate mumbled something to the effect of fuck you and hell yeah mixed together.

"I'll call you tonight," Arianna said to Pam.

"You better not."

Arianna stood next to Nate as the SUV made a right and disappeared down the street. "Are they gonna be okay, Nathan?"

"Yeah, they're gonna be fine."

"Location, Mr. Jackson?"

"You're not ready for the intel." Nate kissed Arianna's forehead. "Go get ready. I'm gonna edge the yard a little bit."

Arianna cleaned up and put herself together. The dress was a little tight but she took comfort in the effort. She zipped up the sheath before looking into the mirror, fully dressed, something she vowed to always do before seeing her reflection. Ignorance was bliss, and so was blackout. Nate loved her body, distortions and all. Too bad she couldn't feel the same for herself. Perhaps hiding her scar's true origins had helped along her secretive self-loathing.

Arianna flipped her strawberry-blonde hair into a quick up-do, leaving wisps of hair to glide around her face and neck. The style drew attention to the earrings. The last thing was her lipstick, candy apple red. She looked into the mirror and held the tube up to her mouth.

"If I could melt you into chocolate and cover a marshmallow with you and eat you while you're still warm, I would. Good God Almighty, you're fine as shit." Arianna looked in the direction of Nate's voice. He stood there, his eyes locked on her. "Like you never had my two hard-headed kids."

"If you don't stop, I'm gonna cry, and makeup will smear all over my face."

"You'd still be hot as hell, and you'd still be mine."

"You did it again."

"Did what?"

"Made me feel brand new."

"My job." Nate kissed her forehead. Then he undressed and started the shower. Arianna suddenly backed him to the wall, dropped to her knees, thanked him for her dress, and gave Nate a better reason to take a shower.

As he cleaned up, Arianna called her mother. She told her she'd fly into Knoxville next Friday and be there for the last round of chemo. Her mother was sounding better, leaving Arianna optimistic. They spoke about the kids and Nate's surprise plans.

"Tell my son-in-law I thank him for taking such good care of you all these years."

"You can tell him in person next week." Her mother didn't answer. "Mom?"

"Sorry. Dozing off."

"I'll call you tomorrow."

"Are you making me another grandbaby tonight?"

"Mom!"

Her mother gave a faint laugh.

"You're worse than Nathan."

"Night, pumpkin. Love you. Always have, always will."

"Night, Mom. Love you too." Arianna hung up. *Always have, always will.* Her mother had a way with words, and breast cancer did nothing to change that.

Nate came downstairs in a black suit and a teal tie that matched Arianna's dress. "You ready, Mrs. Jackson?"

"Why yes, Agent Jackson. Are *you* ready?" She slipped on her heels.

"I'm always ready. Nice touch."

"Stockings don't work well with stilettos."

"Makes my job easier."

"I bet it does, sexy boy."

"Let's go before we don't make it out of here."

Nate opened the passenger side of his slick black Cadillac CTS and eased Arianna into the leather surroundings. He filled the interior with jazz almost as smooth as the interior of his luxury vehicle that, unlike Johnny Reese, had come from an honest living.

"My husband is so romantic." Arianna kissed his cheek. "Tell me something sweet, Agent Jackson."

He looked over at her. "Sweet?"

"Yeah, sweet."

"You're the most stunning woman, like, ever in existence, Mrs. Jackson."

"You know just what to say."

"And I'm gonna screw the shit out of you tonight."

"That's my Nathan."

"Don't you ever forget it."

Realizing they hadn't had a date night in a while, Arianna studied her husband, her Nathan, from his warm, sepia-brown skin that resembled the shadows cast on the clouds in a desert sunset, to his brown eyes with their sensual easiness—a softness that made his hard demeanor less intimidating. He may have inherited from his parents a hostile view of life, but at least his African-American father and Brazilian mother had blessed him with natural beauty, including the jaw line and perfectly framed chin which appeared to have been sketched, edited for a seamless transition.

Arianna gently glided her hand down Nate's cheek. In turn, he grabbed her hand and kissed it softly. I love you and I love you too, simply stated without saying a word.

He pulled up to the Mokara Hotel, the Riverwalk's finest.

Nate opened his door and stopped the valet from opening Arianna's door. "I got her," he said. The valet backed up. Nate grabbed Arianna's hand and led her out of the car.

"How did you get reservations?" she asked.

"I called last year."

"You look so sexy in strategic planning."

Nate whispered in her ear. "Hey, I get a great return on investment."

"And I get to see a huge rise in your capital gain," she whispered back.

Nate smiled.

A young, bubbly hostess with a head full of spiral curls greeted them. "Your name, sir?"

"Nate Jackson."

"This way." She led them to the elevator.

Arianna got happy. "Oh no, you didn't, sexy boy."

As they ascended, Nate confirmed his presence. "What's my name?"

They rose to the roof and stepped into the night.

Formal white linens draped the reserved table. A candle, tucked into a floral centerpiece, flickered as if winking, letting them know the night belonged only to them. White satin dressed the chairs, which were angled outward, the setting opening its arms, telling Nate and Arianna the roof had been waiting for them to grace it with their presence.

Arianna was so astounded she could barely walk. Nate pulled out her chair and she sat down.

Soaking in the pleasure of the surprise and absorbing the shock that she was sitting atop San Antonio, Arianna's heart rate leveled. The cool air crawled up her arms. She draped the matching shawl around her shoulders. "You thought of everything."

"Well, you *do* everything, figured I could do my part."

Arianna cradled her wineglass and angled it to her mouth. The motion displayed her long nails and finely crafted French manicure. She sipped and then subtly licked her lips. The wineglass gradually came down to the table, guided by her subtle eroticism. "It's good," she said.

"Life's good," he said.

"Yes, indeed." She slipped out of a stiletto and rubbed her foot across Nate's leg. Up and down, she brushed his shin with her toes, then up his thigh, bringing her toes down, giving him a prelude to the climax.

After dinner, filet mignon of course, the waiter brought dessert, tiramisu. Arianna loved tiramisu. Coffee was its star ingredient.

The waiter asked for their empty plates. Neither responded. Arianna was grinning at Nate and he was too busy returning the implication. Their chemistry spread across the table like satin linens and subtle flames.

The waiter left without the dishes.

"Aren't you gonna eat that?" Nate asked, softening his eyes to set the tone in his voice.

"Why don't you slip it inside my mouth?" she whispered.

"Be glad to." Slowly, Nate slid the fork down the slice. He fed her, watched her lips seduce the fork and caress the bite, five times until the piece was gone. Nate's slice went untouched.

"I have something for you," he said.

Nate dug into his pocket and pulled out a small velvet box. Arianna almost choked on her last sip of wine.

He reached across the table and held her hand. "Ani, until you, marriage was *not* for me. I was the biggest dog on campus. You knew that and you trusted my ass anyway. I didn't think I could ever be loyal to anything other than the one-night stand. Your beautiful soul proved me wrong, and you made it so goddamned easy to be faithful."

A tear fell from Arianna's eye. "Before I met you, I thought I would have to settle. I never thought I would meet somebody like me who had estranged parents, or who saw past my awkwardness to still want me. Or who could have related to wanting more out of life than just getting by. Thank you for not making me compromise."

"And thank you."

"For what?"

"For being woman enough to save me from myself." He handed Arianna the box.

She opened it and discovered the four-carat, marquise-cut diamond solitaire set in a band of fourteen-karat white gold. "Nathaniel."

"I couldn't afford it ten years ago. But I can now and then some. It's only fair."

"Fair?"

"Ani, you are so humble. I could buy you a plastic band from a gumball machine and you'd wear it. You deserve a ring that represents how happy you make me."

"Thank you, baby. I can't even move."

"Here." Nate removed her original ring and slipped the new one on her finger. Looking at the diamond reminded Arianna she had come a long way from her poverty-stricken upbringing. Defying her racist father was the best move she'd ever made. She wished her daddy could see that a white girl reared in a Tennessee housing project could marry into another race and prosper nicely. She wanted to make it tangible, put it on a plate and smear it in his face.

Nate grabbed her hand. "Dance with me."

Nate held her close under the seduction of the slow, simmering soul coming from the outside speakers. She fell into his chest and rested there as her feet followed his. She breathed in his cologne, almost high off the scent. In that moment, nothing mattered. They were the only people in the world, a couple grateful they'd both been strong enough to fight for what they'd wanted.

The temperature continued to drop, not freezing, but a couple degrees shy of nippy. Arianna slipped her hands from around Nate's neck and pulled them close to her chest, between his body and hers. Nate raised his arms and wrapped them around her shoulders. "You are my world, woman. Kiss me."

They stood in the middle of the Mokara roof, lips locked, not caring who came and who went.

"I know I'm not easy, Ani."

"I wouldn't be anywhere else, Nathan."

"Let's go."

"Where?"

"Surprise. I'll lead."

"I'll follow."

Nate led Arianna to the luxury suite. He shut the door. A fraction of a second later, her dress crumpled hitting the carpet.

Nate moved inside Arianna's body as if he'd never been there; like he had dreamt of her in a past life and just

26

discovered she was real. She got lost not only in the physical feeling, but also in the sheer appreciation he displayed for her allowing him to give her that feeling. Nate raised her above the level of a loved woman. He made her feel as if it were a privilege to touch her, to share a decade of love with her, to share a bond of love with her for their children.

"Hold me, Nathan. Don't ever let me go."

"With both hands, baby. Trust and believe."

Chapter 3

Nathan,

I've spent so much time, the vast majority of the last year, so consumed in corporate by-laws and the legal implications of expanding my business that I haven't stopped long enough to see all you have done for me this past year, this past decade. Every day I spend with you adds some new lesson to my life, makes me grow more and more as a woman and a wife. Whether it is something as simple as learning men hate asking for directions, or that they love to be touched as much as we do, each revelation has brought me more joy than I could ever express. Sometimes I laugh at what I learn. Sometimes I ache for what I learn. But through everything I've learned about you, I know you are one hell of a man and I wouldn't trade you for anybody easy. The scars on your hands remind me that I never have to ask you twice to fix anything. They remind me you have a job you can't discuss, but that same job has bettered the lives of many people. They remind me you have done things to protect people in ways you'd like to forget. I feel safe in your arms because when you hold me, I can feel the softness and the love you have for me, yet at the same time, I know you would kill somebody with those arms before you would allow them to hurt me or our children.

I know this letter must seem sudden and perhaps unnecessary, because our anniversary has passed, but I would marry you all over again, so the timing does not matter. Every day is our anniversary to me. I love you.

Your wife,

Arianna

Nate folded up the letter and slipped it back into the card Arianna had waited until this morning to give him. He set both on the hotel dresser. "Now who's trying to make who cry?"

"I just needed you to know."

"You show me every day. Every day you leave me alone to watch a game; every day I don't have to look for socks; every day the house is clean and my kids look nice; every day you don't bitch about my job; every time I fly home, you're asleep on the couch because you dozed off waiting for me. You might not think I notice the little things, Ani, but I do." He continued to stare at her.

At first she thought it was admiration, but his eyes roamed a couple of times, letting her know something was on his mind. "What is it, Nathan?"

"The promise, Ani. The children. We're missing one. Three by ten was the deal. We're happy; we have money; we have graduate degrees. It's time."

Arianna remembered the promise. Nate had made it clear a decade ago that he wanted three children. Deep down, she wanted another child too. But now just wasn't the time. "I need a couple years, Nathan."

"C'mon, Ani. Not the deal."

Arianna put her hand on his chest. "I need two years. *Please.* Tre is only two and I need this incorporating to take hold."

"Two *years?*" Nate sat on the bed, tapping his leg. Arianna knew he was either feeling disappointed, rationalizing her decision, or a combination of both.

"I want this too, Nathan. Just need some time."

He looked up at her. "Does this have anything to do with my commute to Baltimore?"

"No, not at all. I knew the arrangement when we moved from Maryland. I'm good with you working away. This is me."

Nate sat for a few more minutes, staying quiet. Arianna knew he was thinking it through as he did all things.

He sighed, rubbed his forehead, and got up. Arianna knew this was a sign of concession. "I admit it. It's bad timing for both of us. Things are going on at work for me also and waiting is best." He stroked her hair. "But you don't get off that easily."

"Yeah, I do, actually."

"Now who's funny?" He kissed her lips. "I'll meet you halfway on this. In a year, you throw those pills away. Then we'll have another nine months. Deal?"

She found relief in his compromise. And it made sense. "Deal."

He grabbed her waist and lifted her up, suspending her in the air. "When are you going in?"

"After you make love to me."

"Now that sounds like an immediate plan."

Arianna entered the Gleason Building, hit the ascent button and waited. The Gleason was the tallest building on the Riverwalk; getting a punctual ride rarely happened.

Once she was inside the elevator, her suit made her look like a lone peach in a smothering sea of charcoal grey and navy blue suits. She adjusted her brightly colored ensemble and looped her long, straight hair behind her ear. Through the mirrored wall, Arianna saw a man standing in the corner. She chuckled, remembering a day when the elevator had malfunctioned. She and Nate had been the only ones riding it, and the elevator stayed jammed for about forty-five minutes. They had stood in the same corner where the man was standing now, the wall burning Arianna's back as Nate stroked her like a paintbrush to canvas. The elevator doors dinged. "Good day," she said to the man.

He stared at her oddly.

Arianna sauntered down the hallway, feeling a case of Saturday Night Fever all the way to the glass door leading to her small corporation. She was proud. Damn proud.

"Who are you?" Arianna asked the white woman sitting at the reception desk. Her hair was blacker than toxic smoke and highlighted in streaks whiter than cotton. Her eyes appeared too green to be organic. And her tight, beige sweater popped her perky breasts into place. She appeared to be in her late-twenties, early-thirties.

"Shawnee, your new assistant. You must be Arianna." Shawnee stood up and stuck her hand out, showing how well skinny jeans complemented her hips.

Arianna walked down the hall, leaving Shawnee's hand high in the air, waiting for reciprocity. She stormed into Taesha's office. "Who is that?"

"Surprise!"

"You hired our assistant?"

"Yep." Taesha handed her Shawnee's resume. "Look."

Arianna spent more time than usual looking at the resume. "You call references?"

"One of her instructors."

"How'd she hear about the job?"

"Networking." Taesha smiled.

"Smart girl." Shawnee looked good on paper. Strong typing speed, administrative certifications, previous experience in Texas and California...yet she had a gap in her employment a year back, and had worked her previous job for just four months at a nonprofit facility before interviewing with Taesha. She was, however, a student taking online courses in business and had more computer experience than one person needed, certifications that made the term *computer geek* seem cool. "She looks good in some ways. I give you that." Arianna looked up from the resume. "Driver's license? Social Security card?"

"Yup. I don't have an accounting degree for nothing. I have another surprise too."

"Oh, God."

Eva Sanchez, who rounded out Arianna's quartet of friends, strolled in. "Who is that?"

"Apparently, our newest family member."

"Oh cool."

"So, this was my surprise," Arianna said to Taesha.

"No. Tell her, Eva."

"You are looking at the newest staff surgeon at University Hospital."

Arianna leaned in. "Oh my God, you passed residency!"

Eva smiled big. "Yay! And I'm gonna work right across the street." She nodded in the direction of the main hospital in University Hospital's system.

Arianna gave her a congratulatory hug and watched Taesha do the same. Arianna smiled at their smiles. Her friends, so different, yet so made for each other. Taesha, the promiscuous woman who defied odds and dress codes and could run numbers blindfolded. Eva, the stunning Latina with cascading auburn hair who'd survived the death of Zachary Deleon Sanchez and was still standing, could perform emergency surgery under candlelight if she had to. And Pam, the Ph.D., the school principal and diabetes survivor who'd withstood a hemorrhage and early hysterectomy and lived to tell about it. All her friends—beautiful, educated, and fighting battles very few knew anything about.

"C'mon, let's go to my office."

They walked past Shawnee's desk. She had settled in, put up a few pictures, displayed two plants, and draped a sweater over her chair.

Arianna stepped back. "Sorry about earlier. Crazy day. We'll chat in a bit."

"Okay."

"And Shawnee?"

"Yes?"

"Keep your cell phone out of sight."

Arianna walked into her office. It wasn't a lavish space, but she had acquired some nice furniture from a company that had liquidated all its assets, so she was fortunate enough to have cherry-oak furnishings and Victorian chairs.

She shut the door. "Please tell me you gave her a *contingency* offer pending background."

"Arianna, we needed someone ASAP. You're leaving next Friday to visit your mother, so I figured this needed to get done."

"You don't get it, Tae. What if she does something wrong?"

"It's called firing."

"No, Tae, it's called negligent hiring."

"I don't follow."

"If she has a record of grand larceny, for example, and goes down the hall and steals a computer, we can be held liable."

"She's right, Taesha," Eva said.

"Well, can we just go back now and run it?"

"Yeah, but she's on board now."

"Sorry, Arianna, I'm just trying to unload your plate."

"You already do that. You forecast accurate sales; you handle marketing like nobody's business; and you brighten this place up with...with...with *you*. We all have strengths and weaknesses, Tae. Just from now on, leave me to the employment law and I'll leave you to the numbers."

"Agreed. But just for the record, I screw better than you."

"I doubt that."

They laughed.

"Shawnee will be well-trained by the time you take off to see your mom," Taesha said.

"How *is* your mother?" Eva asked.

"She sounds good. We're optimistic. I just wish I had more time with her."

"I know you do."

Arianna checked the clock. There was never enough time in the day for a businesswoman, especially one who'd spent the morning on her back continuing the celebration of her tenth anniversary.

The afternoon settled into routine. Arianna looked through Shawnee's new hire packet. Taesha had rushed the hire, but handled the paperwork spot on. Despite Taesha's eccentricity, from her need to wear faded jeans with self-inflicted holes, to her desire to highlight her platinum blonde ponytail with Ferrari Red and fandango pink, she displayed a meticulous attention to detail and had the strength to take life's serious blows. At times, though, she was way too spontaneous.

Arianna put down the file and summoned the topic of its contents. "Shawnee? Could you come in here?"

Arianna did her best to turn their conversation into *just* a conversation, and not an interview for a job Shawnee already had. To Arianna's relief, it went well. Shawnee seemed to understand the standards, the conduct expected, and the job description. So far, Arianna was feeling more confident about the hire. She looked at Shawnee's driver's license again to make sure it matched the information written on the immigration form.

Arianna smiled at her. "So, why my company?"

"Who *doesn't* want to work at Empowerment? This place is the bomb. Free smoothies, good benefits. Plus, I kinda heard that you needed somebody yesterday. At least that's what I *thought* I heard when I got a latte the other day and handed my resume to Ms. Skye."

"You heard right."

"Good, cuz I'm broke and I need to keep this job."

Arianna chuckled. "You got it."

Shawnee stared at a framed photo on Arianna's desk. "Your besties?"

"Yep, that's them."

"You have some beautiful BFFs."

"Thanks."

"Anything else?" Shawnee asked. "I would really like to get to work."

"No. Just spend the next hour settling in and we'll pick up tomorrow. And by the way, jeans on Fridays only."

"It is Friday."

"Oh, that's right." Arianna checked the calendar and felt stupid. "Sorry, between work and family, sometimes I forget my own head."

"No worries." Shawnee turned around to leave, but looked back. "Hey, Arianna."

"Yeah."

Shawnee nodded to a picture of Nate in a suit, something he rarely wore. "Your husband looks like a serious guy."

Arianna smiled. "Nah, he's my teddy bear."

"What does he do?"

That's kind of personal. "Federal agent."

"You said that like you meant it."

"Anything else, Shawnee?"

"Good-looking family. You must be very proud."

Arianna felt uncomfortable with Shawnee's tone, which seemed happy and sprinkled with a pinch of spite. "I am."

Shawnee left Arianna's office, and left behind her lingering personal intrusion. Arianna looked down at her breasts after seeing Shawnee's knockers almost take out her tea table at the entry. Then she logged on to her company's Intranet, looking for the background check authorization form.

Evening snuck up the same way all of Arianna's duties were sneaking up due to the growth of her business and its incorporation. Shawnee had long gone home. Taesha had made a trip to the Broadway store. Arianna packed up and planned to repay Nate with dinner plans of her own.

There was a knock.

"Come in," she hollered.

"Hey, Mrs. J," Brian, the delivery man said. "This just came in 'same day', and I forgot these others in my truck."

"No worries, Brian. I don't know why people pay so much to send me stuff."

"Don't hurt them, Mrs. J."

She smiled. "Good night, Brian."

The packages consisted of three envelopes and two boxes. The envelopes were first, invoices from distributors and a couple of new vendor contracts for review. The smallest box contained items Taesha had ordered, including updated statistical software and reference manuals.

Arianna cut open the larger box, the "same day" delivery. It took a minute to figure out the sender. She froze when she read the label. *The Convalescent Center at Oak Hill.*

The cancer had claimed victory. At one a.m., the morning after her anniversary, Arianna's mother had passed. *What the hell? I just talked to her!*

Life seemed to stop. Arianna locked the door, not allowing it to start again. It was just her and a FedEx box in a world full of frost. Shifting through heirlooms and the relics of her mom's life put her in the middle of a whiteout, making her feel lost against the cold air.

A clay handprint, a few self-made greeting cards, and photographs made up most of the contents. The rest were trinkets gathered over her mother's life. A few glass figurines bought from dollar stores, a dream-catcher, and her mother's high-school diploma stained with time.

How could I have let all these years slip away?

Kindergarten, she thought. The handprint she'd made in kindergarten.

A big, brown envelope lay at the bottom. She picked it up slowly, as if a spider had just crawled underneath it. The contents consisted of a simple letter.

Nightmare.

Arianna shook her head, opened her mouth to scream, but pain and shock blocked the sound. She covered her face. All this time. She hadn't been the only one.

The torture. The objects that penetrated her. The quarters each time he'd touched her in her early years, the dollars for each time he'd touched her in her preteens. It all slapped her back into her childhood. The dirt under her fingernails from digging holes to hide the money, vivid enough for her to relive the phantom feeling of grit on her hands. The scar across her breasts began to burn.

Arianna read the letter, the deathbed confession of her mother. For the first time in her young adult life, she couldn't reach for the one person who'd always protected her. Tell Nate? *Are you kidding?* She would rather have tied hosiery around her neck and tightened it until she turned blue and her eyes glassed over.

36

Slowly, she picked up her phone and dialed.

"Taesha." Arianna spoke low, as if somebody had dropped a rock on her voice.

"Hey, wassup? I can barely hear you."

"Where are you?"

"Turning off Broadway Drive about to come back."

Arianna swallowed, controlling the tangy taste, stopping her need to vomit. But, she couldn't do anything about her shaking hands. "Hurry."

Pam received the next call. Eva wasn't far behind.

Chapter 4

Taesha sat in one of the Victorian chairs. Eva leaned on the desk, her back to the edge, her hands clutching the rim. Arianna stood close to the window as she looked out into the city.

Pam read the letter.

Arianna,

I don't mean to be dramatic, but if you're reading this, I'm probably dead. Don't be mad at the staff here. I told them not to tell you how bad off I really am because you and I have such a limited amount of time together, and I didn't want to spend it in tears. I also gave them specific instructions to hold this package until I passed and not to call you when I did. You're gonna need time to absorb this before telling Nate I'm gone. Trust me.

Pam looked at everybody before continuing.

I know about it, sweetheart. I know all of it, the assault, the torture, and your pain, baby. Bianca told me. What a weight for a young girl to carry.

In case Nate doesn't know, I'm having this package sent to your office. I'm assuming he doesn't have a clue about Bianca's father, because I didn't have one until Bianca came and visited me about three months ago. Then she left and shot herself in her car. I cried for days.

I didn't tell you about Bianca's visit because I didn't know if I should bring up the pain. You and I had just reconnected and I didn't want to spoil that. But I couldn't die with what I am about to say, unsaid.

Pam paused and took a deep breath, as if the remaining words of the letter might send them all over the edge.

He's locked up, honey, for other assaults, so he can never hurt you again. This was not your fault. I don't want you playing victim. You're strong and capable despite your childhood. There's much I haven't told you. I suspect there's much you haven't told me. I never wanted to bring up your father so I left it alone. His version of hell was bad enough. The thought of yet another man hurting you breaks my heart. Since you never brought him up, I figured I should keep quiet. But now, you must know, in order to move on.

I hated your dad, as you well know. That didn't change after you and Nathaniel left Knoxville. I know you didn't understand my decision to take him back after I had left him. But it was the best choice to keep everything calm and everybody safe. He never hit me again, not after Nathaniel put him in his place. As hard as it was, I believe having you guys leave me for good was the right thing. Although I missed you so much.

Four months before I got sick, I put your dad in a nursing home. He'd finally been approved for Medicaid. Thank God. Immediately afterward, I started looking for you, but couldn't find you. I made call after call and then gave up and moved into assisted care.

Looking back, I realize that when you were a child, I was too busy hating my life to protect you. I was surprised and somewhat relieved when I finally found you and you never asked about your father. I guess you were too happy to hear from your mama. I will always be grateful for the computer literate staff here, and I guess the Internet. What a powerful tool.

I love you and I will feel forever complete because we got back in touch this last year. I'm sorry your father kept us apart. We both fell victim to a hateful man. Me by choice, you by fate.

Pam paused to pat her eyes. Then she continued with a cracking voice.

Tell Nathaniel I would accept his offer of moving in with you guys if I weren't dying of this cancer mess. I knew he was special the minute I saw him. So young, so present. If you haven't told him about your past, tell him. Don't try to fix it yourself. Even if you can suppress the past, remember: closure, without honesty, is another form of greed. Goodbye, my baby.

Love,

Mom

Pam's hand dropped mechanically. She loosened her grip on the letter and it fluttered to the floor. The somber mood lurked through the office like a hardened felon laughing at the innocent, telling them that, after this day, nothing would ever be the same.

A few minutes later, Arianna broke the silence. "My mother always had a way with words. Wanted to be a poet. How she ended up with my father is beyond me. So many times I wanted to call her, but I didn't have it in me to make her life worse. Growing up surrounded by black people and living with a racist bastard makes for a lonely existence. At least I got to escape it."

"What happened?" Pam asked.

They waited a moment for Arianna to gather herself enough to explain. She sighed. "I was sodomized, sexually assaulted, and tortured from pre-K to seventh grade."

Pam's jaw dropped. Eva looked at Taesha.

"What the hell did you just say?" Taesha asked.

Arianna's voice stayed on simmer. "I needed cash. Both of my parents worked, but we were broke. My mom cleaned up a grocery store and my dad was a janitor. They needed a babysitter, and there was only one other white couple in the projects. Do the math. Nightmare, the father in that family, claimed to be a war hero who couldn't work."

"Nightmare?" Eva asked.

"I named him because of the dreams."

"What dreams?" Pam asked.

"I'll get to that," Arianna said. "When he first started touching me, he would cover my face with a pillowcase. When he was done, he would give me quarters and send me on my way."

She stopped speaking. From the way her friends were staring at one another, she could see they had no idea what would come out of Arianna's mouth next. They were scared to find out, yet too curious to let it go.

Arianna walked away from the window and sat in the other Victorian chair. "So long ago it seems. I was too tight to penetrate, so he would use his finger and small objects. Pens, etc."

"Pens?" they all asked.

Arianna nodded. "As I got older, around eight, he would give me dollars. For my services. This went on for close to four years. I hid the money in the dirt and dug it up when I needed stuff."

"Stuff?" Eva asked.

"When I was little, I needed candy. When I got close to twelve, I needed pads. I got tired of rolling up tissues to stop blood from dripping down my legs."

"This is not okay," Eva said. "He needs to fry."

"I need some water," Arianna said.

The mini-fridge was in the reception area, the place where Shawnee had laid claim, the place where she'd hung a picture showing herself holding a dog. Arianna felt haunted. Intruders had just invaded her world. It was awkward enough explaining these details to her friends. The shame was amplified by what other people would think of her.

Arianna grabbed a bottle of water and downed it like liquor.

Nate texted: *How's your afternoon, baby?*

Arianna didn't reply.

She went back to her office. "I should have followed through at the end. I should have spoken up like I threatened to."

"Um," Taesha said. Her voice was far different from her usual, loud confidence. She sounded mousy, scared, and sad. "What do you mean? How did it end?"

"Don't push her," Eva said.

"I'm not trying to push her," Taesha snapped.

"Yes, you are," Eva said.

"Stop arguing," Pam said.

"Nobody's arguing, Pam. I'm just concerned. Can I be concerned?" Taesha yelled.

"We're all concerned," Eva shouted.

"Please," Arianna said. "Don't yell at each other."

They were silent.

"You're my best friends, so you may as well know." Arianna opened her shirt and unclasped her bra.

A scar, five-inches of what looked like magnified, jagged, pinkish bacteria cells, stretched across both breasts, passing through the cleavage, looking somewhat distorted, obviously due to her breasts having developed as she'd grown older. Its width was about two-inches, its edges amorphous. The scar was slightly raised, with random, vein-like protrusions extending from the main burn.

Arianna's friends gasped as if they were watching a horror movie, as if The Blob were seeping over Arianna's chest.

"He burned you?" Pam asked.

"It's chemical," Eva, the good trauma doc, interjected. "Isn't it?"

Arianna nodded. "Lye, I think. Drain cleaner probably. He poured it on me when I finally told him to stop."

"I'm gonna cut his heart out," Taesha yelled. "I swear, one stab to the chest."

"I don't know how, but I finally got strong enough to say no. We were in the bathroom. He'd tried to force my head down, make me do oral. Guess he thought I was old enough to do it finally. That was it. He went into a rage when I defied him and he tried his damnedest to penetrate me. But I was still too tight. He took a cold curling iron and put it inside me. He kept opening the clamp and shutting it, trying to stretch me."

There wasn't a dry eye in the room.

"My only saving grace is that he never got himself inside me. I remember so clearly the last attempt. He slapped me. He plugged in the curling iron, then held watch over me, so I wouldn't run. I almost tried, but I simply froze. Once the curling iron was good and hot, he came to me, spread my legs." Arianna clenched her teeth. "That was it. I clicked. I fought like hell. I kicked him, slapped him. The curling iron fell out of his hand. He punched me, and I almost landed on it. Before I could gather myself, he came at me with a container of *something*, maybe drain cleaner. I can still smell it, my flesh burning. He flung open my legs and tried to thrust himself inside me. I screamed, both ends of my body on fire. He covered my mouth and tried to grab the curling iron, but then he stopped abruptly. The bastard had the nerve to orgasm as he was trying to kill me. I bit his hand so hard I had his blood on my teeth. He pulled away, his semen all over the place. Then he stuck a water gun inside me and threatened to do it again, next time with a real gun, if I told anyone. After that day, he never bothered me, but he did threaten to make my life hell if I said anything. It worked."

"Did you get medical help?" Eva asked.

"Yes. Nightmare told my father he'd told me to behave and that in a show of defiance, I tried to pour the chemicals on him and he blocked my hand. My father made me tell the ER staff I'd been trying to fix the toilet and spilled the stuff and didn't say anything because I was scared of getting in trouble. I don't know how they believed that crap. When we got home, he slapped me for being so defiant to my elders and told me I'd better not tell my mother."

Taesha squeezed her eyes as she pinched the bridge of her nose. "Okay, I'm lost here. This bitch happens to have a can of drain cleaner, opened, ready to pour? In the midst of trying to rape you? What, he's a good multitasker? Arianna, this isn't plausible."

Arianna cocked her head, got defensive. "You calling me a liar, Tae?"

"No. Absolutely not. I just think there's something else at play here. That's all." Taesha took a breath. "I just think...I don't know...he was waiting for the opportunity or something."

There was a moment of silence before Arianna spoke. "Geeze, I don't know. I never thought that far into it. I just know it hurt like hell."

"From what you've described about him, it is plausible," Pam said.

"It's more than plausible, Pam," Taesha snapped. "It's a fact. Look at it."

"Chill out, Taesha," Pam said. "We're all upset. Don't lash out at me. We're on the same side."

Taesha and Pam began to bicker. Eva broke it up. "This isn't helping anything. Stop it, now." She looked at Arianna. "What Pam and Taesha are saying does make sense. Why the hospital didn't investigate, well, *that's* what's not plausible."

"We lived in poverty, Eva. We had no insurance. The ER didn't care."

Eva looked away and snapped. "Well, they should have." Then she spoke low. "Bastards."

Taesha changed the conversation's direction. "I knew it seemed odd you wore shirts to the pool."

"Why didn't you tell us?" Pam asked.

"My nightmares literally stopped the day I met Nathan." Arianna's eyes began to fill. "The night before we met, I hadn't slept again. I went to the store that morning to get something for my headache. And there he was. Been next to him ever since. As long as I could move further away from my childhood, it was like it never happened."

"So, how did Nate react when you told him?" Eva asked. "I hope better than that stupid hospital your father took you to."

Arianna didn't respond right away. Then she dropped the answer like a porcelain vase on a laminate floor. "He doesn't know."

The women looked at each other.

"Excuse me?" Taesha said. "How in God's name can he *not* know? You can't exactly hide this, Arianna."

Arianna looked at each of her friends. "I didn't have to hide it. I kept it from him the old-fashioned way."

"You lied," Pam said.

Arianna looked down and nodded. "I didn't have a choice."

"Why?" Eva asked. "As close as you two are."

Arianna sighed and mumbled. "Oh Lord, how do I make you guys understand this?" She gathered herself. "When Nathan and I started dating, we were so young. My father put us through holy hell. Plus my impoverished environment didn't help. That was *enough* for Nathan to deal with. I couldn't put eight years of sexual assault by yet another sick man in my life on top of it. I just couldn't. I was already ashamed." Arianna took a breath. "Nathan knew my dad had beaten me and my mother. Saying that I'd stayed out late and that my father punished me was easy. And I didn't have to reveal my escapades for money."

"Escapades?" Taesha backed up. "You were a little kid in a ghetto. Stop placing this blame on yourself, Arianna."

"You guys have no idea all the crap that bastard stuck up in me. His mouth *everywhere.* "

Eva tried to be the voice of reason in a sea of high emotions. "Okay, you're a lot older now. Let's think this through. Nate can handle it."

Arianna shook her head defiantly. "No...he can't."

"You sound sure," Pam said.

"There's more," Arianna said. "I almost *did* tell him, once, when I realized we weren't kids anymore. I knew I had to man up and be grown up about it. But something happened and..."

"And what?" Taesha asked.

"I, um, had this plan to sit him down one night. Darius was three. Nathan had just started with the DEA. I had just opened my shop." Arianna blinked, soft tears fell. "I figured, new moves, new life, no old secrets."

"What happened?" Eva asked.

"Nathan came home that night...*different.* That's the best I can explain it. He was detached, almost in a daze. Turns out, he'd been collaborating on some case with the FBI for a while." Arianna could barely get the words out. "They found a couple of girls chained in a basement in a house they'd raided. They were half-dressed in dirty nightgowns, blood all over them, the whole nine, guys. A dead baby was on the floor, placenta still attached. It was horrific apparently."

"Good God," Taesha said.

"I heard about that," Eva said. "One girl survived, right?"

"The girl who'd given birth was dead. The other girl was *near* death, sprawled on the floor, cradling the dead baby. Can you believe it? They'd been starved; they were living in absolute squalor. Nathan couldn't sleep for weeks. Everybody involved had to go to counseling within the department; it was *that* bad. Nathan was questioning his career."

"Oh wait, I remember that story too. I was in Atlanta visiting my mother," Pam said. "It was heartbreaking."

"It did something to Nathan's mind. I can't tell him what happened to me now. It'll break him in half." Arianna instinctively rubbed her chest. "He won't snap back from that incident, *or* the betrayal from my lying, for so long."

"Does he even know it's a chemical burn?" Eva asked.

Arianna shook her head. "No, he thinks it's a burn from a big curling iron. An accident."

"Arianna," Pam said. "It doesn't take a doctor to know *this*"—she nodded toward Arianna's chest—"isn't from a curling iron and that it's no accident."

"Yes, it does take a doctor," Eva said, "if you want to deny something badly enough. You take the reason you're given and you run with it. Who wants to picture somebody they love being tortured?"

Pam stood still for a moment, seemingly taking in Eva's insight. Then she nodded in agreement. "Yeah, I guess you're right." She looked up suddenly. "But what does Arianna do now?"

Before Eva could respond, Taesha chimed in. "Okay, I'm confused again."

Pam shook her head at Taesha's terrible timing.

46

She continued anyway. "How do you look at this scar every day and make it through?"

"I almost don't sometimes. Some days are better than others, though. I don't look at it often. I don't stand in front of the mirror naked, if I can help it. It's something that I've accepted, I guess. It's like I will it to be gone and it fades away and I focus on my family. Nathan doesn't speak of it much. Guess it's something he's adjusted to as well." Arianna looked down to the letter where it lay on the floor. "Sometimes he takes his hand and softly rubs across the scar in the dark, as if he's telling me I'm still beautiful. Every time he does it, the guilt rips through me." She spoke low in her revelations. "I knew this would catch up to me. Now I have my dead mother begging me to tell Nathan the truth. Now I have to live with the fact that more girls suffered because I didn't say anything. Now I get to drown in open wounds all over again."

Again, there was a moment of quiet. All the girls, Arianna was sure, were taking in the horrific details and trying to process them, or worse, picture them. "Tell us about Bianca, Arianna," Taesha said.

Pam snapped. "Stop forcing it, Tae."

"You got one more time to snap at me," Taesha replied.

Eva spoke to both of them between clenched teeth. "STOP."

Arianna put up her hand. "Guys, this isn't helping."

"I *told* you guys that," Eva said as she glared at Pam and Taesha.

They were quiet once again as Arianna spoke. "Shortly after the end, Nightmare's wife had a baby, Bianca." She pounded her desk. "I didn't even *entertain* the idea that he would harm his own daughter too." She shook her head in gut-wrenching guilt. "God, if I had just said something sooner, she wouldn't have to endure it."

"You don't know that," Eva said. "And he's the bastard. Not you."

"Doesn't negate my silence. And it's too late now." Arianna did the math. "She couldn't have been more than sixteen when she killed herself. If that."

"You can't keep this on your shoulders," Pam said. "It's gonna snowball, Arianna. If you keep this bottled up, the pain you're feeling is going to affect your marriage. I'm surprised it hasn't already."

Arianna put the letter in her purse.

"What are you gonna do?" Taesha asked.

Arianna picked up Nate's photo, the one she'd snapped of him at a cookout a few years back. He was standing next to Marcus, beer in hand, a smile on his face, complete with his signature cap, Tony Parker jersey, and black basketball shorts. He'd looked at her, only briefly, when she'd called his name. She'd clicked before he could turn away.

As Arianna stared at Nate's image, she realized his force, his strength, his protective nature had kept them close, kept her sheltered from Nightmare. The way they made love soothed the pain of the sodomy that had maimed her tiny body.

But now, as the layers peeled away, she realized that evading the memory of Nightmare through ignorant bliss was nothing more than borrowed time. The way she never carried quarters. The way her hair stayed sleek straight because she couldn't bring herself to use a curling iron. Nightmare had always been there, asleep, waiting to touch her again, waiting for a moment to resurrect his dominance, magnify her deceit.

"Arianna?" Pam tried to bring her out of her trance. "What *are* you gonna do?"

Arianna looked at her friends, one by one, and then at the picture she was holding. She'd been so unfair to her husband. Her mother had known about this bastard; now her friends knew. And Tennessee law enforcement, while they didn't know about Arianna in particular, knew of Nightmare. Funny how things could get worse in the span of an hour, Arianna thought. Not only was she keeping a secret from Nate...she was now making him the last to know.

She took a deep breath, and once again, relived the night when Nate had come home hollow after seeing children in chains. She sank into the chair and looked up. "Sweet

Jesus, I *do* have to tell him now. I can't keep this hidden anymore."

Arianna, Pam, and Taesha glanced at Eva for the final word. Eva quickly glanced back at all of them, one by one. "Why do you guys always do this to me?"

"What should I do, Eva?" Arianna asked.

Eva looked out the window. She was the most intelligent one, most reasonable mind in the bunch. After a few moments of pondering, she responded. "Tell him." She pointed at Arianna. "You gotta get help too."

"I can't worry about myself right now. My husband's life is about to fall apart and there's nothing I can do to stop it."

"Slow down, Arianna," Eva said. "I didn't say tell him in the next five minutes. You have to plan this out."

"No. I have to do it before I change my mind." Arianna looked up. *God, help me.*

The silence that followed spoke of the anxiety the girls could never express.

Chapter 5

That night, Arianna arrived home later than usual. Nate and the boys were playing in the den. Nate was on his stomach, and Tre was trying to stomp on his back, falling down in the process. His plastic letters were scattered all over the floor. Darius complained about Tre's loud screams of joy; he couldn't hear himself think about his March Madness brackets. He was also arguing with Nate over team placement in the Final Four.

Arianna stood next to the couch and watched her happy, rambunctious family. She fixated on her men with a distant smile, as a tear almost ran down the side of her face. She stared at her babies until life seemed to slow, Tre jumping up and down, Nate groaning with each hit to his back, and Darius saying his witty quips always bordering on back talk.

"Hey, babe," Nate said. "Look who your son picked to win it all." He looked at Arianna. "You okay?"

"Yeah."

"How was your day?"

"Fine."

"It doesn't seem fine."

"Did you feed the kids?"

"No. I was waiting for you."

I can't tell him with the kids here. What the hell was I thinking?

"Mommy."

Keep it together, Arianna.

Arianna looked down and smiled at Tre. "Hey, baby."

Nate walked up close to her. "Something has you rattled. I can see it."

Arianna looked at Darius reviewing his brackets, and Tre running around in dizzying circles, oblivious to pain because Nate and Arianna had created such a peaceful haven in their home. They were a team—one that had overcome seemingly insurmountable odds. Maybe they could overcome this too...maybe.

But it would have to wait until she could better plan things and get Nate alone.

Arianna opened the fridge, trying to act normal, but her shaking hands wouldn't comply. "Nathan, could you take the kids to get something to eat?"

"What about you?"

"I'm good."

"You must have had a terrible day, babe."

Terrible isn't the word. "You can say that." She smiled at Nate, cupped his chin, and kissed his lips. "But it's better now." Arianna couldn't stop the visible vibration no matter how much she tried.

"You gotta come better than that. What happened?"

Arianna hesitated. She didn't answer.

"Ani?"

In that moment, facing her husband, and looking into his eyes, she realized that Eva was right—she needed a plan before crashing in Nate's world.

Arianna grabbed his hands and tried to think of a logical explanation that would satisfy him. Instead of lying, she did the next best thing—diverted his attention with a legitimate question that had nothing to do with the topic at hand. "Would you be upset if I decided to be a stay-at-home mom?"

Nate backed up. "Good Lord, what went on today?"

"This incorporating thing is tough." Another truth wrapped up in the wrong shell, like an authentic taco stuffed into a hamburger bun.

"You wanna quit working?"

"Just tossing the idea around. I have been since Tre was born." Another truth that was, well, true with bad timing. Since they'd discovered Tre's speech challenges, she'd thought maybe a career was selfish. Nate had convinced her to keep it. Now it was her hail-Mary to satisfy his inquisitions.

"I'd support whatever decision you made. Hell, I might even get laid more."

"Whatever, silly."

Arianna received a text from Pam. *Just thought of it. Do I need to come get the kids? We're going for pizza as usual and can keep them overnight. You know Marcus never minds.* ☺

She replied: *Thank you. Yes! I feel like I can't even breathe. Maybe I can talk to Nathan tonight after all.*

Thought you were going to do that anyway.

Well, I am now. With the kids gone, this is my only shot.

You sure?

I think so, yeah.

Be there in two minutes. Already in the car. Talk in a sec.

Arianna put down her phone, stared at it, and realized more than ever, the depth of her friendships. "Pam wants to take the kids for pizza with Marcus."

"We can all go. I'm starving."

"No." Arianna snapped.

"Excuse me?"

"I'm sorry. I just want some time alone with you, okay?"

Nate took a step back, seeming to analyze a rare moment of Arianna snapping at him. "Uh, okay."

"You alright, Nathan?"

"Are *you* alright?"

"Just want to decompress from the day."

"Yeah, you need to, for real."

A few moments later, Pam knocked, and broke up the awkward moment. Nate answered the door, staring back at Arianna until he left the kitchen. Her outburst had clearly jolted him.

"Hey...Nate," Pam said.

"Uh, hey."

Pam smiled and walked in stiffly, as if her robotic parts needed oil. She picked up Tre, and started a random conversation with Arianna. In turn, Arianna noticed Nate staring at the two of them as they talked in choppy sentences about the weather, pizza, and shoes.

"Why do I feel like I'm in a movie where aliens have taken over everybody's brains?" Nate said. "Because you two are acting weird as shit."

"Weird?" Pam asked.

"Women." Nate walked out and headed to the truck. Darius followed.

Arianna took a deep breath and exhaled. "Pam, I'm scared out of my mind."

"I know. And I'm not making it any better."

"It's okay. None of this is easy. Just go before Nathan gets more suspicious. Do you need clothes for the boys?"

"Nah, we have plenty."

"Tre is working on the letter B." Arianna escorted Pam to the door, gave Tre kisses, and waved to Darius.

Pam gave a last word. "You sure about this?"

"Yes."

"Call me if you need me. I'll have my phone close."

Arianna smiled. "Thanks."

Pam walked out and got in the truck.

Nate came back into the house as Marcus drove off. "Well, you got me alone, woman. Now start talking. Whose ass do I gotta kick for pissing you off?"

Arianna sat quietly for a few moments, trying to talk herself out of the reveal. Ten years of deceit. No matter her motives, her need to protect her family, her need to keep Nate sheltered from more carnage, lies still held their own faulty merits, and like bad investments born of good intentions, can't be unloaded without losing everything. But she had enough sense to know when the time had come to fess up. The thought of Nate never looking at her the same again shattered her, and she fought not to fall apart. The last thing Nate needed to see was panic before the explanation.

"You look serious. Is this really about this stay-at-home thing?" he asked.

Arianna didn't acknowledge the question. Instead, she got up and headed toward her purse. The letter would say it better than she ever could.

Her intestines felt like they'd come undone and had retied themselves too tightly. Her stomach stung and her neck tingled. *Please don't hate me, Nathan.*

Arianna reached inside her purse, hands shaking, still not acknowledging Nate.

"Ani, you're scaring the shit out of me right now," Nate said.

Nate's cellphone startled her more than any ringtone should. The contents of her purse scattered all over the floor. She scrambled to pick everything up as Nate looked at the caller ID, sighed, and then answered as if he hadn't wanted to. "Boss, what's up?"

Arianna frantically gathered her items and tried to gather her composure before standing up. She watched Nate sigh deeply, then shake his head and roll his eyes—another call, another frustration, another East Coast headache.

After about three minutes of ranting, Nate hung up with his boss and made his own call. From the way he was venting about crime versus bureaucracy, she could tell he was talking to his partner, Dave. "Can you believe this shit, man? They know to get a warrant first..."

Nate started pacing, something he often did when he was upset at the job. Arianna slyly slid the letter into her shirt, walked upstairs, and slipped the letter into her nightstand, hoping to vault it away permanently. Who was she kidding? Nate couldn't shoulder *another* issue, and he could never see the letter. But she couldn't destroy it either, because it contained her mother's last words.

Arianna came downstairs and heard Nate ending the call. "Talk to you soon, G."

"You okay, Nathan?"

He sighed. "Yeah, it's just the job. Every day there's either pain or anger. And I don't get the luxury of choosing which poison I'll swallow that day."

She thought of the girls in chains. "How are you with everything?"

"Everything?"

"You know."

"Ani, I. Am. Fine."

"You sure?"

"Yes. I don't wanna talk about it. I want *you* to talk to me."

Arianna swallowed, her nerves revved up again. She had to tell Nate at least part of it now. "Sit, baby."

He sat beside her. "What's wrong?"

She hesitated, then spoke. "My mother died."

"What! When?"

"A couple of days ago. I heard from the convalescent center at work today."

"I thought she was doing better. What the hell?"

"I did too."

"Jesus Christ, when's the funeral?"

"We're not going, Nathan."

"Why?"

"My father."

"His fat ass can go to hell." Nate seemed to catch himself. "I'm sorry. I know he's still your dad. I'm just...this damn job."

"It's okay. I'll say goodbye in my own time, my own way."

Nate studied her face as if her answer wasn't good enough, or even rational. She'd just lost her mother and was acting like the cat had just gotten run over. "You sure this is what you want, Ani?"

"Yes, I'm sure."

"Ani."

"Please!" Arianna put up her hands in another unfamiliar outburst. "I can't handle my father's hate. I can't."

Nate softened his stance, but appeared to be, yet again, cautious at her snappy demeanor. He said nothing else.

"I'm sorry, Nathan, I'm taking it out on you."

"You don't have to apologize." He held Arianna tightly, and kissed her forehead. "At least you were able to reconnect with her before she died."

"That I did."

He said sweetly, "What do you need?"

Her tears formed, and she melted in his arms as always. "I need you to be okay."

"Me? Ani, you are so unselfish."

I don't feel unselfish. "Just keep holding me."

In the comfort of Nate's warmth, Arianna tried to forget the tragedies of her detriment and her deceit, his agony and his anger. She knew Nate was growing tired of senseless searches and dead victims. She caressed his torso, lost in his presence. "Make love to me, Nathan."

"Oh, Ani," Nate whispered. "That's easy."

Nate took her upstairs and laid her down gently. He touched her, felt the scar as always. Then he kissed her chest and began to suck on her breasts. His openness to her disfigurement gutted her, raised the guilt over her secrets, and raised her awareness of the pain in his heart from the many tragedies of his career. What she needed most that night, her husband's love, she couldn't receive. Her onus wouldn't allow it.

"I can't." She jumped off him. "I'm sorry."

Arianna ran to the bathroom. The commode was cold against her palms. Trying to vomit on an empty stomach did nothing but remind her that all day she hadn't eaten. Saliva trickled out of her mouth as the uncontrollable heaving tightened her abdomen. Each jolt of her throat brought a lapse in breathing, then the need to rapidly exhale. She gripped the porcelain, taking in a steady stream of air as if pacing herself with each step on the track.

So devious, Nightmare's plan. A poor child would do anything for a couple of dollars. Easy. Get the money, go inside, and give up your innocence to survive the ghetto. End up a grown woman, hunched over a commode, reliving the ghetto.

Nate walked into the bathroom. He lifted Arianna's hair back so vomit wouldn't stick to the strands. She finished heaving. Nate flushed the toilet. "Come here."

He and Arianna stood in front of the mirror. Nate turned on the faucet and let the cold water turn warm. He grabbed a washcloth and wiped her face.

Arianna brushed her teeth while Nate wiped down the commode. He put the rag in the hamper and washed his hands.

"I'm sorry for freaking out, Nathan."

"It's been a sad day, Ani. Don't apologize to me for being human."

"We can try again."

"Not tonight, baby. It's too much. Let's just go to sleep."

The Jacksons went to bed, Nate on his side, Arianna in his arms.

~~~

"Hey, pretty girl."

"Get away from me!"

"Let's make up for lost time, shall we?"

Arianna woke up in response to the jolt of Nightmare pulling her to him. She looked over to Nate realizing he was sound asleep. *Thank God.*

After ten years, Nightmare had returned, and with him, all the tainted skin Arianna felt she possessed and blatant reminders of how she'd deceived her husband all these years. She curled up in the fetal position, realizing her happy world had been too good to be true.

Then, Nightmare's return hit her, made her realize the purpose for her mother's letter—to say goodbye. Helen Statton had died and robbed Arianna of any chance to build the bond they'd lost when her father had separated them.

Arianna buried her face in the pillow, and silently tried to cry herself to sleep. It didn't work. The memories of her mother surfaced, her struggles, her lifelong pains.

But she also thought of the good times they'd had together, impoverished or not. The times Arianna's mother had done her nails, the nights she would keep Arianna motivated to stay on track when school had become too much.

The whimper turned into a full-scale wail, and Arianna could no longer hold it in. She felt Nate's arms shelter her as she wept for her mother, wept for her mangled memories.

April

"What do you want from me, Ani? I love you. I'm concerned."

"Just stop pressuring me to talk, Nathan."

"I knew skipping your mother's funeral was going to do more harm than good."

"Don't lecture me."

"I'm not trying to."

"Just leave me alone for a while."

May

"Late again, Ani?"
"Bad day. I'm going to bed, okay?"

June

"Would you please just talk to me, Ani?"
"I can't, I just...I can't."

July

"Shit, is it me, Ani?"

"For the last time, no. I'm just overwhelmed, Nathan."

"I'm not stupid."

"What do you mean?"

"You didn't start acting like this until your mother died. Do you blame me somehow?"

"Blame you for what?"

"I don't know. That maybe I took you from her when we moved away. Shit, I'm grasping at straws here. Help me out."

"No, of course not. I'm just dealing with a new corporation."

August

"Where are you going, Nathan?"
"I gotta get some air."

September

"It's a nice night, Ani. Wanna take a walk, baby girl, talk?"

"No, I have to reconcile the quarter. Maybe next weekend."

October

"Not tonight, Nathan."

"You said that last night...and the night before that."

"I'm sorry. I'm just really tired."

"I'm trying to be supportive, but this is getting old, Arianna Rae."

"Where are you going?"

"The guestroom."

Chapter 6

Halloween complemented the Jackson household nicely. It was the one night adults could pretend. A man could wear a mask and be something, or someone, he wasn't.

"I'll take Tre," Arianna said. "You can pass out the candy." She handed Nate the candy bowl. He shoved it away, shy of spilling the Tootsie Rolls onto the floor.

"I got him. Let's go, Tre."

"I can take him, babe."

Babe. Whatever. "I said I got him." He spoke low enough to whisper, but harsh enough to let her know he didn't want to whisper.

Seven months was all it had taken to unravel a once beautiful, sensual marriage. The nights of soft music, satin sheets, and silk linens seemed a lifetime ago.

"Don't forget his jacket," Arianna said.

"It's not cold enough." Nate walked outside with Tre, or rather, the White Power Ranger.

Each house told a story. The dark ones, those without illuminated porch lights, signaled passersby to stay away. Nate wondered about the deeper meaning, why the families in these homes wished to be left alone. Before, he hadn't questioned such trivial matters. Wedded bliss had kept him confined to his happy world. Analyzing the degree of unhappiness in others hadn't been necessary. Now Nate needed a benchmark. How many men were staying in marriages out of obligation? Were the non-trick-or-treating participants rebelling against the meaning of the night, or were they miserable and not wanting to celebrate a damn thing?

The houses decorated with Dracula and Frankenstein seemed festive. The orange lights framing the lawns of a few of his neighbors were a nice touch. Were those families happy? Did those men work tirelessly to hang the decorations to appease their bitchy wives?

Strange what a strained marriage could make a man think.

Three blocks down and an undetermined number to go. Tre was carrying his plastic pumpkin and Nate was holding the cargo pillowcase.

"Over there, Daddy." Tre ran across the street.

Nate trotted to catch up. "Give me your hand, Tre."

He passed Darius. At first, Nate didn't notice him. Then he heard Dracula. "What's up, Dad?"

"You get any chocolate?"

Darius handed off a snack size bar and went on with his friends.

"Be careful," Nate said.

Four more blocks. Tre ran up to Marcus's door. Before hitting the driveway, Nate could hear the ghastly noises coming from the stereo. "Trick or treat."

Pam filled Tre's pumpkin with an unfairly generous portion of candy. Nate reached into the bowl and grabbed a Milky Way. "Where's Marcus?"

"At work. It's a late one," she said.

Nate nodded. He didn't reply, didn't engage in conversation. "Thank you," he said, treating Pam like another neighbor.

Tre ran to the next house. Again, Nate trotted to catch up.

"Okay, that's enough now. Let's go home, champ," he said. He hoisted Tre onto his shoulders.

All Tre wanted to do, it seemed, was hurry home to show his mommy how much candy he'd gotten. For Nate, the joy of anticipation wasn't there, the feeling one parent gets when wanting to see the reaction of the other parent at a child's good news. He didn't care. Instead, he walked block to block, mindlessly heading home.

The porch light was off and the house seemed dark as well. Nate took Tre down from his shoulders and they walked inside. The empty candy bowl was in the sink. Darius was in his room. Arianna was asleep. Nate checked Tre's candy for homemade items and potential dangers and gave Tre two pieces. Then he prepared Tre for bed. Arianna had apparently checked Darius's stash. Good thing, because it was halfway gone.

"No more," Nate said to Darius. "Go to bed before you throw up everywhere."

A quiet home allowed Nate more ammunition to realize that things weren't the same. Halloween used to be an experience. The Jackson home used to be the one with orange lights and scary music, the one with skeletons hanging from trees and sinister spiders in bushes. Now it was one of the houses he'd analyzed, one of the places that had been decorated last year, so something must have happened this year.

He peeked in the master bedroom. Arianna lay on her side. Sleep made her look innocent, like the devoted, sexy wife he'd married. How easy it would have been to lie down next to her, to kiss her bare shoulders, to drop each strap on her nightshirt. But he couldn't. She'd reject him just like she'd done ninety-five percent of the times he'd tried since March; or he'd get the other five percent, the times she'd reluctantly spread her legs, and he'd monotonously work for his inconvenient orgasm.

He thought back to the night she had come home, shaken over her mother's death. Arianna's emotional landslide had to be attributed to that, the loss, the inability to have her mother in her life. But that wouldn't explain it all.

There was more. Otherwise, avoiding Nate didn't make sense.

Arianna moved slightly, and her camisole shifted down her chest enough to reveal the scar, the one her father had given her at the hand of a curling iron, the one they had both adjusted to as part of her past that would never define their future. Nate zeroed in on the wound, and then thought back to college, reliving meeting Arianna's mother and father, loving her and loathing him. Memories of dating Arianna in Knoxville consumed him for what seemed like years as he stood at the bedroom door.

Then, going off what he knew about Arianna's mom, her need to see Arianna succeed, it hit him—Arianna had something to prove to her mother, a post-mortem dying wish, powerful enough to swallow her whole and consume her time. That had to be it.

Nate continued to stare at Arianna's body, reliving memories of meeting her when she was just eighteen and helping her to unravel her impoverished life. He thought back to the reveal of her scar, how frightened she'd been. Then his thinking suddenly shifted, as if he'd been lifted up and suddenly dropped, as impossible as that seemed.

Jesus, how come I didn't see it?

Arianna feeling the need to prove herself to a maternal ghost might have been part of it—but her shutdown was due to another person, Nate was sure of it now—her dysfunctional father.

He shook his head. The death of Arianna's mother had triggered the pain, the nightmare of her father's abuse. That was it.

Nate approached Arianna quickly, but stopped when he realized the spontaneous move could do more harm than good. Trying to talk to her about how her father had burned her wouldn't be as easy as taking candy from his son.

I have to figure out a way to bring this up.

Nate got ready for bed. He wanted to reach out to Arianna in his revelation, but without bringing up the pain. While the best he could offer her was his warm embrace, her cold shoulder would be too much to handle. Nate couldn't take the torture. He'd been living in hell for seven months, physically, emotionally, and with the heat of his job, professionally as well.

The couch beckoned. Nate lay down and watched a movie before dozing off.

~~~

"Tonight's gonna be real fun, pretty girl. Fitting, don't you think?"

"I don't want to play anymore."

"That's too bad. I'm just getting started."

"Ouch."

Arianna jerked and opened her eyes. She felt an anxiety that had become a constant in the night. She looked over to Nate's side of the bed. He was gone. Arianna checked all over and found him on the couch. This jarred her deeply; Nate was no longer waiting for rejection to sleep elsewhere. He'd become proactive, avoiding it altogether, a sign they were growing further and further apart. At some point soon, she'd have to stop the breakdown or face the inevitable—she and Nate wouldn't make it.

Arianna was drowning in the horror of Nightmare, too traumatized for real intimacy, and too selfless to hurt her husband.

That night came back to her, the one that had caused her husband so much devastation, the night Nate had come home a shell of his former self, a hollow man at the hands of a sadistic bastard who'd ravaged innocent girls and left them to die in a basement.

She went back upstairs.

The small carry-on travel bag in the closet caught her eye. She'd forgotten Nate had told her he had to leave tomorrow. She wasn't sure how much of that was the truth. While she did believe he had to leave, she questioned whether it was due to his job, or to a reprieve from the woman who used to be his loving wife.

I can't let him leave like this. Arianna walked backed downstairs and lay down next to him on a couch too small for both of them to comfortably sleep. Arianna took the hit in the position, sacrificed comfort to be next to him. She clung to him in her desperate need for his presence, and in her commitment to sparing him the same pain she endured.

When Arianna woke the next morning, Nate was gone, his carry-on gone as well.

Winter

"Dad, are you and Mom alright?"
"Sure, Son. Grab your coat."
"When do you leave again?"
"A couple days."
"You're gone a lot more now."
"I know."

Spring

"Daddy, Mommy go to carnival."
"Not today, champ."
"Daddy go bye-bye soon."
"I'll be back before you know it."
"I get sad."
"Daddy gets sad too, Son."

Summer

"Spending more time away from home isn't gonna solve it, Nate."

"I don't know what else to do, Marcus."

"When are you coming home?"

"Few weeks."

"You can't go on like this forever."

"No shit."

Fall

"Hey. Boss, what's up?"

"Sit down, Jackson."

"Damn, why are you being so nice?"

"Just sit down."

"Okay...what is it?"

"That kid you're fond of in your mentorship program. Jeremy Banks... There's no easy way to say this. He's dead, Jackson."

"J-Bug?"

"I'm afraid so. They found his body behind a dumpster near his home."

"No...no...NO!"

"I'm sorry, Jackson..."

"Nah, that can't be. I just saw him the other day. Shit, I helped him put a shed in his backyard. You sure it's him?"

"Yes, Jackson."

"Can't be."

"Sit down. It is."

"I want to see the body."

"No, you don't. Trust me."

"I need to be sure."

"Jackson, don't do this. You sound like a parent in denial."

"Don't lecture me, Agent Greene."

"Look, I know you're upset. I get it. But if you don't back away from my desk, and calm down, I *will* handle you...that's better."

"This can't be happening. He was doing so well."

"You knew this going in. You know these streets."

"He had a shot at a productive life."

"And you did what you could."

"Who did it?"

"Who do you think?......Jackson, talk to me."

"Reese needs to get got."

"Soon."

"Not soon enough."

"I told you to sit down, Jackson. Keep your head."

"I'm not that stupid, Boss. I'm not gonna blow a years-long investigation."

"Where are you going?"

"Home."

~~~

"Ani, I'm drowning here. The walls are closing in at work. I need my wife back. I can't do this anymore. I lost one of my kids. In Baltimore."

"Not tonight. I'm tired."

"Are you even listening to me? That's *not* it. You think that's all I want? I mean I want *you* back. Your support, your faith in me."

"I didn't mean it like that."

"Look, I'm gonna get right to it. We have to discuss your father. We have to lay this to rest."

"Wh-What about him?"

"Calm down. I'm just saying, about how you got the scar, and how you're freaking out all the time. We have to deal with it."

"Nathan, stop! I don't want to talk about this."

"Where are you going?"

"I have a meeting."

"Are you serious right now? I come home in pieces, and you leave?"

"I gotta go."

Chapter 7

Zachary Deleon Sanchez
Devoted Husband
Dedicated to Justice

Nate waited at Zach's grave for Marcus to arrive. They often came here to find peace, to block out the world in a sea of quiet. No one made noise in a cemetery.

The eleventh anniversary had come and gone with no balloons, no Mokara, and no pregnancy. Six months shy of their twelfth anniversary, which was sneaking up on them every day, probably wouldn't be a celebration either.

For about five seconds, he thought about leaving, making an excuse to vacate the graveyard due to Marcus's tardiness. But he couldn't. He was drowning, and he needed to talk to his friends, one alive, one dead. Zach's headstone set the tone for another life Nate felt had gotten cut short—his own.

"What's up?" Marcus caught his attention as he pulled out the other metal chair from an adjacent tree. Nate had pulled his thirty-minutes ago.

Nate unloaded. "I can't do this anymore, Marcus."

"Your marriage?"

Nate shook his head. "Yeah. After all this time, she still won't talk. I tried bringing up her bastard dad and she freaked out." He fell silent, staring at Zach's headstone. "I'm out of options to heal us."

Marcus too looked at Zach's headstone. "You know Zach's mother is a psychologist. What advice do you think our boy would give you?"

"Counseling is a joke. I've been through it. Besides, Arianna won't even speak to me. How could we get through something like that?"

"You do make a good point. But maybe you should try anyway."

Nate quickly changed the subject, trying to get closer to his last-resort decision and further away from therapy. "We haven't had sex in four months."

Marcus snapped his neck in Nate's direction. "Seriously?"

"Yup."

"I knew it was bad, but goddamn. You're not getting *any*?"

"This is the longest stretch. I don't even want to initiate anymore. Hell, when I do get it, it's bland as hell."

"What are you gonna do?"

Nate didn't answer. He kept tapping his foot in the dirt and sighing like the Spurs had lost the NBA championship by two points in triple overtime.

"Jesus, you're gonna file for divorce."

Nate looked at him as if he were crazy. "What? And leave my kids? Hell no."

"Then what?"

Nate turned away. It took him a minute to process what he was about to say. Vocalizing his intent would make it real. "I met someone."

"What?" Marcus asked. Then his eyes opened wide. "You didn't."

"Not yet."

"Who is she? In Baltimore?"

"Nah. I don't want you to know who she is. Keep you out of it."

"I'm married to Arianna's best friend. Goddamnit, I'm already in it."

"I'll protect you."

"Protect me? Jesus Christ, what do you want me to do that I'll need protecting?"

There Nate was, contemplating the choices that would define what he'd become and unravel what he'd worked so hard to overcome. He missed Arianna's touch and comfort. Nate thought it ironic. Arianna had always been the one to express her feeling of safety with him, that he sheltered her from the cruelty of life. But she was the one who'd protected *him* from the evils of the world, giving him a safe place to land whenever he'd needed to fall, providing a warm place whenever he'd needed to come in from the cold. Now that warmth and safety were gone. "I need a ride."

"This is a bitch ass move. You know that, right?" Marcus said.

"I don't wanna do this to Arianna. I'm in love with that woman, man. The last thing I need is for you to judge me."

"Pam and I have problems too. But damn. I would never cheat."

"Please come off your high horse. This is about so much more than sex. It's about being wanted, Marcus. And there isn't a damn thing anyone can do for Ani if she doesn't want to get better. I'll just have to ride it out. But damn, I'm still a man. My ass has gotta get laid. I gotta feel the touch of a woman."

Now it was Marcus's turn to absorb the moment. Nate watched him look around, sigh, and look around again. He took a good ten minutes to think about it.

"I will help you, Nate, but only because I know you'll do this shit without me anyway, and end up doing God-knows-what. But I'm gonna tell you, right now, I don't like this shit and I damn sure don't agree with it. It's beneath you, and it's beneath me."

"Thanks. I owe you."

"What do you want me to do, exactly? Drive you? Where?"

"I'm still putting it together. It's been some years since I've cheated on anyone."

Chapter 8

Nate unlocked the door and entered room 108. The tenth visit, the ninth time he'd promised never to visit his old ways, the first time he'd decided to stop making promises he couldn't keep.

He knew the risks. Marriage, job, and pride all at stake, following a dysfunctional path he'd learned from his father, yet holding to the belief that *this time*, his pain validated his choices, even though his illicit actions had vanquished his right to hurt.

It was five-thirty in the morning. Nate shut the door to room 108.

The fan was off. The air smelled like a load of wet clothes left for a week in a washing machine. The room was muggy, adding to the stench. Nate set the air-conditioner to high. He always let it run until the room felt like a meat freezer. It was a habit he'd been spoiled on since leaving for college. He couldn't stand to be hot. Growing up, Nate, Sr. had kept a tight hold on money. Electricity had been closely watched, and the light bill—pure evil.

The temperature in the room had become a source of contention. Nate liked it freezing. His mistress wanted it sweltering. They would often bicker over heat and other small things.

Arianna called. Nate stared at the photo ID, allowing her smile to take him back to happier days. A time when they'd both laughed and when Nate had understood the meaning of depth in simple things. A moment when he'd snapped a shot of his beautiful wife smiling at the thought of getting a caramel sundae. He stared at the woman his wife used to be, hoping her soft facial features would give him a sense of morality.

He let the call flow to voicemail, realizing the only thing staring at a two-year-old picture could do for him was remind him it was time to upgrade his phone. "You can't say I didn't try."

He ripped up this morning's motel receipt and dropped the pieces into the rusty commode. The ink smeared away and then he flushed. Alone, and with his thirty-nine-dollar proof erased, he waited on the familiar bed. Every corner of this raunchy motel room, room 108, told a forbidden story of Nate recapturing his manhood.

"She better c'mon," he said as he looked through the curtains.

Had traffic delayed his mistress? Did she have a point to prove? He didn't care. By five-forty, she was late. Nate used the downtime to erase Arianna's unheard voicemail and reply to a text from Marcus letting him know he too was getting sick of catching dumb-ass criminals.

Another call came in from Arianna. He turned off the phone.

Today was veering from routine. Nate had never needed to pass time in the room because his mistress had always been on time. Finding something to do before dawn in a dive motel was hard. The television had no reception, so that was out. What was he going to do, complain and get another television?

Her being late made Nate feel bruised. And his ego was a sensitive deal. He needed something masculine.

Push-ups seemed appropriate.

His body broke the plane between his shoulder blades and elbows with seasoned precision. He teased the floor with his chest, getting close enough to cause the kind of static he would open himself up to if Arianna ever found out he was cheating. Fast and fierce he counted.

The burn set in at close to eighty-five. Thinking of Arianna sitting behind her desk propelled him to suffer, but the notion of *no pain, no gain* did nothing to assuage the guilt. He cursed himself until his arms shook, then stopped the pointless exercise. Plus, he'd begun to sweat.

"Girl, you got fifteen minutes and then I'm out."

He read the newspaper. A DEA agent had to stay abreast. City crime was small scale, but no less important than shutting down major drug cartels. Clues to major crimes always brewed under the local headlines. Perhaps something would open up a lead to the major drug operations in the country's ports.

Oh, the irony of his actions. All the traveling he'd done, all the time spent away from Arianna, safely on what felt like the other side of the world. No wife to check up on him, no kids to drag him home. Isolation to do whatever he'd wanted, and not once had he touched another female. Nights he would shut the curtains, then lie down in a hotel room blacker than burnt coffee, fighting the urge to take a nice young lady (pick one) up on her offer, to take her back to the room, to screw her senseless; the internal battling he'd done in the name of loyalty to a wife states away, and now he found himself cheating a few miles down the street from home.

Nate checked his watch and cracked the curtain. No sign.

He stroked his goatee. "I'm out."

As he was making a quick stop to the bathroom, she knocked on the door with the usual code: two quick taps, a three-second pause, two quick taps. He flushed, and prepared to rehash the rules. Rule number one: Always be on time.

He opened the door, ready to fire away.

But when she walked into the room wearing a fuchsia mini-dress that coated her well-proportioned body smoother than the syrup on a candy apple, he reconsidered. And when she dropped the overlay, defining her strapless attire, he shut the door behind her.

Mistress moved in on his mouth.

"You know we don't kiss. I don't know where the hell your lips have been," Nate said. "I don't know why you keep trying."

"I'm not a quitter."

"Funny."

"You don't know where the rest of me has been either, but you run up in it."

"Condoms. Why are you so late?"

"I don't think you have the right to ask me that until you make me an honest woman."

"Six months into this, you wanna get honest. Really?"

"I told you last time, I'm changing."

"Let's get on with it."

"Fine." She pushed him onto the bed and stripped the lower half of his body.

Mistress wiggled out of her clothes, then made her way to Nate's lips again. He turned away.

"What would you like?" she whispered.

Nate stared at the outdated television. The silver knobs, the scratched framing. The lower standards from what he'd grown accustomed to. "You know what I gotta have."

She guided him inside. Nate closed his eyes and dreamt of another bed at another time, when Arianna used to guide him inside. Back then, there was no reason to close his eyes and focus on anything other than the woman he'd made his wife. Arianna would lean down to kiss him, and he would slide his hands down her sides as she lowered herself to reach his lips. By then, his hands would be at her waist. He would slide one arm across her back and one just below her cheeks, allowing her to stroke him as they kissed, as they left the technical troubles of marriage behind to focus on being lovers above all else. He would hold her, not letting her up for what seemed like hours.

He lay there on his back, allowing each stroke with his mistress to grow more intense, more pleasurable for his physical hunger. The wetter she became, the more he felt at ease because her orgasm was guaranteed. But holding her? Nuh uh. Kissing a woman he didn't love? No way in hell.

"You are so good, Nate. This is all yours."

"Prove it."

Nate grabbed her hips, anticipating the justification for his infidelity. Her body contracted wildly, thereby validating his parking pass. Her piercing screams worried him because the parchment-thin walls allowed other people to hear, but he would have worried more if she'd kept quiet. He needed the evidence of an amazing performance. He needed a guarantee he hadn't created Arianna's sudden inability to perform. Deep down, he knew as much, but as a guy, a bruised ego was a bruised ego, despite another person's culpability.

"Why'd you stop?" he asked.

"It just feels so good."

"This isn't all about you."

"I got it covered." She rode him with double-jointed hips that seemed to go in every direction, letting him know she was doing most of the work. She slammed into him until he closed his eyes and reached his hollow satisfaction. Once done, he could see her gloating with a false sense of power, and he didn't like her cocky attitude. He always fought not to make a sound with her because he wanted the upper hand, and letting her know she was good would give her too much power to dominate the affair.

After he unclamped her, she grabbed her purse and went into the bathroom. "Don't I always take care of you, Nate?"

"Just hurry."

He stared up at the water-stained, foam-tile ceiling, and over at the peeling, off-red carpet, until his mistress came out of the bathroom. Nate looked away from her, gathered his clothes, and went into the bathroom.

"You are so wrong, Jackson," said half the man to his other half. Nate was learning how hard it was to scold yourself when one part felt guilt, one part felt justified, yet nothing felt whole. When he looked into the chipped mirror, the only concrete thing he knew was that he needed a haircut. His fade was losing definition.

Nate finished cleaning up, put on his black button-down shirt, and walked back into the room. He gave his mistress a blank stare as he continued to play tennis with his feelings of guilt and justification.

"Go," he said.

"Where's my ring?"

"Excuse me?"

"I told you last time. I want my ring. Your wife has one."

"That's because she's my wife."

"Then why are you here?"

"Good question."

"Don't get smart. I told you, you need to make an honest woman out of me."

"My ride will be here soon."

Nate looked through the crack in the thick curtains. Marcus was waiting in the truck. Nate opened the door and remembered the room key. He walked to the table to grab it. It was gone.

"Be back at eleven," she said, holding up the key. "I'll take an early lunch."

"What?"

Nate had firm rules. He checked in at five-thirty in the morning, checked out by seven-thirty. He controlled the key and always paid cash. He never drove his own car and, if his mistress told anyone about the affair, he would deny everything. She spoke to no one and never showed her face walking in and out of the room.

"It's becoming clear you're not gonna leave her. Come back or your wife gets an earful from me."

"We agreed no strings."

"I'm changing the rules."

"You can't change rules I've written, sweetheart."

"Wanna bet?"

"You can't threaten me either." Nate shook his head.

"I just did."

"She won't believe you. I'll see to it."

"You wanna take that risk? You wanna see her take your retarded child away?"

Nate sucked in his abdomen, tightened his body, and fought like hell not to punch her in the throat. His mistress may have been a cruel and nasty woman, but she was still a female. "He's not retarded. He has an articulation disorder. Fuck you."

"Be here, or else."

"What's gotten into you?"

"Me and my power. I'm running things now. Any more questions?"

Nate fell silent. He didn't want to lose control. But after staring down his mistress, he realized he couldn't lose something he'd never had.

"That's what I thought," she said.

Nate left without another word.

Chapter 9

Nate donned his shades and walked toward Marcus's idling vehicle. *I just did*—the threat from his mistress—inched across his mind like the words on an antiquated screensaver. His back felt a creepy itch, the kind you get when you've left something behind you can't grasp, something you can't undo, and something you can't direct. Damn, he thought. Never go back to old ways with a new breed of woman.

Marcus met him halfway. He stared sharply at Nate, the way a parent would threaten a misbehaving child in a grocery store.

"What's wrong with you?" Nate asked.

"What took so damn long?"

"Had some hiccups." Nate walked off and approached the truck. "Let's go."

"Hold up."

Nate stood there as Marcus caught up. "What is it?"

"I'm catching heat, Nate."

"What do you mean?"

"My boss wants to know why the hell I'm starting to come in late almost every other Friday. He called me in early and wanted to know what was going on."

Nate kept watch on room 108. "I thought you had that handled."

"I thought I did too. I'm gonna get written up if it continues."

"Okay, let's talk about it on the road."

"We're not alone."

"What?"

"I couldn't leave by myself."

"Excuse me?"

"Just play along." Marcus opened the door. "Nate, this is D.J."

Nate stared at a white man with reddish-brown hair, cut in a low white-boy fade coming up to a spiked crown. He was solid and muscular, yet somewhat lean, and wearing Levi's and a black T-shirt with the words *Linkin Park* flashing off his chest, his arms sleeved in tattoos. Nate deducted that this man must be Marcus's partner, since Marcus had told him his partner was white. Whenever Marcus had a bad day, he would vent to Nate about not having anything in common with him and how he kept asking for another partner.

Nate slammed the door shut on the man waiting inside. "Are you trying to get me caught? You can't do this. This isn't Zach!"

Nate looked out into the street, trying to stop the rage building in each muscle. He gazed around the low environment as he desperately thought of what the hell to say to this white man who, undoubtedly, wanted to know why he was at a motel worth less than a single star.

Across the road a pawn shop was opening its doors. Adjacent to it, the gas station with the cheap, inadequate gas was starting to get business with the older-model cars, ones built tough enough to withstand anything, even less-than-clean fuel. Down the way was another cheap motel. Nate wondered if another lost DEA agent was there, looking for absolution through sex.

Seeing Marcus's partner enraged him, true, but not for the breach of trust between best friends alone. It introduced Nate to shame on a new level. His BFF judging him was one thing. To be judged by a strange Caucasian male, someone who Nate felt was probably looking at him like he was trash, pained him to his gums. Nate had painted his own image, shaped his own character; hence, he'd set himself up for failure, lit the path for people to make him feel less than a man.

Nate felt powerless, because he'd just given his power to an insane mistress and an unfamiliar white dude. But worse yet, he was beginning to realize he'd also given his power to Marcus, because he was at his mercy for rides.

"Why?" Nate asked.

"I needed cover. I couldn't be unaccountable again."

Nate thought of his mistress, who he assumed was peeking out the window, snickering at her new-found control as she toyed with him, making him wonder when she was going to emerge to shed her aloofness. Nate looked at D.J. "Get in the back."

"Uh, what?"

"Do you want me to place you there?"

"D.J.," Marcus interjected. "Just get in the back."

D.J moved to the back. Nate got in, but not before glaring at D.J. hard enough to leave an impression of contempt.

It's unraveling.

Losing control was profound for Nate, because he always directed and executed what he thought was his destiny—excelling in high school in Houston, then choosing the University of Tennessee—weeding out many other schools to study communications and criminal justice—before commissioning into the Army as an Intelligence Officer with the National Security Agency located in Maryland. Before he'd figured out his next life move, the Drug Enforcement Administration had contacted him and invited him to apply.

Now, for once, he found himself seeking refuge from others.

"Your ring."

Nate took his wedding band out of his pocket and put it on his finger.

"Your shirt."

Nate fixed the buttons on his shirt.

"Your badge?"

"Got it, damn."

"I'm getting tired of paying attention to your details."

"Would you stop?" Nate glanced in the back.

"He can't hear me."

"Drive."

Marcus got on IH-37 to head toward downtown. "I can't believe I agreed to this."

Nate sighed. "Here we go again." He noticed D.J.'s green eyes stabbing at him from the rearview mirror.

Marcus brought his voice up to normal. "When are you going back to Baltimore?"

"Sunday."

"You Vice?" D.J. asked.

"DEA."

"I thought you were Vice. I thought that was why we picked you up from the room."

Nate looked back. "You honestly think I'd screw a hooker for the goddamned job?"

"You tell me."

"I'm a federal agent. Nothing compromises my job."

"Then why are you here?"

Nate looked at Marcus, then faced the front. "See what happens when you bring in a third party?"

"I told you I had no choice," Marcus said. "It doesn't matter... it's just business."

Nate took this as a subtle reminder to stay cool. D.J. didn't know the personal nature of Nate's stay.

Nate looked over his shoulder. "I had some information to gather for my next trip. I live here and I commute to Baltimore."

"How? Fly?"

Nate bit his lip, contemplating whether or not to play along. He hated to be interrogated; yet entertaining D.J.'s questions gave him an opportunity to redirect the conversation, away from the motel, away from dirty secrets.

"No, I walk."

"They put you up?"

"Yep."

"That's a lot of federal funds."

"It's also a lot of drugs off the streets."

Marcus began talking to D.J. about a case. Nate checked his cell phone. He always turned it off right before his illicit romps. Separating the motel from reality could only work if he cut off the outside world.

Nate listened to two new apologetic messages from Arianna. "She said her engine's sounding funny again." He tapped the phone on his leg. "It's probably nothing. She's trying to get me to come home. This is why I stopped listening to her damn messages."

"Last night Pam told me I was minimizing her pain. Why do women say dumb shit?" Marcus asked.

"Because women *think* about dumb shit." Nate looked at Marcus. "What are you doing?"

"Nothing."

Nate had caught Marcus making a cutting motion at his throat with his finger while looking in the rearview mirror.

"You got something to say to me? Say it," Nate said to D.J.

D.J. kicked back, arms folded. "Just wondering what's so special about you the United States Government would waste so many taxpayer dollars."

Nate lunged toward the backseat and got in D.J.'s face. "Well, Mr. Treasury Secretary, why don't you cut off my funding and take your ass to East Baltimore and catch Johnny Reese and his merry band of the most dangerous criminals ever to walk Baltimore by your goddamned self."

Marcus reached over and grabbed him. The truck swerved as Marcus fought traffic with one hand and Nate's hostility with the other. "You need to end this. It's killing you. Now turn your ass around before I get in an accident or worse yet, get pulled over by a colleague."

"I can't believe you put this dude all up in my shit," Nate said.

"Drive yourself from now on. I'm done," Marcus said.

Marcus pulled into a parking lot near the Alamodome, approached Nate's luxury sedan, swerved, and then backed in beside it.

Nate frantically patted himself down before realizing he still had his wallet. "Oh Jesus, thank God."

"What's wrong with you?" Marcus asked.

"It's nothing."

"Nah, you're more edgy than normal."

"Get out with me," Nate said. He glared at D.J. one last time.

"Why?" Marcus asked.

"I don't need an audience."

Marcus and Nate got out of the vehicle and walked a few feet away.

"Nate, I gotta get back, man. What's up?"

"You remember the summer after we graduated high school? When we went to Galveston before we both left? Set those goals of a good life and a good education by thirty."

"Yeah, and we made it. So?"

"Did we?"

"Oh my Lord, I hate when you get all Aristotle and shit."

"What happened? We struggled, worked hard, saved every spare dime, learned the markets, invested, stayed in school. We married hard-working, ambitious, educated women."

"What are you getting at?"

"Look at us. Between dual incomes and investment incomes, we pull in, what, two-hundred-plus a year? We're not even thirty-five yet."

"Well, Pam and I don't rake in *that* much, but enough to be comfortable."

"Enough to live in Stone Oak and have excellent credit."

"I gotta get back to the job. What's your point?"

"Why am I struggling to be happy? I was happier when Ani and I were sacrificing *everything*."

"Rough patches, Nate. We talked about this before you decided to cheat. We have to believe we can fight through them. Even with our best intentions, we were still young. Wives were never in the plan. We deviated. Hell, we were both married with children just after we were legally old enough to drink. Problems are gonna pop up. But shit like this isn't helping either of us."

"That's easy for you to say. You're still happy. Pam still screws you."

"Not like she used to. Things are different. But I deal with it."

Nate's voice got loud. "That's just it. I don't want my marriage to be something I have to *deal* with. I just want Ani to be the same. Back in the day, we survived on little sleep and even less money for years, hardly went anywhere...but we were so, so strong. Now, I can buy her the world and it's not enough to make it right. I gotta make it right. I *have* to make it right, Marcus."

Marcus sounded impatient, ready to get back to work to prevent a write-up. "You have to stop *screwing* another woman first. Now you wanna get all remorseful."

"I've always been remorseful. Don't go there. I know this affair has to end."

"Your ass is in rare form today."

"I have to put us back together and I'm running out of time."

"Nate, what happened in that room this morning?"

"She threatened to tell Ani. She's dead serious."

"Intelligent move, genius." Marcus shook his head. "I'm no cheater, but common sense tells me you don't pick a side chick who knows your wife!"

"Shhh. I didn't say they know each other. Anybody can find out that type of shit."

"Yeah, whatever. Do I know her, Nate?"

"No, damn."

"Just making sure. Never know with you."

"I don't need the sarcasm right now. I need your support. When you're faced with the reality of it all, it hits you. Ani's my baby, Marcus. I can't lose her."

"Well, you gotta do something because I'm done. You didn't tell me they knew each other."

"I'm ending it. I mean, for real."

"You better not make it worse."

"I just screwed another woman on my anniversary. It can't get any worse."

"Just handle it, and for God's sake, don't let this get out."

"I'll contain it." Nate got into his car. "But you gotta handle him," he said, referring to D.J.

"I got it. Where're you off to?"

"Barbershop."

~~~

Marcus climbed into the truck. "Don't," he said to D.J. before D.J. could ask any questions. D.J. made a comment about needing to get back to work. Marcus said nothing. He was thinking about that split-second sliver of opportunity, the one where he'd opened the door to D.J.'s presence and his own glance at the motel. It was in those few moments when Nate was looking at neither Marcus nor the building, that wrinkle in time when Marcus had looked toward the window of room 108. He'd briefly caught a shadowy glimpse, not enough to identify Nate's mistress, but a vision of mannerisms and silhouettes that could write the prologue to an epic novel. Marcus had played it cool with Nate, not wanting to make a bad situation worse, and not knowing for sure if he was right. But the pinging in his head wouldn't let it go. *I've seen her somewhere before.*

Marcus drove back to work, talking only to himself in his own head. The room had been dark, so he couldn't make out the complexion. He'd seen her eyes and a few seconds of her walking past the crack in the curtains. He may not have been able to pinpoint who she was, or if in fact he actually knew her in more than passing, but one thing was for sure: He knew crazy when he saw it.

Chapter 10

It was now approaching eight that morning. Arianna sat in her SUV, clutching the latest in self-help books. *Secrets That Shatter: How to Develop an Honest Marriage.* Damn, she thought. Analyzing the mess she'd made of her life wasn't on today's schedule. But somehow, it always worked its way in.

For the last two hours, she'd found herself alone at the park, contemplating her choices, praying under the dawn, desperately needing something to hold onto. She hoped God was lending His ear to her, the same way the Texas sun would soon lend its warmth to the March air. "Lord, I need you."

Months of planning for her twelfth wedding anniversary had come down to twelve remaining hours. Nightfall lay ahead regardless of Arianna's fear. But praying gave her hope that Nightmare might vanish along with the daylight, allowing her to become the wife Nate had lost when she'd misplaced his manhood.

She finished her prayer, ending with a soft "Amen." No more crying, no more crying. Holding back tears was proving difficult. She needed God to strengthen her and soften Nate. Would He do both? She doubted it, but it was worth a try. The Jackson household wasn't exactly a church-abiding entity. Maybe next Sunday.

Jesus had never been a priority in her upbringing. But she knew enough to believe in Him, and hope was all she had left. Nate had also had some exposure to the Word, maybe not enough to make worship a routine, but enough to keep a Bible on the coffee table. Nightly prayers with the children were Arianna's and Nate's contribution to the grace of God. An occasional *Thank you, Jesus,* for an avoided accident or a pay raise was the limit to their religious activity. Arianna praying for herself meant things had gotten bleak.

She thought about the calls she'd made this morning and the apologies she'd given to an answering machine for the regret of having left Nate aroused again. Would he move back into the master bedroom if she begged? How much was too much?

"Hey again, Nathan," she spoke sweetly. "Um, I need you to pay the daycare when you pick up Tre. I dropped him off earlier than usual and I guess I was rushed. Call me when you get this. Again, I'm sorry about last night. I know you're tired of hearing that, but I mean it."

She hung up, again asked God to intervene, and then got out of the Jeep.

The robust aroma of freshly brewed coffee permeated the outdoors. She took a deep breath before greeting her friend—the faded, black tar track. She fixed her ponytail, whisking her hair through a rubber band. The park lights towering over the field died one by one as she stretched, dressed in a pair of pink Nike jogging pants and a white cotton T-shirt that read "Shot Caller" in grey letters. "One-one thousand, two-one thousand," she murmured as her top rode up her stomach to reveal the low body fat she'd worked so hard for, the skinny shape Shawnee had so eloquently reminded her she had.

She bent sideways and represented an upside-down J as her muscles elongated for thirty seconds.

The first mile began. Headphones channeled classic rock to her mind. Janis Joplin echoing privately through her headset allowed her to briefly forget the world existed.

"Faster, faster, Arianna," she huffed. "Man up. Put the past behind you. Nate never has to know."

She'd been a runner since high school. Shortly after beginning her junior year, Arianna had walked to the field house after school to meet a friend. They were going to go look for part-time jobs. Her friend had been late, so Arianna had sat on the bleachers, watched football practice, and occasionally gazed at the joggers who were using the track surrounding the field. After ten-minutes of waiting, she'd walked off the bleachers, thinking of ways to avoid home. Walking the track for one loop turned into running the next, walking another, and then running another, until she had run herself smack into the middle of a track and field scholarship.

Even though Knoxville was her hometown, she'd stayed in the dorm. Her classmates thought she was stupid for spending her scholarship money on room and board. What they hadn't realized was that Arianna felt liberated, like she was living worlds away from hell, even though the housing projects where she grew up were only a few miles away. It hadn't mattered much anyway. She'd met Nate a week or so before starting her freshman year. Soon after, she spent most of her free time with him, and he was a senior with an off-campus apartment.

Arianna's Nikes pounded the ground. She questioned herself with each step. Would it have been that embarrassing to run into Nate's arms, the way she'd wanted to so many times, and cry in his comfort?

Not a day had gone by that she hadn't rationalized the decision to stay silent. The implications of what she'd done and the silence she still desperately held onto made each day worse. When she'd first gathered her friends in the office, the risk of telling Nate was less because she could have lied. She knew that victims of heinous crimes sometimes blocked out painful memories. This information could have been the foundation of a good lie. The arrival of her late mother's letter had suddenly triggered forgotten childhood memories. Nate would never have to know she'd deliberately left him in the dark about the raging scar across her breasts.

Perhaps now, with *another* lie, she could tell him. What would be the harm in waking up (all of a sudden) after a bad dream, all the memories flooding back? Or how about lying and saying she'd feared for her own life and now the lives of her children? When would it have been safe to justify her changing from devoted wife to lying bitch?

Now she found herself at her last stand, her strained marriage reaching its revelation, turning her into a one-woman pep rally to get wet enough to perform. Arianna knew of no deadline on satisfying a man's physical needs. At what point could Nate cheat and be justified? Worse, instead of running around the track, worrying about her marriage ending, she was supposed to be at home, waking up at two a.m. to a quiet house, searching for Nate, who would be found downstairs, their third newborn over his shoulder as Nate snored. Even though the pact was childish, Nate's desire for a happy marriage and another baby were far from immature. He wouldn't stay much longer if Arianna didn't change.

As she passed her midway marker at two-and-a-half miles, the muscle cramps smoothed out and she caught a second wind. She increased her speed, trying to out-run the thought of Nate running out of her life.

Two more miles down, and one-half to go, she sprinted to the end, not letting up as the shock absorbers in her Nikes earned the two-hundred dollars she'd paid for the shoes.

Arianna walked a few steps, then placed two forefingers on her neck. While counting her pulse, she noticed the increase in traffic. The sun signaled her day had begun. She'd also missed her target heart rate. With her competitive spirit broken, she walked off the track. Every skipped beat exaggerated her fear the night would not go as planned.

Arianna ended the run with some light stretching and then headed home. Normally, she would shower in her private bathroom across the street in the Gleason Building.

But today was different. This could be her night to shine, but only if Nate were willing to give her another last chance.

She got into the Jeep and dialed again. "Hey, baby. Just seeing if you're home. Call me back. I'm on my way home. Maybe we can talk."

Chapter 11

Arianna had been left to shower alone.

Last year's anniversary had ended in a huge fight, with Nate leaving the house and staying the night at Marcus's place. Since Nate's whereabouts this morning were unknown, and Arianna hadn't seen or talked to him since he'd left the house this morning, history would repeat itself if she couldn't turn things around.

She walked past Shawnee's desk. "How goes it?"

"I'm fine. At least God woke me up this morning."

Whatever.

Shawnee had become an enigma, hard to decipher and a much different person from when Taesha had hired her. She'd begun showing up late, taking excessive personal calls, and she was discourteous most of the time. Then in the last few weeks, Shawnee had started reading the Bible daily, attending church every Sunday, and passing judgment to the point of discrimination against those who didn't follow Christ. How, Arianna wondered, could somebody who'd just found God remain so rude?

Arianna wanted to fire her. But Shawnee was good at the job, and with the resurrection of Nightmare, Arianna barely had enough strength to handle unforeseen corporate conundrums. There was no way she was going to throw in self-inflicted problems.

She had learned two important things in Taesha's hiring of Shawnee, things she hadn't learned in business school: never hire out of desperation and always put your foot down if it doesn't feel right.

She sat down and fired up her computer. The twenty-inch, flat-screen monitor had a picture of Nate and the boys as its background. She smiled at the screen and then spilled her coffee.

"Damnit," she yelled. She shifted items on her desk and patted the desk down with tissues. The office phone rang.

"Mrs. Jackson," she answered while still wiping at her mess.

"Do you need me?" Nate asked, deep and decisive.

Arianna's skin tingled like ladybugs were on her flesh. "No. The truck's fine. I had minor trouble and I called you too quickly. I forgot you have that conference at this hour."

"Can you be home a little early?"

"For you, yes."

"I'll see you tonight."

"Happy Anniversary."

"I sure hope so, Ani."

"I love you."

No answer. Nate had hung up.

He's at his limit.

Taesha walked in. She wasn't her usual candid self, full of sarcastic banter. That had faded long ago. Today her firm face made her look like somebody who'd had too much Botox. "We need to talk," she said, her voice like stone.

"Profits?"

Taesha set a manila folder on the desk. "We're good."

"You don't seem happy about it."

"We've always been honest with each other, right?" Taesha asked.

"Yeah. What's up?"

"I think you should step down."

"Where the hell did that come from?"

"Maybe from that coffee you just spilled everywhere."

"That was an accident."

"Arianna, we are going to go under if you don't get it together. You're not stupid. You gotta know that."

Shawnee walked in with a delivery of roses, and Arianna perked up like a freshly watered flower. She dove for the card like a bridesmaid competing for the wedding bouquet, but her eyes filled as she read: *I enjoyed our date, Love Davion.*

"Here." Arianna passed the card to Taesha. "I'm not stepping down."

Taesha flicked the card, appearing hesitant in what she was about to say. "Then I have no choice."

"No choice in what?"

Taesha looked into the full-length mirror hanging on the wall. Then she reached into her pocket, pulled out plum lipstick, and colored her lips. She tightened her platinum ponytail and adjusted her breasts. A long look, side to side, of her biracial body, and she was complete. But she didn't carry the bubbliness of past primps. She looked sad, as if this was her last romp with Arianna's mirror.

"You're avoiding my question, Taesha. And what are you preparing for?"

"I'm getting ready to Skype with Jerome."

"You're lying. And what happened to Davion?"

"Davion is so Dallas. Jerome is taking me to Mexico this weekend. And I'm entitled to a fifteen minute break." She rolled her eyes.

"Mexico. Jerome is really taking you places."

"You are not in a position to judge me."

"I'm not judging you. We used to joke like this all the time."

"Do you know what it's like to watch somebody you love unravel like a ball of yarn thrown in a sewer?" Taesha asked.

"What's this about? Where are you going? And don't tell me a Skype call."

Taesha flung her hands up. "A job interview, okay?"

"You're *leaving*?"

Taesha pleaded. "Arianna, you are one of my best friends. I *love* you. But my career is gonna tank if you don't get your head on right. Don't you see that?"

Shawnee walked in again. The way she glanced at Arianna and then to Taesha, it was apparent there was more going on than a petty girl fight. "I can come back." She shut the door.

"That's another problem," Taesha said. "We have a secretary who wears her big ass on her anorexic shoulders—"

"Taesha."

"—but you won't fire her because you don't want to create more work. The old Arianna would have canned her ass last year."

"*You* hired her."

"I was wrong. I admit it. But don't blame me because your pain is stopping you from letting her go. I've been by your side since you shed your first tear over this shit."

We will never speak of this again. Arianna remembered the words she'd said the day she'd shredded the evidence. Her tone of authority had been that of a mafia leader, holding a cigar, demanding compliance. But back on that day, she'd forgotten one detail. Her friends were just as hard-headed as she was. On a weekly basis, they'd brought up her past and the urgency of telling Nate until Arianna felt like screaming. None of them had been sure which was worse: the torture Arianna had endured or the anxiety over Nate finding out.

"Can we squash this? Eva's coming in," Arianna said.

Eva opened the door. She looked at them the same way Shawnee had done. "Heeeey. Sorry I couldn't make the run this moooorning... is everything alright?"

"The pity party is getting old," Taesha said.

Eva was standing in the middle of an impasse. She put out one arm in Arianna's direction, flanking herself with a friend fighting to keep the man she loved, and the other arm toward Taesha, the friend fighting to get the woman to love herself.

Taesha walked toward the door. "That's your friend," she said before slamming it shut.

"You wanna tell me what just happened?" Eva asked.

"Taesha wants to quit."

"Can you blame her?"

Not again.

Eva continued. "I would give my eyesight for one more night with Zach. At least you have a second chance. Make it right."

"Nathan will never be the same."

"Look, it's just you and me here." Eva locked the door and strutted back to Arianna's desk. "Arianna, we are way past this now."

"What does that mean?"

"This is about more than Nate's feelings. This is about *you* too."

"That monster put foreign objects in me. And I let him."

"That bastard doesn't define you. Do you actually think Nate would look at you differently?"

"No, of course not."

"Then what?"

"I look at *myself* differently. Don't you get it, Eva? It seemed so easy to tell a catastrophic lie about my scar and my past, and glance over it so much it became an afterthought. Now, the lie is in my face and has been for two years."

Eva didn't respond. She simply listened.

"It seemed so easy: satisfy Nate with a plausible cause so he doesn't mention it—at all. It worked. He treats me like I'm normal."

"You *are* normal."

"All I do now is stare at the damn scar and find reasons to hate myself."

"Arianna, look at me."

Arianna looked at her beautiful, Latina friend. "What is the worst thing that could happen if you tell Nate?"

"He'll hurt worse than ever."

Eva nodded in a pregnant response. "Okay, true. But at least he'll hurt in the truth. And that, you can heal from."

Arianna sat quietly. It was her turn to listen.

"Taesha is about to leave your company. Pam is so caught in the middle, she's about to choke. Darius isn't the same, and *you...*you're about to disintegrate." Eva leaned over and grabbed Arianna's hand. "Trust me, my dear, dear friend, this situation can't get any worse."

Arianna slumped into the chair and looked around. The office seemed to personify itself. The "E" on the bookcase looked as if it were passing judgment on her actions. The framed diploma once representing pride and accomplishment hung crooked, expressing disappointment with her poor representation of the Alumni of the University of Maryland's graduate program. The Victorian chairs and coffee table took her back to the Mokara, throwing in her face how happy she'd once made Nate. Pathetic, she thought. Now inanimate objects were judging her.

The monitor defaulted to her screensaver. The change in image caught the corner of her eye. Family pictures fell, one on top of the other. Too bad happiness didn't come with a system restore button. One simple push of the key could erase her viruses and take her back to the Mokara where she could start over.

"Even if I did tell him at this point, I wouldn't know where to begin."

"You just begin." Eva flashed a reassuring smile. "But like I said two years ago, in this very office, plan it out. Set some time away for you two to be alone. Away from life. It'll be okay." She checked her watch.

"You gotta go, don't you?"

"I don't want to leave you like this."

"It's okay. I get it. I do. I know the stakes."

Eva got up. She nodded to the door. "You need to figure out a way to stop the best accountant in Texas from leaving this company."

Arianna flashed a reflective smile, thinking about her eccentric accountant and soul sister. "She's always there for us, isn't she?"

"Yep. Always. Now be there for her. "

Arianna shook her head in acceptance. "She's right about Shawnee. I need to fire her."

"Maybe that's not a bad thing. Her attitude stinks."

"That it does. She's not the same person she was at first." Arianna sat silently as she mulled over the last two years and all the fallout since her late mother's letter. "My mother once told me a lie is like a cancer."

"How?"

"It metastasizes until you can't stop it."

"You *can* stop this, Arianna." Eva checked her watch again.

"Eva, go. I know you have to. "

Eva clutched her purse. "We will continue this talk." She left in a hurry, making Arianna feel worse. Eva was about to be late because of a lecture.

Arianna reached over to her policy books, to read up and refresh herself on the rules she'd written. She spoke to herself. "I gotta grasp some control."

The HR manual was thick and heavy, the section on terminating employees, straight forward.

Shawnee had to go.

Chapter 12

The sway of Pam's voluptuous hips spoke of a woman who knew she had skills, though her overactive pride caused her to make risky moves... like telling the superintendent she had the expertise to fill the position of Stone Oak Middle School Principal, plus a little extra, so the superintendent better not blink because Pam would soon be coming after her job too.

She pressed her fire-opal nails into the car alarm remote. She settled into the driver's seat, looked in the rearview mirror, then ran her hand down her shoulder-length, freshly relaxed hair, smoothing down the strays. An all-true female, Pam often said about herself. Like most women, she'd tried all the tricks. False eyelashes, concealer, heavy foundation, weave, you name it. But she was never comfortable in what she felt was somebody else's manufactured skin and often wondered why females of any race had to pretend through artificial means. But she didn't judge the look. She did, however, have a huge problem with women who toted plastic personalities: those passive-aggressive, manipulative females who smiled and laughed at anything just to get attention, and who played stupid games just to push buttons and control reactions. She was a polished woman, of course—hair done, and enough makeup to light up her face. She just happened to be a well-respected professional who had an aversion to fake bitches.

She dialed Marcus before pulling off. He didn't answer. She sent a text. *I slayed it.*

He immediately replied: *I expected nothing less* ☺

The prompt response via text let Pam know that Marcus was once again somewhere at a scene, probably looking at a dead body, and couldn't take her call. She wondered how much more cop he could take.

After a twenty-minute ride from Northeast Independent School District Headquarters to the Stone Oak Community, Pam pulled up to the front of the school and turned into her reserved parking space.

She often thanked God for unanswered prayers. Her childhood dreams hadn't included becoming an educator, much less an administrator in the field of education. She'd wanted to become a painter, an artist with an abstract touch. But art school eluded her, thanks to her military father moving her to Italy right before her senior year of high school. Maybe Milan, she thought, would carry her dream overseas. She held on, waiting for the opportunity to apply anywhere art would set her free.

Meeting Marcus at nineteen had diverted her attention and given her a new dream. She'd decided to change her major to literature/education at a local American university to keep closer to him. She achieved her bachelor's degree and married Marcus on base. They left Italy for San Antonio after Marcus's brief, three-year stint. He'd had enough Army for a lifetime. Both went to school in the evenings and on weekends, as Marcus worked his beat and Pam taught English at the school she now helped run. So far, each time she parked in "her" space at the school, she knew what she loved—impacting kids and running the show. Finally being able to move into the upper-class community of Stone Oak and cutting her commute hadn't hurt either.

The lack of students outside surprised Pam. The lunch period had started five minutes before she'd arrived, and the picnic tables were usually full a few minutes after the bell.

She walked into the school. Emptiness filled the large foyer except for the backpacks littering the floor. Toppled tables and collapsed chairs entangled each other. Trash cans had been flipped onto their sides, scattering debris.

Screams came from the cafeteria. Pam had a sinking feeling in her gut. She knew it was another fight.

Looking through the open double doors leading into the cafeteria, Pam found a crowd of students pushing each other in what appeared to be a struggle to get an upfront view. She ran around the obstacles in the foyer, squeezed past the vacuum-packed students, and saw a trashcan rolling across the cafeteria. Lunch monitors were calling for staff. Apparently whatever was going down had just happened. Pam was not surprised. As the assistant principal, she was in charge of discipline. Whenever she left the campus, she would come back to an incident report. This time she'd come back to witness the incident.

Laughter indicated some were amused. Others stared without moving in what appeared to be shock. Those who shook their heads in pity didn't get involved.

A few sixth-graders ran through the crowd and stopped the trashcan. A student crouched down to the opening. Darius and two other students reached inside the can. By the time Pam reached them, the sixth-graders, to the chagrin of the booing crowd, had rescued Ben, a special needs student.

"Who did it, Darius?" Pam asked.

"Over there." He pointed. Four students smiled and waved, proud to take credit for the incident.

"I hate this school," Darius said.

"Don't let stuff like this bother you. You used to love coming here," Pam said.

"I used to love a lot of things." Darius walked off with his friends.

The school nurse escorted Ben to the clinic.

Teachers and cafeteria monitors broke up the crowd. Some students gathered in line for food, and others had begun eating before the disruption. Whether sitting or standing, the students replaced routine gossip with the incident and talked as if it were breaking news.

"Faggots," Raul, one of the bullies, shouted in Darius's direction. Darius and his friends stopped.

"Turn around and walk to my office," Pam said to Raul. "Now." She placed a semi-forceful hand on him, strong enough to push him forward, soft enough to escape a potential complaint from a parent in denial—a parent of a kid who did no wrong.

Ronald, Darius's best friend, caught up with them. "What did you call us?"

"Get to class, Ronny," Pam said.

"I called you faggots," Raul said.

Darius approached Raul. Pam motioned for help.

"You pick on a weaker kid and you're calling us faggots?" Darius said. "Dumb."

"Suck my dick," Raul said.

Ronald was on him before the help could arrive.

Students started to gather again. Darius jumped between Ronald and Raul, trying to convince Ronald that Raul wasn't worth getting suspended over. That was before Seth, another kid who'd orchestrated the trashcan incident, punched him in the face.

Darius hit back. The brawl began.

A teacher pulled Darius off the student who'd punched him. "Let me go," Darius said. He fought to get loose.

"Calm down," the teacher said. "Don't make it worse, Darius. You're already gonna be suspended."

"I want my dad," he said. "Call my dad."

Staff ordered the crowd to disperse. Teachers directed students back to class. Darius, Ronald, Raul, and Seth found themselves sitting outside Pam's office while they waited on their parents.

Pam's office was small, a tease to what she'd interviewed for. The goal was getting across the hall, where the boss she couldn't stand earned his pay as the principal. A burnt-out man who'd lost all reason on the road to retirement, he had little patience and routinely made it known he couldn't wait to give up the job. That was fine with Pam. AP's were known as the bad guys, the ones called on to wash the dirty laundry. The principal made the rules affecting the educational institution, paving the way for success. Pam was ready to step into a role involving more praise, less punishment.

"Dr. Carter," her secretary said. "Raul's parents are here."

"Send them in."

She made quick use of the meeting. Three days suspension and an appointment for a hearing to assess his ability to attend public school. Somehow the parents believed his punishment was unfair. They objected, threatened, stormed out, stormed in, objected, and threatened.

Pam held her ground. Next.

Chapter 13

Nate cut contact with the outside world. Avoiding Arianna and the rest of civilization gave him time to think. All morning he'd been driving around the city, learning his confession, practicing the speech. Maybe he could end the fling and focus his attention on his marriage without ever confessing. For a moment, that was his decision. But Nate wouldn't be able to look Arianna in the eyes and tell her how much he loved her when he'd be constantly looking over his shoulder, wondering how well his jilted ex-lover held grudges.

How did a man—with everything going for him, even living in a gated community—end up aimless, parked outside a dirty motel, thinking about the day he met his wife, number forty-six on his belt, a woman he never thought he could love?

He still wasn't sure.

Something had clicked inside Nate when he'd lost his virginity, making him vow a life of infidelity. Maybe his father's philandering ways had slipped into his genes. Perhaps as a horny fourteen-year-old kid, he'd discovered a lust for sex. Maybe he liked how he made number one scream that afternoon and wondered if he could make the next girl scream louder. Nate savored the challenge, started comparing each young lady to the next. As an adult, he waged war on monogamy. Nate took the term *whore* to a new level, vowing to never screw the same woman twice.

He'd tasted all flavors. Black, Asian, Hispanic. But not white. He never dreamt of it or planned on it. Caucasian hadn't turned him on, until he met Arianna standing in a grocery store in Knoxville, Tennessee. And even then she wasn't supposed to stop his insatiable need to screw every woman he became attracted to. Yet, Nate soon learned that nobody could explain love.

He knocked on the motel room door.

His mistress opened it. "How does it feel, not holding the key to everything?"

"Let me in."

"I said eleven. Now you have to pay for another day."

Nate's blank stare and stone face complemented his cold eyes as they perused the body in front of him, laced in a hot-pink bra.

"We can't take long now," she said.

"We won't."

"Alright." She took off her bra. "We'll make up for it next time."

"Get dressed. There isn't going—"

The phone in the room rang for the first time since Nate and his mistress had been meeting at the motel. "Who did you tell?"

"Nobody."

"I'll ask again. Who did you tell?"

"I said nobody. I wouldn't do that to us."

"Get dressed and get the hell out."

She put on her clothes while Nate stood watch, as if she were a student in alternative education.

"I didn't tell anyone, baby."

"I'm not your baby."

"You will be." She placed the key on the bed, smiled at him, and ducked her head on the way out.

Nate couldn't run after her to finish his talk about ending the affair. That would have caused a scene he didn't need. Instead, he sat on the bed, wondering what he'd become, wondering how sick she really was.

The phone in the room rang again. "Shut up," he screamed. Eventually it stopped. He grabbed the key, glanced around at the disgust he'd created, and then left to check out.

The motel clerk took the key. "See you next time, Mr. Brown."

"There won't be a next time." Nate paid the late check-out charge and left.

He drove in complete silence on I-10, heading toward El Paso, still unreachable. He hadn't closed the affair, which meant another confrontation with his obsessed mistress. His nerves were also racing over the phone call to the motel room. He wondered if it was coincidence or if somebody knew his dirty secret. What about Arianna? Would she forgive him if he confessed? Perhaps she would understand why he cheated. Maybe it would make her open up and explain why she'd turned away from him. Maybe not.

The loose ends were choking the life out of Nate.

He heard a horn, alerting him to the fact that he'd swerved into another lane, two seconds shy of taking out a family. Pulling off the highway was the smartest move. "What the hell am I doing?"

He called Marcus to see, in the off-chance, if he'd called the room. In a matter of seconds, the phone signaled him to eight missed calls from Marcus and fifteen from Arianna.

He called Marcus.

"Where the hell have you been?" Marcus asked.

"I needed time to think."

"Pam and Arianna have been trying to reach you."

"Why?"

Marcus filled him in. Nate learned Marcus had called him at the motel, but he had no time to feel relieved. "Where's Darius now?"

"Sitting in front of my wife's office waiting on his dad. You need to call."

"I can't. I'm thirty minutes outside of town. My location will be another thing I have to explain, which means more lies."

"What are you...forget it. I don't even wanna know. Get your ass to the school."

Nate hopped back onto the highway and headed home.

Chapter 14

By the way Seth's parents stormed out of Pam's office, anyone could tell Seth had also been suspended. Because of how the parents were hollering, Pam had given him the same punishment as Raul. His parents were demanding to see the principal. They waited on the opposite side of the administrative area.

Pam walked out of the office. Arianna was sitting next to Darius, watching Seth's parents stomp their feet and berate Pam.

"Did you find my dad?" Darius asked. Pam looked at Arianna. Arianna looked at Darius. "We've left messages. He'll be here if he can make it."

"I guess maybe now I'll get assigned to Alternative. Maybe he'll show up then," he said. He stood up.

Arianna ordered him to sit back down. "Are you suspending him?" she asked Pam.

"No. I think given the circumstances, he and Ronald deserve a second chance."

"A second chance?" Seth's mother yelled. "You're suspending my son but you're giving them a second chance?"

Pam ignored her. She motioned Arianna and Darius into her office.

"What happened?" Arianna asked.

Pam broke down every detail. Darius sat there, rolling his eyes and slouching in the chair. Arianna told him to sit up straight. He scooted up and tucked his hands in the kangaroo pocket of his powder-blue pullover.

The principal stormed in, leaving the door ajar, without consideration of a knock. "You're not suspending them, Dr. Carter?"

"No disrespect, but I don't think you have all the facts."

"I don't need all the facts. Fighting is fighting. And I have some very angry parents ready to go downtown. You *will* suspend these two. Now." He eyed Darius. "I'm sick of kids like you giving this school a bad name," he barked.

"Sir, respectfully, watch your tone with my son," Arianna said.

"If we don't practice discipline, then delinquents like him grow up to be bigger delinquents." He stepped closer. "Understand, Mrs. Jackson?"

"I'd appreciate it if you stepped away from me."

"So would I," Nate said.

The principal twitched. Everyone in the office stared in the direction of the door. Darius smiled.

Nate walked in and stepped in front of Arianna. His hand brushed her side and stayed there. Arianna looked at Pam, not knowing what to do. Pam's eyes widened. Neither had seen Nate show Arianna affection in months.

Nate stood calm, the picture of self-discipline. "Scream at my son or step to my wife one more time, and I'm gonna become a problem for you."

The principal softened his stance.

"The way I see it, if you suspend my son, my wife and I are gonna go over your head. But if you don't"—Nate nodded to the chairs outside of Pam's office—"they will. So you have to ask yourself: Who would you rather give you a bad name? My guess is you don't want a federal agent with a top secret security clearance to call you out."

Darius smirked. Nate looked at his son. "Don't get too happy because you are *not* off the hook. And sit up straight."

The principal stared at Pam. "Darius and Ronald may go back to class." Then he looked at Nate, and left.

Pam shut the door.

Nate motioned Darius up, but kept a concrete face. "Why'd you hit him, D?"

Darius explained.

"You helped a kid out of a trash can?"

Darius nodded. "Yes."

Arianna and Pam smiled.

"He hit me first, Dad."

"I got you. All I ask is that you use your head, understand? As long as you do that, I'm fine with it."

"You mean I can fight?"

"No. I mean you can do what you gotta do, to do the right thing. Never become somebody's punching bag, but never be a bully either."

"I get it, Dad."

"And if I ever walk into a room, and you're sitting down with a cocky little attitude like you're on the block, I'm gonna fly off the handle."

Darius's eyes filled. "I just want it the way it used to be."

"We're gonna work on it," Nate said. "Now pick up your chin and get back to class."

Darius headed for the door.

"D?"

"Yeah, Dad?"

"Pull up your pants."

"Yes, sir." Darius shut the door behind him.

Pam sighed.

Arianna sensed her frustration. "It's over. You handled the parents well, Pam."

"Thanks, but this is nothing. Wait until I have to explain this to Ben's parents."

"I can only imagine," Arianna said.

Nate nudged her arm. "Let's go, baby girl."

Baby girl.

Pam and Arianna looked at each other. Who was this guy and what had he done with Nate?

For the first time in two years, Nate grabbed Arianna's hand. Pleasure and comfort shot through her body like a jolt of electricity on speed. Damn his touch felt good.

Nate had *shown up,* as he would say.

The last time his hand had been that decisive was the day she'd met him at an airport, the day he'd grabbed the hand that wasn't holding onto a big metallic balloon.

Arianna followed him out of the school.

His appearance elicited memories and unmasked hidden clues. A year ago, when she'd had a flat tire, stranding her on the side of the road, Nate had arrived ten minutes after she'd called him. Eight months ago, when Tre had woken up screaming that his ear hurt, Nate had had the engine cranked before Arianna could get dressed. Two months ago, the day of Darius's parent-teacher conference, Nate had postponed his flight to Baltimore to attend because Arianna had gotten caught up at work.

These were the times she'd taken his presence for granted, the times she hadn't stopped to realize he'd *always* shown up, in spite of his anger and frustration.

Then she thought about the subtle movements. How she would wake up in the middle of the night to pee and, even though they weren't speaking, Nate had thought enough to put down the seat since he'd last used the bathroom. The times Arianna would remember the oil change only to look up at the windshield decal and notice Nate had already taken the Jeep to the lube shop.

He'd always been there, despite the fights she'd instigated to keep them separated, despite the extra effort she'd given to magnifying his flaws: towels on the bathroom floor, whites mixed with darks, sodas in Tre's lunches, Xbox at midnight with Darius, elevated pushups using her dainty footstool.

Not perfect by any means, but Nate had never lost respect for Arianna as a woman. Consuming herself in the hyper-vigilance of making sure he stayed at bay had blocked her from seeing that when it counted, when sacrifice was at its highest, Nate had always been a man, even though she wasn't treating him like one.

Arianna stood in the middle of her epiphany. "My God, you always show up."

Nate didn't need commendation. "When it comes to my family, I'm always gonna show up."

Arianna fought to keep her breathing uniform, the tears hidden behind her eyes. For her, love, until that minute, had never been defined or fully understood. Superficial love was easy to relate to because it involved little sacrifice. Arguments weren't deal-breakers when the biggest concern in a marriage was the Mokara or the Four Seasons. It was easy to hold onto love when problems were confined to who got to pay the daycare on time when there was plenty of money in either wallet. Love was easy to communicate when everyone was home by five-o'clock every night.

Real love was a man too tired to stand, yet who couldn't go to sleep on his anniversary without his woman. Real love was saying *Ani* in spite of. Real love was showing up, stepping in front of a wife (who'd long ago killed your spirit), just to take the heat. Real love was the sword that could slay nightmares. Real love equaled sacrifice.

Nate was real love in Arianna's world of made-up monsters.

"I've been so stupid," she said. *How could I have been so stupid, not having faith in you?*

"I haven't been the sharpest tool in the shed either, Ani, believe me."

"You haven't called me baby in so long. I forgot what it felt like."

Nate hesitated, as if something was on his mind. "I just know what I have, that's all." He looked at his car. "I need to get Tyson home."

Arianna giggled. "I'll get home as soon as I can."

They stood next to her car as if they were saying goodnight on a first date.

Nate leaned in and kissed her. One kiss led to another and another until Darius's parents were making out in front of his school. "C'mon, guys, I gotta be here every day. Show some decorum."

They pulled away from each other. Arianna laughed, but she noticed that Nate was more subdued. "I'll see you tonight, okay?"

"Okay." Arianna watched Nate walk to his car with his head slightly down, as if he couldn't shoulder the cross he was bearing. *I've hurt him so badly. I have to rectify this.*

By the time she made it up the elevator, Arianna's mission had taken priority. Her purpose: fire Shawnee and then go home to take back her life. Her anxiety built like a lethal virus, but determination to bury her past for good that night fueled her.

She walked around the corner to Shawnee's desk and found her in front of a mirror touching up mascara and putting on lipstick.

"What are you doing?" Arianna asked.

Shawnee looked up. "Getting pretty. You do it."

"I'm also the boss, in my office, working my butt off when I do it. Antics like these are why men don't take women seriously in business."

Shawnee shrugged.

"Shawnee, you're fired. I'll pay you for the rest of the day, but please leave. I'll also mail your discharge letter."

Arianna expected a reaction, at least an apology. Shawnee remained calm. She grabbed her purse and said nothing.

"Would you like to make a statement to put in your file?" Arianna asked.

"Bless those who persecute you; bless and do not curse them."

Arianna got loud. "Excuse me?"

This prompted Taesha to come out into the reception area. "What's going on here?"

Shawnee got out of her chair with a reassured grace and, in a sinister voice, stepped close to Arianna: "Romans 12:14. Read your Bible."

Her tone chilled the air. Arianna realized, from the way the woman had changed, that what lay beneath

Shawnee's words was more than a love of Scripture; they created a warped sense of the Word and a judgmental confidence that could only come from somebody who had turned to the Bible *not* for salvation, but to find absolution in anger, a misguided belief that whatever acts had been born from revenge, vindication, or the quest for completion were justified. Did Shawnee truly love God? It didn't matter. Despite her beliefs, or how close she felt to the Lord, all Arianna could feel was threatened.

"Get all your belongings and exit the building. Security will meet you at the elevator."

Shawnee left without another word.

"What the *hell* just went on?" Taesha asked.

Arianna explained the fight in full detail. "She doesn't even care, Tae."

"Well, she will when somebody calls us for a reference check. Let her pray on that. At least she's finally gone."

"I don't need this right now. Look how she left this place. Documents everywhere."

"We'll take care of it."

Arianna looked seriously into Taesha's eyes. "I'm sorry. I've let you down. I've let a lot of people down. That crap ends tonight. I don't know how I'm gonna do it, but I will find a way to tell Nathan about Nightmare. I have to."

"You sound determined."

"I haven't been fair. Good intentions go stale after a while, I get that now. I guess I didn't realize that until it came into perspective seeing Darius hurting and watching Nathan be...so, so *Nathan*."

"I heard Nate raised Cain."

"He did." Arianna walked quickly into her office.

Taesha followed. "So, how *is* Darius?"

"He's fine, a little shaken, but you know my son is strong." Arianna sat at her computer. "Two days in-house suspension though."

"What are you doing?"

Arianna started typing, her fingers shaking. "I have to respond to this meeting request and send a couple of emails since Shawnee is now gone." She looked up suddenly. "Can you deactivate her email privileges?"

Taesha went around Arianna's desk and stopped her from typing. "Arianna, I got it. All of it. Take a breath."

Arianna inhaled deeply. "I don't know what happened to me, Taesha. It's like I'm a different woman. Or like..."

"Your old self?"

"Kinda, I guess. How can that be?"

"Revelations come in many ways."

"I have the best man in the world." Arianna checked the time. "How could I have done this to him? How could I have lied to him all this time and not seen it?"

Taesha nodded. "Well, I'm not a shrink, but break down what happened."

"I just woke the hell up, Tae." Arianna explained her epiphany. "In twelve years of marriage, I've *never* seen Nathan like that. I mean, I knew he was protective, but good *God*. He almost slammed Darius's principal straight into the wall."

"It turned you on."

"Yes, but it was more...*so much* more than that. It was like...like I'd just met him and he was defending my honor or something. You should have *seen* him come up in there, ready to take *anybody* down. And the way he kissed me at the car...whaaat?"

Taesha was standing there smiling. "I think I got it. You fell in love with him all over again."

"Stop, Tae. That's silly. I've always been in love with him."

"It's been rekindled though. It's all over your face. It's different. It's rewound."

"I do feel like I did when he first kissed me, before these nightmares, before my mother's letter."

Taesha shook her head. "Makes sense."

Arianna thought about her feelings, the butterflies in her stomach at the thought of her husband. She froze and looked up at Taesha. "Oh my God, I did. But *how* is that possible?"

"Look, I may be a hoe, but I do believe in love, and I do believe you're not supposed to know the answer when the feelings are genuine."

"All this time. I'm not having nightmares because of Nightmare himself."

"You're not?"

"No."

"Then why?"

"I'm having nightmares because I'm not telling the man I love the truth."

"I see. And when did you become Freud?"

"I'm serious. Think about it." Arianna started patting everywhere on her desk and turning her head like she were watching a tennis match. "Okay, so much to do. I gotta get out of here. I gotta talk to my husband about everything. I don't wanna lose this feeling because I know he feels it too." Arianna abruptly looked up at Taesha again. "Oh my God, it's my anniversary. I can't do it *tonight*. Besides, not with the kids there. You know I can't do that. I have to get Nightmare out of my head for just one night."

"Slow down, Arianna."

"What do you mean?"

"Yes, you need to tell Nate. We've all said that. But we've also said you need to get help too. Telling Nate is the beginning, but it's not the ending."

"Taesha, I have not had this feeling in two years. Just let me have my moment. *Please*."

Taesha must have seen the desperation in Arianna's eyes. She smiled and scaled back her lecture. "It does feel good to see you so excited."

"I love that man, Tae."

"I know you do."

Arianna noticed the concern. "I wanna make it through the night of my anniversary in my husband's arms, Taesha. I can't do that if I'm thinking about therapy and Nightmare. I have to focus on Nathan and my marriage."

"Just keep the idea open. If not for you, then Nate."

"He's the last person who will go to counseling."

"You never know."

"Taesha, I need my night. No more therapy talk."

Taesha put up her hands. "Okay. You win...for the weekend." Then she smiled slyly. "You're gonna wake up the neighborhood, aren't ya?"

"I hope so. If I can get Nightmare out of my head."

"I think you will. Love trumps fear. Hashtag Fuck Nightmare."

"That's right. Fuck Nightmare."

"You don't even sound right, Arianna. Stop it."

They giggled, and Arianna fled out of the office, trying not to notice the apprehension that had returned to Taesha's face.

Chapter 15

Arianna pulled up to her house at seven p.m. and took a quick glance around her utopia, around all she and Nate had built. It wasn't dark, but the sun had set enough to spark the track beams Nate had mounted around the perfectly smooth bushes. The neighborhood gave off an awe-inspiring sense of peace with its nice homes and quiet corners. The air was cool and the clouds were moving in, scenting the air with the upcoming rain.

The house represented years of working together as a team, a culmination of balancing children, classes, and homework. Luckily for Arianna, Nate had carried the bills with his military paycheck while she'd gone to school, with no summers off and a heavier than average class load. Times were tough because Nate had continued his graduate studies while he worked. This left Darius in Arianna's hands most of the time. Once she graduated from the University of Maryland, she opened her first coffee house in Baltimore, located on the Inner Harbor. She'd been able to spend a year at the business before they'd moved back to Texas. She was going to sell it, but Nate had encouraged her to keep it. She hired a manager, and Nate looked in on the store whenever he was in town. Not a day passed that she wasn't grateful she'd listened to him.

Nate opened the front door and stood in the doorway.

She ran straight to him and almost knocked him over in her embrace. "Hi."

"Hey yourself. Shit." Nate reciprocated her embrace. They mauled each other in the doorway, stumbling into the kitchen, leaning against the counter, falling onto the floor, until the past two years of pain and agony faded into a new beginning, allowing Nate and Arianna to revel in each other as if they had never experienced a rift. Nate almost had her shirt off, his tongue on her collarbone, under her moans and sighs.

"Dad! Mom!"

"Oh, hell." Nate quickly jumped off Arianna. "Damn, I forgot we had kids. Hey, Son."

Arianna quickly buttoned up her shirt. "Hey, baby. How's your arm?"

Darius shook his head. "You two oughta be so ashamed of yourselves. I'm just gonna order a pizza. C'mon, Tre." Darius climbed the stairs, Tre toting Elmo by his leg. "Daddy on Mommy."

Nate looked at Arianna. "That was *so* inappropriate."

"You wanna make out again?"

"Yep."

Down they went.

Arianna turned off Elmo's World and turned out Tre's light. She walked into Darius's room and said goodnight to her prize fighter, after he'd devoured everything he wanted from Stone Oak Pizza and Wings, thanks to his parents' embarrassment.

Nate was in their bathroom finishing up shaving, bare chested and with his lower body wrapped in a towel. Arianna stood in the middle of their bedroom, staring at him, her love dripping from every orifice. He locked eyes on her. She approached him. "I have so much to make up for. I haven't treated you right at all."

129

Nate's eyes welled up. "Please don't. I haven't been perfect."

She leaned her head on his arm as he cleaned his blade and put it up. "You're *my* perfect, Nathan. I just want to tell—"

Nate put a finger to her mouth. "Don't go there. I don't want an explanation."

"It's been a tough two years."

"Ani, you know me. I'm a simple guy. I don't want circumstances and reasons. I just want us normal again."

They kissed and continued what they'd started downstairs, this time in the comfort of their king-sized bed. Nate lifted Arianna up as he sat up, allowing her to straddle him, both sitting upright; she bit his lip as her body traveled his under the caress of his hands and the anchoring of his body to hers. Arianna's hair draped his shoulders as he brought his hands to her neck and guided her mouth to his. Nate kissed his wife until her body seized under her massive uncontrollable outpouring of how her husband had made her feel. His grip on Arianna let her know how much he had missed their intimacy.

"Thank you, Ani."

"For what?"

Nate couldn't help but chuckle. "You're *so* not a guy." He flipped her over to achieve his own tender satisfaction. He could barely rein in his profanity in his pleasure as he reminded Arianna of how good she felt.

She spoke sweetly into his ear. "I have something for you."

"That makes two of us, Mrs. Jackson."

Before they could exchange their gifts, Arianna had fallen asleep on his chest, and he wasn't about to disturb her.

Chapter 16

Pam wrapped Marcus's plate in foil and placed it in the oven. Another late night, more worry about Marcus's stressful job. She began loading the dishwasher while glancing at the clock for the fifth time since Gwen had said good night.

She turned off the kitchen light, then realized she couldn't call it a night without talking to Marcus, without knowing he would soon be on the way home.

"Hey, when are you coming home? I want to tell you about my interview."

"I'm wrapping up some things at work. I'll be home soon."

"I'll wait up."

"I know you will. One of the things I love about you, babe. But you have another long day tomorrow. Get some sleep."

"Not without you. And no more discussion herein will be entered into."

"I don't know if I should be scared or turned on."

Pam laughed. "Turned on."

"I'll hurry."

~~~

Zachary Deleon Sanchez
Devoted Husband
Dedicated to Justice

Marcus remembered the day they'd served the warrant. The expression on Eva's face when she'd answered the door. Three years ago, Zach killed while trying to arrest a man charged with beating a five-year-old boy to death. A woman had found the remains of the child in a ditch near a dumpster. Skeletal, starved, thrown to the ground. The case had consumed the whole department. And then, by luck, they'd gotten a lead—the father. Zach couldn't wait to bring him in.

The look had said it all. The way Marcus had shaken his head when Eva asked why he was there. "There was an explosion, Eva."

Cemeteries were scary places at night, even for a grown man. The wind, the creaking of twigs, symbols of the things unseen shadows and restless souls could cause. While this idea was preposterous from the perspective of a person who didn't believe in ghosts, the environment of a cemetery left the possibility open that maybe there was something to be said for life after death.

Marcus looked at his phone, thought of the lie he'd just told his wife about his whereabouts. He wondered, as far-fetched as it was, if Zach could hear him. The wind tickled his neck as if Zach were there, telling him to pour out his soul.

"Nate done lost his mind and done pulled me into some shit I can't get my ass out of."

Marcus sat there, venting to Zach, his friend since his first day on the force. He mentioned his guilt over helping Nate cheat, and that led to his disgust over Eva's choice for a new husband, Kyle, the one neither of them could stand, the miserable replacement Eva married in a quick courthouse wedding.

"You out here talking about me?"

Marcus looked up. "Why are you even here? I've never seen you visit."

Eva sat beside him. "I come here about five times a week."

Eva stared at Zach's last name, the name she still carried, the name she'd refused to drop when she married Kyle Ridgeland, the cop Marcus loathed the most.

"Why are you here so late?" she asked.

"Just needed some air."

"Miles away at a cemetery?"

"Yep." Marcus watched Eva brush off Zach's tombstone.

"I had a dream about him last night. He reached out for me and then he was gone."

Marcus cut his eyes toward her, yet said nothing. Couldn't she just come back later and let him vent in peace?

"Let it out, Marcus, I know you want to."

"I'm done trying to figure you out."

"We need to end this."

"I didn't come here to argue with my dead partner's wife."

"Just know I did what was right."

"Right? Really? You had my partner cremated and his ashes thrown into the ground. You didn't even afford us the opportunity to say goodbye."

"Please try to understand my side for once."

The peace Marcus was searching for that night had turned into a revival of his uneasiness surrounding the questionable nature of Zach's death. Instead of having a quiet conversation with his deceased friend, Marcus stood up, more stressed now than when he'd left home. "There's a mandatory forty-eight-hour waiting period in Texas to cremate a body. That wasn't strange to you?"

"There was nothing left of him, Marcus." Eva stood up. They began to argue in what was supposed to be a place of rest. "What do you want from me? I was destroyed."

"And they knew that."

"Here you go with your conspiracy theories."

"Nobody saw his body, Eva! You're his wife and they wouldn't even let *you* see him."

"That's not fair to the city, Marcus. They offered. I declined."

"They persuaded you to decline."

"My husband was *charred.* They spared all of us with a quick cremation."

"Did the ashes look like Zach? Oh, no, they couldn't have, because THEY'RE ASHES."

"Marcus, you've been chasing ghosts for so long, you can't even process reality."

"Ghosts? This has nothing to do with my mother, and I'm not saying Zach's still alive. But the handling of his body wasn't right. *Something* happened in that house."

"Like what?" she asked in an exhausted voice.

Marcus looked around the cemetery and then back at Zach's headstone. "I don't know yet."

"Yet?"

"YET."

"You have to let this be, Marcus, please! I can't let it go if you can't let it go."

Marcus felt a wave of conflicting emotions—sadness for his loss, anger at Eva's choices, empathy for her pain, anxiety over not knowing exactly what had happened. Watching Eva wail over Zach brought him back to the moment his boss had told them they'd found the body. In the hours prior, they'd at least clung to the far-fetched hope that maybe he'd found shelter and was trapped.

"I didn't mean to make you cry. But he wasn't *just* your husband. He was my friend, my partner. I left him in that house alone. I live with that all the time."

"That's what this is, Marcus. It's your guilt talking. Can't you see that? Nothing strange is going on. The explosion mutilated Zach. The city was protecting us from the pain."

When they'd followed the tip, Zach had knocked on the door. Nobody answered. He kicked the door in and went inside with Marcus. Shortly afterward, Marcus looked through the window and saw their suspect running across the grass. He ran after him, leaving Zach in the house. Then the house had exploded.

"What has Nate said about it?" she asked.

"Nate's so consumed chasing down his own demons, he can't even deal with it."

"I can't take you guys hating me anymore. You have to let this go."

"We never hated you. We just don't understand your decisions."

"This is why I ran straight to Kyle. When I had Zach cremated, none of you could understand. Not even my best friends. Kyle gave me comfort in a world of judgment."

"He's no good for you, Eva."

"It's better than being alone."

"Right." Marcus knew that, for whatever her reasons, she was lying not only to him, but to herself as well.

He also realized that tonight he wouldn't be able to finish his conversation with Zach about how much Nate's affair had affected his life. Rehashing the explosion left Marcus wondering who was behind the cover-up, and worse, whether there was a cover-up at all. Did the SAPD and the City of San Antonio really have his, Eva's, and the public's best interest at heart? It was too much to fathom on an evening when all Marcus wanted to do was talk to Zach, not defend his speculations surrounding his partner's death.

"I gotta get out of here, Eva. But I don't wanna leave you like this."

"It's fine."

"It's not fine. C'mon. Another night."

"I need to be here. Some alone time with him will do me good."

"Ridgeland know you're out here?"

"Not a clue."

"Is he hitting you? Say the word, I'll take his ass down."

"I can handle Kyle. Are you gonna be okay?"

"I don't know."

"Please let my husband rest in peace. Give yourself some peace too. Zach loved you like a brother. He's in God's hands now. Let him go. He'd want you to live."

"Yeah, well, life sucks right now."

"Marcus, wait, don't leave like this. We can talk about what else you're going through. I'm not Zach, but I can listen."

"Eva, there are only three people in my life who truly understand me. One's dead. One is currently screwed up in the head, and the other has enough on her shoulders. Believe me, that's a conversation I don't want."

"Well, I'm here."

"Well, I'm out." Marcus looked back. "Just so you know, if your pathetic replacement of a husband so much as turns his head wrong, he's done." He walked through the cemetery, heading toward his car. Looking back at Eva, he saw that she had taken his place on the ground. She'd settled in, obviously intending to stay there for a while. That woman was an enigma to him. Despite her explanations, Marcus couldn't reconcile how Eva had gone from loving Zach while he was alive, to disrespecting him after he died.

He received a text from Nate. *I feel guilty as hell.*

Marcus thought about all the help he'd given Nate to pull off his side activity. He looked at the text message again, tired of Nate's insanity, tired of his own inability to come to terms with Zach's death.

"You're not the only one, Nate."

Chapter 17

"Hey, pretty girl."

Wearing a three-piece black suit, Nightmare came out of the shadows, walking on a bed of fog. Arianna had nowhere to run. She wondered if she was in an alley, or a warehouse, and how she'd gotten there. A streetlight came on, draping the scene in haunting illumination. She was between the buildings of her impoverished neighborhood, next to the big gutter. As Nightmare got closer, he opened a cape and cloaked her in things she'd like to forget. She backed away from him, he yanked her back.

Arianna jolted awake at Nightmare's tight jerk.

Good God, not tonight too.

She got up and crept to the bathroom to shake off the latest encounter. She washed her face, took a breath, and did her best to compose herself. It was still her anniversary, and she'd overcome Nightmare's grip long enough to ring in the evening nicely with a renewed spirit. But this latest encounter with an intangible evil reminded Arianna that her ordeal wasn't over and that she still had a hard conversation ahead.

When she walked back into the bedroom, she noticed a black jewelry box on Nate's nightstand. It was similar to the box her ring had come in, the one Nate had given her at the Mokara. Slowly, trying not to wake her husband, she picked it up and opened it, revealing a stunning, fourteen karat gold necklace holding a charm engraved with the names of their kids. The thoughtful present helped Arianna keep Nightmare in the shadows of the past for at least a little while longer.

"This is absolutely unreal," Arianna mumbled to herself, low enough to respect her husband's slumber, but involuntarily loud enough to fail at her attempt.

Nate sat up and checked the time. "You couldn't wait, woman?"

She smiled. "No."

He motioned her down to him. "Come here. Let me see it."

Arianna lifted her hair and Nate clasped the chain.

"I don't know what to say, Nathan."

Nate kissed her. "You don't have to say anything, Ani."

"When did you get it?"

"You want the truth, huh?"

"Uh, yeah. That would be the best choice."

"About ten hours ago."

Arianna shook her head in disbelief. Nate had done it again. "I don't know if I can beat this." She reached inside her nightstand drawer and pulled out a brown bag, not caring whether Nate wanted to go back to sleep. "Remember I said I had something for you?" She dangled the bag. "It's not much, but I wanted you to have it."

"You're lucky I love you, woman." Nate rubbed his eyes, sat up, and pulled from the bag a gold-framed, five-by-seven, refurbished picture of his late maternal grandmother and himself. The picture's symbolism made Nate recall the day his mother had abandoned him. He remembered picking the photo out of the gutter after his mother had sped off. This water-damaged photo was the only relic of his grandmother. Nate thought it had gotten lost in the move back to Texas from Baltimore. "Where was this?"

"I found it about ten months ago in the bottom of a box in the basement. I didn't tell you because I thought it would make a good gift if I could find somebody who could restore it."

"You've been working on this for almost a year?"

"Well, it took a few months to find somebody who could work with the photo. I had to mail it off."

Nate couldn't close his mouth. "I can't believe you did this for me with all that went on this year." He looked at her, astonished. "This is amazing."

"I had to do something. Besides, you have everything a man could need, so I figured more cologne would be overkill."

He looked at the photo, his eyes watering. "I still remember the day my mother walked out like it was yesterday." Nate put the photo on the nightstand.

"I can't even explain it," Arianna said, "but something happened to me today when I saw you walking in front of me at the school. I realized that I was turning away from the one person I should have been running toward."

Nate's eyes studied Arianna in the light radiating from outside through the half-open blinds. He ran his hand across her stomach.

"Daddy."

He quickly looked in the direction of the door. Then he looked at Arianna. "Does he ever sleep?"

Arianna couldn't help but giggle. "No."

"Let me get him settled down." Nate opened the door.

"Daddy, Elmo."

"Elmo's asleep, Son. Let's go."

~~~

Nate came back into the room and found that Arianna had lit the fire and, to his surprise, a Citronella candle. She came out of the bathroom wearing the short, red nightgown he'd bought her for their second wedding anniversary. "Do you ever get rid of anything, woman?"

"Nothing *you* give me."

"I see that." He looked at the candle. "We don't have mosquitoes in the house, Ani."

"Yeah, well, this is kind of impromptu, so this is what I have. It smells like lavender though."

"Only you can light an insect repellent candle and make it seem sexy as hell." Nate started at her feet, moved his eyes up her waist, to the scar across her distorted cleavage, and to her face. "I've always thought you're the sexiest woman in the world."

"Whew, that was close." She walked toward him seductively, grabbed his shoulders for support, and leaned into him.

Arianna opened her mouth just a little bit. Her lips whisked against his. Then in a decisive, sultry maneuver, she took in a slight puff of air, much like taking a sip through a straw, as she closed her mouth and puckered at the same time, pressing into his lips, planting a kiss on him so powerful it seemed to give off a magnetic charge. Before he knew what had hit him, Nate's mouth was uncontrollably drawn to hers with powerful reciprocation. "Damn, I missed all this."

Nate grabbed the back of her neck and slipped his tongue into her mouth. She clung to him like a drowning woman reaching for the only life raft in sight. They kissed as if they were a reunited, post-war couple during the times when love and sacrifice trumped everything.

He walked her to the bed and she fell onto her back. The shadows from the window blind danced across her shoulders and outlined her body in moonlight and black stripes. The fire crackled and the shadows danced as they reconnected again after months of mental and physical separation.

Nate's passion for his wife became relentless. He couldn't help but take her. After a few moments of being wrapped up in their own private world, Arianna shrieked as she held tight to him, calling his name.

As he looked down at her, she stared back at him in a way that let him know, at that moment, no other man existed. Her soft touch triggered Nate to detonate. His arms gave out and he fell on her as his body reached the pinnacle he'd been striving for, completion, in more ways than one, for the second time tonight.

Arianna spoke in a wispy cracked voice. "I couldn't make it without you."

Nate held Arianna until she fell asleep, their love reconnected. As he stroked her head, he hoped for two things: that she would keep her word and remain the sensual, vibrant woman she'd been before their rift, and that his guilt over meeting a woman at a motel would lessen, because it was about to tear his guts out. *Your horny ass just couldn't wait.*

Nate got out of bed feeling too agitated to sleep. He went into the bathroom and stopped at the mirror. His self-hatred over his decision almost sent his fist straight into his reflection. He gripped the towel rack. The heat rose through him as he thought of his significant deceit with an insignificant woman, and his total disregard for his family. *Fuck me.*

Before Nate realized it, he was holding a towel rack in the middle of the bathroom, drywall falling to the ground.

Chapter 18

Marcus woke to blue sky, the sun beaming in, highlighting his expensive living room and reminding him of how far he'd come in life. The trust he and Pam had built, the bond they'd shared since Italy, since he'd first introduced Gwen to her on their third date. He thought of how she had never hesitated to take her on, to help Marcus in his quest to be an effective parent at such a young age. How could he have taken that loyalty, that blind faith, and turned on Pam in a complicit action to help Nate cheat on her best friend. In his eyes, accessory was no better than infidelity.

Pam came downstairs, dressed in jeans and a spring sweater, a cross between business casual and Saturday shopping. "I don't know why I can't just teleconference this from home."

Marcus chuckled. "Because your boss wants to make a good impression with the district. Having all of you in the same room shows his authority."

Pam grabbed a cup of coffee. "It shows me that he has no life." She checked the time, and then her phone.

Marcus had an inkling of what was on her mind—Arianna, and how her night had gone. But he didn't want to delve. Staying away from the Jackson marriage in all regards was his safest bet. He came up behind her and draped her in his arms. "How long is your meeting?"

"With my boss, you never know."

"I can relate to that."

"What are you gonna do all day, free from divas?"

Drown in guilt. "Not sure. Hit the gym. Go over cold cases."

"You mean a particular cold case."

"You caught me."

Pam sighed. "Marcus."

He backed away. "Don't start. We're having a good morning."

"I'm not starting. I just hate what this does to you."

Marcus thought of the original suspects in his mother's disappearance and the case files he was going to peruse once again. "It's therapeutic."

"Right, Marcus."

"Would you feel better if I reconciled my expense report and got reimbursed instead, so you can buy shoes?"

"I'd feel better if you had peace."

"I have you and Gwen. I have my peace. I just want answers." He kissed her cheek. "But seriously, I do need to work on getting my reimbursement this month. A brotha gotta pay for them braces."

"Speaking of Gwen." Pam reached into her purse, and suddenly panicked as she shifted through her items. "Crap."

"What's wrong?"

"Gwen's extra inhaler. I can't find it."

"Calm down. You'll find it. She has one with her, right?"

"Yeah, but she loses it sometimes. The last thing she needs is for her mother to lose the backup." Pam was growing more frantic. Then she looked up suddenly. "Your truck. I dropped my purse that day, remember?" She grabbed her keys and shot out the house. Marcus smiled in the moment, thinking that Pam was probably panicking for nothing, and also realizing how much she truly loved a child she didn't have to raise.

Pam came back into the house a few minutes later, calmer, quieter, and carrying the inhaler and a small piece of paper.

"Told you," Marcus said.

Pam smiled and put the inhaler into her purse. She held onto the piece of paper and paused for a moment. "Baby, you know I trust you, right?"

"Yeah, no doubt, why?"

Pam handed him the paper. "I found this under your passenger's seat digging for the inhaler. I have to ask. Any wife would."

Marcus grabbed the receipt out of her hand. His stomach almost plummeted through the floor—the motel. Nate had gotten sloppy. He stared at the receipt, read the date, and realized it had been in his truck for a while. It must have been a morning that Nate had forgotten to flush it. He was so fixated on the incriminating evidence, he forgot that Pam was standing in front of him, looking at his reaction.

"Marcus, no way, right?"

He looked up at her and quickly gathered his bearings after realizing how guilty he must look. "Of course not. How could you think that?"

"It's a no-tell motel receipt, Marcus. What if you found one under my seat?"

Keep it cool, Carter. Marcus fought like hell to think of a non-truth that wouldn't constitute a direct lie. "I was just helping out a fellow officer who thought he'd be spotted undercover." He kissed Pam's forehead. "I would never cheat on the best thing that's ever happened to me."

Pam smiled. "I know. I just saw it and...you know. It was just odd."

"I get it. We're good, babe."

"Can you amend your expense report and add this?"

"What?"

"You get reimbursed for this, right?" Pam read the receipt again. "You paid cash. You couldn't use your card?"

"Best not to." Marcus was starting to realize that you don't need a big shovel to dig a big hole. One lie always had to lead to another one. Now he had to find a way to justify spending their hard earned money for work without seeing a dime in return. "It's probably too late to submit it. I'll see. I forgot."

"College needs all the breaks we can get." Pam checked the time, quickly kissed Marcus, and grabbed her purse. She muttered about how she didn't want to spend Saturday morning in a meeting to discuss what had happened yesterday with Ben and the trashcan, and then spend hours bickering over developing a more comprehensive plan to tackle the bullying when it could wait until Monday. "I'll pick up Gwen on the way home."

Marcus blurted out, "Just saying, I didn't cheat. I'd never do that."

"I never *once* thought that. Believe me, if I suspected you, all your shit would be on the lawn right now. We're good, babe. Enjoy your day."

Pam left. Marcus held the receipt, feeling worse than he'd felt thirty minutes ago.

~~~

Pam got into her vehicle, reflected on her conversation with Marcus, then immediately picked up the phone to call Arianna. She dialed one digit and then put down the phone, realizing that she had to let the morning play out. This anniversary was vital to her best friend, and she didn't want to cloud it with a shade of grey. *Maybe it is just an innocent receipt.*

Chapter 19

Nate jolted. Arianna removed her cold hand from his warm back. "Sorry. Didn't mean to wake you."

"What's wrong?"

"Nothing. Sounds silly, but I just needed to touch you. Go back to sleep. I'm gonna take a shower."

"Your fault I'm so sleepy." Nate put his head back down. "Give me a couple more hours, and then feel free to touch me again. Just make sure you have bacon and you're naked when you do it."

"You're so crazy, Nathan."

In the bathroom, Arianna stripped, then fumbled for her apricot body wash. The lack of organization under the sink gave the shower the time it needed to fog the bathroom, allowing the heavy steam to slap Arianna with warmth when she slid open the metal shower door. Before stepping inside, she noticed the two holes in the wall, and the absent towel rack. *What the hell? Again, Nathan?*

Arianna didn't want to wake Nate up for a towel rack, so she did the next obvious thing. She looked under the sink, a little further back where Nate had put the towel rack the last time he'd bumped it and loosened it from the wall.

Arianna chuckled, thinking that Nate had put it back up incorrectly the last time and had bumped it again. *Another good reason to renovate the bathroom, make it bigger, and get my spa tub.*

Arianna stepped onto the non-skid flowers and let the hot water comfort her. It washed over her closed eyes, and she savored the sting from the initial heat. She poured out the velvety smooth body wash, feeling the coolness of the thick substance that filled her palm like a rippled pyramid. The creamy soap turned to lather as Arianna rubbed every inch of her stomach. She jumped, taking in a quick breath, as she felt Nate's hands sharing the warmth. "You really think you can put the words *shower* and *I'm gonna take a* in the same sentence and expect me to fall back asleep?"

Nate cleansed Arianna's body as she rested the back of her head on his shoulder, his caresses bringing her passion to the surface. Her knees became weaker as her breathing became stronger. She pressed against him, wet from her desire as well as the shower.

Nate's blue-collar hands moved around Arianna's body, polishing her sense of completion. He pressed her firmly against the rose-colored tile, her back to his front, immobilizing her. She savored every stroke.

The feeling of Nate's arms overpowered her in the afterglow. It had been so long since they'd been able to enjoy true intimacy. "I'm sorry for causing so much distance. I just want to stay like we are now, forever."

Nate held her until the water turned cool. She knew Nate too felt overwhelmed. He gripped her tighter until her shivers and goosebumps prompted Nate to cut off the shower. "Look at me."

She looked at him as she shivered. Nate grabbed her robe and draped it around her. "No looking back, understand?"

Arianna nodded, knowing what was to come. "I don't want to look back either."

"We just have to make sure we make *us* the priority."

"I will. I promise."

"Me too." They held tight to each other. "Did you have something planned today?"

"Just my family, baby. I missed this. I missed you." She paused. "I thought maybe we could go do something with the boys today, and then let the kids go to Pam's house tonight. We can reconnect and...talk." She could barely get it out as the reality of the morning-after started hitting her. They still had to deal with Nightmare.

"Would you mind if I spent the day alone with the boys? I want to take them fishing. I haven't exactly been Father of the Year. I need it. They need it."

Arianna chuckled. "Okay."

He kissed her and kissed her again. "I could do this all day."

"Me too."

"But I need to get at it if we're gonna survive I-35."

Nate's phone alerted him to a text. He reluctantly broke away and checked his phone.

Arianna realized she had an entire day alone to sit and stew in her thoughts. Eva had to work; Pam had a Saturday meeting; and Taesha had a Saturday meeting to work some guy. The downtime would drive her crazy. "You know what, Nathan? I think I'm gonna check out that new gym. You still have those free passes?"

Nate appeared distracted. "Uh, passes?"

"Yeah, the ones that were slipped in the front door the other day."

Nate sent a response and quickly put down his phone. "Uh, yeah, they're on the dresser."

"No, they're not."

"Uh, check the junk drawer."

"Are you alright, Nathan?"

"Yeah, I'm fine. Just work...*again*."

"You need a vacation."

He spoke low. "Don't I know it." Then he perked up. "Wait a minute. The track star's going to a gym?"

"Hey, I do my squats."

Nate laughed. "You do know we work our asses off to not have to worry about free."

"It's okay. I'm gonna do a little shopping first, so I won't get there until eleven anyway, when the deal starts."

"God help the cashiers." Nate dressed in long cargo shorts and his lucky fishing T-shirt, tan with a picture of a big fish on it. Arianna put on a track suit, taking her back to her college roots. As she dressed, she tried her best to drown out the inevitable, the revealing of Nightmare to Nate.

Nate grabbed his wallet. "Here, pay cash. Stay off the cards. I just paid the last one off. And pick me up a can of WD-40 too. I need to fix that squeaky-ass hinge." He gave her a kiss. "I gotta get the boys up. Oh yeah, get some of that edible wax shit because you're gonna be licking it off my chest later."

"You sure do seem in a hurry, babe."

"Traffic. I just told you."

"Oh yeah, thirty-five. You better go."

"Don't you gotta get going too?"

Arianna wasn't in a huge rush. But when she thought about it, the last place she wanted to be was in an empty house pondering nightfall. She needed to clear the hell out.

Arianna gave Nate a kiss, reminded him to ease up on the soda with the boys, and then told him to drive safely to Austin. "Hey, what time do you think you'll be back?"

"Late."

"Okay, well I think I'm gonna ask the girls if they want to go eat on the Riverwalk tonight. I think it will do us all some good to get out."

"Good idea." Nate seemed uninterested.

Arianna chalked it up to the job. "Try to relax, Nathan."

He smiled at her. "I will. Now go enjoy yourself."

~~~

Get in the car. Get in the car. Get in the car.

When Arianna drove off, Nate rushed from the window and called Marcus. He'd texted him earlier saying, *Pam found your receipt. Call me when you can.* "What the hell happened, Marcus?"

"You got sloppy, that's what."

"Oh, shit."

"I handled it."

"Look, I'm headed to Austin. Wanna roll?"

"Yeah, Pam has to go in to work for something. And Gwen doesn't wanna be bothered with me."

"Be there in thirty."

One minute to throw off covers, one minute to shake beds, one minute to put ice on Darius's back, one minute to shake beds again, two minutes to tickle Tre, eight minutes to eat cereal, one minute to brush teeth, five minutes to get dressed, four minutes to pack clothes, three minutes to straighten up.

They were out the door, on schedule, the boys running to the truck with three minutes left to drive around the corner to Marcus's house.

Nate's phone rang. Two seconds to check the caller ID, three seconds to breathe, four seconds to pray, one second of realizing this moment was inevitable.

Chapter 20

This is definitely not Nate's gym.

Arianna toted her gym bag. She gasped at the modern technology of the fitness center. The nautilus machines looked like spaceships, and the free weights glistened in glazed black. To her left stood a towel rack stacked high with plush terry cloth towels, right next to an automated blood pressure machine. The floor was laid out in red, white, and charcoal tile, which matched the background at the smoothie bar. Overhead, patrons ran around the circular track while looking down to the open first floor.

Arianna heard a man's voice. "Can I help you, pretty lady?"

She spun around and saw her reflection in sea-blue eyes. His frayed muscle shirt matched the blue mesh shorts that stopped below his knees. He wore a white baseball cap backwards, leaving a hint of sandy brown hair. His Caucasian skin showed the veins in his well-earned biceps. A small scar was etched above his brow, angled just enough to be cool, looking so right. The dominate jawline added pure loveliness. Handsome, smooth, confident, and to Arianna, surprisingly not the man she'd just made love to in the shower.

He reached down and took the flyer out of her hand. "Would you like a tour guide?"

"I think I can find my way," she said.

"If you need anything, my name's Anthony."

"Nice to meet you."

Anthony looked her over. "You run?"

"Yeah, a lot."

"Pays off, doesn't it?"

"Yes, it does."

"You act like you have something on your mind."

Arianna thought of Nightmare. "Just life. Guess that's why I'm here."

"To let it go."

Arianna let out a deep breath. "Pretty much."

"Would you complete this form showing you took advantage of my offer?"

"So, this is *your* gym, Anthony?"

"I own it. My manager runs it during the week because I have one of those damned nine-to-five things."

"Yeah, have one of those." Arianna placed the form on the counter and began writing down her information.

"Your husband must like blinding other men."

"Excuse me?"

"That rock you're wearing. It looks nice on your pretty hand."

Arianna looked at her ring. "I got a good one, that's for sure."

"The man or the bling?"

"Both." Arianna was starting to feel uncomfortable, and her accentuation of the "b" in *both* proved that. She'd almost spat in Anthony's face because she'd pursed her lips so tightly.

"Cool." Anthony picked up the card Arianna had filled out and began reading it. He nodded. "Well, Arianna Jackson. Enjoy my facility."

She stepped away to tour the gym, walking further and further from the regret of filling out a simple form. Anthony had said her name as if he owned the rights to it. Giving in to instinct, she looked back. Anthony was staring at her. Normally, interest from other men didn't faze her. Arianna's heart belonged to Nate, and Anthony's passes did nothing to change that. But this time, the words lingered because she felt so creeped out. Anthony didn't seem to be watching her—he seemed to be studying her. Or maybe this was his way of dealing with an attraction. It didn't matter. What Arianna wanted she already had at home.

She walked down a wide hallway. Aerobic steps and huge mirrors were in most of the rooms. To her left was a room dedicated to spin bikes with women struggling to go nowhere. Racquetball courts faced her. Arianna had extra energy, so she played herself in three rounds of racquetball, a gym activity she felt comfortable performing.

Then she hit the sauna and showered.

Arianna could have showered at home but she loved the sensation of cool water on hot skin. The sensual combination turned her shower into a steamy erogenous paradise. She hadn't masturbated in years. Since the shower stalls were private, and nobody else was showering, Arianna took advantage of the opportunity.

She emerged from the locker room clean and self-satisfied.

Anthony came out of nowhere. "Well?"

"Geeze."

"Startled you?"

"A little."

Anthony looked around. "You like?"

"I'm not a gym person, but I like. I would bring my husband, but it's kinda modern for his taste."

"Not the old-school, paint-chipping-off-the-walls and ripped-up-weight-bench gyms, huh?"

"Yeah."

"Seeing that big-ass iceberg on your finger and how fine you are, I imagine he works out a lot."

"He holds his own."

"I hold my own."

"I gotta go."

"Get with me if you want personal training."

153

"I don't need it. My husband knows how to work my body just fine. You have a nice day."

"You too."

Arianna walked out of the gym, sneaking one last peek at Anthony through the windows. *Creep.*

Chapter 21

Nate and Marcus found a picnic area at Travis Lake and settled in. They agreed to talk at the lake once the boys were safely fishing. This made for a tense, quiet ride up I-35, because neither Nate nor Marcus was adept at the art of filler conversations. Darius had slept during the ride, leaving Tre to ramble on about his new Spiderman fishing pole.

Nate checked the bait, and then the boys went down to the water. The men stared at the lake.

"Where was the receipt, Marcus?"

"Floorboard."

"What the hell did she say?"

"She gave it to me, a little shaken by it. Accepted my excuse."

Nate was skeptical. "That simple."

"My wife trusts me, Nate." Marcus shook his head. "I don't know if I should feel validated, or guilty as sin for lying to her."

"I know. I'm sorry. At least you didn't screw another woman."

"Doesn't matter. I'm in this as thick as you are." Marcus quickly glanced at Nate. "You *did* end this shit, right?"

"Didn't have to. She did."

"Seriously?"

"Yep. She called me right before I picked you up. Said she'd been up all night thinking and didn't want a man she had to share anymore, so it was over."

"Sounds too easy. She's up to something."

"I don't think so. There was something final in her voice."

"How do you feel?"

"Free."

"How was last night?"

"Man, Ani broke my ass off," Nate said, not giving his mistress another thought.

Marcus's eyes widened. "Did she finally tell you what's wrong with her? Talk about her parents at all?"

"Nope. But she seems normal now."

"Just like that? No reason?"

"Said she let life get in the way, and that she woke up and realized what she had."

"Now, *that* is too simple."

"I have to believe her. She's my wife."

"Aaaand six months ago, you were racking your brain to figure out why your marriage was tanking. Now you just don't care?"

"Nope. Things are good now. I'm leaving it like that."

Darius and Tre ran up to Nate for help untangling Tre's fishing wire. Nate fixed the wire and explained how to cast a proper line, and Tre gave him a hug. Darius tried handing Nate a receipt and the change from the park concession stand where he'd bought sodas. Nate told him to keep the change and reminded him not to tell his mother about drinking soda at nine in the morning. Darius put the change in his pocket along with the receipt, and off the boys went.

A text message from Arianna got his attention: *Hey sexy boy*

Nate replied: *Sup baby girl?*

As he waited on her response, he again realized Arianna was somewhere in love with him, trusting him, believing in her Superman. The affair may have been temporary, but the guilt would last forever if he didn't unload it. And he would live with the silent legacy, day in and day out, watching her smile, stepping in front of her when he'd have to shield her, making love to her until dawn, holding her, making her think she'd been the only one since their wedding, lying to her with his body language.

"What's wrong?" Marcus asked.

"I'm gonna have to cop to what I did in that motel."

Marcus panicked. "It's gonna unravel everything. I'll go down too."

Arianna texted back: *Did my men catch anything yet?*

Nate didn't acknowledge Marcus. He stared at Arianna's words instead. He thought of the restored picture, the time and thought it had taken to pull it off. All this time she'd gone cold, she'd never lost her commitment to the man she loved. His mind flashed to the motel, and the guilt almost made him cry.

"You can't do this, Nate."

"I don't have a choice. I'll keep you out of it."

"Pam and Arianna aren't stupid!"

"Lower your voice."

Nate and Marcus were arguing back and forth when Tre yelled, "Daddy, I can swim!" He trotted into the water.

Nate dropped his phone and flew off the bench. Marcus was already running toward the lake.

"Darius, grab him," Nate screamed.

"I'm trying."

"Damnit, Tre. Don't do this to Daddy!" Nate shouted. "I'm gonna kill you as soon as I save you."

The water rose chest high on Tre. He screamed for his daddy as the water continued to rise. Nate got closer; Tre went under water. Darius was panting for breath and appeared confused as to his next move.

Nate ducked under the water, didn't see Tre. He screamed, pleaded, cried for Tre, as if that would make him appear. As Nate's world drowned, Marcus swam out a ways to look further. Nate took another dip under—there was Tre. He got Tre's arm and pulled him up. Tre almost coughed up his lungs, crying and hollering at the same time. "Daddy! Daddy!"

Nate held him tight. "Daddy got you. Daddy's here." He looked at Darius. "Darius, please find my phone. I dropped it near the bench. And get the blanket and your brother's bag out of the truck."

Darius made his way to the bench to find the phone. Tre was still crying.

"Hush now," Nate said. "It's okay."

Nate's heartbeat slowly returned to normal, but his breathing hadn't calmed. He cradled his baby boy, put his head down, and gave the Lord a private moment of gratitude. The affair was now, indirectly, affecting his children.

Nate caught eyes with Marcus. The stare was understood. Arianna needed to be told. This fiasco needed to end before it turned into a tragedy. "I'm sorry you're in this, Marcus." He looked at Tre. "I'm sorry for all of it."

"I know that," Marcus replied with a more understanding tone.

"Mommy is going to be mad at me," Tre said.

"No, she is going to be mad at Daddy. Let's keep this our little secret."

"Can I get ice cweam?" Tre asked.

It was one of those moments when the mood couldn't help but change.

"Are you bribing me?" Nate chuckled.

"I don't know."

"You keep your mouth shut and I'll buy you a whole franchise." Nate kissed Tre's forehead.

Five minutes had passed. Tre was shivering.

"Where the hell is Darius?" Nate asked.

"He's coming," Marcus said.

Darius returned with the blanket and the bag.

Nate covered Tre. "What took you so long?"

"Sorry. I had trouble getting the door open."

The park's restroom was considered clean by public facility standards. Cement grey with black commodes and a wet floor. Nate helped Tre change his clothes while trying to keep him off the floor until he could put his shoes back on.

Nate held him up in the air; Marcus tied his shoes. Nate was grateful he'd listened to Arianna. She'd always told him to pack extra outfits for everyone.

Fishing was over for the day. Nate played it safer. Tre went to the swing set and Darius ran over to some older kids and started playing freeze tag. Darius seemed different, not as responsive, but Nate attributed his attitude to Tre ruining their time to fish. Marcus and Nate cleaned the bench and packed up their fishing equipment.

"Boys are tough," Nate said.

"Try girls," Marcus said.

Nate smiled at the thought. "I guess."

They loaded up the truck.

"When are you gonna tell her?" Marcus asked.

"I guess tonight."

"That soon?"

"I have no choice. I can't put this off."

Marcus nodded. Nate noticed him looking at Tre. "I guess it does need to be said."

"Do you think she'll leave?"

"Arianna? No. Pam? She'll leave long enough to get a machete."

"Funny."

"Honestly, no. But Arianna will be devastated and Pam will never look at me the same."

"I think it's better than how we're living now. I have to believe I can heal everything."

Marcus stopped loading. "Look, you're my boy. I'm gonna be there regardless. But the issue is not your affair. It's why you had it. You can't heal the root."

"Maybe if I tell her, she'll tell me."

"I hate it when you think. I've said it before. This is beyond your scope. I'm no fan of counseling, either, but you guys need help."

"I told you, she won't open up. And it won't work."

"That's it?"

"What else would it be?"

"You tell me."

Nate looked across the landscape, hoping Marcus would just leave this counseling shit alone. But Marcus knew him too well. He stared Nate down until he came clean. "It will hit my insurance, Marcus."

"Now we're getting somewhere. Claims leave paper trails."

"Yep."

"Pay cash."

"It's too much of a risk. The last thing I need is the DEA finding out."

"Finding out what? That you made a mistake?"

"Drop it. I'm not going."

Marcus shut the trunk of Nate's Tahoe. "Look, I didn't want to bring this up because I know how you feel about it, but...if you change your mind, I know a guy."

"A guy?"

"A doc. Yeah, he, um, he works on the DL for us. A few of my colleagues have seen him. Doesn't leave a trace. But he is good."

"I don't know. I gotta think about it."

"Nate, you have no other option."

"I said I'd think about it." Nate looked toward the playground. "I'm gonna go swing Tre."

Salvaging the rest of the day for the kids took little effort. Travis Lake was a huge recreational area. The place where they'd been fishing was part of a huge landscape, with a thick, dense wall of trees surrounding grassy fields. On the other side of the trees were other areas to play games and enjoy park food. Tre was content on the swings, and all Nate had to do with Darius was keep him fed between his running spurts.

"Legs out when going up and in when coming down, Son," Nate said to Tre.

"Woah," Tre said.

After a couple more hours, Nate and Marcus called it a day. Everyone piled into the truck, except for Nate, who stood outside the driver's side door and stared at the trees. His instincts were always on.

"What's wrong?" Marcus asked when Nate hopped in.

"I'm not sure. I could have sworn I saw somebody watching us." He nodded in the direction of ten o'clock.

"Nobody's there. Damn, you're paranoid."

Nate backed out of the parking spot. "Oh hell, where's my phone?"

"In the console," Darius said.

Nate picked up the phone and noticed a small crack in the screen from when he'd slammed it down earlier. "It better turn on."

"Yeah, Dad, we know you hate to have the phone turned off."

"Excuse me?"

"Just saying. You're well-connected."

"I sense an attitude," Nate said. "What's the rule?"

"The only person allowed to have an attitude is you."

"Exactly." Nate turned on the phone and checked for missed calls and messages. He had no alerts. He put down the phone and began driving to the nearest ice cream parlor, leaving the trees and his gut instinct behind.

"I have a sleepover tonight," Darius said.

"You never said anything about a sleepover."

"Ronald and I planned it yesterday. Can I go?"

Nate figured a break from Tre would do him good. "Sure. But next time tell me sooner."

"Let's go catch a movie after we drop him off," Marcus suggested. "Tre would like that."

"Yeah," Tre shouted.

Nate agreed. It would help him prepare for a talk that, after Tre's run-in with a body of water, had become a necessary pain to inflict.

Chapter 22

The San Antonio Riverwalk enchanted its evening crowd of party-goers and feel-gooders with its captivating variety and sleight of hand. The Walk's decorative lights glimmered like Christmas in spring, while multicolored tour boats beamed passengers to other worlds, first enveloping them in a forest of trees and then, a few feet later, surrounding them with the modern beauty of glass walls at Rivercenter Mall.

Past the dancing waves, dinner tables with umbrellas in bright hues splashed Downtown San Antonio with the essence of childhood. Lovers kissed. Onlookers drifted under the arched bridges where marriage proposals were known to take place.

The lit lampposts made tourists and locals feel caught up in a fairy tale, while their wallets crashed and burned at shops offering everything from overpriced ice cream to souvenir T-shirts. Scenic high-rises and hotels dominated the river's landscape.

It was the perfect spot for young people on first dates to fall in love or for middle-aged couples to celebrate twenty-year anniversaries. It also served as a place for friends to chill out over Margaritas.

Arianna and her friends decided on barbeque, and the best barbeque in San Antonio was at the County Line. They had to wait a few minutes for an outside table, but their timing fell right. They took the best spot on the promenade, within a few inches of the river and an outdoor heater. They received excellent service, despite the full capacity Saturday crowd, and had a sexy waiter to boot. The lights reflecting off the river, a light breeze, and a mariachi band set the perfect tone. Arianna looked over the water, to the Gleason Building. *Wow, I have offices up there.*

They were exquisite, each in her own way. Arianna shaped her new, black, low-rise skinny jeans nicely, pairing the pants with a pastel yellow tank top under a long-sleeved, midriff cover-up. Pam showed off her coral capri pants and matching jacket. Taesha magnified her eccentric vibe with faded red jeans and a black-and-white-striped shirt. Eva, the consummate professional, played it safer with a mocha-colored Ralph Lauren sweater and Levi's. They settled in for a good meal as Arianna tried to settle her nerves.

"Just got a text from Nathan. They'll be home soon." She looked at Pam. "You're gonna keep the kids tonight, right? So I can try this again? You sure you don't mind?"

"You've asked me five times in the last ten minutes," Pam said. "Yes. The boys are always welcome at the house. You know that." She said nothing else and looked around the Riverwalk, appearing to be people-watching.

"What's wrong, Pam?" Eva asked.

"Nothing."

"Doesn't look like nothing," Taesha said.

"I'm just worried about my husband shouldering everybody's issues."

"What do you mean?" Eva asked again.

"Just problems at work. Everybody always looks to him to solve everything. It's weighing on him."

"I hear you on that," Arianna said. "Nathan feels the same way."

Pam nodded in agreement and changed the subject. "I hope I hear something soon from my interview. In the meeting today, my boss indicated he wants to retire sooner rather than later. The whole incident involving the trash can sent him over the edge."

"I bet he is tired," Eva said.

Pam looked slyly at Arianna. "We're all tired." She looked down at her phone.

Arianna noticed. "Okay, what's up with you, Pam? Your mood is more than about Marcus and his stressful job."

"Yeah, I agree," Taesha chimed in. "This is much more than your stressful job."

"I guess it's just finally sinking in that when you tell Nate about Nightmare, I'm gonna have my own questions to answer. Guess I didn't think about that until today."

"I'm so sorry to put you in that position, Pam."

"Don't misunderstand me. I *want* you to tell him. I just know Marcus will realize that I knew the whole time and didn't shed any light on why you shut down the way you did." Then Pam seemed to go on the defensive, as if she was holding something in. "But it's not like I lied to him or anything, right? I mean, keeping a secret isn't the same as directly helping you hurt Nate through a complicit action."

"Uh, okay," Arianna said. "I'm not trying to hurt Nate and you didn't make me keep Nightmare from him."

"I'm not implying any of that. That's my point."

"Whatever is making you feel this way, you are absolutely correct, Pam," Eva said. "You have nothing to feel guilty for."

"Oh, I don't feel guilty. I just know Marcus isn't gonna be too happy, as if I did something wrong."

The waiter came around and started pouring water. The women stopped talking. Arianna noticed Taesha staring at Pam as if studying her.

The waiter left, and Taesha got straight to it. "Why don't you tell us what's really on your mind, Pam?"

"What do you mean?" Pam replied.

"I know emotions. And I definitely know pissed-off when I see it. What did Marcus do?"

"He didn't do anything."

"You sure?"

"Taesha," Eva said in a tone that told Taesha to take her voice down a notch.

"I'm sure," Pam replied.

"I see."

Pam shook her head. "Why do you do this, Taesha?"

"Do what?" Arianna asked.

"Push," Taesha replied as she stared at Pam.

"You do seem awfully edgy," Eva said.

Arianna watched Pam and Taesha stare each other down. Then she peered over at Eva, who looked just as confused as Arianna felt. "What the hell is going on?" she asked.

"That's what I'd like to know," Taesha said.

"Let it go," Pam said. "Just stuff between Marcus and me."

"Stuff?" Eva asked. "Oh God, are you guys having problems?"

The evening that was supposed to be a stress reliever/girls' night out was turning into a failure to launch. Instead of being nice, it became an onslaught of inquisition into the state of the Carter marriage.

Pam asserted that she and Marcus were fine, just perhaps needing a vacation. She seemed convincing to Arianna; Eva also seemed settled with Pam's response.

Taesha wasn't so sure. But the women had come to accept Taesha for the conspiracy theorist she was and for her relentless assaults for the truth whenever she felt a front coming on. "You don't believe him."

"Excuse me?" Pam said.

"You've checked your watch six times in the last fifteen minutes, Pam," Taesha said. "Wherever he says he is, you don't believe him."

"That's ridiculous. He's with Nate," Pam said.

Arianna backed up her story. "Nate put Tre on the phone earlier, said Marcus hasn't caught any fish." She chuckled.

"Well, then, that settles it," Taesha said, obviously not feeling settled.

"Okay, fine," Pam said quickly and decisively. All the women stared at her, now realizing something else was going on. She sighed. "I found a rec—"

"OH MY GOD!" Eva shouted and suddenly stood up.

The women jumped out of their seats and looked across the river at the sound of the screams. "What the hell!" they all yelled.

People began looking up to the sky, others looked down. Some ran, some prayed. Everyone saw that a person had just fallen from the top of the Gleason Building and into the afterlife. The body had landed on the cement near the water and then rolled closer to the edge of the river.

"Is that—" Taesha shook Arianna's shoulder, forgetting all about their discussion and Pam's near-miss revelation.

"This can't be happening," Arianna said.

Chapter 23

The darkness blinded Arianna, protecting her from picturing blood on her hands. She walked barefoot across the warm plush carpet until she reached the hard, cold, tiled kitchen floor, wondering how much pain Shawnee had felt when she'd hit the concrete. Images of bodies falling from the sky would now be added to Arianna's repertoire of nightmares, and her mind prepared to do double-duty.

Despite the blood and the awkward position, Shawnee had lain there peacefully, her soul in a better place, while her physical being gazed up at the sky. Her dress had ridden up the leg that had bent backwards, painful for Arianna and the rest of the living to see. One of her stilettos had lain next to her; the other had fallen into the water. The blood from her broken body had seeped into the river, turning the water red. The image of a metallic silver heel floating in a contrasting crimson sea would plague Arianna the most, or maybe Shawnee's open eyes would sear into her memory, prevailing over all others.

~~~

The small glow from a scented outlet in the den provided the only bright spot in the Jackson home. Nate was waiting for Arianna on the sofa. He'd just turned off the television, just tuned out the relentless reporting of Shawnee's fall. Under normal circumstances, the fact he'd had an affair would not go over well; with Shawnee's death, the truth would break Arianna in half. He drank his Crown Royal and Coke as if a cocktail would make his words easier for Arianna to swallow.

"Why are you sitting in the dark?" Arianna's voice cracked.

"Waiting for you."

"Kids asleep?"

"I dropped Darius off at Ronald's. Tre dozed off at the movies."

"My little man missed the movie, huh?"

"We all did after Marcus got the call."

"Sorry I'm so late. After I showed Marcus and his guys Shawnee's desk, I stayed and helped them find what I could about her. I hung around in case they had any questions."

"Baby, we need to talk."

Arianna started crying. Nate shut up and opened his arms. He knew that he needed to open up. But tonight, given Arianna's brittle body and profound pain, there was no way he was breaking her further into fragments.

"I fired her. It's my fault," Arianna quavered. "She jumped from the Gleason, Nathan. She was sending me a message."

"You're the fairest person I know. This is not your fault. It's gonna be alright." He kissed the top of her head.

"I'm so drained, baby."

"It's been a long day for everybody. Let's go up. I need to be at the airport early tomorrow anyway."

"You can't delay it?"

"Not this one."

Arianna brushed her teeth and took off her clothes. Nate pulled the covers down on her side and she slipped into bed. He slipped in beside her. She migrated closer to him, kissed his collar bone. Nate knew she was sad.

"You didn't push her off that roof." He closed the gap between them. "Stop carrying the blame."

She grabbed his hand and brought it to her chest.

He kissed her. "Never forget how much I need you, even if you feel the need to."

"Why would you say that?"

"Just that I'm not perfect."

"You're my kind of perfect, Nathan."

Nate held her close. "What on Earth did I do to make you love me so much?"

"You never faltered."

"What?"

"All the drama with my family, my need to resist you, my past, my poverty. You were always there to fix my car, save my mother, help me however you could. Then when I walked away from you, I knew for sure you wouldn't want me back. But you didn't hesitate."

"You mean the dorm?"

"Yeah."

"From day one, I knew you were special, different, just the way you carried yourself, baby. I wasn't stupid. I knew what I had. You were the diamond in a world of, shit, I don't know, fake cubic zirconia and cheap, flimsy glass." Nate stroked her hair. "*I* got carried away that night, Ani. That was on *me*."

"But I wanted you. It got real and I couldn't handle being exposed."

"Listen to me, baby girl. I knew better. I got too close. My hands had no business even on your stomach."

"I tripped out because of the scar, not *you*. You went a long time without touching me."

"Should have gone on longer. That look of fear on your face took a long time to leave me."

"You never told me that."

"I'm a guy, there're a lot of things I didn't tell you about that night."

"Like?"

"Ani, I can't."

"Please."

"Let's not go there."

"Talk to me. You seem so edgy."

You have no idea. "I scare myself, Ani."

She glided her hand down his cheek. "Why?"

Nate hesitated, but felt too gripped in her soft eyes to refrain from telling her of his sheer anguish. He finally opened up about what had led him down a black hole after she'd cast him out, and how irrational he could become. "When you said you didn't want to continue with me, I took it *seriously*. I pictured you eventually moving on with somebody else. Just the thought of that *alone* made me completely illogical. I'm better now, because I'm older and more mature, but deep down, there's this *rage* that rises up when I think of somebody taking you from me. And now the boys. I think these extreme thoughts. If I lost you guys, or if somebody killed you or something, I think I'd leave a trail of destruction and then kill myself."

"Baby, we're not going anywhere."

Nate's heart flooded with a concoction of love, fear, and guilt. Each beat brought with it the angst of losing Arianna. He felt it in his soul and the blood running through his veins. He could barely handle the hemorrhage of emotions, and he began to shake a little, heart beating faster than he'd like. His sadness for Arianna's pain added what was needed to send him over the edge, and the only thing Nate could do to stop an emotional explosion was to bare his soul.

"I got home that night and I realized I'd lost you. Something possessed me, I swear to God. I sat in my apartment alone and all I wanted was you, to the point of complete obsession. I thought I'd gone crazy. It's a miracle I didn't tear up my house."

"What happened?"

"I'm still not sure. At first, I just wanted to hold you, talk to you, listen to you whispering and moaning in my ear. Then that made me want to kiss you softly like I did that first time in my truck."

"That's not crazy."

"I snapped, Ani. The phone rang and I thought it was you. A wrong number was my reality check that you were out of my life, and I couldn't do anything except crave you. Then my thoughts went all over the map. I went from wanting to peck your lips to slopping you with my tongue. I wanted to pound you as you cried out for more, and then listen to you beg me to lighten up because it was your first time. I pictured your pretty ass having my kids. Then I pictured you sexing up somebody else and I couldn't take it. I couldn't."

Nate could barely get the rest out, yet he couldn't slow it down. He was nearly hyperventilating.

"I grabbed a knife and stabbed my couch over and over again, at just the *thought* of you dating another guy. I pictured him harming you and all I wanted to do was beat the brake dust off of him. I felt sharp pain and I looked down and my knuckles were bleeding. I'd punched everything I could find."

"It's okay, Nathan." Arianna held him as he shook.

"I was so messed up. I got drunk as hell. I called Marcus and told him he was forever in my heart—I still hear about it to this day. I fell asleep thinking about your smile and woke up at three a.m. realizing I couldn't make it without you. I put my house back together the best I could, so I could get you back. Then you come knocking on the door at five a.m., soaking wet from the rain and exposing that damn scar. All the women I'd nailed, and I swear to God taking your virginity was the best sex I've ever had. I loved you so much, I thought I was gonna explode."

"You did actually. A few times."

"It was next level, baby."

"My rock. I embarrassed the crap out of you in the hall. Then I kicked you out. When I finally came to my senses, I showed up to your place unannounced and revealed this *thing* on me." Arianna welled up. "And you turned around and asked me to *marry* you that same morning after making love to me. How can I *not* love you?"

Nate's body swallowed hers as he constricted almost all her air. "I'm *so* hard to be with. I'm overprotective, crazy, irritating, jealous as hell, possessive, controlling, and I don't apologize for any of it."

"You forgot kind, sweet, compassionate, comforting, romantic, sensitive, respectful."

"I'm not sensitive."

"Yes, you are. We gotta get them all, Agent Jackson. Let's see...exceptional lover, great kisser, wonderful father, fantastic provider. My husband. My best friend."

"I'd give my life to save you and my children, you know that?"

"This is what I mean about wives getting it wrong. This is what happens when a woman finally wakes up and realizes the best thing that's ever happened to her is standing in front of her or sleeping beside her."

Nate wanted to confess, especially now. He wanted to admit his debauchery to the woman who'd placed her world and her trust inside of him. But his fear of losing her was too strong. "Just remember that no matter what I do wrong, I love you, with all that I am."

"You hardly ever say that to me."

"But you know it's always there. I swear to *God* I will strangle somebody with their own intestines if they mess with you, Darius, or my Tre Tre."

Arianna rubbed Nate's arm and leaned in to kiss him. "Make love to me, Nathaniel. Everything you want. Everything you need. Live your obsessions. Play out your private thoughts. Turn me inside out. My body is yours."

"Ani, I can't. I want you so badly right now, I'll hurt you."

"Take me, please." Arianna shook, she cried, she moaned, she begged for his touch. "I gotta have it. Take me back to that morning. Take my virginity again. Hold me like you never wanna let me go. The kids are gone. Nobody will hear me. Take me. I need you to take me there."

Nate fully understood what Arianna wanted, what she needed. Take me. Their code word for the early dawn when he had taken her virginity as she lay wet and shaking underneath him. The morning he opened her up to a world that existed only to them. Nate knew the times when Arianna wanted sex, when she craved sex, and when she just all out yearned for her husband to immerse her in his love. Tonight, with every whimper and every tear she shed, what she wanted was for him to take total possession of her body and soul.

Nate slipped in and out of his beloved wife's body, aware that with every stroke he was making her feel safe, and reminding her that she was, without exception, loved by a man who'd give his life for her and their children.

"Take all of me, Nathan."

"You sure, baby?"

"Yes. Now."

Nate lifted Arianna up, then lay her down. His hands mangled her hair, his mouth bit through her flesh. Their sweat proved relentless; their positions abundant. Arianna flung her head back, screamed, clawed, kissed every inch of all of him. Nate gripped her tightly, as if she wasn't an inch from his body. The lamp smashed against the floor; the mattress separated from the box spring. Nate rushed Arianna against the mirror; the contents on the dresser scattered to the floor. Her nails cut deep into his shoulders.

Arianna followed Nate's commands until he knew he'd taken her completely away—away from life, away from death. Her only focus, pleasing him.

Nate gave Arianna all of himself without question, without hesitation, wherever he wanted to and as many times as he needed to, so he could forget his own hauntings. He was cut; she was relentless. His back bled; she cried out for him. The sheets were soaked and the room destroyed. One final screech and they collapsed, utterly exhausted.

Arianna found herself on the bed, on her back, her breathing as hard as his. Nate glistened in the moonlight; sweat dripped down the hills and valleys of Arianna's body. He hovered over her like shelter in a hurricane. Hours of being all to each other came down to a moment of complete quiet. Nate brushed the matted hair from her face, feeling so guilty he could have vomited a pile of remorse as Arianna's devilish softness danced all over the room.

"I love you, my Nathan."

"As much as I hate that name, hearing you say it never gets old."

"I wish you didn't have to leave this time."

"Keep looking at me like that and I'm gonna get fired, because I'm not gonna go."

"Let me turn away."

"You better not, beautiful."

He came down to her lips for a sweet nightcap before placing his head on her scarred chest and resting in post-coital serenity, calming down, breathing deeper, slower, clinging to his wife and his borrowed time. Arianna fell asleep as he rocked her.

Nate closed his eyes. A tear escaped one corner and landed on the pillow as he thought about his broken vows. *Lord, what have I done to my family?*

Chapter 24

Marcus crouched beside the chalk outline. He scanned Shawnee's landing position from head to toe. A few whispers floated around him, but most onlookers had either gone home or up to their hotel rooms to sit in front of their windows and watch law enforcement examine the scene. The media had thinned as well. A couple of rival reporters remained, staking their spots as close to the scene as the yellow tape would allow. An entire section, marked from bridge to bridge, had been cordoned off.

Marcus stood up. With an analytical stare, he scaled the Gleason Building, starting at the bottom. The building's height was creepy, almost sinister.

He strolled away from the crater Shawnee had left and then walked around the yellow tags, making his way to the Goliath known as Gleason.

"Talk to me," he said to the building.

Marcus often thanked his grandfather for the gift of perseverance. They had a special bond born out of his mother's disappearance. His grandfather made sure that once Marcus (or *Froggy,* as he'd nicknamed him) became successful, he would stay grounded.

His grandfather often spoke his wisdom. "I may not have good credit, but I have street credit, and this can buy you anything if you treat people right."

D.J. walked up to Marcus after following the crime scene investigators who had swept every square inch of space.

"Nothing," D.J. said. "No blood. No security breaches reported. Just a suicide note on the ground. I was gonna bag it, but I thought you'd wanna take a look."

He gave Marcus the note. *Forgive me Father for I have sinned*, it said.

"Prints?" Marcus asked.

"Nah. Just a small, wet piece of paper. It was near the air-conditioning unit on the roof. There's no identifying source, and we don't know how long it's been there. We bagged it."

"Video?"

"None. They've been working on the ventilation system up there. All power was cut from the roof tonight to begin work."

"Tonight?" Marcus looked up at the top of the building. "Who has the construction contract?"

"Gotta check."

Marcus took another look at the suicide note. "Tomorrow, we question everyone on the damn payroll."

"There's no sign of a struggle, no prints anywhere on her body, no unusual bruising on any limb. She jumped. It's clear as day."

"If she'd jumped, she would have landed on the awning at Dick's. Did anybody find a cell phone? Purse?"

"Nothing. The press is gonna want a statement."

"Suicide for now. Shut 'em up so we can do our jobs."

"Before we go digging deep into this girl's life, let's see what the autopsy report says. Tonight, we'll notify her next of kin, maybe pick up some details, and then go from there. We have enough real homicides on our plate," D.J. said.

"You really think this is a damn suicide?"

"I do. Why she landed there? Who knows—wind?"

The workload already had Marcus driving from story to story, witness to witness. Victims found in alleys, innocent bystanders shot in drive-bys. Corpses needing justice, families needing closure, promises he'd made to both. "We'll do it your way, for now. Anything from the autopsy and it's on."

"Fair."

Kyle Ridgeland approached them. There he stood, the bastard who was always questioning Marcus, always throwing in his face his conquest—marrying his late partner's wife.

"Caught a good case, huh?" Ridgeland asked.

"Why are you here?" Marcus asked.

"I came to lend a hand if you need anything," Ridgeland said.

"We got it," D.J. said.

"Just offering."

"Should have known ebony and ivory over here wouldn't want assistance," Ridgeland said. "You boys got this here covered, huh?"

Marcus stepped to him. "I am not your boy."

D.J. backed Marcus up. "Work the case, partner. He's not worth it."

"Your days with the SAPD will come to an end, Ridgeland," Marcus said.

"I'm shaking," Ridgeland said. "I'll tell Eva you said hi." He left.

"I. Do. Not. Like. Him," D.J. said.

"That makes two of us. Let's get this done."

Chapter 25

This lane is for passenger loading and unloading only. Violators will be towed at owner's expense. This lane is for passenger loading and unloading only. Violators will be towed at owner's expense...

Arianna pulled up to the Delta curbside check-in. "Well, this is it."

"I could have driven myself, Ani, and parked in Long Term. You didn't have to get up."

She looked in the backseat at her sleeping children. "They wanted to get up."

"Aaaaaaand now they're knocked out."

She smiled at her children, but her mouth drooped when she saw Nate's face. "Be safe."

"I will."

She fixed his cap. "I feel like I lost two years. Don't wanna say goodbye."

Nate took one last glance at his kids, then looked at Arianna. "Give me a kiss."

"Daddy, bye-bye."

Nate looked back. "Daddy goes to work, okay, champ?"

"I go."

"No, Daddy goes, okay?"

"I go."

"Not this time."

Tre started getting agitated. "I go!"

"No, Tre, you can't go."

"I go." Tre started to whimper. "I go."

Nate dipped his head.

"Nathan."

Nate looked at Arianna.

"Go get your flight. He'll be fine. We're gonna work on five-letter words today."

"I love you guys."

"We know."

"Bye, Dad."

Nate looked at Darius. "Bye, man." He opened the door and looked at Arianna as if something had been left unfinished. "I'll be home a soon as I can."

Arianna watched Nate walk into the airport in his grey sweatpants, white hoodie, and his backward cap. *There's never going to be a good time to tell him.*

She spent the rest of Sunday being an adult—chores, grocery shopping, cleaning. The gym's track found her competitive spirit this afternoon. The creepy owner wasn't there, allowing Arianna to run freely.

Pam, Taesha, and Eva had gone swimming. She'd declined.

It was now early evening, and Nate should have checked in by now at least.

"Mommy, Daddy?"

"Daddy's working, remember?"

"Plane."

"That's right. Daddy got on a plane."

"Mommy work."

Arianna scooted from her desk to let Tre sit on her lap. She was preparing her weekly reports early. "Yes, Mommy is working too, see."

"Oh."

"Where's your brother?"

"I get him." Tre scurried off.

Arianna watched him scoot away. She wondered if he would ever begin talking in complete sentences. While she enjoyed Tre's toddler spirit, he wasn't a toddler anymore, and she worried that he may never talk equivalent to his age.

Thinking of Tre's vocal challenges made her think of Nate, and his patience and unconditional love he gave to his kids—the nurturing, the teaching, and the constructive discipline when they needed it—all the things that made him a great father.

This prompted her to look at her phone. Not a word from him. Nate usually texted *I'm here* or something else quick and easy to let her know he was safe.

In deep thought, she put her elbows on the table, clasped her hands, and pressed them against her mouth. She blew into her hands. *Why haven't you called, babe?*

"Mom, you need me?"

"Just curious as to what you were doing."

"Watching T.V."

"Anything good? Wanna watch movie?"

"Mom, stop."

"Stop what?"

"Mom, I love ya, but let's stop pretending that we can be 'whole' without Dad."

Arianna gave Darius a soft look. "I miss him too. But we can still have fun."

"Yeah, right. It's never the same when he leaves."

Arianna got up. "C'mon."

"Where?"

"Your room. 2K."

"Seriously?"

"As a heart attack."

Darius didn't move.

"Let's go, Son, chop chop. Unless you're scared."

"Mom, you *so* don't sound right talking junk."

Darius tried to teach his mother how to use the controller, what the A, B, X, and Y buttons represented. He tried to explain how to shoot the ball and manipulate her chosen character. "I got lost, Son."

"At what point?"

"When you said, 'This is the controller.'"

"Oh my God, Mom, you're gonna get me kicked. Here, one more time."

Arianna spent the evening with her children. She didn't make any baskets, and she couldn't grasp the buttons on the controller, but she still managed to save the evening.

Before departing Darius's room, she gathered their trash, the soda cans and empty bag of chips. She looked back and saw Tre asleep and Darius close to slumber. "Thanks, Mom."

"You're welcome, Son."

"Mom?"

"Yeah, hon."

"Am I wrong to want Dad to quit his job?"

"Well, you're not *wrong* to want your dad here." Arianna thought of her reticence when it came to telling Nate about Nightmare. "But protecting people is who your father is. Does that make sense?"

"Yeah. I still miss him though."

"I miss him too."

Arianna left her boys to sleep and went downstairs. She threw away the remnants of their impromptu party and she made some hot tea. Then she heard a knock at the door.

"How come you haven't answered your phone all day?" Taesha passed her and came into the house.

Arianna shut the door. "Just needing a break from life. What the heck is wrong with you?"

"I screwed up. I screwed up."

"How?"

"Last night on the Riverwalk. Remember Marcus's partner?"

"He's the shy guy, right?"

"Yeah, D.J. He gave me his number at the crime scene after everybody left."

"Really?"

"No, I just like making shit up. *Yes.* I called him and met him at his house."

"And you screwed up because you slept with him like normal?"

181

"No, that's the confusing part. I was all messed up over Shawnee, crying and shit. Then I came onto him like the fabulous whore I am, and he wouldn't give in. But he asked me to stay for dinner anyway, so I did."

"Okay, first of all, don't call yourself a whore. And secondly, some men actually just want good company."

"We had chicken."

"Chicken?"

"Late-night chicken he called it. It was so good. I've never had anything that juicy."

Arianna wanted to laugh at her comment and Taesha's rattled demeanor. "I knew you liked him."

"Why would he do this? Why would he be that nice to me?"

Arianna thought of Nate. "Because not all men are jerks, maybe?"

"Seriously, why me?"

"I'm gonna give you the same reason Nathan gave me when I asked *him*. Why *not* you?"

"You weren't a fun-loving *woman*."

"No, but I do have an unsightly blemish that kinda makes me look an alien. And it doesn't faze Nathan at all. If D.J. sees something he likes in you, give him a closer look."

Taesha searched Arianna's face. "I need to go talk to somebody who isn't as sprung as you."

"Stop, Taesha."

Taesha stopped, fidgeted. "I don't do this."

"Then why are you doing it?"

Taesha flung her hands up and started stepping and side-stepping. "Arianna, I don't want feelings. I don't want to doodle on my calendar. I don't want to hide nightmares."

"I don't either."

"Oh, God, I'm sorry. I didn't mean it like that."

"It's cool. I get it. You don't want to be vulnerable."

"Exactly."

"I think it takes more strength to be weak than to be strong sometimes. Depends on who's worth suffering for, Taesha."

Taesha searched her face *again*. "Okay, I'm done talking to you."

"What's your alternative? Sleeping with men simply because they're hung?"

"I know but...hey, you think D.J.'s hung?"

"Oh my God, Taesha. I'm going to bed."

"I'm serious. I'm dying here. This dude is like *wow*. And I feel really weird and ...susceptible. Oh, crap, I'm using big words like you."

"There's nothing wrong with it as long as you have a man worth your weaknesses, Taesha."

"Nate's hung, isn't he?"

"Goodnight, Tae."

"Can I spend the night?"

"Sure, but you don't have clothes or anything, do you?"

"Yeah, my bag's in the car."

"Of course it is."

Taesha ran out and almost tripped in the doorway. Arianna watched her, remembering how giddy she had felt the first time Nate kissed her. She pressed her lips against her fingers and the feeling registered with more than just her mouth.

Taesha made quick work of settling into the guest room. She talked Arianna into a coma over D.J. until Arianna's head dipped in her weariness, almost landing on her knees.

Arianna started a fire in her bedroom fireplace and then slipped into bed, exhausted. She pulled Nate's pillow close and scooted to his side, feeling the coolness and the remnants of him. The conversation with Taesha made her miss him that much more tonight, made her long to sit beside him for a late-night chicken dinner. She dialed his number, yearning to hear his voice, her patience worn thin waiting for contact. *This is Nate. Get at me.*

Arianna left a sweet message, asking him how come he hadn't contacted her. Then she lay in their bed, in the room that had laid witness to so many intimate moments, from Arianna's water breaking with Tre, to Nate throwing up on the beige carpet one night when he was sick, the night he'd acted like a child, begging Arianna to take his temperature.

The fireplace burned with a sensual flame, a fire that had seen many nights of passion and pillow fights, kisses and kinky shit. The bay window, the place that Arianna turned to look at her husband as his semen slowly dripped after marinating in her the night before. The foot of the bed, the place she and Nate would sit when he'd had enough of his job, the times she'd convinced him how much society needed his sacrifices. And yes, the bathroom, the place Nate would migrate to when he got tired of hearing Arianna talk about her friends to the point that he felt like he was participating in a sleepover complete with hot chocolate and marshmallows.

She made a last attempt, listened to Nate tell her to get at him, and then she curled up in the sheets and fell asleep, leaving the fire to die on its own.

"Hey, pretty girl."
"Get away from me."
"Thought I was gone?"
"No! Stop! No!"

Arianna sat up and took in the sharp smell of dying heat. The firewood flashed hints of orange as it breathed in its last minutes of life. She looked out the window into the night. Nightmare was as brazen as ever. After futilely checking for a text message from her Nathan, she lay back, wishing she was in his arms.

She turned on the television, needing some type of noise.

Shawnee's death had taken up part of the news hours over the weekend, but just enough to show an older picture Arianna assumed came from her dad's house, some footage, witness accounts of a body falling from the sky, and of course, the presumption that a woman who'd recently been fired jumped from the building where she'd worked, so the message was clear that the victim wished a final hurrah on her employer.

How sad it seemed that a vengeful suicide didn't bear as much coverage as a vengeful murder.

Taesha knocked on the door, then opened it. "You okay in here?"

Arianna didn't want to mention the nightmare, didn't want to start another conversation over her bad dreams. "Just thinking about Shawnee."

"I know. She wasn't my favorite person, but she didn't deserve that."

"Why is it that every time I make up my mind to tell my husband about my past, something far worse occurs?"

"You've only really tried twice."

"But still. I'm over here worried about keeping secrets, and another woman is plunging to her death because she's too sad to live."

"It does put things in perspective."

"Maybe it's a sign that Nathan won't be able to handle it."

"Now you're reaching."

"Yeah, I am. I just don't know for what."

"Look, Arianna, this is going to sound crazy, and random, but do you think Marcus is cheating on Pam?"

"No, of course not. Why do you ask?"

"She had that look tonight. I think that's what she was gonna tell us."

"Really?"

"I don't know. Maybe."

"It's been a long day, Taesha. Let's go to sleep before we imagine them in divorce court."

"You're right. Good night."

Taesha shut the door, leaving Arianna to analyze every detail of Pam's demeanor just before Shawnee's fall.

The whole day had proved too much and yet just enough. The agony caught up in Arianna's need to clam up about Nightmare was killing everyone around her, she believed. Maybe not directly, but indirectly, this savage secret was drowning her and taking everybody else down too. She couldn't explain it. Things weren't like this before. This couldn't go on. As hard as it was, Arianna was finally starting to see that she needed help. Yes, reliving Nightmare in the daylight, on a counselor's couch, could infest her with all of who he was in the dark, at least for a little while. But at least with Nate away in his brief absences, she could sneak in a few sessions. Just to see—it couldn't hurt, right?

Arianna got up and opened her laptop. She did some preliminary research, found a couple of good names, a couple of what she felt were therapists worth the trial. *I want my life back. If this is what has to happen, then fine.*

Chapter 26

This is Nate. Get at me.

The call went straight to voicemail, letting Arianna know Nate had turned off his phone. "Nathan, where are you? Call me. This isn't like you."

Monday morning found Arianna sitting at her desk, looking at the sun's rays shining through the plate glass. Guilt over Shawnee's death had her hyper-sensitive. Ironically, though, she felt relieved that Nate's voice had come on without a ring. The ten times prior, she had left messages after umpteen-something rings. Nate had to be alive in order to turn off his phone.

His lack of contact prompted her to do something she'd rarely done.

"Good morning, DEA, Mrs. Keys."

"Hey, Nancy," Arianna said. "Is my husband in?"

"Well, hi, Mrs. Jackson. I haven't heard from you in a while."

"Yeah, it has been a while. Is Agent Jackson there?"

"He's unavailable. Would you like his voicemail?"

"No. So he made it there, right?"

"Yes, of course. I'll tell him you called."

"Thanks, bye."

Arianna hung up and mentally backtracked from Friday. It had been an emotional weekend for them, a time of deep reconnecting. She relived Saturday night and Nate's openness, his emotional eruption. It was still affecting her. As intimate and beautiful as that moment was, something had triggered Nate into a panic over his fear of losing his family. Plus, when they'd said goodbye before his flight yesterday, he'd acted like he was going off to war, as if things would never be the same. *Where are you, baby?*

She checked out the weekend revenue. Disgusting, she thought. Why did it always take negative media attention to spike sales for a company? Why did an employee's suicide have to lead to a rebirth of profits?

Taesha came in, escorting D.J. "This is the handsome detective from Saturday night."

Arianna nodded and saw D.J. blush. "It's Detective Pratt, right? You're Marcus's partner."

"Call me D.J.," he said.

"Would you like some coffee?" Taesha asked.

"Sure, but can you leave the office today?"

Taesha smiled and looked to the side. Then she looked at D.J. "We're a coffee company."

"Oh, yeah. Oops."

"And what brings you our way?" Arianna asked. "Besides Taesha's warm personality?"

D.J. took his eyes off Taesha. "Sorry, got sidetracked. Do you have a better local address for Shawnee Redman? The address we have is no good. She broke the lease on her apartment last month."

"Not that I know of. She mostly used a PO Box. She told me she didn't trust her mailman. The only other address she gave us was her father's in Katy, as the emergency contact."

"We contacted him. How about another phone number besides the cell number?" D.J. asked.

"No. She told me she didn't use a home phone. I didn't question it because I rarely use mine. What about her mother?"

"Her father said they were estranged and that he would inform her. I know this is a long shot, but have you discovered a purse?"

"Purse?"

"Yeah."

"No."

"Well, did she change her direct deposit recently?"

"No. Why?"

"Just seeing if she had any other bank accounts besides the info you gave us. A life insurance policy?"

"No."

"So, no plans with beneficiaries of any kind?"

"No."

"Okay, well, thank you, ladies, for your time. Just needed to tie up loose ends before closing the case."

"Are you alright?" she asked him as she caught him looking at Taesha, *again*.

"Yeah, you have to forgive me. Been working on this all weekend and it's been a hectic morning. It's a suicide, but we have to be thorough."

"Have you found *anything*?"

"We found out she doesn't do much but buy books, pay her bills, and service men."

Taesha looked at D.J. as if he was talking about her.

"Excuse me?" Arianna said.

"She led a simple life. No enemies that we can ascertain, but we've had guys come forward and say they've, you know, been with her at random places. They didn't even know her real name. Recognized her face."

"That's sad," Arianna said. "I'm surprised men would come forward."

"Why?"

"Wouldn't they be afraid of becoming suspects?"

"Exactly. They came forward to plead their alibis. We humans do a lot of things when we're scared."

Arianna could relate completely. "True."

"Her only friend was her father, it seems. The neighbors at her old apartment said she was nice, but a loner.

Never let anybody in. They did say they thought she was depressed."

"It's sad to live that lonely," Arianna said.

"Been there. Still there, I think sometimes."

"I think we're all there once in a while."

"Explains the pills."

"Pills?"

"Yeah, we found antidepressants in her desk."

Arianna looked down and then to the side.

"You didn't know," D.J. said.

"Nope."

"Well, I've probably told you more than I should have. It was nice seeing you ladies again."

"I'll walk you out," Taesha said, seemingly sad.

"And that coffee?"

Taesha smiled at him. "And that coffee."

"I like your platinum hair, that's cool," D.J. said to Taesha. "I really enjoyed meeting you the other night. Don't normally meet nice women at crime scenes."

"Uh, yeah, let's go."

They left the office.

Arianna glanced through Shawnee's application and resume. Until now, the details of Shawnee's life had never entered her mind. She had graduated from a California high school and, according to the work history, had spent her life in California. But her father lived in Texas. The natural assumption was that her parents had divorced and she'd lived with her mother growing up. Why estranged? Arianna realized she didn't know Shawnee at all. It was clear Shawnee had been looking for something to complete her life. Maybe that's why she'd turned to God while she turned to men.

Arianna called Nate again. "Nathan, it's me. I could really use hearing your voice right now, babe. Please call me back. I'm worried."

Taesha came back into the office.

Arianna did her best to smile over her concern for Nate. "That was a long coffee break, Taesha."

"I think he likes me."

"I think it's mutual."
"At least mine knew my name, right?"

One Week

"You alright, Pam?"

"Why wouldn't I be, Marcus?"

"You just seem distant."

"A lot on my mind."

"Your interview?"

"Uh, yeah. She said I interviewed well, but I haven't heard anything."

"You will."

"Maybe she was blowing smoke. Sometimes it's hard when you have to decipher the truth."

"Anything else you wanna talk about?"

"Nope. I'm good."

Chapter 27

Another week passed. Nate never called Arianna. Every time she called him, he didn't answer. He responded one time with a text that said: *I'm fine. Just need some time.* In a couple of hours, her staff would expect her to mourn the loss of Shawnee at a small memorial service. Shawnee at least deserved some respect. How could Arianna grieve genuinely, with such angst in her heart over Nate's silence?

A millennial named Jenna Logan, a young lady with olive skin and light-blond hair highlighted in purple, replaced Shawnee. When the trendy girl showed up in hot-pink pants and a shirt that read *Screw Society*, Arianna vowed to never let Taesha make any more hiring decisions. Yet, Arianna refused to fire her. She didn't want another suicide on her hands, especially of a bright-eyed, innocent girl, as rebellious as she seemed.

Jenna yelled through the door. "You have a phone call, Arianna. He sounds kinda hot."

Arianna instantly picked up the phone. "Isn't it funny about phones? They actually work when you pick them up," she hollered. "I was worried sick about you."

"The party you are calling is pissed. Please hang up and I'll try this call again," Anthony said before hanging up.

Arianna remembered the voice. She sighed and waited for the second call, realizing this was the last thing she needed. "How'd you get this number?"

"A little better. Did you stop working out, or did my gym not meet with your approval? Did you find somewhere better to tone your arms?"

She swallowed, and contemplated hanging up. "I see you read my fitness card."

"Seriously, I like to check on my patrons."

"Thank you, but I'm not your patron. I didn't join."

"Can I be honest?"

"Well, that's better than being deceitful, right?"

"I know I came across as somewhat of a crass jerk when we met, and I know you're married. I just wanted to let you know that you are really, really, pretty, and I enjoyed meeting you."

That seemed like a genuine compliment to Arianna, something she desperately needed in that moment. "Thank you. That is very sweet. But I do have to go."

"We can all use a platonic friend of the opposite sex once in a while. Call me sometime."

"Nice try."

"Can't blame a guy."

Arianna refused to cross his line, but couldn't help a guilty smile. "Bye, Anthony. You have a good day."

"You too, Mrs. Jackson, you know, with you being married and all. Take care." Anthony hung up.

Arianna adjusted herself, brushed her hair, and pinned it up.

Taesha walked in. Arianna saw a stranger, a woman in a charcoal suit with hair smooth as melted white chocolate and very little makeup on her flawless face. Arianna studied her, looking for clues to justify her theory that aliens had abducted Taesha.

"What?" Taesha asked. "I'm showing a little respect."

They were about to walk out, but Jenna yelled again. "I think the same hottie's on line two."

"Hottie?"

"This guy won't let up. Hold on." Arianna picked up the phone. "What did I tell you?"

"Bad day?" Nate asked.

Relief poured into her soul. Nate was okay. She sighed. "Nathan. Thank *God.*"

"I'm back."

"You're home? You're a day early."

"I'm going to grab the boys and eat lunch with them. Then I'll be home."

"Are you alright?"

"I need to talk to you. How about in a couple of hours?"

"What's wrong?"

"Babe, just...we'll talk then." Nate hung up.

Arianna stared at Taesha.

"What's the matter?"

"Something is very, very wrong with my husband."

Chapter 28

It was a small service in a Catholic church. The pianist played some calming notes. The orchids and other flowers Arianna had ordered lifted the mood. None of the staff had really known Shawnee. The managers showed up, Arianna was sure, out of sheer obligation. A few employees just wanted out of the work environment while on the clock. As she looked around, Arianna realized that Shawnee hadn't associated with hardly anyone at Empowerment; however, the way she'd died would have jolted anybody into feeling some sadness for a life cut so short.

Eva showed up for support, but with her husband and Marcus's and Nate's arch-nemesis, Kyle Ridgeland, adding some unspoken tension between her, Arianna, and Taesha. Of all places, she couldn't leave him home. Arianna maintained her professionalism. The way Taesha rolled her eyes at Kyle, it was clear professionalism was the last thing on her mind. Arianna told Taesha to play it cool. She was already consumed with wondering what was wrong with Nate. She didn't need a fight between Taesha and Kyle on top of it.

"Shawnee had no friends, Tae. Why?"

Taesha took her eyes off Kyle and looked at Arianna. "You have to stop this. You heard D.J. She led a secret life and had her problems."

"Yeah, but you run around with guys and have friends."

"I was fortunate to find friends who don't judge me, Arianna. That's rare. That type of friendship is worth putting up with the shit I eat from your husbands." Taesha looked back over to Eva and Kyle. "Zach was the only one who didn't treat me like I had a disease."

"I don't understand how she could have been so Catholic and so loose."

"It's called battling, Arianna. She didn't find religion until near her death. Maybe she was finding peace."

The music got louder, and the priest went to the podium. He quoted some verses on God's grace. Then Arianna got up to speak to her staff. She looked around the church. For the first time, it hit home that she was a leader to many people.

She looked at Eva and Kyle. The body language was clear. Eva did not want Kyle there. Kyle, much older, seemed out of place with her. Either that or she just didn't look right with anybody but Zach.

"Thank you, everyone, for coming. I wish I knew enough Scripture to cite a verse or two because that would make it easier to think of something to say about a woman I never took the time to really know."

Arianna looked at Taesha and the audience. "What I can say is that while I didn't know her as personally as a CEO probably should have, Shawnee taught me that suicide is never the answer. And if we can be so brave, maybe we can step forward with our problems and open up before we turn our own bodies against us... or maybe we can step back and not be as judgmental when things don't go our way."

She paused. "This is probably not the time, but then it probably is. It's no secret that I fired Shawnee the day before she died. And I know you're probably asking why we're here, spending time honoring a former, terminated employee. Well, this is my attempt at bravery, I guess, and I hope that you follow my lead." Tears welled in her eyes. "My mother once said, 'Closure, without honesty, is another form of greed.' I can't walk away from this without acknowledging my part in it, and it's my hope that all of you, no matter what you battle, find the courage to be honest with yourselves and those around you."

She paused again, composing herself. "In the coming weeks, we will be having a suicide prevention seminar that I encourage all of you to attend. If you can't attend, we'll have copies made for you to watch when you can."

Arianna looked at Taesha. "A couple of years ago, a young woman was sitting in my reception area. She smiled and held out her hand and introduced herself. Her name was Shawnee. In the beginning, she brought donuts and laughter to our daily grind. Always on time for work, always with a quick, sassy comeback. Then, no more. She was the woman we hired, but she wasn't the woman we fired. Get between whatever it is that's changing you and tell it to turn around because it has no place here. Thank you."

Arianna stepped down.

"You have a lot of people in your corner, Arianna. You need to know that," Taesha said.

The priest stood to take over the service. Before he could speak, Kyle's cellphone rang.

Taesha snapped. "You can't turn that fucker off?"

"Taesha!" Arianna shouted.

"Sorry, sorry, Pastor...Father," Taesha said.

Kyle answered, undaunted by his environment. "I told you I'd be in," he yelled.

Nobody seemed to know what to do. Eva looked down and shook her head, then rolled her eyes as if she'd had enough. Arianna tensed up. From the way nobody flinched, they'd tensed up too. The priest just stood there, mumbling. Arianna knew he was praying.

Kyle stood up. "Tell me now, Captain, what?" He was silent and then spoke louder than before. "Suspended?! Pending investigation? This is some shit Carter invented, right?"

Again, more silence, except for the priest, who had begun to pray loudly for peace in his church.

"I didn't assault her, she wanted it."

Eva stood up too. "What the hell are you talking about, Kyle?"

Arianna tensed up further. No way in hell could this end well.

"You know what? I quit." Kyle hung up his phone. He looked around the pews. "Don't all of you sit here with your happy lives and judge me."

"We'd like to pray for you, young man," the priest said.

"I don't need your holier than thou bullshit."

He glared at Eva and yanked her arm, trying to force her to leave. But she didn't move. Nobody moved.

Eva looked at the priest, at Taesha, at the crowd, at Arianna, and then back to Kyle in that order. Then she looked up, spoke a few words, apparently to the Lord, looked down, and crossed herself. "You're done terrorizing me." She looked at the priest. "I know God hates divorce. But this is one I think He'll condone." She looked back at Kyle. "Get out of my air," she said. "And get out of my church."

"You will regret this, Eva."

"All I want from you is a place to send your papers."

"You can't touch what you can't find. Tell Carter I said that shit."

Kyle left the church. The doors slammed, then the only noise was the air conditioning unit humming quietly in the background. Even the priest seemed unsure of how to gather the troops and continue on. Arianna tried, told everyone to please take a breath and focus on the service, so they could continue celebrating Shawnee's short life.

Taesha left the pew and asked the pianist to please get up. Arianna watched, trying to figure out Taesha's intent. Then Taesha began to play. Arianna froze at the revelation of her friend's musical talent as she stroked the keys and belted out lyrics in a relaxing rendition of *Hallelujah*.

Eva walked over to Arianna and broke down in her arms as Taesha sang.

"Kyle was so sweet to me after Zach died," Eva said. "That's why I married him. I know it was quick, but I felt so alone. Then I realized I was still alone, just sleeping with somebody else."

Arianna held her, wondering what Eva had gone through and what *she* was about to go through when she walked through the doors of her home.

Chapter 29

Zachary Deleon Sanchez
Devoted Husband
Committed to Justice

Marcus sat on the metal chair, kicking the dirt beneath him. He'd just gotten into a fight with his boss over Kyle Ridgeland's phone resignation, which had led to Marcus flinging accusations at him about how the circumstances of Zach's death had yet to add up. He subtly accused his boss of covering something up, and his boss told him to walk it off before he didn't have a job. Marcus made a comment about how he needed the truth, and how his boss needed a treadmill. D.J. had intervened before the boss could say those three little words, "You are fired." He had convinced their boss to calm down, and then walked Marcus out of the shop.

Marcus heard twigs snap behind him. He immediately looked back and saw Pam, who hadn't been herself since a couple of weeks back. "What are you doing here?"

Pam stood with her arms folded. "Went to your job. D.J. said I'd find you here."

"Something happen?"

"You could say that." She walked closer to Marcus. He got up and offered her the chair. Pam declined. "I called Taesha to let her know I couldn't make the memorial. I was slammed at work. Then she mentioned Nate had called Arianna in a panicked state and told her to be home soon."

"And?"

"I didn't get where I am being stupid, Marcus. So let's stop."

"Stop what?"

"I knew it, Marcus. I knew it when I found the receipt. I knew it when you said you were helping a fellow officer. I think, deep down, I didn't want to believe it, so I chalked up your excuse to the truth. Tried to anyway."

"What are you talking about, Pamela?"

"I almost said something to my friends the night that girl died. Maybe it was best Arianna didn't find out that way."

Marcus realized what Pam was saying—the receipt. She'd suspected Nate the whole time.

Pam continued. "Today brought it into focus, into honesty, Marcus. Nate essentially disappears for two weeks, and comes back needing to talk to his wife."

Marcus stayed silent. He couldn't deny it, but he didn't want to solidify it either.

"Instinct is a powerful thing, you know?" she said.

Marcus still didn't respond.

"How long has Nate been cheating, Marcus?"

"How did you really find out?"

"You just told me."

Marcus froze, feeling as though he was about to go into cardiac arrest. If he dared tell another lie, he'd be buried next to Zach, and Pam would be holding a shovel. "Six months, here and there. It was nothing heavy."

Pam nodded. "I see."

"Pam."

"How did you get involved?"

Marcus didn't want to answer. "I drove him."

Pam's eyes widened. She leaned in. "You *drove* him?"

"Let me explain how it went down."

Pam didn't give him the chance. Instead, she slapped him, almost sending him into a nearby tree. "I figured you knew, and somehow helped him, but good God, Marcus! Not only did you lie to my face, you took him to her. Geeze, I don't even know you anymore."

"It's more complicated than that."

"Nah, it all looks pretty simple to me." She looked around. Marcus could tell by the squint in her eyes that it was taking everything she had not to slap him again. "I can't believe you drove him."

"I didn't have a choice."

"And I don't either." She started walking away.

"What does *that* mean?"

She looked back. "I need some space."

"You're just mad." Marcus went after her, but she refused to be slowed down.

"Marcus, let me go."

"I didn't have a choice but to help him, Pamela."

She stopped, snapped her neck toward him. "Yes, you did." Pam stared at Zach's headstone, then looked at Marcus. "You haven't been the same since he was placed here. You're drowning in Zach's death, and you're choosing your dead partner over everything you claim to hold dear. And now you're helping Nate to your own detriment."

"That's not true."

"Then why are you here...*again*?"

"There're things you don't know. Nobody knows but Nate and me."

"No shit, Marcus."

"Wait."

"No. I'm going to make sure my best friend is okay, no thanks to you." Pam trotted off, leaving Marcus to flounder in the truth while his phone demanded an answer. He looked at the caller ID and almost threw the phone across the cemetery. Work was the last thing on his mind. "Yeah, D.J., what's up?"

"The M.E. called, said she tried to call you earlier."

"Yeah, I'm not exactly in a receiving mood."

"She ruled Shawnee Redman's official cause of death as a suicide."

"How?"

"Well, our vic had the anti-depressants in her system. Plus, the doc said a whole bunch of other technical stuff."

"Like what?"

"A variety of things, Marcus, shit, I'm not a coroner. From what I understand, there's no sign of trauma and no prints to indicate anybody else was with her, I guess. Plus the suicide note."

"Nah, there's more. There's gotta be."

D.J. hesitated, didn't answer.

"D.J., I don't have time for this."

"She was pregnant."

"Uh, excuse me? How can she rule this as self-inflicted when the woman was having a kid?"

"See, this is why I didn't wanna tell you. It is what it is, Marcus. Case is closed. Let's move on."

Marcus received a text from Nate. *I'm scared as shit. I'm getting ready to spill it.*

He replied to Nate while trying to hold the conversation with D.J. *I already know.*

"Marcus, you there?"

Marcus snapped. "Hold on."

Nate replied: *How do you know?*

"I'm sick of this shit!" Marcus yelled.

"Who do you think you're screaming at?" D.J. asked.

Marcus spoke through clenched teeth. "I'm not screaming at you, dude." He replied to Nate: *Not getting into this right now.*

Nate's reply: *Pam know something?*

"Jesus Christ," Marcus said. *Later Nate.*

"Look, I just need to know that we're on the same page with the Redman suicide," D.J. said.

Nate sent another text. *I might have to stay at your place.*

I'll call you in a minute.

Maybe she won't be that mad.

"Marcus, we need to come to an agreement on this and move one. We still gotta double we gotta deal with."

Marcus still didn't respond to D.J. *Just lay it out, Nate. Don't make her think it's her fault.*

Why would I do that?

Marcus sighed, the eruption building. *Just saying. Don't do it.*

"Marcus!" D.J. screamed, obviously feeling that Marcus was ignoring him.

I'm not that stupid, Marcus.

Marcus lost it. "FINE, D.J! Shit! It's a suicide! We'll move on!"

D.J. seemed to calm down. "Okay, partner. By the way, everything is cool at work now. Wanna get something to eat? Oh, yeah, did Pam catch up with you?"

Marcus stared at the phone before turning it off and throwing it across the cemetery. After a couple of minutes of standing there, huffing, he mumbled, "Shit, I need that."

It took ten minutes for him to find his phone. Then he headed to the Jackson home.

Chapter 30

"Nathan?" Arianna called out. She walked through the house when he didn't answer and found him sitting in the den.

Arianna stared at her husband, realizing how much she'd missed him and how troubled he looked. He admitted to taking a cab home and then getting his car to go see the kids, not just because he wanted some time with his children, but also because he didn't want to face her just yet. He needed that drive, he said, maybe the last one where he would turn off the highway to head straight to her arms.

Last drive? Arianna was confused, naturally. He'd just made love to her like she was the only woman in the world, then he'd taken off seemingly without a care, and now he was acting like they were over. "Nathan, what's wrong, baby?"

"Sit with me," he said.

Nate reached out for her hand, grabbed it, and led her beside him. He asked her to let him speak. Arianna sat down, knowing that something big was on his mind that he couldn't wrap his head around. She felt his heart pounding when she leaned into him.

Nate told her about the first night he'd arrived in Baltimore. He'd gone to the park to clear his head. That was the first sign. Why did he need to clear his head? He'd just unloaded his soul and, in his hope, his seed, into her right before he'd left. But she let him continue without interruption because, from the way he was playing with his hands, Nate needed to get whatever it was out of himself immediately before he burst. Arianna thought maybe this had something to do with Baltimore back *then*, back to the haunting that Nate couldn't escape.

He told her about a seventeen-year-old African-American kid who'd approached him and demanded his wallet. Arianna was not ready for that. It brought her back to the reality that Nate's world was a dangerous place, even for law enforcement. Sure, there was crime in San Antonio, but it was light compared to Baltimore.

"This kid had a gun aimed at my chest," Nate said. "All I could think was to ask where his father was. He said he didn't have one. I subdued him, took his gun, and told him I was a federal agent. He lost it and broke down in front of me."

Nate too looked like he was about to break down. He told Arianna that he sat the kid on the bench and talked with him until Nate had to turn him in for a previous robbery at a liquor store. He looked at Arianna, with all seriousness, and told her the kid said he wished that Nate was his dad.

"I'm not surprised, Nathan. You're a great dad."

Nate snapped. "Stop complimenting me. I don't deserve it."

"Excuse me?"

"I am so removed from the man I should be. I love you and our children, but being around this kid reminded me of how much I've let myself down. Growing up, I never wanted this. I never wanted a white woman. I never wanted the suburbs. And I never wanted a three-car garage. But now I have it all and wouldn't trade it for anything."

What the hell was going on? Nate had never raised the issue of black and white. The theme of interracial difference had never crossed their marital path. Other than her father shooting at Nate when they were dating, no strife from dark to light had ever existed in their world.

"Please don't take this wrong, Ani. I don't regret you, ever."

"No, it's worse." Arianna took her hands off Nate and stood up.

He looked up. "What?"

"You regret not regretting me."

Nate stood up. "That's not true, Ani."

"Yes, it is. It's like you've come home realizing that life with this white woman is making you less black."

"You're way off, Ani. Let me finish."

"Finish what? Let you finish making me feel like I'm a liability to your Baltimore legacy?"

"You have to let me finish."

"People in Baltimore don't care that you're well-off or that your wife is white. The only thing they care about is that you genuinely care about them. Nathan, that whole damn city loves you, and for good reason. You're sitting here attacking our relationship because of a perception that doesn't even exist."

"Can I finish!"

Arianna shut up, stood still, and watched Nate fight a breakdown worse than anything she had ever seen. Nate put his hands behind his head and gasped, as if he was trying to get energy from the air to spill what he had to say. Then he grabbed Arianna and squeezed her so tight she could feel his pressure against her bones.

Nate held her as if he would never see her again.

Arianna rested her head on his chest, heard his rapid heartbeat, felt it pound her cheek. "Always remember what I said. Never forget I need you, even if you feel the need to. Promise me."

"Nathan, what's wrong? Please talk to me."

"First, you have to promise me."

"I promise."

Nate didn't speak, which amplified Arianna's panic; when his hands began to shake, he engulfed her with worry.

Twelve years. In the time she'd known him, she'd seen many emotions: anger, joy, pain, sadness. But extreme fear? Never.

"My God, Nathan, what's wrong?"

"I've been trying to say that I gave my life to the most beautiful woman in the world, took myself away from everything I knew, only to screw it up. No more, no less. I will never regret anything about you, even when you begin to regret me."

"What did you do, Nathan?"

Nate gripped her, she gripped him, both gripped in the moment. "Oh, God, baby, I had an affair. I am so sorry."

"What?" Arianna felt suspended, like she couldn't feel her feet on the ground or move. Her pulse beat out of her throat. She looked away, her mind sailing through the past two years. Nate backed up.

Could he have been joking? It had to be a joke, right?

Not a chance. The tear in Nate's eye said he was stone serious.

Images of another woman touching Nate's flesh ground her heart into hash. Arianna entered another world where nothing was familiar. She was little again, the vulnerable child being assaulted. Pain jabbed at her heart the same way foreign objects had jabbed at her small womanhood. She was back in the whiteout, the blizzard assailing her face, blinding her from finding her way through.

Questions began to form, and with them, more pain. Who was the other woman? How long had it been going on? Did Nate love her? How did Arianna not know? Was this why Nate had expressed discontentment with a three-car garage? Did he get a taste of a black woman and now he was questioning his life with Arianna? Did he find something he was missing in her?

Arianna's heart felt squeezed, like an arm inside a malfunctioning blood pressure cuff, cutting off the circulation. Every breath came hard; the air seemed dry.

She transformed into somebody she'd never known: a vindictive bitch.

She began to scream. "You bastard!"

~~~

Nate sat there, stewing in his shame, respecting Arianna enough to let her insult him, over and over, as she talked about how no-good he was, how he couldn't screw, how his dick was too small, and how, out of pity, she'd allowed him to think it was big. He kept composed under what he knew was her attempt to not fall apart completely. Her words were childish, but Nate was mature enough to understand what was going through her mind—his penis—and the visual of him penetrating another woman with it.

Arianna ran through the house like a mouse through a maze, still screaming, venting what he expected to hear. Nate knew the power of anger and the consequences of rage. Anyone could succumb to it, commit childish acts, regress back to high school, and say stupid things. Anyone could also get out of control with it, blur the boundaries between right and wrong.

So Nate prayed. "Lord, please don't let her go to the basement."

Apparently, Arianna's voice could be heard outside, because Marcus stormed inside. "So, I guess you did tell her."

"Ya think?"

Arianna pushed Marcus out of the way. Then she did the unthinkable—she ran down to the basement, descending on the weapons.

Nate ran after her, Marcus close behind. Nate needed to stop her from reaching the small arsenal in the cabinet next the washing machine.

Nate kept the key high above the cabinet. Arianna had reached the cabinet when he grabbed her hand.

"Do you really think I'm crazy enough to shoot you, Nathan?" She broke down. "I just want to get away from you."

Arianna cried until she couldn't speak. Nate draped her in the protection of his arms and listened to her muffled bellow. She fought to get free. But he was her Superman and his presence overwhelmed her. She stopped fighting him.

Nate turned her around, and she soaked his neck and shoulders with her runny nose and watery eyes. He said nothing, except for an occasional "shhh," as he stroked the back of her head.

He heard Pam's voice speaking softly. "Oh God." Nate looked back and saw her at the stairs.

Arianna seemed to run out of air to sob any longer. Nate lifted her head once she'd calmed, revealing her face marked with lines of black mascara. She sniffled, wiped her nose, and tried to gather her composure. "Is she black?"

Nate backed up. "Excuse me?"

"Is she?"

"Everything you've put me through, and you think this is about race. Great."

"You came home talking about regrets over my being white. I console you over your issues, and then you throw a damn affair in my face. What am I supposed to think?"

"I was feeling guilty and everything was hitting me. I never said I regretted marrying you. YOU said that. In fact, had I not loved you so much, I wouldn't have married you and put you in this house."

"Because you were never interested in white girls, right? I'm special?"

"You're acting very insecure."

"You just told me you had a goddamned affair! What the hell am I supposed to be, confident and self-assured?"

"You're turning this around and using race as a reason to not see the real reason."

"You opened the door, idiot."

"Idiot? Really? You're calling me an idiot?"

"Hey, if the shoe fits."

"If—"

Nate stopped. He had to before he said something so hurtful he couldn't take it back. He had given Arianna plenty of room to express her pain. So far, he'd been a bastard, a terrible man, and a lousy lover with a less-than-desirable package. Now, he was an idiot. Despite his understanding and his belief that the affair *was* stupid, he couldn't take any more insults. He felt the need to defend himself start rising up inside him. Nate backed up, knowing his best course of action was to get the hell out of the basement. If not, he would throw blame in Arianna's face and really be an idiot.

He walked to the stairs, thinking he would talk to her when she calmed down.

"Get out," she said.

Nate stopped. "What?"

"Leave the house."

"Excuse me?"

"I said leave."

"Baby, please, let's just talk this out."

"Get out, Nathan. Yesterday."

Nate looked at Marcus; they both looked at Arianna. She in turn looked at Pam, and then back to Nate.

"No. I'm not leaving my kids, Ani. I'm not leaving you. No. I refuse."

Pam walked past the men and headed toward Arianna. "You sure this is what you want?"

Nate hung back, praying for Arianna to change her mind.

~~~

Arianna looked down, processing the scene and the events that had just happened. It took a minute for her to respond. Thinking of Pam's demeanor at the Riverwalk, and Taesha's references to Marcus cheating, she spoke in a whisper. "You knew."

The women began talking low, soft enough to let the men know this was a conversation not meant for them.

Pam replied, "I had a strong suspicion. But I wasn't sure if I should plant that seed in your head."

Arianna began rationalizing how much of an insane maniac she'd just become. "I probably wouldn't have told me either. I just made a fool out of myself. Please tell me I didn't just get caught up in crazy white girl syndrome."

"You're hurt."

"Did I cause this?"

"Of course not." Pam looked back at the men, then at Arianna. "What do you wanna do?"

"I'm not blameless, Pam."

"Nobody's gonna think less of you if you want Nate to stay."

"I'm gonna look weak."

"This is your marriage, your husband. Nate's not some deadbeat guy, even though I want to strangle him right now. *Both* of them."

Arianna glanced over to Nate and quickly looked away. She briefly mulled it over before once again picturing Nate inside another woman. "He can't stay, Pam. I can't take the visual. Not now."

"Okay then. Let's get you out of this basement." Pam walked Arianna up the stairs, holding onto her shoulders. Pam whispered to Marcus, "Get him out. I'm gonna stay the night here. That's the best thing for all of us."

"Ani, we can talk this out," Nate hollered.

"Nate," Marcus said. "Go."

"I'm not leaving my kids, Marcus."

"Look where we are, Nate. Arianna almost grabbed a gun."

"She wouldn't."

"You don't know what she would have done. Look at her mental state. Give her some space."

"I need to do this my way."

"Whatever. I need a drink."

And with that, Marcus left.

Nate stayed in the basement, quiet. Not a sound came from upstairs. Marcus was right. Nate was the last person Arianna wanted to see.

He walked up to the kitchen and sat at the table, hoping maybe he was wrong. After a few minutes of realizing that Arianna was not coming after him, he left in his luxury car, wondering how he would explain to Darius that pain is an equal opportunity affliction, and that sometimes even educated, professional people act on raw emotions and behave like insane morons. Perhaps, Nate thought, breaking it down like that would help Darius cope should he ever find out that, for a brief moment, and however implausibly, Nate had believed that Darius's mother had actually had the desire to kill his father.

Chapter 31

Marcus pulled up to D.J.'s place. D.J. had bought Marcus his drink, the first time they'd associated off the clock. Marcus hadn't wanted to wrap himself up personally inside another partner, especially because he had to deal with what he felt was the total deceit surrounding Zach's death. Because of that, he'd built a wall, blocking out D.J., chalking it up to black and white, when the truth was the only thing black and white. Marcus missed Zach.

But he needed a break, and D.J. had his back today, at the risk of his own job when the boss had told Marcus to walk off his attitude.

After leaving the bar, Marcus dropped D.J. off at his apartment complex in the Medical Center area, a nice community known to house doctors and other highly paid professionals. D.J. had saved money, and his tiny apartment made for lower rent. Plus, he was a widower and lived alone, so the smaller square footage suited him fine.

"Nice crib," Marcus said.

"Hey, I'm trying to be like you one day, partner."

"I don't know if that's a good thing right now, man." Marcus felt completely deflated. "My best friend's life is crumbling around him. My wife hates me. And I feel like I'm paying for a debt I never owed."

"You mean that taxi service you provided Nate?"

Marcus looked over at D.J., didn't respond. Picking up Nate at a motel left him with little means to excuse it away.

"You actually thought I was stupid, Marcus?"

"You sound like my wife." Marcus sighed, then let it all out. "I'm the one that's stupid." He shook his head. "I can't believe I got in it this deep."

"Loyalty isn't always easy, partner."

"Tell me about it."

"It'll be alright. Trust me."

"How can you say that?"

D.J. pulled a photo out of his wallet and showed Marcus. "Because my wife used to tell me that stars can't shine without darkness."

Marcus stared at the picture, then at D.J, then back to the picture. "She was black?"

"Yep. African."

"Didn't see that one coming."

"Nobody ever does."

"She's pretty, partner."

"She was the sweetest lady you'd ever meet too."

"How'd she die?"

"Not right now. Let's save that one for another night at the bar, huh?"

Marcus knew that D.J. was either being unselfish in giving Marcus time to sort out his own problems, or that D.J. wasn't ready to face his own. "Gotcha."

"Well, let me get on in here. Bought me the digitally re-mastered Gunsmoke series on Blu-ray."

"Nice."

D.J. hopped out of the car. "Hey, look. I'm not Zach, but I can listen."

"I don't know how much more I can shoulder."

"You've been hit with a lot of shit. I know."

"I almost quit after Zach died. The grief, the doubts, the distrust I have for the Department now."

"But you didn't."

"Nope. Nate convinced me to stay on; said Zach would have wanted that. Even if it meant putting up with assholes like Kyle Ridgeland. Now look at it."

"Why do you think the brass is covering up details about Zach's death?"

Marcus shook his head. "I have no idea."

"Well, you're not alone in this. In any of it. In the midst of all of your problems, who is the one person who'll always be there for you, no matter what?"

"Don't say you, because that shit would be too weird."

"Your kid, Marcus. The whole world can crumble around you, and nothing will change the fact you're dad to a little girl who adores you."

"Thanks, partner."

"No problem." D.J. looked at the complex. "Well, Gunsmoke's calling. See you tomorrow, partner."

"Bet." Marcus watched D.J. walk into his apartment. Then he drove off.

The quiet ride home allowed for poignant thinking. Marcus battled memories, fighting to forget his own betrayal at the hands of his ex-girlfriend, Gwen's biological mother, Charlene. It had rained that evening. Wet and tired from a long day, he'd met her at a restaurant for news she had to share. "I'm pregnant, and I'm aborting it because I'm married."

Three bullets in one loaded sentence changed his life. Marcus learned a lot about himself that day, including how he'd become the stand-up guy his grandfather had reared. There would be no abortion. And he would become a single father, no matter the battle.

After learning that Charlene's husband was his company commander, Marcus had confronted him and used the power of persuasion that only blackmail, embarrassment, and public humiliation could bring. A risky move for sure, one that could have cost him a career. But Marcus gambled that his commander's reputation was more important to him than retribution. He was right.

Years later, an old army buddy told him that Charlene had developed a bad drug addiction and left Italy without a word. Marcus had learned the pain of infidelity, brutally.

He thought about his missing mother as he drove closer to home. This prompted him to think of Nate. "Even though you don't remember your mother, at least you can say you love her. I remember mine and can't stand her," he would often say.

Marcus drove down US 281, made a left onto Stone Oak Parkway, and headed into the higher end of San Antonio. Pam's truck was gone, as he thought it would be because she was staying the night at Arianna's. But Nate's car was there, and he was sitting on the porch with a six-pack at his side. "I didn't mean to tear up your marriage too."

Marcus nodded. "Where you been, man?"

In guy talk, *we cool.*

"Picked up Darius and Tre. Took them to the park. Told them I'd be gone for a while. Darius didn't take it well."

"Would you?"

"I'm worried about him. My tore-up marriage is affecting him and my leaving is gonna make it ten times worse. He's already been acting worse since the fishing trip. He feels like Tre gets most of my time. Now Darius believes he isn't gonna get any time at all."

"C'mon. Nothing's gonna get figured out tonight."

They went into the house. Nate put beer in the fridge, except for two bottles. He handed one to Marcus.

"I found out something interesting today," Marcus said.

"What?"

"Kyle Ridgeland quit. The bastard was called in to face the music and ran like a little bitch. Doesn't matter much though. His accuser recanted."

"Why?"

"He fled, can't find him. She freaked. Eva said he's gone and she only wants contact for her divorce. I told her so." Marcus changed the subject. He'd had enough of Kyle Ridgeland for one day. "What did Arianna mean by you opening the door?"

"Oh, when she called me an idiot?"

"Yeah, that."

"I tried to soften the blow, but it backfired."

"How?"

Nate explained the incident in Baltimore with the young kid he'd helped. "Seeing that kid made the remorse hit me like a bus. I was trying to explain to her the guilt I had. I meant well in explaining it."

"Well, she's trippin'out."

"I love that woman, man. I made that clear to her. Maybe I did deliver the message wrong."

"She's hurt. She never thought you'd cheat."

"I'm sure there's a pow-wow going on at my house. How many times do you think Taesha has threatened to kill us?"

"Enough for me to make sure I lock every window and door in this goddamned house."

Chapter 32

"Come here, little girl."

"No!" Arianna screamed. She sat straight up, eyes unfocused. Her chest rose and fell with fear. She looked at Nate's empty side of the bed. Finally, her vision cleared. It was two in the morning, and she realized she'd cried herself to sleep.

The sheets were damp with sweat. Nate was gone and Nightmare eagerly filled the void.

Nate's car, not in the driveway; his wallet, not on the dresser; and his stock portfolio, not on the ottoman next to the recliner they used to make love on. Arianna wanted to assume he was asleep downstairs so she could nudge him and then guide him upstairs like she used to. Now she was left to her own thoughts and the fears surrounding the childhood she had kept so secret.

A noise sounded in the hallway. Arianna froze, her mind caught up in a cycle of wishing Nate was there protecting her from harm. The loneliness at night that had come from his job had never created this morbid feeling. Nate was gone for a different reason this time, and this wasn't loneliness.

This was pure emptiness.

Arianna peeked out into the darkness, her heart pounding. She wanted it to be Nate coming up the stairs, but she knew better. It was Tre, holding his dinosaur and sniffling.

"It's gonna be fine," she said.

"I want my daddy."

Arianna took Tre back to his room. He asked why they couldn't call Nate like they normally did when he got scared. Arianna lay with him without an answer to give. She finger-combed his hair until he fell asleep, and then got up with the reality check that she was on her own. There would be no more late night talks, no more arguments, and worse yet, no more pre-dawn wake-up calls with Nate on top of her, kissing her awake like Sleeping Beauty. They had just gotten a second chance to get it right, and now it was gone.

She returned to her room, let her nightgown fall to the floor, and adorned herself in one of Nate's cotton T-shirts. She rubbed her shoulders and bent her neck sideways to catch a whiff of his scent. She didn't know if she should be sad, mad, both, none. All she knew, despite what he'd done, was that she missed him. "He's the father of my children. I gotta find a way to forgive him," she said to herself.

Arianna decided to go on a safari into Nate's world. His wardrobe was organized to a T, suits on one side, athletic clothes in the middle, casual wear on the other end. The shelf was home to his baseball caps. Arianna thought about how Nate shook the walls when he shouted at the television.

Pushing his *Sports Illustrated* magazines to the side, she noticed what looked like a red tackle box at the back of the closet. Moving it made a loud screeching sound like nails down a chalkboard. It had been a while since the box had been disrupted.

Medals and certificates of valor in Nate's name touched her heart. She angled her neck, smiled, then lifted the pull-out divider and saw pictures of the kids with her, as well as cards Tre had drawn. She shifted them around until she found the letters she used to write to him. Tears moistened the words, so Arianna packed up the box and tucked it back.

Nate's toasted bronze Hugo Boss sweater fell on top of his hand weights as Arianna pulled her arms away from the top shelf. She brought the sweater to her face, and the fragrance of his cologne saturated her senses. She held it close, comforted by the thick softness. With every breath and every tear, she questioned her decision not to tell him about her past.

Arianna had rationalized Nate's mistress as black because he would find common ground with her. But in the back of her mind, she knew her withdrawal from him had triggered the chain of events now unfolding. Being white was not her choice, so thinking Nate had strayed for race reasons stripped her of blame.

Arianna slipped into bed. She rolled over to smell Nate's pillow, savoring the scents imbedded in the cotton. She held it to her body, remembering the countless times Nate had tried to make love to her, only to be greeted with rejection.

"You're a selfish bitch, Arianna. You ran him straight to her." She picked up the phone and was about to dial when she suddenly pictured Nate having sex with some random woman. She saw his naked body stroking up a stranger, as if Arianna didn't matter. Her sense of dignity spoke to her. *He just had a damn affair. I can't just run into his arms.* She put down the phone and cried in the dark, in the confusion of not knowing the right answer or the right next step. Arianna believed she didn't deserve the pain of an affair, but Nate hadn't deserved the need for one either. But did telling Nate about Nightmare really matter anymore? The damage was done. However, the urge to pick up that phone wasn't done either. *I've never been so confused in my life.*

Arianna heard a knock at her door.

Taesha peeked in. "We thought we heard some commotion up here." She turned on the light and came in with a gallon of chocolate ice cream and four spoons.

Pam and Eva followed behind, Pam with whipped cream and Eva with caramel topping.

Arianna prayed that sugar would quell some of her confusion.

~~~

Nate lay on Marcus's couch with the den window cracked. He remembered the times he would fall asleep in the den and wake up close to dawn to find Arianna sleeping on his chest. He would kiss her until she woke up, and they would make love as the sun rose.

Insomnia set in. Nate walked around the den, looking at all the memories in Pam's gold frames. Pictures of Arianna and the kids were placed around Pam's decorative candles and vases.

He looked over at the home movies, turned on the television, and put in the video of Gwen's birthday party, shot in Italy.

The film made Nate wonder why so much fuss was put into a celebration the guest of honor wouldn't remember well. He watched the video, recalling arguing with Arianna over the subject, twice.

Arianna had cut the cake. Nate was impressed that she and Pam had hit it off so well when they'd first met at his wedding. It had been Arianna's idea to go overseas for the birthday party.

Nate smiled at the television. He watched Arianna serve the small guests while she asked what flavor of ice cream each wanted. He thought of their life together and how they had been in happier times.

"She was right, Jackson, you are an idiot," he mumbled. Then he reached for the phone and began to dial.

"Give her some space, Nate," Marcus said. "You're gonna make it worse."

"I thought you were asleep."

"And I thought you were somebody breaking into my house. Hang up your phone before she calls you an idiot again and I have to hear about it."

Nate put down his phone. "Marcus, she ignored me for two years. Was I *that* wrong?"

"I don't think it's about right or wrong at this moment. It's about pain and getting past it. Give it some time.

Don't you have something big going down in Baltimore soon?"

"Yeah. We're taking down Reese."

"You need to get right in the head for that, or his ass will take *you* down. Go to Baltimore and get that handled. Then deal with this."

"It doesn't feel right leaving it broken. What am I supposed to do? Leave and not talk about it?"

"Let her process it and come to you. Right now, if you hound her, it's gonna make it worse for you, and you don't need that. Your head has to be clear, or you'll come home in a bag."

"Did she leave me for good, Marcus? I mean, she's just angry, right?"

Marcus sighed. "Ah, hell, here we go. No sleep for my ass tonight." He turned on the light and grabbed two beers.

April

"Dad, when are you coming home?"

"Not sure, Son."

"You're never gone *this* long."

"I'm sorry. I wanna be home, but I can't right now."

"It's not the same."

"I know."

"It's not fair."

"I know that too."

May

"You've lost a lot of weight, Arianna."

"I haven't had much of an appetite lately, Pam."

"Have you and Nate talked at all?"

"Not much. He has something major going on in Baltimore right now. Said he has to focus. We agreed to talk after that."

"Any idea what you're gonna do?"

"I've decided to get help with or without Nate. I have to now."

"What happened?"

"You know Shawnee's death made me see things more clearly. I told you that, remember? Made me want to get help for my marriage."

"Right, I know. I remember."

"Well, today, Darius made me see that I need to get help for *me*."

"How?"

"He told me in his loving-son way that I looked like death, and all I needed was one of those scythes and a black hood to complement my look."

"Damn."

"My kids are seeing it. I have to get a handle on this. Do you know anybody? I searched some names, but I'm not sure."

"I can get you a good referral."

"Thanks."

"By the way...Would you mind if I stayed the night at your house tonight."

"Are you alright?"

"I just need to run away from home for a minute."

"What's wrong?"

"I feel like death."

Chapter 33

"DEA," Nate's voice resonated. He stood outside the door of the row-house, his team waiting behind him on what was left of the white steps. The paint, olive on the bottom half of the walls and red on the top half, continued to peel, as it had over time, reducing the look of the building to skin scaling away from a blistering sunburn. It was on Federal Street, and not uncommon. These places housed broken awnings, broken porches, and broken dreams on the streets of East Baltimore.

Nate and his team had come dressed for battle, prepared for war. They looked like infantry soldiers dipped in oil. Black boots, cargo pants, bullet-proof vests, helmets with protective shields, gloves, and nylon raid-jackets with 'DEA' plastered on the back in big, bold silver. The letters hung with authority, screaming at the few onlookers who'd seen the team pull up.

Nate had the search warrant in hand. Armed, he felt in the zone, pumped, ready to clean house and take down anybody who got in his way. But Arianna's beaming smile and soft facial features kept getting in the way of complete focus.

"Nate? You cool? You seem out of it."

"I'm good."

Nate checked the door. As expected, it was locked. He gave diplomacy one last chance, received no response.

"Let's do this," he said before kicking his way inside.

The quiet made the house seem empty. But this was unlikely, unless an exit existed in the basement the DEA was unaware of.

After the all-clear, two agents went down to the basement while three others walked down the hall and proceeded up the stairs. Three had already gone around to the back of the house. One agent, Jonathan Simpson, stayed on the first floor with Nate.

The blueprint they had studied wasn't geometrically complicated. The small first floor consisted primarily of three spaces: a living room in front, a kitchen in back, and connecting the two, a walkway the size of a foyer. From the front door, the house stretched longer than it was wide, allowing several narrow houses to connect to each other on a single, city block.

When Nate had entered the house he'd found himself in the square living room. Immediately, he felt strange and stopped. Canvassing the area, he noticed the kitchen in the back, down the hall. The hallway itself seemed narrower than Nate had expected. At ten-by-ten, Nate thought the living room was small enough, making for a cramped abode.

Nate crept to the kitchen.

A stove and old cabinetry rested against the back wall. The back door was near the right corner. If someone were to enter from this door, that person would face the staircase.

"This isn't right," Nate whispered.

The size of the hallway and the width of the staircase were supposed to match. They didn't.

Nate walked back into the living room. To his right, a couch rested against the wall and a floor model television caddied in the corner. A stereo system sat on top of the television. Long, thin speakers, which looked expensive, were positioned on either side of the television.

Lining the left wall in the living area was a sofa table. A couple feet farther, to the left, was the door leading to the basement. Beside that door was a closet door.

He looked at the dirt in the corners and then at the foil hamburger wrappers in the trash. He breathed calmly, trying to escape the consuming thoughts of his family's well-being, the family he hadn't seen in weeks.

Simpson signaled to Nate that the closet was empty. No word from the rest of the team. Nate's nerves didn't like the calm. No raid had ever gone on this long without resistance. He hoped they'd gotten it wrong and his team would soon emerge empty-handed. Nate may have loathed miscalculated raids, but those were better than planned ambushes.

He walked back into the living room, focusing on the television. For a second, Nate thought somebody might be behind it, perhaps crouched in the corner. There were no shadows, no movement.

He noticed something else. The television was old, framed in bulky wood, but the speakers were long and sleek, state-of-the-art.

That's odd as hell.

Nate picked up the universal remote and pushed the power button. There was no power to the television, but the stereo and the speakers lit up like a chandelier hanging in the foyer of a five-star hotel.

"Oh hell no," Nate whispered to himself.

His eyes trailed the speaker wire around to the back of the television. There was no connection. Nate backed up and pointed his weapon at the screen.

"Come out with your hands up," he screamed.

Nothing happened.

"Come out with your hands up," he screamed again. Then he heard a gun jam, the sound coming from the direction of the television.

Nate fired into the screen. The glass shattered, exposing a hollowed-out television and a now-dead drug smuggler.

A fellow agent screamed from the basement, "On the ground, now."

Nate descended and discovered a massive and well-maintained stock of marijuana plants, cocaine, which the press later would coin as having a street value of approximately $200,000 for ten kilos, and a few assault rifles. Normally cocaine would not be found in a grow-house, so Nate assumed the dealers had a failed plan at another location.

His agents had the basement secured, with two men on the ground.

"They were inside the walls," an agent said. "They came out when they heard fire." He pointed to the hole in the wall, which had been finely crafted as a holding area between the wooden panels framing the building and the finely cut sheetrock posing as a camouflaged door.

"Where the hell do they think this shit up?" Nate asked.

He heard several more shots and Simpson screaming for him. He ran back up to the first floor and found one of his agents, Jay Campbell, on the floor, dead. "What happened?"

"The bastard was in the couch," Simpson said. "Jay came down, and then this guy came out of the couch and fired."

"Where'd he go?" Nate asked.

"I didn't sign up for this," Simpson stuttered.

"Where'd he go!" Nate screamed.

"Upstairs." Simpson nodded.

"Call for help," Nate shouted before running up the stairs.

"I am."

The second floor consisted of three bedrooms, their doors positioned in a U shape. The bathroom was to the right off of the top of the stairs. The hallway stretched about ten feet. The floor was quiet, but now Nate knew better and he was ready to fire on anything that moved. An agent was on the floor in the hall, another agent was on the floor in the second bedroom, and the third, Agent Wood, was checking the pulse of the agent sprawled out in the hall.

A member of the cartel was facedown on the bathroom floor, dead.

"He's gone," Wood said. "They're both gone."

Nate couldn't believe what was happening. He had never lost a man in an operation. Maybe his state of mind had him unfocused, and this had caused him to lose three in one swoop.

"How about the master bedroom?" he asked.

"It's clear."

Nate looked at the body on the bathroom floor. "Is this the guy who just ran up here? I heard several shots."

Wood appeared puzzled. "Nah. This dude here came out the smaller bedroom. Nobody else has been up here."

"Simpson said another guy came up."

"Oh yeah, that's right," Wood said.

Nate squinted, and was about to question Wood about his sudden memory loss when he heard a child whimpering in the master bedroom. He gave Wood a hesitant stare before walking into the bedroom. *No, please, not again.*

A girl, maybe four years old and in a purple flannel nightgown, sat with her arms wrapped around her body.

Wood followed. "She wasn't in here when we cleared the room."

"She didn't just appear."

"She wasn't here. I'm telling you."

"Check the closet and cover the room."

"Hey there." Nate put his gun in his holster and crouched in the corner. She appeared to be healthy, yet frightened as hell. Nate's anxiety settled down. At least she looked unharmed.

"What are you doing?" Wood asked.

Nate waved him off and told him to do as ordered.

"What's your name?" Nate asked the little girl.

She didn't respond.

"My name's Nathaniel. Now what's yours?"

"Abigail," she cried. "I'm scared."

"I'm one of the good guys. I'm not here to hurt you."

"My Daddy said you guys were trying to take food out of my mouth by hurting his store."

231

"That's not true. You need to let me take you out of here."

She didn't move.

"Please," Nate said.

Abigail opened her arms. He scooped her up, his back to the closet. He caught a glimpse of Abigail looking over his shoulder.

"Daddy," she shouted.

Nate turned and faced Reuben Guerro, the most wanted man out of Nueva Laredo, Mexico.

"Surprised?" Guerro pointed his weapon at Nate. "Expecting Johnny Reese?"

"Nothing surprises me, Guerro." Nate was stunned, but he couldn't let Guerro know he'd been caught off guard. He'd thought the DEA was fighting a local drug lord who was getting his supply from across the waters, because the Inner Harbor was a prime port for illegal activity into the Northeast. The war on drugs with Mexico normally went down in Texas because Nueva Laredo bordered Texas.

Nate was thorough in his research and in his recon, but he also delegated a lot to his team—people he trusted. Nate assumed advanced technology was allowing for strategic growth in the drug trade in a way the DEA couldn't detect. The thought that somebody on his team had dropped the ball was incomprehensible.

"Daddy, don't shoot," Abigail said.

Nate slid Abigail down his body and shielded her behind him.

"You think you can protect my daughter?"

"Someone has to, you sick bastard."

"You're the cockiest unarmed man I've ever met. By the time you pull your gun I'll have you strung up on a light pole."

"If you wanted to kill me, I'd be dead already."

"True. The power of choice, Agent. Damn, I love America."

Intense gunfire came from downstairs. People were shouting. Nate heard enough to decipher that a second team

232

was downstairs and more members of Guerro's cartel had emerged.

But from where?

"You seem surprised," Guerro said. "You need to do more homework, Agent."

"Where were they hiding?"

Guerro had a smug look. "The house next door. Let's say we did some home improvements. Ask Wood."

Nate stared at Wood in shock.

"We, we...we needed the money, Nate. I'm sorry. Nobody was supposed to get hurt," Wood said.

"You sold out for a dollar. A DOLLAR!"

"You Americans are so stupid, so gullible, so greedy," Guerro interjected. "You really think your fellow Americans won't turn on you for a dollar? Shit, it was easy getting your guys on board. Reese took some doing, but we gave him an offer he couldn't refuse. Plus knowing your trusted 'team' would feed you false information helped sway him. Isn't that right, Wood?"

Wood didn't answer.

"You're of no use to me anymore." Guerro abruptly shot Wood in the head. Then he pulled out his cell phone and handed it to Nate. "Suspender la incursión." (Suspend the incursion.)

"Que está fuera de mis manos," Nate replied. (It's out of my hands.)

"Then you're of no use to me either...kneel."

"No. In a second this floor will be crawling with agents."

Abigail's arm peeked out from behind Nate. Guerro shot at her. She screamed and hid deeper behind Nate.

"You black-hearted bastard," Nate said.

Simpson and two agents from another team came upstairs. They pointed their guns at Guerro and told him to drop his weapon.

"I told you," Nate said.

Simpson looked at Nate, then toward the two other agents. Whirling around, he shot the two other agents in the head at point-blank range.

"Don't tell me," Nate said, "you too?"

"I'm sorry, Nate. I needed the money."

"So I hear."

Simpson looked away.

"Jay had a wife and three kids," Nate said.

Simpson didn't acknowledge the statement.

"How did the rest of the cartel get in?" Nate asked.

Again, Simpson didn't respond.

"Answer me," Nate demanded.

"We drilled through the wall in the downstairs closet to create an opening to the other row house. Please understand, Nate, I didn't wanna kill you."

"Turn around and kneel. Hands behind your head," Guerro demanded of Nate. "Or she dies."

Nate had no other choice. He knelt beside Abigail as he tried to remember the 23rd Psalm.

"The Lord is my shepherd. I shall not want...I shall not want," Nate said. He would have given his life to remember the words.

"En verdes pastos me hace descansar," Abigail whispered in his ear.

Nate looked at her astonished. "He makes me lie down in green pastures."

"He leads me beside the still waters," Abigail whispered again. "He restores my soul."

Nate placed Abigail in front of him so his back could shield her. He held her close as he mentally said his goodbyes. Memories of Arianna, Darius, and Tre whisked in and out of his mind.

"You ready to die, Agent?"

He leads me beside the still waters. He restores my soul.

"Answer me," Guerro demanded.

He leads me in the paths of righteousness for His name's sake.

"Answer me!"

Though I walk through the valley of the shadow of death, I will fear no evil, for thou art with me. Thy rod and thy staff they comfort me.

"You got five seconds."

He prepares a table for me in the presence of my enemies. He anoints my head with oil.

"Shoot him, Simpson."

"I can't."

My cup runneth over.

Nate heard a shot. Simpson's twenty-three-year-old body fell beside him. Abigail screamed. Nate flinched. Reality crept into his mind like a tarantula crawling on his heart, making Nate wonder if and when its fangs would pierce him.

Guerro stood behind Nate's head. He pressed the barrel into his scalp. "Say good night to your children."

Goodness and mercy shall follow me all of the days of my life.

"Lights out."

And I will dwell in the house of the Lord forever. Amen.

The shot was loud, decisive.

Nate opened his eyes, realizing he was still in one piece.

"You alright?" Laticia Malone, a fellow agent, asked him.

"Yeah. Thanks."

"They've taken it to the street." She started running downstairs. Nate yelled, telling her he would be right behind her. He wasn't sure what he was about to walk into and he couldn't leave Abigail screaming and alone upstairs.

"What the hell is Jackson doing?" an agent asked a couple of moments later.

Nate ran outside, smothering Abigail, who was wearing all of his protective gear. He sprinted for two blocks and reached the safety of the mobile command center.

"Here!" Nate handed her off. "The window was boarded up. I couldn't get her out the back way and I couldn't leave her alone in the house."

Nate started to take his vest and helmet off of her.

"I wanna keep them," Abigail said.

"Baby, I would give you the shirt off my back, but right now I need to stay alive." Nate took his gear, put it on again, and went back into the war.

"Where's Malone?" he asked.

235

"Inside."

Nate ran in, stepping over one dead body, almost tripping over another.

"Agent Jackson," somebody whispered.

Nate looked around. Another agent was pointing to a closed door. They crept toward it. Before Nate could open the door, he heard a voice behind him. "Nate."

Nate turned around. A cartel member had one arm around Laticia's chest and a knife to her throat. "Let's make a deal. You let me walk outta here and she lives."

"No." Nate instantaneously fired, taking a shot at redemption. The dude went down.

"Damn," an agent said.

"Now that's more like it," Laticia said, stepping over the dead body as if were trash.

Nate fired behind her head again.

"Damn!" she shouted.

"I thought I saw something move," Nate said, this time shooting directly into the closet. He opened the closet door. "Let's go," he said to the cartel member he'd just shot in the leg.

"How'd you know?" Laticia asked.

"I didn't, but after today, I don't leave anything to chance."

The battle ended. After escorting the last remaining, living drug pusher outside, Nate walked back inside and canvassed the carnage. Shell casings carpeted the floor. Blood had given the row house a fresh coat of paint.

"Jesus," he whispered.

News cameras captured nine dead agents and ten dead traffickers covered in sheets. Brass walked the area. Law enforcement lined up the surviving cartel members. A few members had on dirty T-shirts. Some had on no shirts at all. Two were in suits. All had been caught in the tail end of Operation Clean House.

The Baltimore Police, SWAT, and other government agencies had representatives on the scene. Numerous kilograms of cocaine, semiautomatics, pot plants, and stacks of ten-thousand-dollar bundles of hundred-dollar bills had been confiscated.

Interviews were taking place and people were fighting to get on camera, trying to look more important than they actually were. Nate took off his gear, leaned against a squad car, and watched the politics.

"Excuse me." Abigail tugged on Nate's pants. "Can I have it now? The shirt off your back?"

Nate chuckled. He took off his DEA shirt and gave it to her. The small girl's eyes lit up. He smiled, winked, and directed her back to the social worker assigned to her.

Turning, Nate rummaged inside the cargo van for a shirt. He picked up a solid black T-shirt and slipped it on.

Laticia walked up. "You posing for the DEA calendar?"

"Not exactly."

"Remember, you owe me your life." She winked. "And a drink."

"I'm a married man," he said.

"Please. Everybody knows that shit is dead."

Nate snapped. "It's far from dead."

"Just keep your ass alive long enough to get a divorce." She rubbed the back of her hand down Nate's arm. "I'm serious."

Nate jerked away.

Laticia winked and stepped off. Dave walked up at the same time. They traded glances.

"Well, aren't you a little predator," Dave said.

"I prefer vulture." Laticia stared at Nate. Then she swished away.

"Little fast thing there," Dave said as he watched her walk. He turned to Nate. "You alright?"

"They got Jay," Nate said.

"I know. Is it true we had traitors?"

"Yep. The only thing I hate worse than a dirty criminal is a dirty cop. If I'd known..."

"You didn't know and you did the right thing. I wouldn't have guessed a hollow television," Dave said.

"That *was* some clever shit." Nate nodded.

"Two years of planning and Reese is still in the streets."

"Nah, it's worse. He's not in the streets. He's in the wind."

"Even though it turned out badly, we still did a lot of good tonight. C'mon. Let's gather the rest of the crew and get out of here." Dave nudged Nate. "First drink is on me. We'll get Reese."

They started walking to the command post.

"Be careful. That Malone is a firecracker," Dave said. "She wants you like a cat craves milk."

"You are so not good at metaphors," Nate said.

"Damn, this is gonna get ugly with headquarters. I heard a dozen inspectors are already on their way to investigate what went wrong. Cigarette?"

"Nah. You know Arianna made me quit after Tre was born."

"That's right. The good ole missus. So, how's the mixed couple?"

"Funny."

"I try. No change?"

"We haven't talked."

"Jackson," Agent Greene shouted.

Nate and Dave stopped and waited for him.

"Goddamn, he's pissed," Dave said.

Agent Greene caught up. "You mind telling me how Guerro sent you to your knees?"

"Boss, c'mon, that's not fair," Dave said.

"Am I talking to you? Go wait over there."

"Um, okay then. I'll just be right over there." Dave left.

"Can you please chew my ass out tomorrow?" Nate asked. "I almost died tonight."

"If I get time to think about it and then chew your ass out tomorrow, I guarantee you won't like it. You *never* put your gun down. You know that."

Nate mumbled, "News travels fast." He looked over at Laticia. *She's fine, but she could never hold water.*

Agent Greene continued his rant. "Remember what I told you about modeling for others."

"She's a child," Nate yelled.

"It's the job!" Agent Greene fired back. "You think she doesn't see guns every goddamned day? Shit, her father was Ruben Guerro for chrissake."

They both looked around and composed themselves.

"What the hell is going on with you?" Agent Greene asked. "You're snappy, irritable, hard to be around...I mean more than usual. And you damned near got yourself killed."

"Arianna left me."

Agent Greene paused before responding. "Was it your fault?"

"I would say so."

"Then why the hell are you still standing here? Fix this shit and come back right, before you kill yourself or somebody on our side." Agent Greene walked off, then looked back. "Have you ever had to live with a fatal mistake, Jackson?"

Nate wanted to say, it depends on the context, but he knew what Agent Greene meant. "No, sir."

"It's not fun."

Agent Greene left.

Dave came back when it was safe. "Guess you're not having that drink."

"Guess you're not either. I need a ride."

"Hey, man, by the way, you alright? I know you had a little girl involved in this."

"I'm fine. And I really wish people would stop asking me that."

Chapter 34

"Hi, pretty girl."

"I have to go home now."

"In just a bit."

"Please leave me alone."

"Come here, sweetheart."

"No, go away. Go away."

Arianna woke up, thanks to her ringing cell phone. Her heart was beating with the fervor of an axe to a petrified tree. Rationally, Arianna knew she was awake, but for a split-second she thought maybe she was still dreaming, maybe caught in that moment when she wasn't quite lucid enough to know for sure. The phone kept ringing as the feel of Nightmare slinked around her shoulders. She patted her face and began understanding that she was in her bed, in the midst of reality, and in more ways than one. Nightmare was gone, but so was Nate.

The phone stopped ringing and started again as Arianna searched all around the bed for it. She found it on the floor, and almost didn't answer. But she couldn't resist. She took deep breaths to calm her panting before answering. "Kinda late."

"I know," Nate said. "But all I ask is a few minutes."

"Are you alright?"

"No. I had a very shitty day at the office and I just wanted to hear your voice, even though I'm the last person you want to talk to."

"You assume a lot. If I didn't want to talk to you, I wouldn't have answered the phone, Nathan."

There was a pause. "We agreed to talk after Baltimore."

"We did. But I didn't know it would be at four a.m. You have me worried. Did something happen?"

Nate didn't respond. All Arianna heard was his breathing. It was loud, choppy, and frightening.

"Nathan, you're scaring me."

Nate still didn't respond.

"Please talk to me, Nathan."

"Look, I swear I'm not trying to gain sympathy, but I..."

"I *what*, Nathan?"

He didn't answer.

"I *WHAT*, Nathan?"

"I was two-seconds shy of getting shot in the head at close range today, execution-style. Losing you is gonna kill me in more ways than one if we don't deal with this."

Execution-style. The incident in the park, with the young man, when Nate had intervened was scary enough to picture. The image of Nate kneeling on the ground with a gun to his head, hardened criminals surrounding him, made the previous incident seem minor. For the first time in over two years, Nightmare became an afterthought. "My God, where are you?"

"Can I come home? That's all I need to know."

"Yes, of course. How long will it take for you to get here?"

Arianna heard the front door open. She ran downstairs and straight into Nate's arms, clinging to him as if he were a buoy in the middle of an angry lake. Nate reciprocated as if he too would drown without her.

Then Arianna backed up and quickly patted his face and upper body, as if she might find an injury. "You sure you're okay?"

Nate nodded. "Close call, but I'm okay."

"You hungry? Want something to eat?"

"No, baby. I just want to be here." Nate looked her up and down. "You've lost some weight, Ani. Are *you* okay?"

"Things haven't been easy."

He spoke low. "I know. I get that."

Nate broke away, put his keys and his wallet on the kitchen counter, and pinched his eyes with the thumb and forefinger of his right hand. Arianna could tell he'd had a long flight and an even longer day. She began to make coffee. Nate stopped her, told her he just wanted a shower and some sleep.

"You wanna go up, Nathan?"

"I wanna talk first. We can't keep going like this."

"You sure? Maybe after you rest."

"Ani, take a breath. I didn't die. I'm standing right here. I'm okay."

Arianna relaxed under Nate's reassuring voice. Then she spoke softly as she sat in a kitchen chair. "Come sit down."

"I'm good. I've been sitting for the last few hours." Nate took a deep breath and, true to his personality, got straight to the point. "Ani, I used to walk through the front door and you'd be all over me. I didn't even have time to drop my keys. Then one day, bam, it's all gone after a letter. We used to talk for hours at night. We've had sex in every corner of this house." He looked around the house and pointed at random places. "Have you seen how big this bitch is, baby?"

"Nathan, I'm sorry I shut you out."

"You know what? I don't even care about that anymore. That's not even our problem now. If I hadn't cheated, we'd be fine. I have to live with that."

It is a problem, more than you know. Arianna wasn't sure what was consuming her more—Nightmare or a nameless woman. "What was she like?"

"Oh God, don't do this, Ani. Not tonight."

"You have to give me something."

"It had nothing to do with race, if that's what you're thinking."

"I know that, Nathan. I was upset."

"She was willing, Ani. That's all I got."

"Nathan."

"Don't cry." Nate looked her up and down again. "It's bad enough I have to come home and see firsthand what I've done to you."

"I'm surviving, Nathan."

"I never wanted you to have a life you had to *survive*."

She stood up and approached him, tears flowing. "It's so hard to think of you with somebody else." Arianna felt tempted to drill Nate, but she kept picturing a gun barrel to his head and that changed her thoughts. Knowing more than she'd like about the affair could ruin any chance at working through it. His survival and their connection trumped her desire to know who was on top and who came first.

Nate looked at the boys' school portraits that Arianna had stuck on the fridge last year. Then he continued. "I was so confused and lost, Ani. I still am, honestly. I get that losing your mother broke you in half. But *I* didn't kill her. You treat me like I did. Then I assume her death triggered some kind of pain, but you clam up when I bring it up. You put me through two years of dry hell. I didn't think you'd ever be the same. All I do is question myself. What is my role in this? What did I do wrong? Am I failing my family somehow?"

"You did nothing wrong." Arianna stared at her worn-out husband, feeling guiltier for allowing him to smother inside his relentless speculation and maddening confusion.

"Apparently, I made it worse." Nate tossed up his hands. "I got weak, stepped over the line, and then, all of a sudden, you seemed back to normal after that incident at Darius's school. As if your mother never died. At that point, not only did I have to deal with the guilt of cheating, I had to deal with the fact that I didn't need it to begin with, if that makes sense."

"I get it."

"Now, we're just back to square one. And I don't know what to do. I'm afraid to touch you because you'll flip out. What brought you around the first time? Maybe we can start there."

"You. I realized what I had. Plain and simple."

"Me before I cheated though. With all this, I feel like we'll never be the same. I can't stand this shit." He suddenly wrapped his arms around her and wouldn't let her go.

"Hold me tighter, Nathan."

Nate tightened his grip. "I need you to get past this, Ani. I need you to come to terms with your parents' *whatever.*"

Arianna held to Nate, breathed in all he was to her as she breathed in the lasting scent of faded cologne and dried sweat, all the smells comprising her working man. "I *will* get past this." She backed up and lifted Nate's head. She looked into his eyes. He had that tired look, one speaking of nights of no sleep and days of constant contemplation of what he couldn't understand—her.

"What do you need, baby?" Nate asked. "I'm begging you here. And you know I don't beg."

Arianna felt this was her perfect opportunity to bring up what Nate hated most. "Nathan, I need to ask you a question and I need you to be open-minded before you answer."

"I'll do my best."

"I want us to go to counseling. I *need* us to go to counseling."

Nate immediately let go of her and stepped out of her personal space. "I knew you were gonna say that."

Arianna turned to face him. "Nathan, please. You asked. This is it."

She waited for his answer. Nate was an absolute man, no frills, no processes, just decisions without drama. She knew that in his mind, all she had to do was make the decision to be happy. He could carry the rest.

"For tonight," he said, "will you settle for me *thinking* about it?"

Arianna nodded. "Yes, I will. I'll accept that."

At least she hadn't gotten a flat-out "Hell to the nah" like she thought she might.

Arianna realized something profound in Nate's reply. Despite the pain of this ordeal, and Nate's reluctance to fully comply, he was growing into a more open guy from this experience. And, she assumed, he too knew they needed professional help.

"Thank you," she said.

"You don't have to thank me." He grabbed either side of her face. "But you do have to kiss me."

"Is that so?"

"Yup." Nate backed her up, all the way to the top of the stairs and to the bed.

Arianna's head hit the pillow softly. Nate's lips hit hers a fraction of a second later. His arms stayed in push-up position as he blanketed her mouth. Arianna had no thought of betrayal, or pain, just a sense of urgency to forgive her husband and submit to his warmth. But she had to take it slow and relish the innocence of what their love had once been, and not enter into a moment of provoking the incubus through Nate's penetration. She knew her mind that Nate's affair had elevated Nightmare back to his throne, and she didn't want to go through another cycle of rejecting her husband. Tonight, she needed Nate's gentle touch, to savor the abstinence in getting close again.

"Nathan, I don't wanna give you false hope," she whispered. "I'm not ready for this. It's just all too much right now."

"If screwing you was my goal, I'd have you naked already." Nate fell on her. "Hush. I also love you for your mind, you know."

They laughed like old times, because it seemed like new times were just beginning.

Nate swaddled Arianna in his warmth. They made out until Nate's weariness overcame him, prompting him to fluff the pillow next to her head.

He stroked Arianna's cheek with his thumb. She turned her head and kissed him twice more, realizing his point. Their marriage meant a hell of a lot more to him than good sex.

"How long are you home for?"

"Not sure. I have to fly back early tomorrow morning, though. I forgot something. I'll be back late tomorrow night. Then I'm all yours."

"That's a lot of flying and hassle. It can't wait?"

"Ani, believe me, with my job, the commute is a walk in the park. And no, it can't wait."

Nate stretched his arm across Arianna's chest and closed his eyes. His breathing slowed, the rhythm evening out. Arianna knew he'd fallen asleep. She snuggled closer, trying to sink into his skin.

Arianna closed her eyes, thinking of the battle with Nightmare. *Bastard, this is one war you're not gonna win.*

Chapter 35

Arianna slapped the newspaper onto her desk when the saliva began to project. She held her coffee mug with one hand and covered her mouth with the hand she'd just freed from the paper.

The thick, bitter-sweetness of Empowerment's latest coffee experiment gagged her, and she continued to cough.

Taesha slapped her on the back. Arianna cleared her throat and grabbed a tissue to wipe the projectile spit off her mouth and hands. She cursed Taesha for her sore throat and what felt like a broken back as she stared down at what was left of the new drink, Black Cherry Almond Crème.

"We've been selling this?" Arianna asked.

"Not yet."

"Needs something a little acidic to neutralize the glucose level badly."

"I bet you have one of those secret Frankenstein laboratories or some shit in your basement."

They laughed.

"You're in a brighter mood than I've seen in a while," Taesha said.

"Nathan came home last night."

"Did you stand your ground?"

"I put my tongue all over his face."

"I see. Did you tell him about Nightmare?"

"Not yet. I've asked him to go to counseling. I'm giving him room to process it."

"And if he refuses?"

"He won't."

"It's Nate. Let's hope."

"He'll come through. I know him." Arianna rolled her eyes in retrospect. "I can't believe I threw race into it."

"He just wanted to get laid. Doesn't matter what color she is, all pussies are pink."

"Aaaaaand we are done with this conversation."

Jenna came into the office, carrying information that quickly diverted the conversation like a plane needing to land immediately. "There's an *Anthony* here to see you?"

Arianna looked at Taesha. "What in God's name does he want?"

"Anthony from the gym? Hashtag *stalker* for real."

Arianna told Jenna to send him in.

"So, you're Anthony?" Taesha asked.

He nodded.

Arianna wasn't thrilled with his impromptu visit. "Give us a minute, Tae."

"Yeah, handle that shit." Taesha left.

Anthony watched her walk out. "She's a tough one."

"She's a friend." Arianna kept cool, stern, but not unkind. "How'd you find me?"

"Your bio, remember?" He looked her up and down. "So this is your business attire? Pretty sharp."

"This is creepy. You know that, right?" She glanced at his grey business suit. "And why are *you* dressed in a suit?"

"How soon we forget. I told you I have a day job."

"Anthony." Arianna spoke in a business-like tone, matter-of-fact, bottom line. "You seem sweet, in a totally psychotic kind of way, but you can't be doing this. Why are you here?"

"I need your help. You're a businesswoman. I'm a businessman." Anthony tossed a flyer onto her desk with details of a community health fair his gym staff wanted to sponsor. "I'd like your help with planning this event. Would you be so kind? It's scheduled for the end of summer. Maybe you could throw in some coffee and/or concessions."

"You think I don't know what this is?"

"What is this?"

"A ploy."

"Ploy?"

"To get inside my head."

"I don't need a ploy. If I wanted to get inside your head, I'd be there already."

"Oh, you would?"

"Read my business card attached to the flyer."

Arianna read it. Anthony was a doctor, a clinical psychologist. "A doctor who owns a gym. You don't see that every day."

"You know how many professionals own, or at least invest in, gyms? It's not uncommon and it's very profitable. I can name at least five colleagues across the country who dabble in the business of fitness."

Arianna wasn't interested in Anthony's profits, or in anything else he had to offer. "A therapist hitting on a married woman. That's not cool."

"I'm not hitting on you. I'm here for business for my gym."

"Right."

"Man, you are tough too."

"I have to be."

"Why?"

"Life."

"Okay, I wanted to see your pretty face. There you go."

"Better, but it won't get you anywhere."

"I know quality when I see it, and I know when it's not appreciated."

"Oh, let me guess...marriage counselor."

"Was. I mostly work in prisons now. But I guess that's the same thing, right? Marriage and prisons?"

"How would I know?" Arianna was growing more and more frustrated. Even though Anthony was starting to seem

249

like a genuinely nice guy, he was stepping way over the line, especially for a professional man. He was either lonely, or unfulfilled, or both. "You know nothing about me. And I have to get back to work."

"I know you answered the phone a couple weeks ago ready to curse me out for not calling. Pretty easy to decipher who you thought I was."

"Okay, that's enough. Thank you for stopping by, but you need to exit my office."

"Why the hostility?"

"I'm not hostile, but I am faithful." Arianna kept looking at the door. She expected Taesha to run in and make some excuse to get all up in her business.

"Expecting somebody? Your husband about to walk in?"

"He's out of town."

"I see. So, you gonna help me?"

"Excuse me?"

"With my event."

"I can't."

"Your husband?"

"Well, I don't think he would take too kindly to us working together knowing you want more than work."

"Whoa, okay. Many assumptions here."

Arianna had reached her limit. Her thoughts were on strengthening her marriage, not stroking Anthony's ego or sparing him hurt feelings. "Goodbye, Anthony."

"Question first. Are you going to tell your husband about my visit?"

Arianna didn't answer right away. This startled her because she actually found herself contemplating the question instead of dismissing it. Nate had expressed to her, the night Shawnee died, how volatile he could get when it came to his family. She didn't want to admit it, especially to a rival man, but Nate was, at his core, irrationally insecure. They were already headed for some rocky waters in counseling. She wasn't going to add a needless complication. "No need. And very inappropriate for you to ask."

"Okay, I'm sorry. I'm over the line coming here like this. There is just something about you I can't shake."

Arianna's cell phone rang. "You need to find a way. Now, please leave." She picked up the phone without hesitation, while staring at Anthony. "Hey, baby."

"Hey, gorge," Nate said.

Anthony looked down at the flyer and mouthed *please reconsider*, then left. Arianna pulled Anthony's business card off the attached flyer. *Dr. Anthony Carone, L.C.S.W., L.M.F.T.*

"You alright?" Nate asked.

"Yeah."

"You sure?"

"I'm always alright when I talk to you."

"Nice answer. But what's wrong?"

"Just miss you."

"You saw me yesterday, Ani." Nate laughed

"And I can't wait to see you *today*." She smiled.

"You really love me, don't you, woman?"

"Oh yes."

"I'm just letting you know I'm getting ready to board. I'll be home soon."

Anthony's visit prompted her to revisit her request. "Have you given any more thought to therapy?"

"Can we discuss it tonight?"

I hope that doesn't mean no. "Sure."

"I'll see you soon. I love you."

"Did I hear you right?" Arianna attempted a joke, the long-running one where she'd always said Nate didn't tell her he loved her enough.

"Yes, sexy smart ass. I see some things are back to normal."

Arianna smiled. "I love you too."

"Ani, listen to this."

"To what?"

Click.

Arianna couldn't help but laugh. She and Nate hadn't shared a joke in so long. Something as small as a simple quip and a funny hang-up let her know that, in the midst of all this heartache, there was hope. She sat down, got on the Internet, and searched counselors. Her phone rang again. She smiled, thinking it was Nate. It wasn't.

"Hey, Pam. I might not need a referral. I think I just found somebody."

"Get to the hospital."

"Why?"

"It's Eva."

~~~

The terminal at BWI looked like a sidewalk during a New York City rush hour. Passengers were walking in droves to gates and concessions. To Nate, the people were blurry images in rushed photos, hazy snapshots of things hard to decipher. He couldn't focus. The guilt he felt made everything about life look like nothing more than smeared dots. One thing about reconciling with Arianna, he now had a front row seat to the fallout—her pain and his regret.

"I appreciate the ride, but you didn't have to sit here with me, G," Nate said.

"What else do I gotta do besides stay white and pay child support until I die?"

Nate laughed. "I don't know. Maybe paint another masterpiece in all that spare time Greene doesn't give us."

"That would be some trick."

"Tell me about it."

Why don't you ever rent a car, Jack?"

"I don't know. I guess the same reason I won't rent an apartment. I love it here, but my home is in Texas. Besides, when I'm here, I only do work-related stuff, and I can use a government car for that. Hell, if I want to relax or anything, I can just walk the Harbor."

"I don't know any man besides you who'll come to Baltimore alone and act like a hermit."

Nate shrugged, like staying in his hotel room when off duty was no big deal. "I'm not alone. I have beer and ESPN."

"True. And you can enjoy it."

Nate nodded in agreement.

"You've been doing this a long time. Pretty soon the DEA is gonna stop paying for hotels and plane tickets."

"They'll continue if I keep taking down notorious drug dealers."

"Well, don't get mad at me, but you gotta stop almost gettin' shot in the head execution-style by notorious drug dealers, to take down notorious drug dealers."

"Don't start. Ani's need to check me every five seconds for bullet wounds is enough."

"So, the mixed couple's working it out?"

"Looks that way."

"What exactly went down between you two?"

"I cheated."

"Get outta here. Seriously, Jack?"

"Yep. And now she wants to go to counseling."

"Damn, I never expected that shit to come out of *your* mouth."

"What can I say? I'm full of surprises." Nate looked to the side. "I didn't realize how much pain she was in until I went home and saw her. She's dropped at least ten pounds. You can tell she doesn't sleep either. I destroyed her. The guilt is eating me alive, G."

"Why did you come back here today?"

"I needed to submit an official leave of absence."

"For how long?"

The airline announced boarding for Nate's flight.

Nate stood up. "As long as it takes. I have to rectify this."

Dave stood up too. "Look, I'm not the best person when it comes to self-actualization or that Maslow shit, but you're a good guy, Jack. Stop selling yourself short. You made a mistake. You've always treated that woman like a goddess. You've always been there for her. Forgive yourself, dude, geeze."

"Thanks, G."

"No problem. I mean, it doesn't help that she's fine as hell and probably gets hit on all the time and could leave you. I mean, she's not *my* type, but some of the guys..."

"You're not helping."

"Sorry, tried."

"Later." Nate got in line.

"Don't be gone too long. I'll miss you and shit."

"Got it." Nate stepped forward.

"Hey," Dave said. "I've been to counseling. It's not that bad. Therapists aren't drug dealers you have to fight."

"I'm not worried about the therapist."

"Then what is it?"

"Arianna will back me into a corner for answers. My wife can never find out who this other woman is. I don't care how repentant I am. She will NEVER forgive me. My best friend too. I will lose my whole life in San Antonio."

"You didn't bang your best friend's wife, did you?"

"What? Hell no, c'mon now."

Dave tossed up his hands. "Okay, just asking. You're the one getting all hyped up."

Nate stepped further. "It's just a mess."

"Messes can be cleaned up, no matter how big. Take a cue from my life."

"I'll try and remember that." Nate turned around and didn't look back.

He came home to find Arianna gone, her blouse and blazer on top of the bed. She had come home late from work before, but this time she'd come home from work, changed clothes, and gone out somewhere.

Nate turned on his phone and saw a text letting him know she'd be late, and could he get the kids from Gloria. He walked across the street to pick them up, thinking of nice ways to turn down cookies and milk, Gloria's attempt to get the scoop about why he'd been gone so long.

Chapter 36

"Dangit," Arianna whispered as she stubbed her foot in the entryway. She tip-toed across the carpet into the kitchen as the clock ticked to its nighttime beat. She slowly brought her purse and keys down to cushion their impact and then crept to the stairs. She didn't realize Nate was sitting on the first step until she almost tripped over him.

"There're cookies on the counter."

Arianna smiled, a welcome activity in an evening full of angst. She grabbed a cookie and went back to the stairs. "Did you eat?"

"Spaghetti under duress."

Arianna chuckled. "Nice."

"How's Eva?"

"Conflicted, confused, chaotic." Arianna sat next to Nate. "Take your pick."

"Sorry, baby."

She kissed him. "Thank you for waiting up."

"What else would I do, beautiful?"

"I don't feel so beautiful."

"I got something to help with that."

Nate led Arianna upstairs. "Nathan, we had this talk."

They walked into the bedroom. "Get your mind out of the gutter."

"What's this?" Arianna discovered an unfamiliar box on the bed.

"A little something I picked up, literally."

She opened the box and pulled out a dusty piece of cement with a heart etched in its surface. She knew immediately where it had come from. It was part of the construction on the plaza where she rented space for her Baltimore coffee house. When she'd leased the property, the building was still under construction. In true Arianna fashion, she'd bent down near a patch of wet cement, poured close to the entrance to the plaza, taken a small stick, and drawn a little heart, symbolizing her accomplishment. She later heard from Nate that the side of the building where the cement had been poured was set for renovations. At the time, she'd mentioned in passing that she'd like a piece of the cement that contained her heart, even though she knew it was impossible.

Now she stood in her house holding the impossible. *Oh my God.*

She put the box on the dresser and then looked at herself in the dresser mirror to see Nate's reflection as he stood behind her. "How'd you do it?"

"They finally started the renovation on the plaza two days ago. Dave's brother is a project manager for the city and he's overseeing the contractors. I told him to make sure he rescued your cement. He thought I was insane."

"That's why you left?"

"Partly. I forgot it when I came home last night. I had to make sure he didn't dispose of it."

"You never cease to amaze me."

"I knew it was important to you."

She turned around, kissed him, and clung to his body. "Thank you. After tonight, I really needed this."

"I can imagine. Eva saw Zach, you said? What's that about?"

Arianna explained again, this time in person and in more detail that she'd gotten a call from Pam explaining that

Eva had been taken to the emergency room. She'd left work, gone to the hospital, and discovered Eva had fainted because she thought she'd seen Zach outside her window. She was given fluids for dehydration and eventually released. Arianna had come home and changed clothes, and then the four ladies had gone for a walk. They stayed with Eva until she finally fell asleep at Taesha's house.

"We couldn't leave her alone."

"So now, Eva's staying with her."

"Just for tonight. Eva refuses to leave the Hill Country. She said she feels close to Zach, and it helps her deal with the fact that she can't divorce Kyle right now. Did I ever tell you he disrupted Shawnee's memorial before he took off?"

"No," Nate said abruptly, almost snapping. "And I don't wanna hear about that bastard. I can't deal with that on top of our issues."

He gazed at Arianna long enough for her to wonder what he was pondering. She wanted to ask again, about therapy. But she thought it best to let him lead when he was ready. He already seemed to be walking a mental tightrope. "I didn't mean to upset you, Nathan."

"I'm not upset, baby. I just want to focus on us."

They stood inside a pregnant pause, Arianna hanging on to hope that Nate would honor her counseling request.

Nate nudged her. "Come with me."

"Where?"

"Downstairs."

Arianna followed Nate back downstairs and out into the backyard. He settled on the swing, put his back up in the corner, stretched one leg across the seat, and used the other as propulsion to rock them. He put his arms out. "C'mon."

Arianna wondered where this was leading. But she did as asked, put her back against his chest, her head on his shoulder. They rocked while enjoying the warm air and light wind. She said nothing, allowing Nate to lead whatever conversation, if any at all, he needed to have.

"That early morning, when I first made love to you. You were so shy, yet you let me do whatever I

257

wanted...despite how nervous you were. It's like you gift-wrapped yourself and just said 'here.'"

"I trust you, Nathan. And this affair doesn't change that."

"Why?"

"Because you confessed. That says a lot."

"But you can't be *free* with me anymore. That kills me."

She felt him tremble slightly and turned to face him. "We can have that again. We just have to work at it."

Nate drew in his lip, as if he didn't want to speak, but must. He paused for a moment before conceding. "Go ahead and find somebody. If you haven't already."

She backed up. "A marriage counselor?"

He nodded.

"Really?"

"We have to find a way to get past this."

"Thank you. *Thank you*, Nathan. I know you hate the concept."

"But I love you more. If this will help you deal with what I've done, I'll take that hit whatever comes."

Arianna felt as if *she* were about to tremble. She'd imagined counseling, had approached the concept of counseling, but Nate hadn't confirmed counseling. Now it was in her face because Nate was on board. It was going to happen.

In simpler terms, shit just got real.

"I need you all in, Nathan. Counseling can get intense. I mean, things can come out that you don't wanna hear."

"I know that. Believe me, I know that."

"Okay."

"Why are you shaking?"

"I'm not." She pecked his lips. "Maybe just a little chilly."

"And that little kiss is so not enough." Nate put his hand behind her head and led her to his lips. They kissed until they forgot life existed outside of the porch swing. Then Nate pressed into her armpits. She released her hands. He flipped her over and grabbed her before she could fall out of the swing. He got up, carried her to the lawn, put her in the grass and fell on her. They continued kissing as Nate laid his entire body on hers. "I'm not losing you over this bullshit. You hear me?"

"I'm not going anywhere."

Arianna wanted to ask him where his trembling was coming from, but she left it alone, realizing that Nate had to work through his emotions in his own way. He too would have to confess things he didn't want revealed, and she knew as much. So instead, she got lost in the moment, relieved they finally had a plan, although she felt fearful of the revelations that would arise from it. She continued returning the adoring kisses Nate was giving her, trying to savor this moment and keep it void of details and real life. Nate kept his hands above her waist, obviously knowing she wasn't ready. He repeated, too many times for Arianna to count, that he wasn't going to lose her and he wanted all of her back. She returned his whispers with those of her own, telling him how they were going to be joined once again, all while hoping Nate could take his own advice to stick it out when the time came for him to sit on the counselor's couch and learn of her nightmares. Nate kept her covered in the grass until Arianna realized how badly he wanted her, and how much he was restraining himself.

"Let's try, Nathan."

"No, Ani, things are good right now."

Arianna whispered in his ear. "I can feel what being out here like this is doing to you."

Nate propped himself up, extending his arms so he could look down at her. "Look at me, baby, seriously."

Arianna gave him her full attention.

"If you're not completely sure you can do this, please, don't put me through it. This is hard enough for me."

The victims, all those other innocent lives Nightmare had ruined at the hands of Arianna's silence. All the pain and torture she'd endured, and how she'd left Nate all alone, cold, searching in a blizzard for the wife he so desperately loved to the point of turning to another woman just to get warm. The visions bombarded her like water from a raging storm. She tried to fight it, tried to embrace the moment as she embraced Nate's body. But she couldn't. "You're right. I can't. I'm so sorry. I just want to please you."

"Ani, you've known me a long time. If I weren't pleased, I wouldn't be here. Let's go to bed."

Arianna followed Nate back into the house and up to bed. She lay down close, reality setting in. Nate would soon know about Nightmare. In the safety of his arms, she wondered what she'd gotten herself into, and how she'd break down to him the details of how this bastard had broken her.

~~~

Nate lay with Arianna on his chest. He realized what he'd just gotten himself into—therapy. He embraced his wife, hoping she could handle what he hadn't yet told her about his affair. Nate's shoulders were growing weary from carrying all the consequences. His mind was growing more worried by the day thinking about Arianna never being the same. Most of all, the constant paranoia over his mistress's identity was consuming him to the point he could barely breathe. Something had to be done.

All this hell, Nate thought, because of a few minutes of gratification in a cheap motel that was a far cry from Heaven.

One Week

"You okay, Ani?"

"I didn't get much sleep last night."

"I noticed."

"What is that supposed to mean?"

"Calm down. Nothing. You tossed and turned and mumbled a little bit. That's all."

"Mumbled what?"

"Don't freak out. Nothing audible, geeze."

"What did you hear, Nathan?"

"I said *nothing*. Damn, Ani, chill out. *Should* I have heard something?"

"Now, what is *that* supposed to mean?"

"Nothing, woman. Shit, just saying...you're over here freaking out for no reason. Believe me, if you were calling out another guy's name, I'd wake you real quick."

"Not funny, Nathan."

"Why are you trippin', Ani?"

"Just don't like to sound stupid in my sleep."

"Women."

"Well then, since I'm such a woman, maybe you should sleep in the guest room until we go to counseling."

"Excuse me? Where the *fuck* did that come from?"

"You don't get it."

"You damn right. A few days ago we were fine. Now these last couple of days, you're a different person."

"Not true."

"Very true…oh…wait…I know what this is about."

"Then why don't you enlighten me, Nathan?"

"My affair. The one you said you could deal with. You're dreaming about this shit, now?"

"Just drop it."

"Of course."

"Where are you going?"

"To my new living quarters, I guess."

"Nathan."

"See you at counseling."

"Now you're just being mean."

"No, just keeping peace. Have a good day."

"Where are you going?"

"Out."

"Where?"

"I'll tell you when you magically transform into my parent."

"Nathan."

"Bye, Ani."

Chapter 37

Marcus made a wish, then blew out the thirty-something candles on his birthday cake. Claps and cheers, for a brief time, filled the Jackson household. Every Memorial Day weekend brought celebration and fellowship to the Jackson home, plus Marcus's ritual birthday carrot cake with double portions of icing. In an attempt to keep with tradition, Arianna and Nate had held the annual barbeque despite the simmering tension.

Arianna had yet to find a therapist. Nate had yet to push her in that direction. They had yet to admit it had nothing to do with the busy schedules they blamed.

Agent Greene had approved Nate's leave of absence request. The few days Nate had been home proved tough. Arianna couldn't look at Nate without thinking of his naked body soothing the skin of somebody else. Strange, she thought. She had handled the affair better with Nate in Baltimore, farther from her and closer to his mistress, than she was doing with him home. His strong presence put the affair in her face.

Touching him made it tangible.

Nate and Marcus, this time with D.J., for whom Nate had buried the hatchet after he'd attacked D.J. in Marcus's car, migrated to the patio, settling into the normal routine as Nate handled the grill.

The girls were whipping up the side dishes in air-conditioned comfort.

"D.J. keeps looking in here," Taesha said. She smiled at him and he smiled back.

"Go talk to him," Eva said.

"Nah, I don't know what to say."

Pam opened the oven door to check on the beans. "They need more married friends so their wives can help clean up."

"That would mean more food to prepare," Taesha said.

"Yeah, true."

"How are you and Marcus doing?" Eva asked.

"We exist."

Nate abruptly swung open the back door.

Arianna looked down and to the side. He passed her, impervious, and went to the refrigerator. The motor kicked in as he held open the door. He took longer than usual to decide what drinks to get. Nate always had his mind made up about his drinks, and seeing that his only choices were between Budweiser and MGD, there wasn't a lot to think about. The kitchen audience stared, knowing he was standing there simply because he could.

He grabbed a six-pack of Budweiser and tucked it under his arm, then grabbed the MGD and placed it in the hand on the side with the Budweiser. He shut the fridge door and walked back outside, lopsided and without a word.

"All I'm saying," he began as he shut the door behind him using his free hand, "is that was a lucky shot."

"Are you guys alright?" Eva asked as she mashed avocados. "He seems mad."

"He's sleeping in another room."

"My God, did you get that therapist?" Eva asked.

"Not yet."

"This is spiraling out of control. What are you waiting on?" Eva asked again.

"Her courage to tell Nate about Nightmare," Taesha said.

Arianna walked to the fridge and got out the mayonnaise. "I didn't think it'd be like this. This affair has complicated *everything*. I'm obsessing over it now. Every move he makes, all I can think about is him interacting with another woman. I actually got online and researched *women in Baltimore* to get some sense of why a particular mistress. He's being patient, but my interrogating him about her identity is killing him. I promised myself I wouldn't do this. I pushed for professional help, but now it's real and I'm scared to death. I'm just not ready."

"What does he say about her?" Eva said.

"Nothing. He clams up, says she was nobody, and walks away. I don't push because I'll open the door to Nightmare. I don't know what to do. I'm drowning. I'm drowning in needing help and drowning in being too scared to get it," she said.

Arianna slapped a spoonful of mayonnaise into her potatoes. Her frustration caused her to use more force than she needed, and she splashed her shirt. She walked over to the sink and glanced out the kitchen window.

Suddenly, an uproar of laughter came from the porch, much like the noise in a sports bar when the home team takes the lead after trailing for almost an entire game.

"I'd love to know what's so damn funny," Arianna said.

They all looked outside. Nate swigged his beer, gave Arianna a stare colder than dry ice, and then turned back around.

"Arianna, for better or worse," Taesha said.

"Would you stop?" Arianna asked.

"I've been around a lot of men. I know facial expressions. Nate is at his limit. I give him a month and he's gone. You have to do something."

"You have to open up," Eva said. "Get that counselor."

Arianna couldn't take much more. She knew her friends meant well, and she knew Nate was indeed at his limit. How could she get her friends to understand that what had begun as a petrifying plunge into silence for the sake of Nate's sanity had transmuted into her knowledge of Nate's inability to process his own fears, his need for total revenge should he have to avenge his loved ones for any reason? Pam, Eva, and Taesha would never truly understand that night months ago, the way Nate had poured his soul and his contents inside of her. The way he had to keep her sheltered under him as he moved. The way he let her know that he was her protector, she belonged to him, and that he wished a motherfucker would try some shit.

Sure, she'd always known his heart would hurt, but until that night, she hadn't thought about his rage toward her assailant.

"You have to speak up," Taesha said.

"It will *crush* him, Tae."

Taesha wouldn't let up. "It's crushing him now."

"Let it go," Arianna demanded.

"Taesha, stop it," Pam said. "Your mouth is the last thing any of us need."

"Pam," Eva said. "That was a cheap shot."

"Nah, let her speak her mind. It never gets to me. I'm not gonna stop. I'm sick of seeing Arianna in pain. She's gonna own this shit if she likes it or not." Taesha went to the computer in the den. "A therapist. Pick one. Now." She looked at Pam. "You're on the verge of getting one too if you snap at me one more 'gain."

Arianna lost it. "I can't do this anymore!"

Pam, Eva, and Taesha froze, much like they had when they'd found out about Arianna's assault. Arianna had a meltdown.

"I know I've gone back and forth on this. But look at it from my position. Not only will Nathan see me as a lying bitch, he will lose everything," she said. "Nathan will find him. Nathan will kill him. His job, his freedom, his heart, his life will be gone, not to mention his sanity. He's my husband. I have to protect him. I know I need to tell him. I've battled it for years. But I don't want to break his heart."

"Let me get this shit straight," Taesha said. "You're gonna sit here, drowning in silence and pain, worsening the broken heart Nate gave you, to spare Nate from his? That's like saving somebody from drowning who threw you in a lake and fell in beside you."

"That's what wives do, Tae," Arianna said. "Sometimes we're the ones who need to take the bullet. "

"And sometimes we need our husbands to believe we're perfect, right?"

"Stop, Tae," Eva said. "All of you."

Taesha kept going, as usual. "You can put all this shit on protecting Nate, and I'm sure some of it's true. But deep down, you're worried about what Nate will think of you."

"What do you expect? That bastard put foreign objects inside of me. And I let him."

"You were a kid," Taesha said.

"Can we just not talk about this right now?" Pam asked. "Can I just get a reprieve from arguing? That's all Marcus and I seem to do now."

Nate walked through the back door. The women were so engrossed, once again, in nightmares and affairs, they didn't realize he was there. "What's going on in here?"

He looked around. It had to have been clear to him from the barrage of emotions the women so clearly displayed—Arianna's tears, Taesha's scowl, Eva's worry, and Pam's confusion—that there was only one logical explanation.

He started to shout. "My affair, again? Seriously?"

"Nate, you need to chill," Taesha said. "It's not what you think."

"Yeah, right." He looked at Arianna, seeming close to collapse. "When are we gonna move on from this? How many times do I have to be consoling, bite my tongue, and shoulder this shit before I'm allowed to defend myself?"

"Nathan, please calm down."

"Listen, Nate," Eva said. "You're flying off the handle for no reason."

Marcus had come into the house when Nate had begun shouting. "Nate, man, you've had too much to drink. Let's calm this down."

"Marcus, please. I can handle my liquor." He looked at Arianna. "When is this gonna end?"

Taesha chimed in and crossed the line. "The side bitch, Nate. Who is she?"

"Taesha!" the other women shouted in unison.

"Excuse me?" Nate asked. "This is none of your business, Taesha."

"You are my family, and I'm making it my business. Tell Arianna who she is, so y'all can move on."

"Get out of my house."

Taesha got in his face. "No. You tell my girl what she needs to know. Now!" Then she looked at Arianna. "Then you're gonna sit his big ass down and you're gonna talk...about EVERYTHING."

Taesha stared Nate down, and then stared at Arianna. She grabbed her purse. "Come on, everyone, we're leaving so they can talk."

"Stop pushing this, Taesha," Nate said.

"You need to man up, SSA Jackson," Taesha shouted. "You don't think this is killing Arianna too?"

Nate took a deep breath, as if he had no more breaths to take, raspy and deep. He looked at Arianna. "The last thing I ever wanted to do was hurt you."

"Let's go, people," Taesha demanded.

"Nah, nobody needs to leave. Everybody's gonna find out anyway." Nate stared at Arianna, then at Marcus, then back at Arianna. "She's dead. She jumped from the Gleason Building the day I told her I would always be in love with you."

The women's mouths had dropped so far, that they wouldn't shut. D.J. looked at Marcus. Marcus bit his lip as if he wanted to knock Nate out. Nobody saw it coming.

"You screwin' with me, right?" Marcus shouted. "Shawnee Redman? My victim? The one I've been scratching my head to figure out?"

Arianna was still silent.

Nate nodded. Marcus turned away, eyes big. He tossed up his hands in complete disbelief.

Nate immediately turned to Arianna.

She stood up slowly. Nate was standing closer to her now, looking like he'd just wrestled a wolf and narrowly won. They didn't quite stand face to face; the top of Arianna's head met him at his neck. She looked up. Every breath Nate was taking in appeared to be a struggle. Beads of sweat bubbled on his forehead.

Arianna slapped Nate with enough force to almost snap his neck. "This whole time I thought she was in Baltimore. I actually felt sorry for *you*. You couldn't find anybody else? Hell, the company next to me has three secretaries. Pick one, Nathan. "

"Like you picked a counselor? It was hard enough for me to admit we needed one. You want me to find and hire the son-of-a-bitch too?"

"Don't change the subject. My secretary? Did you just wanna humiliate me?"

"Humiliate you? My hand is about to fall off and we want to talk about humiliating *you*? News flash. The subjects are the same."

They were silent.

"Why Shawnee?"

"She was a warm body, Ani, in my cold world with you."

Arianna welled up. "That's not fair."

"Isn't it?"

"I'm done."

"Of course you are, Ani. You're the only victim here, right?"

"I want you out."

"Of course, because running is what you do best."

Arianna slapped Nate again. Nate looked away, pursed his lips.

"Why are you still in front of me, Nathan?"

"Ani, I don't want to leave. But *this* isn't fair."

"Give me your ring."

"What?"

"Give. Me. Your. Wedding. Ring."

Everybody in the room, Taesha included, stared at Arianna in utter disbelief. "Whoa, okay now, it's pretty jacked up about Shawnee, but nobody's giving a ring back. You're just so, so mad."

"And you know what?" Nate interrupted, "I am just so, so tired." He stared at Marcus as he gripped his ring finger with his opposite hand. Marcus shook his head no. Nate took off his wedding band regardless and put it in Arianna's hand, then clasped her fingers and looked down. He appeared to be praying, or at least preparing himself for an explosion. He swallowed and looked up, his voice cracking. "I will love you until the end of time. But I'm done begging for the benefit of the doubt. If you don't know by now what you mean to me, Ani, and how badly I feel, you never will. Tell the boys I will work something out with visitation. I'm done being crucified because of Shawnee Redman or any other mistake I've ever made."

Nate hustled to the front door and walked out. Marcus followed him. D.J., who'd been completely quiet, followed behind Marcus.

"Go tell him about Nightmare. Now!" Taesha shouted.

"It's too late."

"You *love* that man. You worship the ground he walks on. Go get his stupid ass, Arianna."

"Since when do you care?" Arianna asked.

"I've always cared. I may be a slut, but I still believe in love. I told you that weeks ago. You're gonna lose him if you don't go after him."

"I lost him before I ever had him. I lost everything the day Nightmare put the pillowcase over my head."

Marcus came back inside the house. "He's gone." He looked at Taesha. "You happy now?"

"C'mon, Marcus, that's not fair. Leave her alone," D.J. said. Taesha glanced at him, he glanced back. Everybody in the room could tell they'd just had a *moment*.

Arianna was shaking with what felt like the magnitude of a California earthquake. Her lip quivered, her eyes closed. She could barely handle the pain. She stood in front of her friends, determined not to break down. Her anger helped her along. "All pussies are pink, right?"

"What does that even mean, Arianna?" Marcus asked.

"Nothing that matters." Arianna walked in the direction of the stairs. "I'm going to check on my devastated children."

Marcus snapped. He made fists as if he wanted to punch the wall, but refrained. He mumbled about how ridiculous this whole situation had become, and how he was more fed up than Nate. "Hold up, Arianna. You're gonna hear this. All of you." He looked at everybody, methodically, one by one. "We are here because of our own stupid-ass choices. And I can't take this shit anymore. Eva can't walk a mile without falling over Zach, or looking over her shoulder wondering if Kyle Stupid-ass Ridgeland is going to show up and cut her. Taesha can give advice, intrude, but can't take any goddamned heat. Nate's gone, probably driving drunk. Arianna looks like she wants to end her life. Pam and I allowed shit to affect us that had nothing to do with us, and now we barely talk to each other." Marcus took a breath. "And our children are upstairs unraveling. Tre's crying. Gwen's scared. And Darius hates the world and has for a while now." He grabbed his keys. "If we don't get it together and stop creating our own problems, we're never gonna be happy. And we will never again be a family. And you know what? If we wanna get real and see this for what it is, we are the only family any of us truly have. D.J. included, with his dysfunctional, white ass." Marcus took one last glance at everybody. "Everybody in this room needs to think about that. What did Zach die for, huh? For us to disintegrate?" He approached the stairs. "Gwen, let's go!" He looked at Pam. "I'll see you at home."

Marcus left with Gwen and dropped the mic on his way out.

"And there goes my ride," D.J. said.

"I'll take you home," Taesha said. Then she looked at Arianna. "Go upstairs. We'll clean up. We got this."

"No. Hold on," Arianna said. She looked upstairs, thinking about her kids. Collapsing, for as much as she wanted to, couldn't happen. *Shawnee.* Arianna had to find a way to break through the shock, the utter disappointment, and the complete betrayal that had happened so close to home.

She climbed the stairs. Tre had almost cried himself to sleep on Darius's bed. Darius looked at his mother standing in the doorway. "He's gone, isn't he?"

"Yes, baby."

Darius nodded. "Could you shut my door?"

"Do you wanna talk?"

"No."

She looked at Tre. "You wanna go with Mommy?"

"I stay here."

"You sure?"

"Mom," Darius interjected. "He's fine. I got him."

Arianna simply shut the door, to avoid stirring up dust, to avoid cultivating any more drama in the day. She knew her son. Just like his father, sometimes he needed to be left alone.

She went back downstairs. "This is my house. We *all* got this."

Arianna led the charge, putting items away, helping to clean up the memories of a Memorial Day better forgotten.

Chapter 38

It was close to midnight. Nate hadn't shown up at Marcus's house since leaving the barbeque; however, Marcus had no time to worry. Gwen had locked herself in the bathroom and had been there for an hour. Earlier in the day, she'd complained about a stomachache. Marcus thought she'd caught the flu. Pam had her suspicions.

She reached the top of the stairs, holding a grocery bag full of supplies.

"The door's locked. Gwen screams every time she thinks I'm going to unlock it," Marcus said.

"Go away, Daddy," Gwen shouted.

Pam moved Marcus over. "Gwen? Honey, open the door."

"I can't stand up."

Pam motioned for Marcus to jimmy the door. He did, but didn't leave.

"Go sit down," Pam said. "Gwen's not gonna bleed to death." She walked into the bathroom and shut the door behind her. The shower rumbled.

Marcus waited downstairs. He paced as if Gwen were undergoing major surgery.

Twenty-minutes later, Pam walked downstairs carrying Gwen's soiled clothing and went into the basement. Marcus heard water filling the washing machine.

Pam came back upstairs. "You don't have to be at a loss for words," she said. "It's natural."

"How is she?" Marcus asked.

"Fine. She's asleep."

Marcus didn't respond.

"Say something, Marcus. We can't pretend today didn't happen."

He shut off the television and headed for the stairs. "What do you want from me? You haven't given me a chance to explain since this mess popped off. Now it's all gone further to shit, so you wanna talk."

"Don't turn away from me, Marcus." Pam started to sob. "I don't wanna be on the receiving end of your wedding band."

Marcus stopped himself cold, but kept his distance. "*You* wedged us. Not me."

"You lied to me."

"Yeah, I did. I was wrong. But you wouldn't even hear me out."

"I'd like to hear you now."

Marcus said nothing. Pam pleaded for answers. Marcus knew that she needed to understand why he would contribute to her best friend's pain, why he would compromise his own values for Nate's compromising positions. He stared at her, thinking of reasons not to delve, but knowing she had a right to know.

"Sit, please," he said.

She did.

Marcus sat beside her. "Everyone assumes I met Nate at school. We weren't even in the same district. When we were nine or so, I met him at a meeting my grandmother's church had started. Some corny shit called Men Without Mothers. She thought guys like me who didn't have moms were missing essential nurturing or some crap. We had to babysit, cook, clean. She believed it would stop boys from growing up emotionless. I had to go because it was my grandmother's group. Nate had to go because his dad used that time to entertain women."

"How come you never told me?"

"Sitting in a room with a bunch of old ladies talkin' about yeast infections isn't something I like reliving."

Pam chuckled.

"It lasted about eight years and ended badly."

"How?"

"I had a friend named Cedric in the group. Everyone knew Cedric's dad had killed his mom. Nobody could prove it."

Marcus's hands began to shake. Pam grabbed one and held it tight. He allowed her hand to remain clenched over his.

"One night, Cedric's father pulled Cedric from the group. Never gave a reason. My grandmother got upset. They argued. Next thing you know, he's lunging toward my grandmother and I'm lunging toward him."

Pam's eyes widened. "Oh no."

"He pushed my grandmother to the floor, and I ran to her. He had his hands wrapped around her throat. I did what I could, but he was strong as shit. He let go of her and came after me. Then a shot rang out. I thought my grandmother was hit. Then I saw Cedric's dad bleeding out his neck. I looked back. Nate was holding the gun. He saved my life and he tried to save my grandmother's life."

"Tried?"

"She didn't make it, Pam. It took Nate a while to get his aim, so he could avoid hitting her and hit Cedric's dad instead. By the time he got it, it was too late. He got the shot off, but my grandmother had a heart attack fighting off Cedric's dad. That's what killed her, so that's what I told you years ago."

"Oh, my God."

"Nate's dad got him a good-ass lawyer. At seventeen years old, Nate stood trial for murder. He was acquitted, but neither of us was ever the same. Nate felt so guilty for taking so long to aim that he became obsessed with the shot. All he did was practice anytime he could. Perfected it."

"Where'd he get the gun?"

"The church was in a rough neighborhood. Nate always showed up with his father's gun."

"Is that why you guys became cops?"

"That night solidified it. That's why Nate is so protective of young males and why he loves that school where he mentors."

"Does Arianna know?"

"I don't know. We literally do–not–talk about it."

"I'm sorry, Marcus."

"I will always have Nate's back."

Pam stayed silent. For once, Marcus knew she had no words.

"I'm tired. I'm going up." Marcus went upstairs to the master bedroom, leaving Pam on the couch to absorb the story.

Marcus took off his jersey, threw it into the hamper, and started the shower. He looked in the mirror and noticed his age. With the day's events, he had forgotten he was a year older.

Marcus reflected on the last twelve months as the steam continued to rise behind the curtain. He'd made no headway on his mother's case. His best friend was disintegrating. His caseload signified that murder hadn't taken a vacation, and he still had no peace with Zach's death. Plus, his own marriage was on the chopping block.

He showered, thinking back to the day Pam had found the receipt, and how no explanations were necessary. Then he thought about Gwen, and how Pam had raised her when she had no obligation to do so. Marcus was doing what he'd always done on the job—looking at circumstances from all sides. But he still had a ping of resentment at Pam's utter disregard of his own reasons for his actions.

When Marcus came out of the bathroom, he found Pam in their bed, lying on her side, facing him. He watched her sleeping, one hand under her head and one on the bed next to her chest. Her closed eyes and her smooth breathing capped the peaceful look, one so soft that it made Marcus think twice about the hard grudges that destroy marriages.

He thought of Nate and Arianna. *I cannot allow us to end up like them.*

Marcus crawled up to his wife.

"I had no business lying to you," he said. "I'm sorry. I don't want to lose the trust you have in me. But you have to allow me room to speak."

Pam opened her eyes, staying on her side, and responded softly. "I remember when Dr. Parsons said I couldn't have children. I used to wonder if you'd be able to handle that. And you always assured me that you could and you would. You never wavered. I should have given you a chance to explain."

"So, we're both wrong."

Pam scooted closer to him. "I didn't say I was wrong."

"Of course not." Marcus smiled and turned out the light. "Now come over here and be right all night long."

"You are so bad, Detective Carter."

Chapter 39

Marcus doubled the coffee grounds in the filter. Heading back to work after Memorial Day weekend took extra effort. Alcohol, money, and free time equaled more bodies to bag.

He answered a knock on the door.

"Are you gonna give me a bunch of shit?" Nate asked.

"You *look* like shit."

"I feel like shit."

"Are you drunk?"

"No, but it was a rough one."

"Did you drive?"

"The shuttle from this place dropped me off."

"Where's your car?"

"Gotta get it."

"Get inside, Nate."

Nate came in complete with his red eyes and wrinkled clothes.

"Where you been?"

"Left my house, went to the store, got enough liquor to help me forget, and then went to a motel and forgot."

"Why didn't you come here?"

"I wasn't in the mood to take what you're about to dish. You have coffee?" Nate went into the kitchen and sat on a barstool.

"How'd you pull it off, Nate?"

From what Marcus could tell, Nate wasn't actively drinking, had stopped drinking a few hours ago. There was enough carryover from the prior night, though, to make Nate a little loopy. Marcus could also tell that he hadn't slept, and this added to the frustration of trying to get any useful information out of him. Nate clearly didn't want to delve, but Marcus could decipher enough to help him find some clarity in Nate's attempt to forget his Ani.

Nate had made Shawnee untraceable, he told Marcus, bought them both burner phones. After her death, he'd smashed his to pieces and wondered if Marcus had found hers. Shawnee didn't have his real phone number. There was no email, no social networking, and absolutely no landlines. Shawnee wasn't allowed to use her debit card within ten miles of the motel, not even for gas. No gifts, no frequenting any of the places he normally went. Nate didn't even have an address to use GPS. He mentioned good talks in the beginning, but also the tension that consumed the sex.

"I didn't even know where she lived, Marcus."

Marcus leaned against the stove and placed his hands on the cold burners. "I saw her, you know?"

"What do you mean?"

"The motel. The last time. I caught a glimpse of her, but couldn't place her because the room was dark. Now, I get it. That stupid office party for Arianna's company. Told you I didn't wanna to go to that shit. If you wanted me so disconnected from her, why the hell did you put us in the same room?"

"You think *I* wanted to go? Arianna pushed."

"I thought you guys were going to see a shrink behind this shit."

"We were." Nate sipped his coffee. "She never followed up, and I didn't force the issue because..."

"Because what?"

"Shawnee's name would have come out."

"Well, you handled that well."

The silence following was understood, Marcus glaring at Nate, Nate feeling ashamed at allowing Marcus to go around wasting time on a case that could have been helped along with some honesty and trust in their friendship. At least Marcus could have understood a motive for suicide.

"I gotta ask you something," Nate said. "If I hadn't been with you at the lake, would you have thought I killed her?"

"No. One thing you love almost more than your family is the damn law."

"You don't know how scared I've been, Marcus."

"About?"

"The motel clerk. I was so afraid that he'd recognize Shawnee from the news."

"I think you're safe there. Someone would have called us by now."

"Plus I always showed up first and paid, so I don't think he ever saw her." Nate squinted. "You have some pills?"

"First, tell me. Did you use condoms every time?"

"I wasn't about to run up in that shit raw. Yes."

"Smartest thing you've done all year."

"Why would you question?...Oh. hell nah, dude."

"Yep. A few weeks along. You didn't know?"

"Not a clue...whoa, wait...this means that woman killed her unborn infant."

Marcus nodded. "It looks that way."

"That poor baby."

"I know."

Nate rubbed his forehead. "I can't believe I lost the love of my life over that woman. Could you please get my dumb ass some pills?"

Marcus went into the guest bathroom downstairs and got Nate some medicine to soothe his head. "What I don't get, Nate? You get pussy thrown at you—don't ask me why—on the daily. Why so close to home?"

"Can we do this later?"

"No. We can't."

Nate reluctantly explained the whole story. One day, he'd gone to pick up Arianna for an appointment for Tre. She was late, and Shawnee was sitting there, in a form-fitting dress. Nate had been at his lowest point, and Shawnee seemed to sense some frustration. They talked, connected, laughed. She seemed genuinely interested in Nate's life, and it was a soothing and a stark contrast to the total disinterest Arianna had shown over the past couple of years.

"Lowest point?" Marcus asked. "Explain."

"There was this kid, in Baltimore, in the mentorship program up there named Jeremy. The streets called him J-Bug. We'd talked a lot in the time he was there. I'd gotten through to him, you know? He was working on prepping for community college."

"That's a good thing, right?"

"Reese tried to recruit him. Word is Jeremy turned him down because of my influence. He went missing after that."

"Damn, Nate, I'm sorry."

"Greene got a call from Homicide a couple days later. My card was in Jeremy's pocket when they found his body. When I came home after that, I *begged* Arianna to talk to me. She left. That was it for me. Felt like nothing I ever did mattered to her, so I decided to meet my best friend in a cemetery and well, discuss an affair."

Marcus and Nate were so quiet, a piece of paper could have dropped to the floor and sounded like an explosion.

Nate shook his head and dropped it down. "After the basement and the things I witnessed back then, I guess I just lost it. Couldn't withstand another young tragedy."

"You mean the chain incident?"

"Yeah."

"It's a lot to take, Nate. I get it."

"I just fell straight into it, you know? Like I didn't even know who I was when I set up the whole affair."

"You made a bad choice, but you're not a bad guy."

"Easier said than thought."

Marcus checked the time. "She hit on *you*, didn't she?"

"How did you know?"

"Our investigation proved that she was a pro at it."

"It was so pathetic. She slipped me an address, a date, and a time, like she knew, like she could read me. I met up with her and set the schedule...damn, what was I thinking!"

"Shhh. You'll wake Pam."

Marcus studied Nate's face. Nate's eyes drooped, his cheeks sagged. It seemed he might soon fall off the barstool in his sadness.

"Man, Marcus, Ani used to suck the *skin* off my dick."

"Okay, c'mon." Marcus led Nate off the barstool. "We'll sort out this later. Figure out what to do about your head."

"It's just a headache."

"I mean the shit inside it."

Nate crashed onto the couch. A couple minutes later, he was out.

Marcus gathered his things and prepared for another day of death. He went upstairs and kissed Pam and Gwen, who were both still asleep. He left a note for Pam not to be alarmed when she saw Nate's big, drunk ass sprawled downstairs.

Marcus went back downstairs and checked on the drunken bag of despondency. Nate was snoring so loudly it hurt Marcus's ears. Marcus watched him, knowing Nate would get a couple hours of freedom before waking up to the cuts and bruises of his broken relationship.

Marcus rushed back upstairs. He went to the bedroom and abruptly turned Pam over.

She jerked. "Did I oversleep?"

"No."

"Then what's wrong?"

"Nothing." He lifted Pam's head and kissed her until he ran out of breath.

One Week

"Nathan came back when I was at work and packed a big suitcase. He's never done that, Pam."

"Why'd you let him leave if you didn't want him to?"

"I'm just saying he packed a suitcase. That's all."

"Okay."

"He's never done that. Just weird."

"You kicked him out, Arianna."

"I know I kicked him out, Pamela. I'm just saying he packed a big suitcase. Geeze."

"You sound upset. I'm gonna stop by after work."

"Do you think Shawnee was pretty?"

Two Weeks

"Daddy."
"Hey, champ."
"Daddy work."
"Yep. Daddy's working. What are you doing?"
"Letter."
"Which one?"
"Teeeeee."
"The letter T. Cool."
"Bro Bro cry."
"Really?"
"Bro Bro sad."
"I know."
"I sad too."
"Tre Tre, I know. Daddy knows."
"Daddy sad...Daddy?"
"I'm here, champ."
"Daddy cry too."
"Nah, Daddy has a cold."
"Sniffles."
"That's right, sniffles, champ."
 "I love you, Daddy...Daddy...Daddy?"

"I love you too, Tre. More than you will ever know. Daddy has to go."

"Daddy sad."

Chapter 40

Arianna cut the blue wire of the edger deep into the dirt, destroying the results of Nate's hard yard work. Shavings of grass bounced off and irritated her bare ankles. She stopped the machine, brushed off her ankles, and wished someone would bring her a cold glass of ice water the way she used to do for Nate. It was mid-June, and Texas already felt like the dog days of summer.

Parched, she started again, but pressing the handle did nothing. She cursed the edger, threw it down, fixed the jam in the wire, and left it too long. It started up, narrowly missing the opportunity to make her shorter. She dug too far into the yard again, so she stopped the spiraling machete and took off her safety glasses. Scanning the yard, filled with the potholes she'd created, made Arianna wonder where the hell Nate got his stamina.

Tre walked out, covered in chocolate. Arianna ran into the house and followed the sweet trail from the front door to the kitchen. Fingerprints and smudges were everywhere.

She checked the clock and realized she'd missed her one o'clock appointment to get the truck serviced. Wiping her forehead, which now pounded, she went to find carpet cleaner. She got down on all fours and worked the carpet. Her oil change and tire rotation would have to wait, not to mention the analysis needed to find out what the obnoxious noise was under the dashboard vent.

She got up with red knees and pulled the magnetic notepad and pen off the refrigerator door to write a reminder to rent a carpet shampooer. On the list was the brown paint she'd forgotten to purchase so she could touch up the rain gutters outside.

She cursed herself and went back to the drudgery.

Later, she leaned on the truck, now realizing why Nate had always told her to put it in the garage before he did the yard. The vehicle was covered in dust and dirt and Arianna wondered, even with her resolve, if she could really do this alone.

She pictured Nate, shirtless, pushing the mower back and forth with ease. She adored watching him stop in the middle of the yard and throw his shirt over his shoulder with all the confidence of a professional landscaper. Arianna's eyes welled with memories, until she pictured him sexing up Shawnee. *Back to it.*

She pulled the mower's chain until it started pulling hers. The machine revved, stopped, and endured her verbal abuse. The cycle continued until she threw the mower on its side. She kicked her SUV's wheels and cursed Nate for cheating on her. Through the pout, the rumbling of wheels and the scraping of metal against the street became louder. Arianna turned to find Gloria headed her way, armed with lawn power.

"You have to prime it first, dear," Gloria said. She bent down in her yellow sweats and gestured to Arianna to come down to her level, close to the mower Arianna was trying to start.

"Here, dear, you push this three times."

Arianna pushed the primer button and heard the gas shuffling. She yanked once and the mower roared. "I'm the man," she yelled as she danced around the rumble. Gloria lined her up. Arianna felt accomplished and ready, like a kid riding a bike for the first time without training wheels. She went back and forth, making crooked S's all over the yard. Gloria grabbed the edger and tried to undo the damage on the corners of the lawn.

Two hours later, both were covered in sweat but had finished the job.

"I'm exhausted. And the season is just getting started." Arianna wiped her forehead.

"June is late for Texas. But yes, dear, you're in for a long, hard battle with the grass."

"How 'bout some lemonade?"

"Sounds delightful."

They went inside.

"Now, dear, promise me you won't try to do the yard in slip-on sandals anymore." Gloria sipped her drink.

"Yes, ma'am." Arianna saluted. She fiddled with her hair, pinning it up, then taking it down, and then pinning it up again, a habit she'd learned from Eva. "Gloria, thank you. It's been a little rough for me."

"Maybe you should hire a yard man."

"I'm determined to do it myself."

"Or does it pain you to think of another man doing Nathaniel's job?"

Arianna shrugged. "I don't know... maybe. I still can't believe he's gone."

Gloria put her drink down. "I wish I had your life sometimes. You're so pretty, so professional. I'm a lowly housewife approaching forty-nine."

"You have a good life, Glo. Sometimes I would love to stay home. But nooo, I had to go and try to be a businesswoman and bark with the big dogs."

"When was the last time you went for a run?"

"A long time. All I seem to do is miss my husband and hate him at the same time. And then I comfort my kids because they miss him too."

"Has he contacted you?"

"Not a word. Guess I asked for it."

"Don't say that. Call him."

"I can't, Glo. I just can't."

"Sometimes it's easier to label something as too hard than it is to work through it."

"I don't know what it is anymore, Glo."

"Love is risk. Remember that."

Arianna listened to Gloria's marital wisdom. Gloria brought over her carpet shampooer and found Arianna a reliable shop to take her Jeep to. Later, they enjoyed Chinese food, and Arianna taught Gloria the art of scrapbooking. Arianna realized she and her old-fashioned, nosy neighbor had more in common than she'd originally thought.

"Now give me Tre," Gloria said. "I'll take him for a night. Take a bath and drink a glass of wine. Think it through in your own time."

Arianna put the glass of wine on the bathtub ledge, then blew bath bubbles out of her hand. She lifted one leg out of the water, grabbed a razor, and rubbed one hand up her leg as she shaved the leg with the other. Her radio rhythm was focused until the beat slowed down—way down—to the captivating sounds of R&B love songs born from the new millennium. Arianna lost her moment. *Seriously? Now?* She threw down the razor and let the water out of the tub. So much for her diva experience meant to escape the feeling of what-the-hell-was-Nate-thinking.

I can't believe Nathan screwed my freakin' secretary.

Lathered in lotion, dressed in panties and a camisole, she knelt to pray before slipping between her barren sheets.

The phone rang. *Blocked caller* displayed on the caller ID. "Hello?"

"Hey there."

"Uh, hey."

"Well, you didn't hang up," Anthony said. "Positive sign."

"You need to stop doing this. I am not available."

"You did put the number on your data sheet."

Arianna fell silent.

"Arianna? Five-foot-five, wants to enhance her calves and upper back too?"

"Stop reading my stupid sheet." She patted her eyes.

"What's wrong? You and your husband having problems?"

"Why do you assume that?"

"Because you're at home and didn't hang up when you found out it was me."

Arianna pondered it. "Good guess."

"His loss."

"Your gain?"

"Yep."

"I love him."

"That's natural."

"Don't shrink me."

"I'm not. You know what you need?"

"What?"

"A good... strong... long... hard... personal training session."

For the first time that evening, she smiled. Anthony's persistence, although strange, was slowly chipping into her resistance. Nate choosing her secretary as a side-chick had helped Anthony along just a bit, softened Arianna's shell enough for her to welcome flattery after feeling flattened. "I'll think about it. How's that?"

"What? For real? Hey, I'll take it."

"Good night, Anthony."

Arianna turned on both lamps, the overhead light, the vanity lights in the bathroom, and two night-lights for good measure. Then she cocooned herself in her bed linens. The room became a blur. Her eyes took their curtain call.

Nightmare entered her dreams. "Your complexion is so smooth."

Arianna wiggled in her sheets. "No."

"You're maturing."

"No. No."

"I like your new short set."

"Stop, please stop." Arianna began to sweat.

"Baby-soft skin." Nightmare kissed her cheek.

"Stop!" she yelled. She sat up, then fell back and looked up at the ceiling. She wondered what Nate was up to and if he were alone too.

~~~

Dave slammed the mug onto the table. The Corona overflowed as he choked. He looked away and then back to his drinking buddy. He leaned in, needing clarification from Nate.

"You went on like that for two years?" he asked.

"Hold your voice down," Nate said.

"Years? As in years?"

"Yes." Nate gritted his teeth. "See why I don't tell your country ass anything? Damn, I screwed up."

"Two years, Jack. Stop this self-sabotage, guilt shit."

"The August before my senior year in college. That was the first time I saw her. We were in a grocery store." Nate smirked. "I had never been attracted to a white girl before. But good *gawd* she was fine. She had these shorts on and this sexy-ass ankle bracelet and a track shirt. Plus that damned strawberry-blonde hair. I just wanted to nail her, one time, I mean to the wall, Graffiti. Didn't care how, didn't give a shit where."

"How'd you get her?"

"You know the fine ones. It's go hard or go home. I had to piss her off to get her interested. Then the idea came to me... spill something on her... get her wet, cause drama. I could convince her it was an accident and then rescue her straight into a motel. I was young and immature. I didn't know what the hell I was thinking. And I just had to take it to the next level." Nate shook his head, trying to forget how badly the scene had turned out.

"What the hell did you do, Jack?"

"I took a two-liter orange soda, shook it up really good, walked by her, and dropped it. It exploded all over her. She knew from the jump it was no accident."

"And she dated you after that?"

"Yep. At first, she was upset, slapped me twice, but by the time it was dark, she was mine and I knew I wasn't letting her go."

"That's forgiveness for your ass. You got lucky."

"Don't I know it. Damn, I humiliated her." Nate shook his head, caught up in the shame he now felt for using embarrassment to get a reaction out of Arianna that day.

"Well, look at it this way," Dave said. "At least it turned out well."

Nate stared at him.

"Oh, shit, Jack, I'm sorry. Poor choice of words."

"It's cool. It did turn out well, for a while."

"I'm sorry about your marriage, man. I thought y'all would make it."

"I did too."

"Ooh man." Dave backed up in his seat.

Nate looked up at the stage. A stripper, Precious, was on the pole holding on with a firm grip, tight enough for her to lift up her body and spread her legs wide so her fluorescent pink thong could tease her masculine audience. The lights overhead flickered in green, yellow, and orange as she wrapped her legs around the pole and slid down. Crawling like a wild beast, she headed toward her prey. She fell flat, rolled onto her back, and let every man in the room know she was highly limber.

"Damn." Dave flung his arms. "Last time I saw titties that big was on my Uncle Lenny."

Nate's eyes never moved from her limber motions. He blocked Dave and the rest of the world out as he tried to forget he hadn't had sex in a male's eternity.

Dave slipped money into her string. He nodded in Nate's direction.

Precious smiled and put the side of her forefinger into her mouth. She licked it sideways as she jumped onto Nate's lap. Nate gasped for air and tried to find enough emotional strength to push her off.

He allowed Precious to undulate her body, up his chest, down his legs. Her eyes were a royal blue, her nose a perfect button. Long nails, high cheekbones. Her hair was braided in cornrows halfway down her crown. Thin spaghetti spirals draped her shoulders. Not much of her was biologically real, not even the quadruple Ds she brought within a quarter inch of Nate's face. He longed for a woman's touch, and was mesmerized by the body, no matter how superficial.

"Is that good?" she asked.

"I can't do this." Nate nudged her off.

He went back to his hotel room, leaving Dave to stand in his dust, calling his name to no avail.

Nate changed into gym clothes, then took in a late-night workout, thinking of his life with each curl, each push, each pull, until muscle failure coincided with how he saw himself as a man—a failure. Nate loaded weight, yanked up, and deadlifted until his knees almost caved. One last drop of the weight, and he left it all on the rack.

In his utter shamble, his need to drive home his mistakes, he caught a taxi to yet another gravesite, the resting place of a young girl and her baby, two people gone too soon, two people he'd found too late to save.

End of June

"Jack, get your ass up and get out of this room."

"I'm good. I'll see you Monday."

"What are you gonna do all weekend? Sit up in here and sulk?"

"No."

"Yeah, right."

"What do you want from me, Graffiti? Pretend I didn't lose everything?"

"Well, look at it this way, Jack. It could be worse."

"How?"

"You could have gotten drunk and thrown up on Greene's Mercedes last night."

"You didn't."

"Yep. See what you miss when you stay shut in all the damn time?"

Mid-July

"Thanks for the meeting, pretty lady. I'm curious. What changed your mind?"

"The numbers you hounded me, again and again, to read. This health fair is an excellent idea."

"I've been saying that. You finally listened."

"Just don't get the wrong idea."

"Oh, never. By the way, would you like to go out with me? Joke...kinda. Sorry not sorry."

"Why are you pushing this?"

"Because you're so damn beautiful and rare. I swear to God, I've never met somebody as captivating as you. I might come across as bold, or forward, but I know what you deserve and what I want to give you, if you'd just give me a chance."

"Anthony."

"Don't answer right away. Just give me a think about it. Oh, and I almost forgot to give you this. Happy Belated Birthday. Remember, you did fill out a data sheet."

"My goodness, Anthony, thank you! I love this bookstore! This is almost as nice as the rap my son wrote for me."

"Rap? That's funny."

"He always raps to me on special occasions."

"Cool."

"Look, this meeting was productive, but I gotta go. Family movie night."

"You're a good mom. Well, see you later."

"Anthony?"

"Yeah?"

"Thank you again. At least somebody remembered my birthday."

"I'll never forget it. Did somebody say coffee?"

"It's too soon, Anthony."

"Well, I know that. We just had coffee at our meeting. Is that a smile? Arianna, are you contemplating...?"

"Okay. Okay. No harm in coffee. Daytime though."

"Deal."

Chapter 41

August, the height of summer, had hit, blasting San Antonio as usual, as if the city had pissed off Mother Nature and could never get her forgiveness. Arianna continued building a new life, and welcomed the sunshine and the heat. Today, her friends were helping paint her kitchen a brighter hue of yellow, in honor of her birthday.

Arianna wondered how Nate had spent the Fourth of July. She was trying to adjust to life without him but he was never far from her mind. Text messaging was her method of choice when she needed to communicate with him. With his voice richer than center-cut sirloin, hearing him speak was too powerful for her to handle. But even with her desire to hear from him and defend that she didn't, Arianna felt there was no going back to him. Shawnee was the ultimate betrayal. Or at least that's what she told herself.

Business boomed. Crushed-ice drinks were a summer-selling icon, and Arianna had started offering cold sandwiches and fresh fruit. Customers received free bottled water with the purchase of food. Using the triple-digit heat to her advantage was paying off.

Her partnership with Anthony was spilling into something more, yet gradually, like drops of water evolving into a soothing rain. He'd helped her gain some weight and trained her with free-weight exercises. Arianna kept their friendship from her children because she knew it would devastate Darius, even if Arianna had no intention of making it anything more. But so far, Anthony had been patient and kind. Her secrets of Nightmare, however, had stayed secrets.

She'd also fibbed to her friends, told them she hadn't had a nightmare in a couple of months. Arianna needed their constant inquisition to stop.

"Thank you guys for this," Arianna said.

"It does look good," Eva said.

The house phone rang. Arianna, unfazed, slowly put down the roller to check the caller ID. Then she came back to paint. "Telemarketer."

"What? No rush to the phone?" Taesha asked.

"I stopped rushing to the phone a while ago."

"Have you heard from Nate at all?" Pam asked.

"Not a word, not even on my birthday. He has totally washed his hands of me."

"What if he did call? You gonna take him back?" Taesha asked.

"Tae, can you for once stop making us overthink stuff?" Pam asked.

"It's not overthinking, it's heavy reflection."

"No," Arianna said. "It's long over."

"Okay then. Be cheerful," Taesha said.

"I am cheerful. You're the one clouding everything," Arianna said. "Just paint."

"Well, I have some good news," Eva said. "My P.I. has a lead on Kyle."

"P.I.? Since when?" Arianna asked.

"Hired him last week. I'm not waiting a year to move on from my deranged husband."

"I hope they find him," Pam said.

"You and me both," Eva said. "I can't get a divorce under abandonment until he's been gone a year."

"That's what I'm talking about. Take charge." Taesha painted Arianna's arm. "You too."

Arianna looked at her arm, then looked at Taesha. "You didn't just do that."

"Whatcha gonna do about it?"

Arianna retaliated, painted Taesha's arm, then got her leg. They went back and forth until their paint fight broke through the overcast of discussing Nate and led to laughter and insane women chasing each other with paint rollers.

"Taesha, you're doing it wrong." Pam painted Arianna's backside. "You missed the booty." Arianna retaliated with a stroke to Pam's leg.

"Would you guys grow up?" Eva yelled. "You do it like this." She caught Taesha's hair. The girls ran into the backyard, armed with paint rollers. Arianna gave a swift stroke to Taesha's shoulder.

"I'm gonna get you, bitch."

Marcus walked out of the house through the back door. "You guys need to lock the front door. Anybody can just walk in."

"Hey," Pam said.

"We need to talk," he said.

"What's wrong?" she asked.

"Not here."

He motioned her inside. Taesha, Eva, and Arianna came back to the porch. Their smiles faded.

Pam wasn't gone long, but long enough to return covered in a different mood.

"What is it?" Arianna asked.

"Maybe we should sit down," Pam said.

"Did something happen to Nathan?" Arianna almost collapsed.

"He retained an attorney, Arianna."

Arianna swallowed. "I see."

"He's also going to, um..."

"Pam, please just tell me what's going on."

"Nate's making a permanent move. I'm so sorry, honey."

Eva put her hand on Arianna's shoulder.

Taesha cursed Nate out as if he could hear her.

"I'm okay. I'm okay," Arianna said. "Nathan's not gonna ruin my day and he's not gonna ruin my life. We're gonna finish my beautiful kitchen and then order Chinese and go shopping."

"That's my Arianna," Taesha said.

"There's a little more," Pam said.

"What?"

"Marcus is waiting outside. He needs your key to Nate's Cadillac."

"This bastard can't come get his own damn keys?" Taesha asked.

Arianna fiddled with her keys, separating the Cadillac key from the chain.

"What are you doing?" Taesha asked.

"Not caving in." Arianna walked outside. She held up the key. Marcus got out of his vehicle.

"Tell Nathan I want the key to *my* truck."

"Okay, this is beyond immature now, Arianna," Eva said

Marcus took the key. "It's on the table."

Arianna didn't move. Her tough act had just blown up in her face.

"Nate's trying to be fair. But hey, you can't see that, right?"

"Marcus," Pam said.

"Out of respect for my wife, I will not say what I truly want to. But know this. You let a good man just walk straight out of your life. And you know what's sad? You love him just as much as he loves you."

"He cheated."

"Like you gave him a choice."

"Marcus, stop," Pam snapped.

"I'll see you at home." Marcus drove away, leaving Arianna cold, shivering, wondering about the legal proceedings that lay ahead while listening to Taesha ramble on about going out and bringing Nate's cocky ass back down to Earth. But she didn't have long to ponder her feelings. Arianna heard a huge crash in the kitchen and ran in behind Pam and Taesha.

They saw broken glass on the floor and Eva breathing heavily.

"What happened?" Arianna shouted.

"The lead didn't pan out. Sorry, Arianna. I just got so angry." Eva grabbed her own arms. "I'm just going to have to wait out the year."

"Did you hurt yourself?" Arianna asked.

"No, just a bruise from hitting the cabinet when I threw the stupid glass. I'm fine. Sorry again, Arianna."

"It's just a glass, Eva." Arianna grabbed her broom and dustpan and started sweeping up the jagged mess. Eva offered to do it. Arianna declined, and made quick work of the cleanup. She had two boys, so taking care of sharp messes was second nature.

Taesha cleaned up the paint supplies. Eva tended to her bruise while Pam poured Eva the glass of water she had intended on drinking before her private investigator called. Arianna put away the broom, quickly washed her hands and then grabbed some lemons, green tea, cranberry extract, and strawberry slices.

Eva had to stop Arianna before she got carried away. "Arianna, I'm okay. Really. Just water."

"Sorry. Used to make Nathan drinks like this when he'd work in the garage. Kinda miss it."

"I'll take one," Taesha said.

"Really?"

"Yep. Do your thing, girl."

Arianna went to work. Taesha began rubbing Eva's shoulders. Pam, to Arianna's chagrin, gave Eva water, the basic edition.

They gathered around Arianna's kitchen table, the smell of paint lingering on the half-finished walls and fully ruined clothes. Taesha continued to massage Eva, extending to her upper back, as Eva kept trying to steal Taesha's drink. Arianna went back to the counter in Eva's regret of not wanting flavored water, and started assembling another drink for her.

Pam searched her phone for Chinese delivery while Arianna began slicing strawberries and lemons. A slow song came on the satellite radio, and she suddenly stopped. *Nathan used to try to get me to dance to this.* A few seconds later, she felt Pam's hands come around and hug her from behind. Arianna put down the knife and clasped Pam's wrist. "What's his plan?"

"He's leasing an apartment for at least a year."

End of July

"Damn, Nate. I thought your ass done fell off the face of the Earth."

"Just needed a couple of weeks to clear my head, Marcus."

"So are you clear?"

"I'm done. I thought my plan of moving would work, make her call my ass. Damn, did that shit ever backfire."

"That was an asinine move."

"But it was the last move I had. She doesn't want me back, Marcus. It's time I stop hoping she does."

Mid-August

"I think we're about ready to put on a good show, Arianna. Thanks for creating the brochures."

"I'm glad I could help, Anthony."

"What's wrong, pretty lady?"

"Nothing."

"I'm a therapist. Spill it."

"Just thinking about my new life."

"Yeah?"

"Yeah. I'm sure Nathan has moved on. It's time for me to move on too."

"I agree."

"You think he's moved on? Sorry...inappropriate question."

"It's cool. Yeah. I'm absolutely positive he has another woman."

"Really?"

"Oh yeah. I see it all the time, especially when they sign leases. But it's all good."

"Of course... it's all good."

"We're going to have fun at the event and not worry about it, okay?"

"Okay."

"That's my girl."

Chapter 42

August came and went without a word from Nate. And life went on. Arianna had regained her weight and even developed some muscle tone in her arms the way she'd hoped. As a runner, her legs were sharp, but her upper body she'd always believed lacking. She straightened her arm and watched her triceps pop. Arianna gave herself a nod. *Not bad.*

She checked out her appearance. She was wearing a conservative casual look. Her marigold jeans matched the sleeveless, printed turtleneck she tucked under a blazer of the same color. Even after Labor Day, the warmth gave her a Texas-sized excuse to dress vibrantly. With her hair in a cute ponytail, a few bangs left wispy, the perfect shade of mango cream on her lips, she looked bubblier than boiling water and felt cooler than an oscillating fan. A night out. She'd forgotten what that felt like, even if it was just a marketing event.

"I'll be back later, Darius. I'm on my cell. Don't go anywhere. And obey Gloria."

"Mom?"

"Yeah, Son?"

"Make sure you have a full tank of gas."

"How are you so mature? It amazes me."

"I don't have a choice. I want to survive living inside this house."

"Cute." Arianna kissed him on the forehead. "On a serious note, I am so proud of you."

"Come home safely," Darius said. "Dad's moved out and somebody has to raise me."

"Now, that's not funny, Son."

"Sorry."

"See you when I get home."

Arianna went into Tre's room, gave him a kiss, covered him up, and turned off the television. She thought about how much he looked like his father and felt relieved that he'd stopped asking for him.

She drove to the gym, taking twice as long to find a parking spot as it had taken to arrive at the facility. A Mercedes pulled out near the main entrance, and she took this as a sign that she was in the right place at the right time.

People eager to shed their old bodies packed the gym. The event offered free blood pressure checks and cholesterol screenings, as well as personal trainers on staff to answer questions. At one end, patrons enjoyed free salads. At another, a boxing ring gave them the opportunity to spar. Kids hustled on the basketball court. Arianna looked around for Anthony and spotted him talking to some parents near the court. He was wearing an event T-shirt and visor like the rest of his staff. He and Arianna caught eyes.

She smiled at Anthony. He excused himself and walked over to her. "Fashionably late. Well, it was worth it."

"Huge success. Congratulations." She smiled.

"Well, thank you, pretty lady." Anthony pinched lint off her blazer. "Your drinks are a hit." One of Anthony's staffers grabbed his attention. "I'll be right back."

Arianna walked through the gym, allowing Anthony to tend to business.

Each room had a different offering. In one a man gave her a fifteen-minute lecture on eating right. In another she picked up smoking cessation brochures for Nate's dad.

What am I doing with these? She set down the brochures.

307

"What's up?" Eva surprised her.

"Hey! What are you guys doing here?"

"We came to check out the gym thingy," Taesha said.

"Health fair, Taesha, health fair," Arianna said.

Taesha looked around. "I haven't seen this many hard bodies in my life."

"Wow, Taesha," Pam said. "Just wow."

"So, this is the crazy crew, huh?"

Arianna introduced her friends to Anthony. Eva hugged him. Pam smiled at him. Taesha nodded at him as if he owed her money.

"C'mon, let me show you guys my facility."

Anthony escorted the women throughout the gym, talked about his vision for the future, expansion, community activities, and the like. He cracked a few psychology jokes. Arianna's friends were impressed. Anthony was witty and well-spoken at the same time.

"Sup, Anthony?" A voice came from behind.

"Hey, wassup, man?" Anthony shook his friend's hand. "Hold on, I'll be right back." He walked a short distance away with his friend.

Arianna and her friends looked on. Anthony raised his eyebrows and nodded to his friend. Both men zeroed in on Arianna, letting her know she was the topic of their conversation.

"Stop staring, Taesha," Eva said. "It's not polite."

Taesha wouldn't take her eyes off Anthony. It was clear she was watching every move he made.

"I don't like this shit," Taesha said. "Maybe your first instincts were right all along, Arianna."

"What do you mean?"

"He's clearly talking about you, but didn't invite you over there to meet this guy."

"Who cares?" Arianna asked. "It's clear that he's letting people know about me."

"This dude has issues and an agenda."

"You think all dudes have issues and agendas," Arianna said.

"Just watch out."

Arianna's friends hung around until closing. They helped clean up, put the remaining food in the staff refrigerator, and packed up the unused coffee supplies. Anthony came out of the staff office wearing a white button-down shirt, black jeans, a gold necklace, a matching watch, and a stud in his ear. Home, apparently, was not part of the evening's agenda.

They all headed to the parking lot. Anthony thanked Arianna's friends, then asked Arianna if she wanted to go out. She hesitated, but then agreed, and asked Anthony for a couple of minutes alone with her friends.

"Well, this is it," she said. "My first date."

"I can feel the excitement all over the parking lot," Taesha said.

"Just try to enjoy yourself," Eva said. She looked in Anthony's direction. "He does look good."

Pam was quiet.

"Pam?"

"I told Marcus I was going to a marketing event. Now I have to go home and figure out what other delusion I can come up with to avoid telling my husband his best friend's estranged wife is dating."

"We're just friends, Pam," Arianna said. "But I won't go if it puts you in an uncomfortable position."

"Just like that?" Pam hugged Arianna tightly, a weird reaction with no reasonable cause. "This is how I know this man will never be Nate."

"Well, I have to do *something*," Arianna responded. "I—"

"I what?" Eva asked.

Arianna sighed. "Look, I love my kids, but"—Arianna shook her head—"I need a break from the house. I feel Nathan everywhere. Hell, his scent is still on the pillows, in the closet, the loveseat in the den, under the sink where Tre spilled his cologne. I *need* this."

Pam studied Arianna's face, then nodded. "I get it, Arianna. I do."

Arianna nodded in return. "I promise you, Pam, we are leaving as friends and we are returning as friends. That's it."

They said goodbye. Eva waved at Anthony from a distance. Pam gave him a half-hearted smile. Taesha looked dead at him, pointed to him, ran her hand down her face to symbolize tears, then pointed to Arianna, ran her forefinger across her throat, and lastly, pointed back at him.

Arianna got into Anthony's truck. He looked at her. "Did your friend just threaten to kill me?"

"Yep."

In the hour it took to reach exit 234C on I-35, Arianna learned about her date through his jazz fusion, which filled the interior with silky smoothness and a hint of hard edge. She watched Anthony's body shift, ever so cool. He squeezed her thigh and left his hand in place. She dared not put her hand on top of his, because it would remind her of Nate's maneuver of flipping his hand over and intertwining it with hers. She rode frozen in indecision, allowing Anthony to leave his hand on her body even though she wasn't sure if she wanted him to.

Arianna wondered about their destination. Austin offered such a variety of choices when it came to restaurants and nightlife, and Sixth Street was a city all its own.

Anthony drove down Sixth, crossing Red River. Arianna glanced at each awning, wondering where he could be taking her. He approached San Jacinto and made a left.

"Now I'm getting a little nervous."

He crossed over Fifth, then Fourth, then Third, before pulling up to the valet at the Hampton Inn. "I need a safe place to park. My cousin is a valet here. I have the hookup."

Anthony got out, shook hands with one of the valets, and handed over the keys. Another valet opened the door to let Arianna out. Anthony scooted him aside and took her hand. They walked around the hotel to Second Street. Arianna kept looking over her shoulder as if she were breaking the law.

They continued walking down Second, then made a right onto Brazos Street.

Arianna realized where they were going. "The Elephant Room?"

"Yeah. Come on." They made a left on Third, crossed over to a bank building, and passed a group of men wearing cowboy hats and boots, a reminder that they were in the capital city. Obviously born and bred in Texas, a true cowboy tipped his hat and said how-do.

"Hello," Arianna said.

They cut a right onto Congress and entered the building, passing the club's neon sign that rested close to the ground in a window, then walked down to the basement.

Rough brick encased the dark jazz club. Anthony spotted a small table in the back of the narrow room. They turned their chairs to watch the traditional jazz band jam. The musicians stood perched on a burgundy-carpeted platform. Arianna tapped her feet on the brown brick.

"So," Anthony said.

"So." Arianna smiled.

"How's work?" he asked.

"Well..."

"I guess you can tell it's been a while since I've dated." Anthony blushed.

"I won't hold it against you. My work is fine." Arianna untangled fallen strands of hair from her earring.

Anthony reached over to help. "There. Now you're perfect."

Humility caused Arianna to put her head down. Anthony lifted it back up. His smile wrapped her in softness, much like being swaddled inside a soft blanket. *Nathan used to look at me like that.*

Anthony took her back to his college days. Four years of football at Texas A&M and a lifelong rivalry with Pam's alma mater.

"Um, Pam graduated from UT."

Anthony held his heart like he was having a heart attack. "Say it isn't so."

Arianna giggled. She and Anthony were bonding surprisingly well. He enthralled her with talk about psychology and how intriguing the human mind was.

She in turn talked about coffee, probably a little more technically than any person should. What other conversation could she start? All she'd ever really known was Nate, kids, and caffeine, tacking on a little scrapbooking, three-mile morning runs, and an insane pack of sisters. Hers had been a simple existence with family and close, close, friends. And that had always been enough.

By the time they left, the temperature had fallen. The chill caused Arianna to snuggle closer to Anthony as they walked to the truck. He put his arm around her.

They pulled up to Arianna's Jeep at three a.m. The early morning stillness caused Arianna to remember Pam's phone call, the one that had occurred at that same hour months ago. She reminisced on how sound asleep her husband had been, and how defined his back had looked in the moonlight. *Nathan.*

Anthony turned off the ignition and placed his arm across the headrest.

"I hope you had a good time," he said.

"I did."

He leaned over as if to kiss her.

Never forget I need you, even if you feel the need to. The words from the night Shawnee died hit Arianna like a cement truck in overdrive. She backed up and tightened her lips.

Anthony seemed gracious about her rejection. He rested his other hand on her thigh. "Why are you so nervous?"

"I've never been unfaithful."

"He's in your past. Let me be your future. You don't need him." Anthony pulled away, respecting her enough to avoid pushing her. "I'll call you Monday."

"Thank you."

"For what?"

"For not pushing me."

He smiled. "You're welcome."

Arianna moved to exit the vehicle.

"Wait," Anthony said.

Arianna looked over at him. "Yeah?"

"Tomorrow morning. The track. You and me. The one by your job. I'll pick you up."

"Seriously?"

"As a heart attack. Sleep's overrated, right?"

Arianna thought of how much she needed a good run. Perhaps the fresh morning air would do her some good. She was uneasy about meeting Anthony again so soon, but at least the track would give her another focus, something to divert her from Nate. And Anthony *had been* good company tonight. Gloria wouldn't mind keeping the kids a couple extra hours anyway. "Okay. You're on." She opened the car door. "Let me go get a couple of hours of rest, so I can leave you in my dust tomorrow."

"Funny."

They laughed as they said goodnight.

Arianna drove home consumed with thoughts of Amaretto Sours, Reaction cologne, and a failed attempt at a second first kiss brought on by her own design. The date with Anthony had gone well, and true, they'd enjoyed some stolen moments when the pain of Nate eased, allowing Arianna to see the sensuality in another man. But the intimacy of Anthony's lips so close to hers made Arianna realize forgetting Nate was harder to forecast than coffee sales. She had no idea when, or if, she would ever get over him. The only concrete thing she knew was that Anthony's tongue was not about to enter her mouth tonight.

When she pulled up to the house, her thoughts went back to Knoxville, to the beach, to the water's edge—to the life she had begun with Nate as he held her on the blanket and told her to slide her tongue across his and to not be afraid. That night, she never imagined she would be parked in front of a home they had shared, reliving the moment, fighting to find some justification for almost letting another man's lips eclipse the memory of when she'd fallen in love with her Nathan.

Arianna went into the house. Taesha lay stretched out in the den. Arianna nudged her. "What are you doing here?"

"Darius called. Said Gloria doesn't know how to play Xbox properly."

Arianna shook her head. "That boy of mine."

"Did you have a good time?"

"It was really nice."

"Nice?"

"Yeah." Arianna sighed.

"Did Anthony behave himself?"

"Yes, Mother."

"So what's wrong?"

"Anthony was so sweet to me."

"That's good, right?"

Arianna let out a desperate breath. "I miss him, Taesha."

"I know. It's written all over everything you do."

"I can't believe I let it get so out of control. I can't even fix it now."

Taesha didn't respond.

"What? No blunt honesty here?"

They fell silent.

Arianna's voice cracked. "How'd it get so far gone? Nathan wants nothing to do with me now. Not even a vehicle."

"Arianna, I don't want to throw shade at you. But this is what you wanted. It's like you make these attempts to cut him out your life, but get mad when he takes you up on it."

"Just once, could you not be this honest?"

"No, because I wouldn't be a true friend."

"Wow, you said that like you meant it." Arianna had tried to lighten the mood, but Taesha was too serious. "What's wrong?"

"Come here." Taesha got up, and showed Arianna the pile of scrapbooks she'd gone through after Darius had dozed off. The pictures illuminated the woman Arianna used to be, from the innocence of her early twenties to the full life of her early thirties with Nathaniel Jackson. The parties, the picnics, the peace that once was, and the friendships they'd developed in San Antonio.

"I shouldn't have intervened like I did on Memorial Day. I get that now."

"Don't do this."

"I haven't been fair to you or Nate."

"That's not true."

"Look, Nate's a hard, hard man and he's making some dumb-ass decisions," Taesha continued, "But at the end of the day, Arianna, it's your baggage that's killing the marriage. Not his. Just like mine is killing my body, not these mindless men who never want anything else from me."

"Taesha."

"I'm here to help you through it. Pam's here to help you through it. Eva's here to help you through it. But none of us can carry it. If you don't drop it, you're gonna feel like crap no matter what relationship you start or which one you end. Look at me. You wanna talk about far gone? I can't even let D.J. take me on a real date. I don't even know what love feels like. At least you do."

"I wanna help you. What can I do?"

"Arianna, you can't do a damn thing for anybody until you do something for yourself. Not me, not Nate, nobody." Taesha studied Arianna's face. "I wanna ask you something."

"Okay."

"Are those nightmares really gone?"

Arianna didn't want to answer, but she couldn't fool the determined woman standing in front of her. "No. I just didn't want to keep answering questions about them."

"So you ran."

"Guess so. Hoped I could just push it down and move on like Nate did."

"Nate could storm through that door, sweep you off your feet, and it wouldn't mean a damn thing if you're not ready to receive him. Same with any man." Taesha scooted up closer as they stood over the scrapbooks. "Get some help, Arianna. Because I am tired of seeing my family in so much pain. Marcus was right. We are all we have."

Arianna nodded. "I get it."

"You've 'gotten it' too many times to count. Take action." Taesha looked at the clock on the wall. "C'mon up. It's late. We'll pick this up tomorrow."

"I will in a minute. Good night, Tae."

Taesha went upstairs. "We're not done here."

Arianna made herself some hot green tea before calling it a night. *It's my baggage.*

Exhausted, she headed straight to her bed.

I'm completely caught up in you, Arianna. Just like I promise to respect you and wait for you, I need you to promise me you won't mess up my head and leave me loving you and hating you at the same time."

"That's easy. I promise."

"I want this to work, Arianna. I need this to work."

"Then make it work, Nathaniel."

"Goddamn, you are so right for me.

Arianna took two more sips of her tea and cut out the light. "Good job keeping up with your part of the bargain, Arianna," she whispered to herself in the darkness. "And you have the nerve to call Nathan an idiot."

Chapter 43

Nightmare flashed a satisfied smile. Normally, he would walk away, leaving Arianna undone. But this time his eyes turned red. His teeth sharpened. His skin began melting. He grew into a hideous monster, something like the Alien with the human features of Jason. Blood dripped from his mouth and eyes. His penis morphed into a dagger as he crept toward her. This time, his words weren't cunningly and manipulatively kind. They weren't distorted compliments to lure her in. They were stones breaking her heart. "Do you really think he wants a deceitful, damaged soul like you? He really won't after I'm done scraping you to pieces." He came toward her.

She screamed for mercy.

"Arianna. Arianna."

Arianna opened her eyes and realized where she was. She gripped Taesha's arm. "Where are my kids?"

"Still asleep." Taesha studied her face. "Oh no, this one was different, wasn't it?"

Arianna panted. "He turned into a demon."

"That's it. Come hell or high water, you're getting help. I'll go make some coffee."

After Taesha left the room, Arianna grabbed Nate's former pillow, hoping somehow it had embalmed his breath and captured his comforting warmth. The longer she held it, the more deeply she regretted not telling him the truth. Despite Anthony trying to convince her that Nate had moved on, all she wanted was her husband. And she finally admitted to herself that her haste to take Nate's ring and kick him out was about more than just her devastation over Shawnee. Nate's choice of mistress was half reason, half scapegoat. Maybe not in that immediate moment; perhaps then it had been anger.

But when all was put away, and the walls closed in on counseling, Arianna knew she had needed an excuse to prevent herself from revealing Nightmare. Now, however, it was ten times worse. She'd hauled Nate through the fire over Shawnee. How would he react when she told him that she'd maximized Shawnee to minimize Nightmare? Nate's potentially insane reaction, her years of shame surfacing and, worse, the silence that had put Nate through hell would now have a voice. Arianna couldn't cope with all the facets of the potential fallout. This morning, with the mutation of Nightmare, she had come to the sad realization of how much deeper her lie had grown and how much more convoluted the affair had become. Telling Nate now, more than ever, seemed a nightmare in itself. *What the hell do I do now?*

Arianna heard a light kick on the bedroom door. She let Taesha into the room and grabbed a cup of coffee from Taesha's full hands. They sat on the bed.

"I feel like I'm going crazy, Tae."

"That's why you need to talk to somebody."

Arianna nodded in concession. "I know. I knew the day I got my mom's letter. Life just kept handing me excuses not to seek it." She thought of her mutated nightmare. "But now, it's gone way too far." She shook her head. "The kids, Taesha. It's a matter of time before they sense something's wrong with me."

"If they don't sense something already."

The doorbell rang relentlessly. Arianna looked at the clock. It was eight thirty. "Who the hell is this?" She threw on some track pants and went downstairs to answer the door. Taesha followed.

"Good morning." Anthony held up a box of donuts. "I figured a little sugar before our run would give us a boost."

Arianna dipped her head at her forgetfulness. "Anthony, I'm sorry. I forgot about the track."

"Why are your eyes red? You been crying?" he asked.

Arianna looked at Taesha. She was tired of lying, tired of nightmares, tired of being tired. "Give us a few minutes, Taesha."

Taesha nodded and went upstairs.

In Arianna's frustration, she almost bared it all at the door. "I haven't been crying. But I haven't been sleeping either."

"What? Why?"

"Just come in. Coffee?"

"Sure."

Arianna led Anthony into the kitchen. He sat on a barstool. She poured him a cup of coffee, then searched for her artificial sweetener, fishing throughout the cabinet, shifting items to find the box. Her nerves caused her to fumble through the pantry less eloquently than she would have liked. Anthony asked her what had her so rattled. "Hold on, Anthony."

Nate's old, expired protein powder was in the corner, hidden behind Arianna's stockpile of plastic grocery bags. She stopped moving grocery items and stared at the tub, allowing a few seconds of picturing Nate in her kitchen to calm her, yet also slap her into the reality that Nate wasn't the man sitting at her kitchen counter, asking her what was wrong.

Again, her thoughts focused on her husband, all the confusion she'd put him through. Yes, she needed counseling, but Anthony wanted to provide more than just counseling, and she knew that. He wanted a relationship. Telling Anthony about her past would be the ultimate betrayal. How could she spill her soul to a friend, business partner, *date*, whatever she wanted to call him, after totally disregarding her husband for two years?

319

Arianna glanced at Anthony. He was looking around her house, obviously absorbing her world. Then the reality of another man in Nate's soon-to-be former home gutted her like a fish to the slaughter.

Arianna found the sweetener and served the coffee to her houseguest, less eager for his presence.

"What's wrong, Arianna?"

She shook her head. "I shouldn't have invited you inside. I'm sorry."

"Don't be silly." Anthony's voice softened the mood, like a velour blanket, draping Arianna's skin. "Talk to me."

"I can't."

Anthony gently grabbed her hand. "Please. I don't bite."

"It's not that simple."

"It can be, sweetie. Whatever is wrong, it's killing you. I can tell."

Arianna sighed under his benevolence and her blatant weariness. Maybe she could get some insight from him without divulging every detail, without feeling as if she was betraying her husband, even though she wasn't sure how long Nate would hold that title. At some point, she had to unload it. "I can't tell you everything. All I can tell you is that I'm having nightmares that won't stop. And I know I need help."

Anthony didn't push for details. "Do you want to describe the nightmares to me?"

She paused before answering, still unsure of what to say. "When I was young, something *bad* happened to me. And the guy who's responsible keeps haunting me."

"Was it ra—"

"Dear God, don't make me say it."

Anthony angled his neck in what looked like profound sympathy. "I'm so sorry."

Arianna thought of the latest nightmare, how she'd been just a few seconds shy of a shredded vagina. "I gotta get rid of this boogeyman. And I don't know where to begin."

"It's hard for me to give advice when I don't know everything."

"Let's just say he's repeating his acts in my dreams."

"It sounds like you do need therapy. And acknowledging that you need help *is* where you begin. Seems to me, you've already taken the first step. Now you just have to keep walking."

She looked down at her coffee cup, then shifted her eyes up to him. "Can you recommend somebody?"

"Well, me, of course."

"You know I can't talk to you."

"Sure, you can."

Arianna stared at him. "Anthony, I'm begging you. *Please* don't push me."

Anthony hesitated before responding, but kept his voice soft and understanding. "Tell me why I can't help you?"

Arianna looked at the pantry, thought of the protein powder that had jolted her into reality. Then she looked at Anthony and answered in a way that she hoped would cushion his feelings. "I need somebody who can be objective. And you know that's not you. I have to separate this from my personal life."

Anthony sighed in a combination, it seemed, of disappointment and agreement, slowly and with a couple of nods of his head. "I get it. I do." Then he grinned at her with soft eyes, in what seemed like signs of admiration and affection. "I'll find somebody good. *Really* good."

"Thank you."

"No problem, pretty lady."

"How does therapy work? I just talk it out?"

"Well, there are methods we can discuss, hypnotherapy, etcetera. It depends on what your therapist decides is best." Anthony squinted, then bit his lip, as if the wheels of his mind were turning, as if gazing on opportunity. "I, for one, am very aggressive in my approach."

"Aggressive?"

"Yeah."

"Explain."

"I make my patients own the problem and face it, literally."

"What do you mean?"

Anthony didn't answer the question. He cut his eyes toward Arianna instead. "Where is this guy? Do you know?"

"Prison."

"I see. Where?"

"Not sure. I just know he's locked up somewhere."

"Texas?"

"Probably Tennessee, I would guess."

Anthony hesitated, then perked up as if he'd had an idea that would save the world. "You know I work in prison systems."

"Yeah, you told me." Arianna thought of the question he hadn't answered. "What does *face it, literally*, mean?"

"I conduct serious, controlled intervention therapy involving confrontation."

Arianna didn't give his comment much personal thought. "Well, you can cross me off that list."

"Why? It's highly effective."

Arianna studied Anthony's eager face. "Why are you looking at me like that?"

"Just thinking."

She backed up, eyes wide, now having a good idea of his thoughts. Anthony wanted Arianna to confront Nightmare. "Oh, heck no."

"I know you don't want me involved..." Anthony paused. "But I think this can work for you. At least show you this guy isn't a supernatural monster."

Arianna almost dropped her cup. She started to shake. Therapy was one thing. Jumping to a face-to-face interaction seemed not only too fast, but too frightening. "*Face* him? Really?"

"Heck, yeah. Let him know he doesn't own you."

Arianna raised her voice. "I just *now* got the courage to seek help, and you want to put us in the same room?"

"I know it's extreme, but if you don't stop these dreams, you're gonna disconnect from society. I've seen it happen. That's why I do this."

"*Now?*"

"As soon as I can set it up, yeah."

Arianna felt as if she'd suddenly fallen with no warning and was now piecing herself back together. Facing Nightmare had never been on her radar, and the shock of this idea left her reeling. "Don't I need to prepare?"

"Prepare?"

"You know, psych myself up or something."

"No. I just need to make sure that you're protected. Which shouldn't be a problem. I can do these in my sleep."

Arianna looked for any reason to avoid this confrontation, to dismiss Anthony's profound and accurate point—that seeing Nightmare in the flesh would make her realize that he *was* just a man—because some points were also double-edged swords. Turning Nightmare back into a man would also send her back to the days of his horrible reign. "I don't need counseling first?"

"Some people do, but you don't."

"Why not?"

"Because you're considered a highly functioning victim. If you hadn't told me you were struggling, I never would have known anything was emotionally wrong."

Arianna thought of her crumbling marriage. "I'm not *that* highly functioning, believe me."

"Why not hit it head on?"

"Geeze, I don't know about this, Anthony."

He talked about how serious the effects of nightmares could become. He told Arianna she could potentially disconnect from society if they got worse. Then he mentioned her children and how seeing their mother frantic could hurt them in the long run, something she already knew.

After fifteen minutes of listening to Anthony's reasoning, and thinking of Darius and Tre, she was almost in agreement, inching her way closer to Tennessee. "This is a *huge* step."

Anthony grabbed her hand. "You *need* this, Arianna."

Arianna sat in silence for few moments, thinking of possible outcomes—what could go wrong, what could go right. Nightmare could send her further into a spiral. But she could also leave the prison having faced her fears and, at the very least, having taken a step further to healing. In thinking of her place in life now, what did she *really* have to lose? If she didn't do this, her life would spiral out of control anyway. "Okay, give me a few days to process it first."

"Process it? If you process it, you won't go. We need to strike while the iron's hot, Arianna."

"You make it sound like it's a battle."

"It is. One you need to fight before you give up all hope."

Once again, Arianna knew Anthony was right. At least in this moment, something was driving her in his direction. Whether it was adrenaline, hope, anger, or Anthony's steadfast advocacy of this idea, Arianna could picture herself standing in front of her manmade, mythical creature and telling him to go straight to hell. She took one more breath before making the decision that could change her life and end her nightmares. "I'll go."

Anthony seemed happy, almost too happy. "I'll make the arrangements."

He immediately began phoning friends in the Tennessee prison system. Arianna gave Anthony Nightmare's real name. He passed it on to his colleagues, and searched the Web. Arianna would have been impressed with his diligence if he hadn't seemed so eager. But she chalked up his haste to concern, wanting to see her set free of her chains.

"Okay," Anthony said. "I found him."

"That quickly?"

"I'm good like that."

"I see."

"It'll take a couple days to set it up though. But definitely doable the middle of next week."

"Next *week*?" Arianna felt another wave of anxiety, her stomach rumbling with the feeling of impending vomit. "That soon?"

"It's okay. You can do this."

In that moment, she almost backed out, but the thought of *finally* ending the nightmare of Nightmare spurred her courage, even though she couldn't stop shaking. "This *will* work, right?"

"My expertise says yes."

She gave it one final thought, one last chance to reverse course, and held strong. "Okay, what's the next step?"

Anthony hopped onto the computer. "I'll arrange us flights. Let's look at tickets."

"Now? *Us*?" Arianna grabbed his arm before he could start to book tickets. "Anthony, stop."

"What's wrong?"

"This is all happening so fast. We don't even have a solid date yet." She brought her hands up and shook them in short, quick strokes. "Just slow down. Remember, I have children to think about in this travel plan."

Her agitation must have been apparent. Anthony took a deep breath and seemed to calm his excitement. "I'm sorry. I just know this can help. I got hyped up, that's all."

"I see that." She walked a few feet away and looked out the window, saying nothing.

Anthony came up behind her. "Look, if you want to wait on this a while, we will. I'll back off. But I do think waiting is a mistake."

Arianna thought again of Nightmare turning into a demon, and knew Anthony's expertise counted for something. While she was fairly confident she wouldn't face a psychotic break, she was sure that another sinister nightmare would send her over the edge of being able to parent effectively. "I don't wanna wait."

"Good."

Arianna swallowed. "But I do need to make my own flight arrangements."

"Why?"

"You know why."

"You don't want me to come with you."

"I have to do this without you."

The disappointment in Anthony's voice was apparent. "Arianna."

"Just like I can't see you for therapy, I can't travel with you either. I know you want to help. And you are. But I *cannot* cross this line with you. We have to find another way to do make this confrontation happen. I'm still married. Please understand."

"So, this is about your husband."

"It's about my family. It's about my self-respect. I need you to *get* this, Anthony. If you don't, then I can't see you anymore."

"Don't say that." Anthony turned her around and zeroed in on her eyes. He responded convincingly. "I'm just being selfish. I'm sorry." He took a deep breath. "I understand. I really do. It's actually refreshing to be around a woman who has class. I have a colleague in Tennessee who can meet you. I just want to make sure everything goes smoothly. Hell, maybe I am pushing you too hard."

Arianna gave him a soft look and spoke sweetly. "I'm not stupid, Anthony. I know myself, and I have to be honest. Whether I had weeks of counseling or not, this confrontation wouldn't be any easier, and I wouldn't be any more prepared. It's going to go as smoothly as it's going to go, with or without you there. But I am so grateful to you."

"Can we at least meet up when you get back?"

"Sure."

"I don't want you to be without a friend."

"I won't be." Arianna looked up, as if looking to the second floor. "I'm gonna take Taesha."

"Taesha? What about your business?"

"I have a next-in-line. And my secretary is more than capable of holding things down administratively for a couple of days." Arianna thought of Jenna. "She's trendy, but she gets the job done."

"I'll be thinking of you."

Arianna smiled at him. "I know." Then she nodded upstairs. "I need to talk to Taesha. We have to hash out a plan for the trip."

"Yeah, of course."

"I'll be down in a little bit. Help yourself to more coffee." Arianna went upstairs to discuss the issue with Taesha, feeling Anthony's eyes scaling her. *This has to work.*

Chapter 44

Nate found himself reading the fine print of his new lease, all twenty pages of it, while standing in his empty apartment. He reviewed the details, including the pet policy and the quiet-hour ordinance.

Rudi, the leasing agent, attempted to make small talk. Nate wasn't interested. He kept his mouth shut and his eyes on the lease.

When he was finished, he took one last skim through the papers and signed for twelve months. His only question was how late the weight room stayed open. Then he handed Rudi the lease and demanded his copy. Rudi agreed and left for the leasing office.

Nate walked alone around his vacant apartment, allowing him solitude to analyze his vacant life.

He went to the kitchen counter and picked up the clipboard with a triplicate inspection form attached to it. A scratch on the living room floor, he checked off. Two tiny chips in the paint in the dining room, he checked off. He made his way to the second bedroom and annotated crayon markings about three feet high. He opened the closet and noticed a small black line on the wall labeled "3 feet 9 inches," and then one above it labeled "4 feet 1 inch." He smiled, not noting this flaw.

His lawyer called, allowing Nate to forget how tall Tre was getting. He walked into the living room, leaned against the wall. "Give Arianna everything," he told the lawyer. "Just keep my ass out of court."

"If you give her everything, she will take everything."

"Can she take my health?"

"No."

"My job?"

"No."

"ESPN?"

"This is no time for jokes."

"Can she?"

The lawyer sighed. "No, Nate, no."

"My ability to reproduce?"

"No...well, yes, if she were clever enough, but that's not the point. Why are you acting so nonchalant?"

"It's just money."

"C'mon, Nate. You're hurting and you're not thinking."

"Are you my shrink now?"

"I'm not trying to be."

"Just make sure I get a fair shake with my kids. Make it happen."

Nate hung up. He grabbed the clipboard and continued with details, checkmarks, and memories. He thought back to how excited his family had been when they'd first moved to San Antonio. He remembered Darius running around his big bedroom before the furniture had arrived, and how Arianna had spent two hours figuring out how to position the patio swing.

Nate threw the clipboard, the papers scattering all over the empty living room. He leaned against the wall, slid his body down to the floor, and sat there, head in hands, for a good hour.

Time was a rare gem. He'd missed so many milestones and memories. To feel better, he thought about the material possessions he had provided for his family. But a ninety-dollar pair of basketball shoes for Darius meant little if Nate wasn't there to compete against him on the court. It seemed ironic. All the stuff he'd worked to buy, and now emptiness surrounded Nate in the name of proving a point.

He called Marcus. "It's done."

"Went smooth?"

"Yeah."

"You good?"

"I will be."

"Damn, your ass is really gone."

"Yep." Nate paused. Then it hit him. Marcus was no longer living around the corner. Another few seconds of silence passed as Nate tried to figure out what to say. "Marcus, look..."

"Nate, stop. I get it. I *hate* it. But I get it."

"I could try to reach out, but she's not gonna be receptive. I moved up here permanently and still not a word."

"I know."

"Marcus, I screwed up, especially picking Shawnee, but I fought like hell for Arianna."

"Fought isn't the word."

"Maybe when it's my turn to have the boys, you can bring them."

"Until then..." Marcus's voice lowered, not completely cracking, but chipping away. "You watch your back."

"You too. I gotta go."

Nate hung up before he could release the true sadness of saying goodbye to his best friend, goodbye to his boys, goodbye to the city where he'd planned to spend retirement with his family and friends, and goodbye to his Ani.

He began facing the reality of never again living under the same roof as his wife, never again enjoying intimacy with her, a rare intimacy born not only of sex, but of a bond so tightly woven that he could express his deepest feelings without saying a word, and never feel required to explain his actions or defend his position—an intimacy that came from never being judged for his flaws, or bitched at for not doing enough, a comfort he could take in knowing that his woman knew him well enough to never doubt he was doing all he could. Nate closed his eyes, missing Arianna, trapped inside his own intimate nightmare.

He grabbed his keys, opened the front door, and walked out of the apartment, trying to convince himself that he was another divorced male needing a way to live up to the notion that at least he had no strings, so he could have fun again. But Nate didn't care about fun. He needed anger because that was the only way he could forget how much he'd loved being tied down to the only woman he'd felt was worth the sacrifice. With each step closer to the sidewalk, he repeated to himself what was becoming a mantra about the inevitable divorce, that it was Arianna's loss and damn her for not accepting the part she'd played in destroying the family.

"As God is my witness, I love her, but I give up."

Nate hit the streets of Baltimore, a new permanent resident, trying his best to forget he had a hole in his heart the size of Texas.

Chapter 45

"One part cream, two parts caramel," Arianna whispered as she wrote. Her recipes came to her whimsically. Whenever the spirit moved her, she would write a recipe like a songwriter might create a tune. Sometimes she would create them based on her mood. If she was angry, she used hot water along with sour tastes such as lemon or other citrus. If she was happy, lots of fruit. If she was horny, lots of syrup and cream. She named her drinks as an expression of how she felt. Her latest, a caramel latte laced with a hint of apple and cinnamon, called "Nervous."

"No, Arianna, we are *not* naming a drink *Nervous*. Stop it." Taesha grabbed the notebook.

"Give me my notebook."

"No." Taesha read the recipe. "And you better add some sugar to sweeten this thing up. Next thing you know, you're gonna throw some shit together and call it *Therapy*."

Arianna grabbed her notebook. "Fine." She started writing again. She added ginger to the recipe and named it "Confrontation."

Taesha looked over at the recipe. "Wow, you got issues."

"Flight attendants, prepare for takeoff," the captain said.

Arianna closed her notebook and locked her tray into place. A few seconds later, she felt the speed of the airplane push her back into the seat. Soon, she would be in the air and, with luck and no stumbling blocks, on her way to closure.

Taesha and Arianna arrived at the hotel around one p.m. and checked in. The suite was comfortable, with two queen-sized beds and a flat-screen television. Arianna fell onto her mattress, feeling free of normal routine. She received a text from Anthony. *There safely?*

"This is alright, Arianna. Look at these towels."

"Taesha?"

"Yeah, what's up?"

"Anthony. He seemed *very* upset that I wouldn't let him come with me."

Taesha stopped perusing the fine things, mellowed out, and sat next to Arianna. "Look, you're not stupid, Arianna. You gotta know he wants to be more than friends. He thought this trip would get him in good...and *in* other things."

"You think planning this was an angle?"

"Partly, mostly...some of it."

Arianna nodded and sighed in acceptance. Taesha was accurate in her assessment. Arianna *was* confused, but far from dumb. "You're right. I think he *wants* to help," she lowered her voice to a level of sadness, "but he also wants more. I saw his eagerness when he started planning this trip. I overlooked it, not wanting to see it."

"You have to decide what you're gonna do when you get back."

"It's just..." Arianna shook her head. "Nate waited until I was ready. I thought maybe Anthony would too."

"Well, first of all, Anthony isn't Nate. And it's a nonissue because you're never gonna be ready to sleep with anybody *but* Nate. You know that."

"If I tell Nate now, I don't even know if it'll matter. I've made such a catastrophe of things."

Taesha paused before responding, more than likely to think of ways to refrain from driving the knife into Arianna's heart with her blunt honesty. Everyone knew Arianna had created the mess. "Let's get through the trip, and then see how it plays out. You'll probably have a much clearer perspective then."

"God, I hope so."

Chapter 46

The gold-framed portrait in Nate's hand had an autumn background. Yellow and orange leaves created a patchwork of warm colors in a forest. Rays from the sun rained down between the trees. Arianna wore a banana-colored sweater with her straight hair framing her face in long layers. She had on soft pink lipstick and sparkles on her cheeks. Her huge smile showed her straight white teeth. Nate ran his hand down the glass before slamming the picture and the expensive frame into the trash.

His carved nameplate, fired in a shiny glaze reading *Nathaniel Darius Jackson, Jr.*, the memento the same lady whose image was now in the garbage had given him, found the same fate.

"What does it matter, right?" Nate talked into the trash can in his government office, as if Arianna could hear him. "It's not like you're ever gonna forgive me anyway."

Nate felt as if he'd tried everything and said everything possible to make things right. He'd finally gotten to the point where he'd gone against all that he'd learned from his dad about standing strong and all he'd tried to instill in his children. Nate had completely, totally, absolutely, positively, and in its entirety, given up.

He gathered the keepsakes he'd collected over the last couple of years. Paperweights once full of love now seemed like dead weight. Nate's little statue of the pudgy golf man ready to swing and the coffee mug he used as his pencil holder never stood a chance. He started throwing all his reminders into the trash. After his mental tirade, Nate looked around at his framed accomplishments, certificates and letters of commendation on one wall, his degrees and his honors accolades on the opposite wall, giving him a reason to boast about how lucky Arianna used to be, and how tired he was of being demonized for things he'd done in the past, things he would do in the future, and things he hadn't done at all.

With the exception of a calendar and the usual supplies, the top of the desk was now barren.

Nate hurried to pack up for the day. His team had planned to meet at the Harbor later, and he needed extra time to prepare to meet them. He was determined to test his single skills. To ensure success, he needed to look good and smell good, and the pickup lines needed to flow off his lips without a ripple. Practice and preparation were essential. He would never let on, even to his closest friends, that domestic life had taken his game.

The plan: don't commit to anyone, much less fall in love. His measure of success would be a full social calendar with no strings. He still had the hotel room. Perfect. He could take pleasure in turning a woman out without worrying she would stalk him at home.

Before leaving his office for the day, Nate did online research into Baltimore lawyers, because he was considering firing the one he'd already retained in Texas. He wanted a smooth divorce for his children but also a thorough break from Arianna. Nate felt the lawyer in Texas was so focused on drawing blood that he was incapable of listening to Nate's wishes.

He set an appointment for the next day, Friday. Before ending the call, the lawyer asked for clarification on one issue, Nate's name.

"Do you want her to keep your last name?"

"Why wouldn't I?"

"Don't snap at me, Nate. I've seen this get ugly before."

"She's the mother of my children. She's keeping my name." Nate slammed down the phone and stormed out of his office, keeping tied to the self-inflicted strings he swore he didn't want.

Chapter 47

Taesha hit I-40. Arianna sat anxiously in the passenger seat, thinking the exit just outside Knoxville would never come. She started to shake when she saw the sign for the cemetery.

Taesha pulled into the parking lot and shut off the engine. "Here we are."

Arianna looked at the headstones. She thought back to the last time she'd seen her mother, the day Nate had driven her away to a new and wonderful life. "She could have had so much more, Tae."

Taesha grabbed her hand and spoke softly. "I know."

Arianna took a deep breath and got out of the car. Then she looked back at Taesha. "C'mon."

"I thought you needed to do this alone."

"Nah, I'd like you there."

The shiny, deep green lawn made Arianna feel like she was walking on top of soft emeralds. Stone statues of angels praying stood along the concrete walkway. Strategically placed trees and mums provided enough shade along the path. She passed two brick pillars. Her stomach unraveled a little more with each step, bringing her closer to the marble headstone. There it was, a long time coming.

"Hey, Mama." Arianna placed a bouquet of white roses in the decanter with a card that read: *Love, Darius and Tre.* She sat down, got comfortable, and tinted her jeans with the Tennessee dirt. For a minute, Arianna said nothing as she realized how close she was currently sitting to the mother she'd last seen alive over a decade ago.

Finally, she opened up. "I'm *so* sorry that I didn't attend your service, Mom. But I didn't want Dad to disrespect it."

Arianna told her mother she'd gone to the hospice to thank the staff for the care they had given her, and in return, the staff had given Arianna the address to the nursing home, in case she had a desire to visit. She'd briefly entertained the idea, but couldn't stomach it.

This led to her wanting to know why things had happened the way they had with her dad, his hatred of people, his loathing of life. Arianna had so many questions, the types of questions somebody wouldn't think of until they'd grown up. How come her parents hadn't had more children? What made her father so hateful? Arianna had heard rumors about how they'd met, that her mother had been a prostitute and ended up pregnant with her, and that was why she'd married Arianna's father, a man much older than her mother. Later, she'd heard that her mother was a scared, lonely woman who'd felt trapped. But her mom seemed too feisty and, at times, too street to come off as frightened. Arianna had never followed up as a teenager because she hadn't wanted the truth back then. Maybe, now that she was older, she would conduct research to find out things she'd never known.

Arianna talked for an hour more, filling her mother in on her life, her family, and her loyal friendships. Pam she gloated on. Eva she praised. Taesha she defended for being crazy, causing some laughter between the women.

When Arianna had no more places left to run, no more fluffy conversations to hide inside, the tears came, along with thoughts of her last conversation with her mother, the last time anything felt completely right. Then the words of the letter, laced with a mother's love and hard lessons, overtook her.

"I couldn't bring myself to tell Nathan. Now it's backfired on me. My husband is gone. I'm trying to be strong. I gotta face Nightmare tomorrow, and all I want is for Nathan to step in and snap his neck. But I know this is my fight. No man can step in all the time and be my superhero. This is all me. I've come a long way, in more ways than one, and I will do this. It's just so hard."

Deep down, Arianna knew her mother wouldn't be mad at her for withholding what had happened, but asking for forgiveness acknowledged her mother's place in Arianna's life. That wisdom made the feeling of reverence concrete, made it something she could almost touch, something she could feel in her heart. It gave her strength, strength to slow the tears, strength to stand, strength to dust herself off and be grateful for all she had accomplished since Nate had left. Arianna could almost hear her: "Get up and move forward, Arianna."

She kissed her mother's headstone, determined to do just that. The two women started to walk off. Then Taesha suddenly stopped.

"You okay, Tae?" Arianna asked.

"Could we go back for a minute? It'd be nice to sit with your mother some more, since I never really got to sit with mine. I guess yours is the closest I will ever get."

Arianna smiled. "Sure."

They went back to the gravesite. Arianna knew Taesha was reliving her mother's drug addiction and her life with her grandparents as a result of her mother's fatal overdose. Cremation had been more affordable than burial, so Taesha's grandparents had made the decision. The ashes had been scattered in the Hudson. Taesha's mother had dreamt of places far away, though she could never leave. At least in death, she could do what she couldn't in life.

But not having a burial spot for her mother had left Taesha with no sense of closure.

The women sat in the dirt again as Taesha rocked back and forth. "Is this weird?" she asked.

"Nah," Arianna replied. "She doesn't have to be alive to be your mother too."

Chapter 48

Nate walked along the Harbor with his coworkers. A few of them were younger than he was and a few were older. Some black, some white, one Asian. A solid team, unified. What happened within the group stayed within the group, as long as Dave could keep down his down-home voice.

The remains of the day brought them outside the Hard Rock Café as evening made its appearance. Waiting for an outside table, Nate looked to the old power plant, trying to decide whether or not to go to the ESPN Zone instead. Then he looked to the Barnes and Noble and thought about buying Arianna a pretty calendar for the upcoming year, perhaps as a peace offering for a civil divorce. He changed his mind.

Thursday made no difference to the mass of people getting a jump on the weekend, nor did the chill. Nate soaked up the double-takes from the vultures who kept admiring him. A waitress brought him a beer and then pointed to the sexy patron who had sprung for it.

Nate tipped his bottle, then tasted his beer as he tasted his freedom.

He'd just sat down when his eyes, roaming over a couple of tables, locked onto "Hawaii." She sat well-endowed. Her skin glowed in Nate's direction as her soft, sleek black hair moved to the rhythm of her neck. She wore the proverbial little black number, but made it unique enough that Nate wanted to take a trip to Honolulu.

Without hesitation, and with very little thought, Nate went back... way back... to his old ways.

Laticia gave him a judgmental look as he got up.

Dave followed, calling for him before Nate could get far. "You're about to tear her up like she's an eviction notice, ain't ya, playa?"

"You really need to stop... but hell yeah."

Surprisingly, Dave became serious. "You sure this is the path you wanna walk down, Jack?"

"It's over, G... my marriage is so dead maggots are eating it."

Dave gave an analyzing nod. "Okay." He went back to the table.

Nate signaled to his island admirer to meet him inside the Hard Rock. He gave her his room number and told her to meet him in an hour. Hawaii didn't offer her name and Nate didn't ask. She must not have cared. She never asked Nate who the hell *he* was.

A colleague had ordered him another beer. Nate enjoyed his drink with his comrades and then left the party to start his own.

This time, it was Laticia who followed. "I'm not good enough, but a complete stranger is? Are you kidding me?"

"Don't make a scene. I don't want my business plastered everywhere. You're good at that."

"Excuse me?"

"I don't want strings. And I damn sure don't want drama."

"Damn, Nate, you're conceited. I'm not in love with you, Mr. Ego."

"No, it's much worse. You're in love with yourself." Nate stared her down, then walked away, nonverbally telling Laticia to get on with her life.

Chapter 49

Nate put on a black muscle shirt and wind pants, something easy. As he'd predicted, Hawaii showed up on time, yet with a surprise...her friend. Five nine, smooth ivory skin. Both were ready to give him a go.

Nate looked them up and down.

"This is Anita. She wants in." Hawaii nodded.

"You can stay, but she's gotta go." Nate pulled Hawaii inside and slammed the door.

"You want me all to yourself, huh?" She winked.

"I'm too old for threesomes. Besides, I don't like her name."

Hawaii dropped her coat. "I must be lucky because you don't even know *my* name."

"Must be."

"Nice room. You don't live around here?"

"No."

She strutted to the chair by the window, crossed her legs, and showed off her heels. Nate grabbed beers for them both.

Her tongue enveloped the bottle. Nate made his way under her dress.

"Slow down. I don't even know your name."

"That's because I didn't give it to you."

"Well, my name's Penny. Like for your thoughts."

"I don't do clichés. And please don't answer questions I didn't ask."

Penny backed Nate up. "I need to know more."

"Like what? You're horny, I'm horny. Let's go."

"Age for starters." She put the bottle back to her mouth.

"Old enough to know what to do. Young enough to keep doing it."

"I like a man who's ambiguous. Diseases?"

"Yeah, I'm very contagious."

"Cute. Hobbies?" She sipped.

"Sports, work, typical."

"No play?"

"Not lately. We almost done?"

"Almost. Kids?"

"Two."

"Romantic?"

"Can be. Have been."

"What's the most romantic thing you've ever done? And don't say make love in the shower. That's soooo played."

"The rain. Actually a thunderstorm."

"Where?" Penny pushed him down on the bed.

"Don't push me."

"Where?"

"Where what?"

"The rain."

"My backyard, if you must know." Nate looked out the window.

"Married? Don't lie."

"Not for long."

"With her? The thunderstorm, I mean." She kissed his chest.

"You're nosy."

"Tell me." She moved her lips toward his.

"It's private." Nate's low mood dipped lower. "And I don't kiss women that I don't—"

"You don't kiss women you don't know, huh? Well then, get to know me." She brushed her lips on his. He pushed her up.

"I don't kiss women I don't love."

Penny kissed him from his neck to his abdomen. "Tell me about the thunderstorm." She ran her tongue around his navel.

"Some things are between a husband and his soon-to-be ex-wife."

"You think she's not somewhere getting off telling another man her war stories? Please. The only thing between you two right now is other people." Penny moved lower, below the belt, twice. "I guess it's too painful for you. Some men are just weak like that."

Nate reached up under Penny's arms, stopping her progress. She looked up.

"I don't feel pain," Nate said. "And I'm sure as hell not weak."

"Prove it," Penny said. "Tell me."

Nate stared into her eyes. "If you must know, we were fighting. She can't stand it when I leave. I flung the back door open and hid inside. She ran outside and I slid the door shut behind her."

"And then?" Penny asked.

Nate sucked his teeth.

"And then?" she asked again.

"I pressed against the glass, gloating like a child."

"Please, continue." Penny kissed Nate's lower abdomen. He closed his eyes, remembering vividly. "And then I saw her, really saw her. Her shirt and jeans stuck to her from the rain as she begged for me to let her in."

"She got soaked?" Penny bit his chest.

"Yeah. I could see her breasts through her shirt. She could tell I was turned on. She stopped begging."

"She stayed in the rain?"

"She put her hand under her shirt and made this face." Nate gestured. "I can't even describe it. Damn, it was sexy. She slid her other hand into her jeans. Her hands moved in harmony with her breath. She licked the glass and got on her knees."

"Do I have to ask what you did?"

"I couldn't do anything but watch her beauty as her hands worked. She slid up, watching me watch her. She took off her shirt and then her pants. The way she wiggled out of them, goddamn."

"No man is worth catching pneumonia." Penny gripped the waist of Nate's pants. "Did you finally let her in?"

Nate rubbed his forehead. "She bent her neck back and then her eyes locked on mine. It felt like I was dreaming. She made herself come and I lost my mind. I flung the door open, lifted her off the patio, and tackled her like she was a wide receiver. Next thing you know, she's screaming my name while I'm pounding her. We were naked in the wet grass, not caring if we got struck by the lightning."

"You remember all that detail?"

"Every turn, every scream, but most of all I remember what she said to me."

"Words don't mean shit." Penny came back up and bit his nipple.

"Sometimes they mean everything." Nate fought his tears. "Especially when your wife says you're so romantic and you haven't even done shit or spent a dime. Or says she feels at home with you. I think that was one of the rare times I told her I loved her."

"You're pathetically lonely." Penny slipped her hand inside Nate's pants. "To tell all this to a complete stranger."

"You do a lot of shit when you're lonely."

Penny massaged Nate in a futile effort to lift his mood, and his blood flow. He lay spellbound in his memories. Penny's mouth made its way down in another effort to arouse him.

"Hold on, Ani...I mean, P—"

"Oh, no you did not. I'm about to put your dick in my mouth and you're gonna call me another woman's name? You *are* pathetic."

"What the hell am I doing?" he whispered before pushing Penny up. "Thanks, but I'll pass."

"You didn't unload your baggage on me for free."

"You don't have to go home." He got up and threw her coat to her. "But you know the rest."

"You're a typical dog."

"You're about to screw a man you don't even know. You deserve to get dogged. It's not gonna work anyway. Do you wanna waste your time and mine?"

"I guess you're right. I hate screwing limp-ass men with issues." Penny fixed her dress and slammed the door behind her.

Nate dialed. Nobody picked up at home, and Arianna's cell phone was off. He called the house again, but the phone continued to ring without clicking over to the answering machine. He was about to call her cell phone again to leave a message, but had a better idea, although he knew it might involve taking enemy fire. *I can't believe my stupid ass was going to let her go.*

He gathered a few personal items and flung open the door.

Dave was waiting outside the room. "Need a ride?"

Nate nodded in agreement, in a way that showed he shouldn't have been surprised. He gave him a small smile. "Thanks, man."

"I was walking past the hotel, contemplating whether or not to storm in here and tell you how stupid you are. But when I saw Ms. Overseas stomp her pretty little ass out the door and down the street, I kinda figured you already knew, and that you would probably want a ride to the airport. If not, I'd have to hog-tie you, throw you in the trunk, and put you in somebody's checked baggage headed for The Lone Star State in hopes your stupid ass would wake up before you landed."

"Trust me, I'm awake."

"Then let's go, Jack. Slow ass."

They headed out. "You got one more time to call me stupid and slow."

"You're not the only perfectly stellar DEA agent in the hall, Jack. Remember that."

Nate started dialing. "Once I make this call, you'll be the least of my worries."

~~~

When Pam's phone rang, she was holding up color swatches while she and Eva decided what colors to use in the makeover of Gwen's room. She ignored the call. "It's Nate."

A few seconds later, he called again. "What do you think's going on?" Pam asked.

"We need to call back. If he's calling *you*, something's up for sure," Eva said.

"We promised Arianna we wouldn't," Pam said. "We can't."

"Shouldn't we call Arianna and let her know?" Eva asked.

As they wrestled with how to handle Nate's call, Pam's house phone rang. Marcus was also home and capable of answering like everybody else. Their first instinct was to run into the bedroom. They did, but froze. Pam and Eva stared at each other in indecision as the phone continued to ring without a lull. It finally stopped.

Marcus's phone was on the dresser. It started vibrating.

"It's Nate," Pam said.

"Let it ring," Eva said.

"Why are you guys circling my phone?" Marcus asked when he entered the bedroom. "I can hear you two downstairs. What's going on?"

"Nothing," Pam said.

"Then why are you guys staring at my phone like you're gonna eat it?" He took his phone. "We're not done," he told Pam before walking off.

"It was bound to come out," Pam said to Eva.

"Whatever it is, Nate is desperate as hell," Eva said.

~~~

"I need to talk to Pam. I need Eva and Taesha too, I guess," Nate said.

"Why?" Marcus asked.

348

"I getting Arianna back and I need help."

"You're fortunate that you made it out of San Antonio alive. Why press your luck?"

"I'm coming home tonight. I need to find out from Pam if Arianna has plans."

"Arianna and Taesha left on business, told Pam they'd be back tomorrow evening."

"Where are the kids?"

"Staying with us."

"Well, perfect then. I'll have some time before she gets home."

"What happened to your new lease on life?"

"Let's just say I woke up."

Marcus couldn't respond. He was too busy listening to the women bicker with anxiety over the handling of Nate's calls.

"Marcus?" Nate asked.

"Let me call you back. I need to handle something."

From the demeanor of Pam and Eva, Marcus knew there was more to Arianna's departure than surveying land for a new coffee house. He asked Pam to have Eva leave. She seemed hesitant, but Marcus's stone face let her know it was a good idea. One look and Pam didn't have to say a word. Eva swiftly left the house.

"This ends now," Marcus said.

"Marcus, she's my best friend."

"And Nate's mine."

Marcus stared Pam down until she broke down. She told him about Arianna's childhood and her planned prison visit. For a minute, he said nothing as the words *sexual assault* sank in. Yes, he felt sympathy for Arianna, and yes, he hurt for her. But he felt stronger pulls in the present moment—fear for Arianna's location, and anger for the double-standard staring him in the face.

"So, it's alright for you to be an accomplice, but let me try it, and I get sent to the electric chair."

"She's trying to find herself."

"Oh, I get it. A man lies, he's a liar. A woman lies, she's trying to find herself."

"Whoa, hold up. Yes, I kept Arianna's secret. But you *directly* helped Nate do the unthinkable, and then you lied *directly* to my face."

"Well, since we're being so *direct*, I asked you if you knew what was wrong with Arianna, and you didn't mention her past, or this excursion she's on."

"At least I didn't drive her to a fucking motel."

The room went silent after Pam's unusual F bomb. Marcus backed up, but continued to stare Pam down. "Don't spin this. Not now. I needed to know this. Nate needed to know this. Do you know how dangerous it is at the Mountain City prison? Do you?"

"They have guards."

Marcus slapped the back of his hand into the palm of the other as he spoke. "It's a maximum security facility. Do you know what that even means?" He checked his watch. "What time tomorrow?"

"I'm not sure. Early."

"Who set this up?"

Pam hesitated, and then obviously realized she had no choice but to answer Marcus. He wasn't about to let up. "A therapist guy she's befriended."

"Befriended. Do you think I'm stupid?"

"She hasn't crossed the line."

"Pam, Arianna crossed the line two years ago when she failed to tell Nate she was sexually assaulted." Marcus dialed.

"What are you doing?" Pam asked.

The call went to voicemail. "Call me before you board. If you don't get this in time, I'll meet you when you touch down."

"You can't tell Nate. Please. I promised."

Marcus put up two fingers. "Two years, Nate pounded his head against the wall trying to figure out what he did wrong."

"Don't. Tell. Him. Arianna will never speak to me again."

"You stripped me of that choice the second you said Mountain City."

Chapter 50

After a layover in Newark, Nate's plane touched down in San Antonio. Because of his sudden urge to fly home, he was at the airlines' mercy regarding available flights. His eyes were red and he had a headache, but he also felt energized, with a fresh focus on life, armed with the determination needed to mend his marriage.

As Nate came down the escalator, he saw Marcus waiting for him. He thought this odd because they usually met at Ground Transportation.

"What's up? Something wrong?" Nate asked.

"Wasn't sure if you got my message and I didn't want us to miss each other."

"I didn't get it."

"Let's hurry. I'm parked in Unloading."

"You and Pam must have had it out pretty bad."

"Something like that. Slept on the couch."

"Shit, you look as tired as I am."

"Yep."

Nate followed behind Marcus, believing that Marcus must have reached his limit. The fight with Pam must have been huge. That was the only logical explanation as to why Marcus was walking and talking like the Terminator.

351

They got into Marcus's truck. Nate felt leery. Marcus kept sighing, rubbing his hand on his thigh, and looking at Nate out of the corner of his eye. Okay, this was getting bizarre.

Marcus merged onto the freeway.

"What the hell's wrong?" Nate asked.

"Let's get home first."

"No. Tell me now."

"Nate, just—"

"Now!"

"Alright, let me get off the freeway."

"You gotta stop driving?"

As Marcus drove to the nearest exit, Nate watched his every move, every expression. He appeared to be a man about to come unglued.

Marcus pulled into a gas station.

"What is it, Marcus?" Nate was now petrified.

"I've made it my mission to protect Gwen from boys. I vowed not to let her date until she's twenty-five. I check out all of her friends, even their parents. And I've never stopped to think..." Marcus paused. "Do I really know the people that she's staying with? Is some pervert watching her, or worse?"

"Did somebody harm Gwen?" Nate's voice was on fire.

"God, I hope not. You don't think about it until it happens to somebody close to you. Then you wonder what your own children are keeping from you. If they've ever been harmed and haven't said anything."

Gripped in the moment, Nate felt afraid to ask what was going on. He breathed in and out, hard, his heart rate speeding. "Did somebody harm one of my kids?"

"No," Marcus said. "Arianna was sexually assaulted wh— "

"WHAT!"

"When she was little, Nate. I just found out. That's what's been wrong with her all this time. Apparently...goddamn, I don't know how to tell you this."

"Just say it!"

"It was really, really bad. I mean years."

352

Nate looked away and then back at Marcus. Questions swirled in his head like equations with no answers, just jumbled numbers and letters with no meaning.

"No way, man. No," Nate said.

"Pam told me. She also admitted that Arianna's gone to Mountain City prison to confront the bastard."

Nate made fists, covered his eyes with them, then opened his hands, grabbed the door handle, fidgeted, rubbed his head, and breathed in deeply, all the while fighting like hell not to punch out Marcus's window. "I knew her upbringing was dysfunctional, but I had no idea she suffered like that. I can't believe she went through that and didn't tell me."

Nate put his head down between his elbows, resting on his knees. Images of a little girl being stripped, beaten, and savagely taken advantage of went through his mind. In his imagination, the girl had blonde hair and innocent flesh. The man was old, dirty, mean, and had the girl pinned in an alley. Nate had few details to go on, so he pictured what everyone thinks of when they think of rape. It was never the neighbor next door.

He lifted his head, then looked down at his hands and cracked each knuckle, one by one. "Do you know what he did to her?"

"No, but it had to have been bad. Pam couldn't even describe it. I am so sorry, Nate."

"You know, if I get my hands on him, he's dead, right?"

"Probably why she didn't tell you."

Clues and missed signals filled Nate's thoughts. The nights Arianna would clam up or ball up in the fetal position had never sparked an inkling that something like this was wrong. The nights he would wake up and discover Arianna in the bathroom or downstairs getting a glass of water hadn't affected him.

"If this happened in her childhood, why did she start freaking out just two years ago?"

"Something to do with her mother's death. I don't know exactly."

"I *knew* it." Nate remembered the night Arianna had told him about her mother's passing. Then he delved deeper into it, picturing vividly the events of that evening in a way he hadn't done before. "Her purse."

"What?"

"She got up and went to her purse. Then my phone rang." Nate thought back some more. "It jolted her. She dropped her purse, everything fell out of it." Marcus listened intently as Nate continued. "Marcus, she was gonna tell me. Probably had something to show me."

"What would stop her?"

"Me." Nate nodded. "The call pissed me off. I started yelling. It probably made her panic."

"You didn't know."

Nate didn't have time to keep processing the pain or the timeline. The most pressing issue now for him was how the hell to get to Tennessee. "I need to get up there with her."

"By the time you get there, she'll be on her way back. The best you can do is call in favors if you have any."

"But she's alone."

Marcus turned away.

"She is alone, right?"

"Nah, Taesha went with her."

"I see. What else? Your mood. I'm not stupid."

"Some guy helped her arrange it." Marcus hesitated. "He's done some counseling or something."

"What. Else?"

Marcus sighed. "Look, I get the feeling that there's more to their relationship."

"Relationship!? Arianna's *dating*?"

"Pam didn't wanna tell me, but yeah, I think so."

Nate got out of car and began to pace. He pounded Marcus's hood once with both fists. He tried a second time, but Marcus stopped him. Nate began to shake and pant. Marcus told him to get into the truck. Nate jerked away and walked off. Marcus screamed for him to come back, his voice drowned out by the busy highway.

For ten minutes, Nate stood at the corner of the gas station. A few people looked and then looked away, consumed in their own lives. He clasped his hands behind his head, moved them to his waist, then down to his thighs. Crouching for a minute, he listened to the life around him while his life fell apart. Arianna was dating another man. When he stood back up, he noticed Marcus trying to get his attention. He didn't move. But after receiving a few more stares, the kind that let him know people thought he was mental, Nate decided to walk back to the truck. He didn't need police pulling up acting like he'd just escaped from the psych ward.

"My guy's there from Knoxville. We collaborated on a case once. He said he'll call once he's in," Marcus said.

"I can't believe I ran my wife to another guy." Nate screamed and hit the window with his fist.

Marcus drove onto the highway. "Do you really think she would screw somebody else?"

"No. But I can imagine what he's telling her. Do you think she kissed him?"

"That's a hard one. I don't know."

"Another dude sticking his tongue down my wife's throat. A pedophile sexually assaulting her. Pull over. I'm gonna be sick."

"You jokin', right?"

"Pull over!"

Marcus cut through the traffic and reached the shoulder. Nate hopped out and hurled on the highway. He stood up straight before realizing he wasn't finished. After a few more seconds of having Marcus listen to him gag, he got back into the truck.

"You done?" Marcus asked.

"I'm good."

"No, I meant, are you done acting like Tre."

"Excuse me?"

"Childish. Do you still wanna be Arianna's husband?"

"I *am* her husband."

"Then take your rightful place, stop vomiting on the highway, and do something about this shit. Federal agent over here acting like a pussy."

Nate wanted to retaliate—wanted to punch Marcus in his throat. But he knew Marcus was right.

He reached for his phone.

"This is Supervisory Special Agent Nathaniel Jackson with Baltimore. I need to speak with Agent Rollins immediately."

"Can he even get guys up there in time?" Marcus asked.

"Let's hope."

Nate waited for the pickup. "Hey, Chris. This is Nate from Baltimore...I'm fine. Listen, I need to cash in on that huge favor you owe me, but I need you and your guys to move on it like yesterday...you handle Tennessee, right?"

Chapter 51

It was now close to eleven that same morning. The confrontation had been thrown off-schedule by four hours because a sudden staff change had been ordered. Arianna had been told that more experienced people had to be brought in just in case something went awry. She kept swallowing to stop herself from becoming sick. But no way was she leaving.

High fences and barbed wire separated her from the years of agony contained within the brick walls. A guard stood with a watchful eye over the compound, making Arianna wish Nightmare would try to escape and be sniped down. Years of his hands on her, his scruffy beard against her young shoulders, his rough fingers, she'd face again.

Arianna looked at Taesha. "This is one visit I *do* have to make alone."

Taesha hugged her with a love that could only come from sisters. "I know. I'll wait near the desk."

A guard escorted Arianna to a private room lawyers used to converse with their clients. Arianna stood near the glass window, wishing for a presence that wasn't there. "Nathan." She spoke low, as if her Superman could hear her calling for him.

A stout guy came into the room. He was older, chunky, white, grey-bearded, with less hair on his head than on his chin. "Mrs. Jackson?"

"Yes."

"I'm Warden Dean. I disagree with this plan of yours, but folks above my pay grade think otherwise. You do what you are directed to do. Are we clear? I don't need any safety violations on my hands. I got enough to deal with."

She nodded in agreement.

The warden left. Guards entered. They had weapons, no visible badges, and were dressed in business casual. Arianna assumed the warden had brought in extra people in case the situation became violent. This way, the guards assigned to the prison wouldn't be distracted from routine.

A man wearing street clothes walked into the room. He had on jeans, a black T-shirt and a tweed sport coat. He introduced himself to Arianna as Detective Nico Jaracobie from Knoxville Homicide, and said he was there to make sure things went smoothly. "Call me Nico."

"My..." Arianna hesitated. She didn't know how to label Anthony. "The therapist who arranged this said somebody would be here to mediate the confrontation."

Nico stared at her. "Yeah, we took care of that."

An older, clean-cut man with salt-and-pepper hair walked into the room.

"That's him?" Arianna asked.

"Sure." Nico stepped up to the man and said something inaudible.

The man stuck his hand out to Arianna. "Hello, Mrs. Jackson. I'm Will. I'll be mediating."

"Hello." Arianna felt a tinge of conspiracy coming from Nico and Will, and was about to question their demeanor, when yet another man entered the room.

He stared directly at Arianna. "You better know your place with my client. Keep your hands to yourself."

"Excuse me?" she asked, wishing even more for her husband's presence.

Nico interjected. "Take a seat, sir. I won't ask twice."

"Just keep her in check." Nightmare's lawyer took a seat in the crowded room.

The door on the opposite side of the room opened.

Will also took his spot at the head of the table.

"You ready?" Nico asked her. She nodded.

"Bring in the inmate," he said.

Guards brought in Nightmare, shackled, through the door. Arianna pierced Nightmare's body with her eyes, hoping maybe her vision could puncture his lungs. She flinched, remembering every touch, every grope, every pain.

Arianna fought to control her breathing. She felt like she was standing alone on a rock in the middle of the Atlantic with a vast hurricane approaching, no shoreline in sight, nothing but blue underneath her and storm clouds above her. One wrong step and she would succumb to the sharks.

Nico seated Nightmare.

Will pulled out his phone, dialed a number, and put the phone to his side. Arianna was so fixated on Nightmare, she didn't care that there was an open line leading somewhere.

"Do you know who I am? You should. It hasn't been that long." Arianna sat down on the other side of the table.

"Yes, I remember you." Nightmare looked down.

"Look at me," she said. He didn't look up.

Arianna looked at his attorney. "Make him look at me."

She fought the urge to leap out of her chair. "Funny, I've had nightmares for years because of you. You're nothing but a shriveled-up old man who needed to prey on little girls to feel like you were adequate."

"What do you want, little girl, huh? A confession? Fine. I did it." Nightmare looked around. "Y'all happy now? You got what you came for? Can I go back to my cell?"

"I wasn't even in Kindergarten yet. And you just had your way."

"You coming here isn't gonna change what I did. Not gonna change that you are just like me. Poor white trash, honey."

"That was it, right? I was poor? I needed money, so you would provide? That it?"

"You didn't complain."

"I was four."

Nightmare looked her up and down, making her sick. "You turned out well. What are you? Some fancy secretary?"

"CEO." As she stared Nightmare down, Arianna could feel the rage building inside her. She could see how he'd been able to prey on her vulnerability and poverty by luring her with a combination of intimidation and money. Anthony was right. This confrontation was working to end her sense of culpability. Her assault hadn't been her fault, she was finally realizing. But her anger was just beginning. "Your daughter shot herself because of you."

"She dead?"

"Yes."

"Was there a lot of blood? I like a lot of blood."

"You are an *evil* man."

Nightmare dismissed her comment. "So, you changed, huh? Grew up?"

Arianna snapped. "In more ways than one." She lunged over the table and pushed Nightmare to the ground. He hit the floor; the chair fell to the side. She crawled over the table, heels and all, and kicked him in the face. She didn't pause to think about how easy this was, about how nobody in the room was restraining her. "I stopped being a little girl a long time ago. You freakin' imbecile."

Nightmare's attorney did *try* to pull her off, but the guards grabbed him and held him to the wall in the midst of his protests that Arianna had violated his client's constitutional rights. He hollered to the mediator, that this was supposed to be a controlled confrontation, but the mediator was standing in a corner of the room now, holding his open phone to his side, looking as if the only right he had to uphold was allowing Arianna to kick the shit out of this dude.

Arianna grabbed a chair and slammed it over Nightmare's back. Nico backed her up. She got in two more decent blows to Nightmare's face before Nico pulled her off.

He nodded to the mediator. The mediator in turn closed the phone.

Arianna and, she assumed, everyone else, thought Nightmare had learned his lesson.

"That's all you got? That barely tickled." Nightmare tried to raise himself up, and got close enough to spit at her.

Every guard in the room drew a weapon, in unison, as if they were performing a professional drill routine in perfect sync. Nico looked at Will; he in turn looked at the guards.

"You so much as lunge at her, you will take a bullet straight in the face," a guard said. He looked at Arianna. "Did he get you?"

"No." Arianna was stunned. She'd expected protection as a civilian, as a therapy patient. She'd never expected to be treated like a government VIP needing an armed entourage.

"I'm filing charges on behalf of my client," his lawyer said. "This is harassment and intimidation."

"Your client raped and murdered twenty women over thirty years," Nico said. "Good luck getting a jury on your side."

"This won't stop me," Nightmare said. "If I can, I'll keep killing. I'll escape and you'll never be free, little girl. I'll torture others, just as I tortured you."

"Threats? Nice," Nico said.

"Shut up," Nightmare's lawyer shouted to his bastard of a client.

"Every time you look just below your neck, you'll remember me. I'll always be your nightmare, little girl."

"Get that trash out of here," Nico said. "Take him back to his cell... Pressing charges, counselor?"

Nightmare's attorney shook his head no.

"Didn't think so."

Nightmare limped back to his cell under the watchful eye of the guards.

"Murder too?" Arianna asked Nico. "When?"

"He's been at this for years. Long before you and I were ever born."

"So, even if I had spoken up..."

"He'd already killed his victims. He raped them for years, until they became teenagers, and then he strangled them."

"But my mother sent me a letter saying he'd raped women, but nothing about murder."

"Mrs. Jackson, if I may ask, did you read up on this guy at all?"

Arianna froze. "No."

"Any online research?"

"No. I couldn't face it."

"We arrested him a few years back, true, but for cold cases. Sexual assault was a part of it; however, he's not locked up for rape. He's locked up for murder. He's been convicted of one of them, and he's serving a life sentence. He's awaiting trial for others. If he's convicted, he'll more than likely get the death penalty. Then he'll be housed in Nashville."

"But he's never getting out, right?"

"Don't worry. He'll never see the light of day."

"Why do you think he kept me alive?"

"Did you fight back?"

"I did. What made you ask that?"

"Are you *not* the same woman who came out of that room?" He started to giggle.

Arianna smiled. "I believe so."

"This guy gets off on intimidation and fear. Your strength took the excitement out the kill."

My strength. "Guess I was stronger than I ever knew."

"In fact, you might be the missing link."

"What do you mean?"

"He wouldn't tell us what finally made him stop. It was probably you."

"Me?"

"You fought back and changed the game."

"No way."

"It's very plausible."

Arianna thought deeper about Nico's revelation. She didn't know a thing about predators, but she admitted that, once she'd told Nightmare no, he had left her alone, albeit scarred. "If this is true, then I actually helped *stop* his reign of terror."

"You spoke up more than you think you did."

Arianna thought back to the day Nightmare burned her. She thought of Taesha on the day Pam had read the letter, and thought of her spot-on instinct. *Nightmare really did plan the acid.*

"What's wrong?" Nico asked.

"Nothing. I just remembered something one of my friend's said. About his evil ways. Every move he made was deliberate."

"Anything you want to tell me?"

Arianna smiled again. "Nothing I can't tell my husband first."

Nico patted her shoulder. "C'mon, let's go so you can leave this behind."

As Nico escorted her back to the waiting room, she felt semi-vindicated. She'd unloaded a lot of anger, but the damage had already been done to her family. Nate was out of her life, and together they'd damaged Darius in the process. And Tre, although too young to fathom the circumstances, knew his daddy was gone.

The rage had to come out. And with this visit, Arianna now realized how strong she really was, and how staring down the devil actually worked. She no longer carried the guilt of things out of her control. However, also she realized that to gain full closure, more steps were needed, and not just counseling.

Closure, without honesty, is another form of greed. Arianna finally understood what her mother had meant. Not telling people the truth, out of a selfish need for acceptance, was unfair. When she kept her burdens to herself, she forced Nate to carry the guilt of thinking he'd done something wrong. Now, if she were to make the decision to close out her past without telling Nate the truth, sure, she would find peace, but Nate would forever live with the misconception that he'd done something wrong to ruin their relationship, and he'd never get closure.

As she headed toward the door, Arianna realized something else profound. She hadn't acted cool or calm, nor had she asked questions to get answers the way Anthony would have. No. She'd acted the way Nate would have, as if he were there, telling her to whup Nightmare's ass.

"Well, thank you, Nico. And thank the warden for putting all this in place."

"Sure."

"Not that it matters, but how'd he get caught?"

"His wife found souvenirs from his kills. She turned him in."

"Jesus...I hope she's okay."

"We do too." Nico looked down the hall. "Look, I gotta get back there. Be safe getting home, Mrs. Jackson."

She nodded and thanked him again.

Nico left.

Arianna fixed her blue blazer, freed her smothered hair from the collar, and walked out of the facility a different woman. However, when she met up with Taesha, she was feeling some concerns.

"Go okay?" Taesha asked.

Arianna described the entire confrontation.

"You go, girl," Taesha said. "How do you feel?"

"Good...for the most part."

"Most part?"

"He's in for murder, not rape."

Taesha's eyes widened. "Wow, huge."

Arianna nodded. "Do you think Anthony knew and didn't tell me?"

"Why you ask that?"

"Just seems like something he would have known." Arianna entertained a callous thought. "He'd made all the arrangements before I told him I wanted to take *you* instead of him. He couldn't back out of the plan."

"What are you getting at?"

"If I'd known this bastard was in for murder, I might not have come."

"Anthony was desperate to get you up here."

"*Assuming* he knew, right?" Determined to see the good in Anthony, Arianna gave him the benefit of the doubt. "I gotta believe he did this for my healing and not just to screw me."

"Arianna, no matter his motive, *you* accomplished this. Not him."

Arianna smiled at her own courage. "That is true. I did it, Tae."

"That's right. Don't let anybody rob you of that."

"You know what else I've come to realize?"

"What?"

Arianna shook her head. "Nate needs to know what happened. No more back and forth."

"You sound absolute this time."

Arianna raised her eyebrows. "If I can stop a murderer, I can tell the love of my life what happened to me."

~~~

"At least she's safe," Nate said. "I'm gonna kill that bastard."

"What are you gonna do now?" Marcus asked. "Arianna'll be home in a few hours."

Nate thought about it for a minute and put his plan together. Darius would be at an Xbox party and Gloria watched Tre on Friday nights. Marcus looked puzzled, asked how he would know the kids' whereabouts. Nate answered that he always kept in touch with his children, a promise he hadn't broken.

"Alright." Marcus tossed up his hands. "What's the rest of your grand plan?"

"Why so negative?"

"Not negative. Just sick of drama."

"Just trust me on this. Can you find somewhere for Gwen to go tonight?"

"She's a diva. Yes."

Nate had it all thought out. He would get a much needed nap, then go to his house tonight and talk to Arianna, lay all his feelings on the line, talk about her anguish, and hold her until she felt strong enough for him to let her go.

Then they would meet up at Marcus's house and hang out like the good days.

"I gotta fix shit with Pam first. I jumped down her throat."

"Text her. Right now. Tell her you love her."

"What?"

"It's time for us to be happy again, man. Text her."

"Now?"

"Yes. Now."

"Fine." Marcus texted Pam. *Love you.* "Happy, Nate? She might not even respond."

It didn't take long for Marcus to receive a return text, and another, and another. "This is not happening."

"What?"

"See what you started? She wrote me a damn book about her feelings, Nate. Thanks a lot."

Nate started laughing. Marcus read aloud bits and pieces of Pam's reply, her analysis of their earlier conversation and how she felt like a hypocrite and how much she adored him, but also how he had minimized her pain and anguish and how she felt jaded.

"She said I minimized her pain. Dude, she used the word jaded."

"Tell her you're sorry...with a smiley face. Women love smiley faces."

"I can't believe I'm taking women advice from you." Marcus did as Nate suggested. He tilted his head back slightly and shrugged at her reply. "Wow." It was clear her response surprised him. "Nate, you might not be coming over tonight after all. I might be busy." Then Marcus received a last text from Pam. He looked at Nate.

"What is it?"

"Arianna texted Pam. Told her she..." Marcus chuckled, "whupped his old, wrinkled-up ass."

Nate couldn't help but giggle himself. "Shit, it sounds like my baby used a *chair* on him."

They laughed for a good couple of minutes before Marcus started calming down. He stared at Nate with what looked like a sense of revelation. "You know what, Nate?

366

Arianna may have been there with other agents, but it was *you* in that room with her."

Nate nodded. "I know." Then he started dialing.

"Who are you calling?"

"A colleague. I have one last thing to handle." Nate waited for Nico to answer. "You have that guy in your custody still?" Nate was referring to the therapist Anthony had contacted in the local area to monitor the confrontation. When the therapist had arrived at the prison, he'd asked for the warden, explained why he was there, and a guard summoned Warden Dean. Nico was present, and offered to greet the therapist and lay down the rules before Arianna got there, giving him the chance to successfully intercept his attendance. Nico had held him in a secluded room, and told him to stay there until he came back.

"Put him on the phone." Nate held the phone while Nico put Anthony's colleague on the line. "This is Supervisory Special Agent Nathaniel Jackson of the Drug Enforcement Administration. You are not to say a word to your friend..." Nate covered the phone and spoke to Marcus. "The fuck's his name?"

"Anthony, I think."

"...Anthony, about what happened at that prison today. Are we clear?"

The man sounded edgy, and was stuttering. "I-I just came here to do a job, sir."

Nate thought about his needing to protect his family. "And I'm doing mine." He gave the gag order a second time and made sure the therapist understood.

"Why do you care if he says something?" Marcus asked.

"I don't. But I don't want Arianna to find out I know about her assault this way."

Chapter 52

It was seven p.m. Marcus was sitting at his desk, reserving the last few minutes of the day to go over details of his mother's disappearance. A decades-old case, a mother Marcus didn't remember because she'd disappeared when he was so young, a pinging he couldn't let go of. He loved the thought of her existence, as if she'd raised him into the strong man he'd become. Where was she?

He checked his watch. Arianna would be touching down soon, and Nate, God-willing, would keep his cool and get his wife back without a brawl neither of them needed.

D.J. remained with him, pretending he was putting the finishing touches on an arrest report. In reality, he was giving Marcus a second set of eyes on a list of potential suspects in his mother's disappearance.

Co-workers trickled out of the precinct until Marcus and D.J. were alone. But that didn't last long. The captain abruptly walked into Homicide. D.J. quickly, yet slyly, subdued the files he was reading and slipped them in a drawer. Marcus minimized his computer.

"Let me guess. Overtime I didn't approve," the captain said.

"Just catching up on work," Marcus said. "You know we're overachievers."

D.J. chuckled under his breath.

"Yeah, I think that shit's hilarious too," the captain said. "Anyway, thought you should know. Detective Ridgeland emerged. He applied to get his old position back in Houston Homicide."

Marcus immediately stood up. "*Houston?*"

"Yep."

"They aren't seriously considering hiring his lazy, greasy ass, right?"

"They're short-handed and his accuser recanted. You bet your ass they hired him."

"What do you mean, 'his old position?'"

"He was in Houston Homicide before here. You didn't know that?"

"Uh, no. Ridgeland isn't exactly on my list of people I care to stalk. Where's he been all these months?"

"I don't know, and I don't care. He's off our payroll. Thought you didn't care to stalk, Carter."

D.J. interjected. "He's gotta point, partner."

"Shut up, D.J." Marcus looked at his boss. "Ridgeland left his wife hanging off a cliff. She couldn't file for divorce because she couldn't find him."

"And that's our problem, how?"

"Boss, your compassion is off the charts."

"So is my curiosity." The captain plopped himself on Marcus's desk.

Marcus glanced at his boss's oversized presence sitting on his desk, and then to D.J., who looked more anxious than his tired partner. Marcus assumed the intrusion involved his mother's cold case. "We're on our own time."

"You're a homicide detective, no such thing. But I could really care less right now. You think I don't know you use company resources to chase a waterfall?"

Marcus was getting irate, but he kept he his cool. "No disrespect, but what is it?"

"Guess where I just came from?"

"Dinner?"

"Funny, but don't lose your day job. Want me to tell you?"

"I'm sure you're gonna."

"High Hill."

"High Hill?"

D.J. interjected again. "The halfway point between here and Houston."

The captain looked over toward D.J. "Glad to know you're so geographically adept, Pratt. But is this your conversation?"

"Uh, no, I guess. Didn't know it was so formal in here tonight." D.J. put his head into a case and pretended not to care.

The boss looked at Marcus. "Now ask me the million-dollar question."

Marcus sighed, cleared his throat, and reluctantly played along. "Why were you in High Hill?"

"Glad you asked." The captain pulled a white envelope from his pocket and placed it on Marcus's desk. It had Marcus's name on it. "To retrieve this. You know who contacted me and asked me to meet him?"

Jesus Christ, get to it. "Ridgeland?"

"Yep. The man himself."

The captain told Marcus that Kyle Ridgeland had called him a couple days ago and asked to meet him halfway; he had a letter for Marcus. Ridgeland didn't want to come back to San Antonio and face the drama. Marcus's boss was a no-nonsense, straight-to-the-point kind of guy who didn't waste time and didn't indulge in drama. Ridgeland had assured him this was one trip he wanted to make. "He said we should read it together. Needless to say, I agree."

The boss didn't take his eyes off Marcus. Marcus picked up the envelope and began to open it. The captain hopped off Marcus's desk and headed toward the door.

Marcus held the envelope. "Where are you going, Captain?"

"I've been doing this job a long time, Carter. I'm not stupid. I said I was curious. I said I agreed I should be here to read that shit with you. But that doesn't make it wise."

"Excuse me?"

"Sometimes the best thing you can do for yourself is to stay ignorant." He put his street hat back on. "I trust if there is anything I need to know, you'll tell me. Good night."

The boss left, leaving the door to slam in his wake.

D.J. relaxed, got up. "Whatever's in that envelope, Captain knows it's not good news."

"With Ridgeland, it's never good news." Marcus opened the envelope. A key fell out and hit the desk. The clank created waves of wonder. Marcus looked at D.J. before reading the short statement.

The black metal cabinet. Bottom drawer. Copy room. Fuck you.

P.S. Tell Eva she can have her damn divorce. I found a new bitch.

D.J. read the note while looking over Marcus's shoulder. "He is a piece of work."

Marcus dropped the letter on his desk. "Let's just do this."

It took Marcus a couple of minutes to open the old, bent cabinet. One last yank and the drawer flew open. Marcus lost his balance and fell back. D.J. looked inside the cabinet and backed up like he'd seen an overgrown insect.

Marcus got his bearings and looked inside, wondering what had D.J. so freaked out.

There it was, the case file from the man Marcus had arrested after the house exploded, killing Zach. It lay on top of other files and documents. Marcus instinctively opened the file. A yellow sticky note was stuck to the left side. *I took out a little insurance policy.*

While Marcus was deciphering the message, D.J. had reached in and pulled out the remaining contents. Evidence from unsolved cases filled the cabinet.

"This son of a bitch," D.J. said.

Marcus found phone records, fingerprint reports, sworn statements, the gamut. He studied the documents with D.J. The yellow sticky note was starting to make sense.

"Marcus, this is evidence from cases that we could have solved," D.J. began ranting. "He hid this from us so we'd look stupid. His jealous ass didn't want to see us succeed." D.J. shook his head. "This bastard commits a crime, and Houston rehires him? Wait until they hear about this shit— detective withholds evidence."

Marcus spoke in heavy voice. "He didn't get the credit."

"Huh?"

Marcus went into detail about the explosion that had killed Zach, how he'd gone after the man suspected of abusing his kid to death after he'd fled the house. "After the house went up, nobody was right in the head. We all tried to function the best we could." He looked at the man's case file and shook his head. "I wanted somebody to pay."

"What are you talking about?"

"I coerced the shit out of that confession. I knew he did it, but I needed that edge, that assurance that he'd fry. Ridgeland was watching from the outside. When all was said and done, I got the attention and Zach got the funeral. Ridgeland got nothing and he always resented it."

"So what is this?"

"He's taunting me. He's letting me know that he can do whatever he wants, and I won't say shit because he'll end my career."

"Damn, Marcus."

Marcus grabbed the documents they'd taken from the drawer. He started sifting through them, recalling cases where he couldn't give families closure or victims justice. "Let's get this stuff organized." He grabbed a notepad and started trying to make sense of what document belonged to which case.

"Partner, we have to talk about this. Ridgeland can't just play you the rest of your life."

"Right now, this *here* is our priority." Marcus raised some of the evidence. "Then we'll figure out what to do."

"We can't let him win, Marcus."

Marcus looked up. "D.J., there are at least five families lost inside this evidence. Let's get them some closure. Then we can talk about that bastard Ridgeland."

D.J. slowly raised his head to agree, although Marcus could tell D.J. felt unsettled from the way he blinked his eyes and folded his arms. "Alright, your call." D.J. pulled out a few pictures that lay at the bottom of the drawer. He went through them one by one, and stopped at one so profound, he dropped the rest.

"What is it?" Marcus took the picture.

Shawnee Redman.

She was standing next to a man. He appeared to be in his late-twenties, early thirties, close to her age, and they were smiling, arm in arm.

D.J. looked closer at the picture. "That's La Mansion Del Rio. Shit, that's here, and look." D.J. pointed to the new carpet. "They just added this a few months ago. This was recent. But she can't be married. We would have found the record."

"Maybe he's married to somebody else. Maybe her pregnancy was a kink he didn't need." Marcus nodded. "I'll be damned. Let's go through that night again."

The men went back to their desks to dig in.

"Goddamn, I'm sorry, Marcus. I pushed to close the Redman case when the M.E. ruled it a suicide."

"Stop, D.J. We're overworked, we're frustrated, and it happens. C'mon. Let's get to work. All night if it takes. It could still be self-inflicted. We just have to be sure."

"Take a breath, partner."

"I can't." Marcus looked at the photo he couldn't seem to drop, and then looked up. "I know what it's like to wonder what happened to your family."

"Well in that case, I'll be right back."

"Where are you going?"

"Evidence. Shawnee Redman. Figured we could start with her. See what's back there. You're paying for the take-out since you're keeping my very fine, white ass here for hours."

Marcus watched D.J. leave Homicide, realizing how much they'd grown as partners and good friends.

A cop opened the door to Homicide. "Carter, you have a visitor."

"I really don't need any more visitors. Who is it?"

Pam walked through the door.

He nodded to the cop. "How come you didn't call me?"

The cop shrugged, as if it shouldn't have been a problem. "I was heading out and she was at the desk. I knew you were busy, thought I'd save you a trip. Won't happen again."

"Chill out. I didn't mean it like that."

"You never mean it like that, Carter." The cop shut the door.

"Hi," Pam said. She looked over Marcus's shoulder to the piles of documents. "Your desk looks worse than mine, babe."

He smiled. "How did you know I needed to see your beautiful face?" Marcus hugged his wife, feeling no need to bring up Ridgeland's antics and ruin his stolen family moment. "To what do I owe this?"

"Well, we didn't talk after last night. And I haven't seen you all day. I missed you. You alright? You look like you're drowning in work."

"Nah, never better." Marcus put down the photo of Shawnee. "As much as I appreciate this conjugal visit, though, I can tell there's something else."

"I got a text from Arianna. She's not alone. Anthony's there too. Nate's at our house prepping this plan of his. I'm torn. It's supposed to be a surprise and now I don't know what to do. She doesn't even know Nate knows she's talking to another guy or that I told you about her childhood." Pam started talking fast, like she was panicking. "She's gonna get blindsided and hate me. I'm so tempted to tell her what's going on." She sighed, took a breath. "Guess I just needed to see you in person to remember where my loyalty is supposed to be."

"The dude's there *now*?"

"Yeah."

"Ah hell, I need to tell Nate, before we have World War Three." Marcus started dialing, not panicking yet. He knew Nate wasn't stupid enough to cause a scene on his own street. But a heads-up would go a long way.

Suddenly, Pam pulled back from Marcus as if an intruder were approaching them wearing a cloak and carrying a knife. Marcus watched her petrified expression. "Marcus."

"What the hell's wrong?"

Pam picked up the photo of Shawnee and the man. She covered her mouth and shook her head. Her eyes were so wide, she looked hypnotized. "Oh no."

"You know this guy?"

"This is *Anthony*. This is the guy."

"What guy?"

"The one at Arianna's house. This is who set up Tennessee."

"Are. You. Sure?"

"One-hundred percent." She stared at the photo. "Taesha was right. He had an angle the whole time." She looked at Marcus. "She's gotta get away from him."

"I'm on it." Marcus screamed for D.J.

"What can I do?" Pam asked.

"Go straight home," he said. "I'll follow you and then I'll go over to Nate's. Do not call Arianna. Do not put her in a position to incite this guy."

"You're scaring me."

"Just promise.

"Can't you send somebody else?"

"Honey, it's my job. You know that. If not this guy, there's always another guy somewhere. Now promise me."

Pam hesitated. "I promise, Marcus. *Please* be safe."

D.J. came in with the Shawnee Redman evidence box. Marcus filled him in, and they rushed out.

Marcus called Nate on the way to his car. Now he was panicked. "Meet me at your house in twenty."

"What? Why?" Nate asked. "I'm not quite ready."

"I'll explain when I see you."

"You know that shit doesn't work on me."

"You gotta trust me. Park away from the house."

"What is it?" Nate persisted.

Marcus hung up. Nate kept calling. He didn't answer.

"Why are you keeping this from Nate?" D.J. asked.

"If you have to ask, then you don't know him very well."

Marcus pulled up close to Nate's house, but far enough away so as not to be seen. Nate's car was parked about two houses down. The headlights were off and the engine appeared to be off as well.

Marcus was approaching Nate's car when Nate got out. They met in the street.

"What's going on?" Nate asked. "Do you know how hard it is for me to sit in front of my house and have patience when another man's truck is parked in my goddamned driveway?"

Marcus didn't answer. He flashed the picture of Shawnee and Anthony. "Recognize the guy?"

Nate stared at the photo. "No. Why are you showing me a picture of Shawnee and this white dude?"

"Because this white dude's truck is parked in your goddamned driveway."

"*This* is her guy?"

"Yeah. And a person of interest."

"Jesus."

"I need you to be cool. Get Arianna out. We'll get him. Do it quietly."

"Marcus, I know. I'm a cop too."

"Right now, you're a husband."

Nate put the photo in his pocket, reached into his glove box, and pulled out some random papers. "I got this." Before he stepped off, he gave a warning. "If you're sure he killed Shawnee, and Ani or my kids would have been in danger, you need to do me a huge favor."

"What's that?"

"Drive him the hell away from here before you tell me."

Chapter 53

Arianna made sandwiches, poured tea into tall glasses, and then put chips in a bowl. It was late, she wanted to be alone, to figure out how to finally tell Nate about Nightmare, but Anthony had shown up unexpectedly. She didn't want to be rude, although she was torn between feeling grateful for his prison connections and her belief he knew about Nightmare's true crimes.

She started a chick flick and sat on the couch. Arianna fidgeted. It was like trying to doze off on a hard mattress, never finding a comfortable position. Anthony was sitting next to her, and her only thoughts consisted of setting up a discussion with her husband.

"Thanks for accepting my invite," he said. "Kinda thought you wouldn't want to see me tonight."

"Well, you kinda came over and invited yourself." She smiled half-heartedly through her lukewarm feelings.

"Funny. But yes, I did."

"I *am* grateful for your help, Anthony." Arianna decided now was the best time to bring up the murders, since Anthony had shown up and was sitting on her couch. "And we do need to talk."

"I know. How'd it go?"

"Not that. Did you know Nightmare was convicted of murder?"

Anthony didn't answer.

His silence told Arianna everything she needed to know. "You did."

"I thought you already knew."

"That's a lie."

"Okay, look. I was afraid you'd back out and keep having these nightmares if I'd told you."

"Is that the only reason?"

"Why do you ask that?"

"I want to trust you, Anthony, I do. But a big part of me is starting to feel like you're just trying to sleep with me any way you can, as if flying me away from here would get you laid."

"That's not true." Anthony pleaded his case. "No. Not at all. I just wanted you to get help." He moved closer to her.

Arianna stood up and backed up. "I don't know what to believe anymore."

He stood up too. "Please, listen."

She jerked away. "Murder is something you should have told me about, Anthony."

Anthony snapped at her, something he hadn't done before. "How long are we gonna keep playing this game?"

"Excuse me?"

"Do you want a relationship with me, or not, Arianna?"

"How did we get on that?"

"You're trying to find reasons to keep me at bay, so, you're coming up with ways to be mad at me."

"Seriously?"

"Yeah, you're deflecting."

"Deflecting? Look here, you think I don't know you're trying to manipulate me right now?"

"Manipulate you? I'm *crazy* about you."

There was a knock on the door. Arianna quickly stepped off. "We'll finish this in a minute."

Taesha had instincts and, more than likely, was standing on the other side of the door, trying once again to save Arianna from herself. But Nate had taught her safety first. Arianna looked through the peephole and felt her stomach drop to the floor. *He's here. Anthony's truck.*

She opened the door, stepped outside, and shut the door behind her. She stared at the husband she hadn't seen in almost six months, the man she realized would never leave her heart, no matter how many trips she took to Tennessee. But she couldn't leap into his arms. He looked pissed, and she knew why.

"Either you just bought a big-ass truck, or you have a man in my house."

Arianna's feet had melted to the ground under Nate's heat. She was too nervous to move. "I haven't done anything with him."

He waved some papers. "Let's do this now."

Nate pulled out a pen and put the document up against the door. Pen scraping paper was the only sound for a brief time as Nate wrote his unique signature of an oversized N and unrecognizable "athaniel," an oversized J with a curl on the end and unrecognizable "ackson."

"I'll get it notarized. Then, in sixty days you can do whatever you want with that dude. Run away with him for all I care. Right now, though, we need to talk about visitation. And seeing that you have some bastard all up in my shit, guess we can't do it here, now can we? My car. Now."

"I knew it. I knew you didn't want me. I'm so glad I didn't call you all those times I wanted to. All those times I fell asleep missing you. All those times I cried out for you in regret."

Nate seemed to wobble, his voice cracked, as if he wanted to do something other than be an asshole. "My car. Now, I said. Right this minute."

"What is up with men thinking they can snap at me?" For as much as Arianna loved Nate, and as much as keeping silent about Nightmare had swallowed her whole, and as much as she wanted to cry out to him, she refused to dance with Nate's double-standard. "You have some nerve,

379

Supervisory Special Agent Nathaniel Darius Jackson, Jr., coming here with divorce papers and trying to pin wrongs on me."

Nate didn't seem to care. "Unless you want me to run up in there and pile-drive your boyfriend, I need five minutes of your time to discuss visitation. In my car. Now. I won't say it again."

"He's not my boyfriend."

Nate gritted his teeth. "NOW."

"Why are you being such a jerk?"

"Now, Ani, or I will seek full custody."

"You wouldn't dare."

"I've taken on dares much more complex. I'm warning you. Now."

"Warning?"

"You want to lose the kids?"

"I'm not going to lose the kids."

"You want to put them through this? Let's go. Car, now."

She followed him to his car, mumbling about how much he was acting like an ass. "Why are you so far down?"

Nate opened the passenger door for her and allowed her to get in. Then he slipped into the driver's side.

Arianna grabbed the papers. "Nathan, this is the back of your lease. I cannot believe—"

"Shut up, woman." Nate took the papers out of her hands, grabbed either side of her face, and kissed her until her hands stopped fluttering, until her body calmed down from being startled. Arianna rubbed his upper back and neck, and repeated the pattern as they kissed, until she almost knocked the vehicle out of gear. Nate pulled back. "Do you *really* think that I could *ever* divorce you?"

"You seemed convincing."

"I can sit here and give you a thousand reasons to hate me right now. I'm stubborn. At times I have a temper. I'm gone a lot. I risk my life. I spend too much time at the gym. I do what I do, and I don't care what people think. I speak my mind. I'm big on my opinions and small on my apologies. I hate chick flicks. I refuse to buy your tampons. I

380

overload the dishwasher, and I let the boys eat cookies and drink soda for breakfast. But I've never let a day slip by, last few months excluded, without letting you know you're the most important thing in my life. I might not say 'I love you' often, but I've never left you guessing."

"Why didn't you just come back months ago?"

"Wasn't sure you wanted me."

"You moved away. I didn't think you wanted *me*."

"Yeah, about that. You don't follow along very well. I mean, that was a straight fail on your part."

"Excuse me?"

"You were supposed to freak out when you realized I was making moves."

"For somebody so smart, that sure was dumb."

"I'm a guy."

"I see that."

"So, you taking me back?"

"Nathan, I never left."

This time, Arianna came for Nate. He held her tight as Arianna kissed his lips, his neck, his ear, anything she could comfortably get to. They felt on each other until Arianna forgot she had a man inside her house sitting on Nate's favorite sofa, forgot Nate had tricked her into getting into his car. The only thing that mattered was that her husband, the father of her children, was home and staying for good. *It's time.*

Arianna pulled back, her hair flying all over her face. She and Nate were quiet. Nate didn't take his eyes away from her as she sat back in the passenger seat and leaned her head back on the head rest. She grabbed Nate's hand and kissed his knuckles. "Oh, Nathan. How could I have done this to you? To us. Shawnee was *such* an excuse for me not to do the right thing." She looked at him, tears forming. "There's so much you don't know. And you're gonna hate me when I tell you."

"Nah, I think that's scientifically impossible."

"I don't even know how to say this."

"You were sexually assaulted. I already know."

Arianna started to shake. "You know?"

"Yes."

She shook harder. Nate grabbed her and held her close again. "I'm not letting you run from me."

Arianna's breathing grew heavy. The clasp of her hands jabbed at Nate's neck because she hadn't realized she was clinging to him for dear life. "I've been drowning in this, Nathan. You don't know how many times I've wanted to tell you. There were days I didn't recognize myself. I went back and forth, do I say something, do I not."

"I love you. You understand that?" Nate asked.

She nodded yes as much as she could with Nate's broad shoulders in the way.

He kept her held close. "I found out today, and I love you just as much now as I did yesterday. You understand that too?"

She nodded again.

Nate placed his hand on either cheek and lifted her head. "I can't believe I didn't catch on. Even Taesha was trying to get me to see, and I just wouldn't look."

Arianna was so overwhelmed with the love and affection Nate was giving her that she damned near crawled up his chest like he was a tree. Nate wrapped her tight in his arms and in his comfort.

"I missed you so much, Nathan."

"I missed you more, Ani. Trust me on that."

"Are you okay?"

Nate's eyes watered. "I don't know." He held her close. "But as long as you're okay, I can deal with it."

"I'm good now."

"I could do this all night."

They made out, again, until they ran out of breath, again. Arianna held on to Nate so tightly, he could barely pull away. When she calmed down, she backed up. "You intervened at the prison, didn't you?"

"Ani, I had to."

"Nobody told me."

"I couldn't let you know who those guards were."

"Why?"

"I didn't want you to find out from somebody else that I knew what had happened to you. I didn't wanna shake you up even more."

"Even when you're not there, you still find a way to hold me."

"What can I say? You're my baby."

Arianna tried to talk while crying at the same time. "I love you so much."

"Come here." Nate opened his arms once again, and there she went. After a couple more minutes, Nate confessed, "I tricked you to get you safely into the car."

"Safely?"

"I need to tell you something. And you need to keep it together. Can you do that?"

"Yes."

Nate showed Arianna the picture of Anthony and Shawnee. "Oh my Lord. How could I have been so stupid, Nathan? I am so naïve."

"You try to see the good in people. That's one of the things I've always loved about you. Just not with other dudes."

Guilt struck her. "I'm so sorry, baby. I was just trying to cope without you. I knew after tonight he wasn't legit."

Nate's mood went from passion to protection like zero to sixty. "What the hell did he do to you?"

"Snapped at me. Long story, I'll tell you." She looked at the house. "Let me get him out."

"*I'll* get him out. You wait here." Nate opened the car door.

Arianna grabbed him before he could move. "No. *I* have to get him out."

"I'm not letting you in there. I don't know what that idiot's capable of."

"Nathan, I respect you. But this is my fight. Wait here." Arianna opened the car door.

"Yeah, that's really gonna happen."

Arianna walked across the grass, holding the photo. Nate followed, telling her to get back in the car. Marcus was standing outside the house and D.J. inside. Arianna walked past Marcus and reached for the door. Marcus grabbed her arm. "Arianna, wait." He looked at Nate. "This bastard has no remorse. Be careful."

"So why is this fucktard still in my house?" Nate asked.

"He didn't do it. Air-tight alibi. Just called, confirmed his story. He was conducting a psychotherapy session in San Marcos. This is all about payback for Shawnee Redman. You know how this has to go."

Nate nodded.

"What do you mean, Marcus?" Arianna asked. She looked at Nate. "What does he mean, baby?"

"He needs our permission to remove him from the home. He hasn't committed a crime."

"Get him out of my house," Arianna said. "Isn't that enough?"

Marcus looked at Arianna and back at Nate again. "We need to tread lightly. He knows about you and Shawnee Redman."

"Yeah, no shit."

"One call to the DEA from him and you're gonna be investigated for misconduct. D.J. is in there, trying to keep him calm, so this shit doesn't go sideways."

"Keep *him* calm? Is that a joke?" Arianna asked.

Nate put his hand on her shoulder, a nonverbal cue that he had this under control. "What does he want?" He asked Marcus.

"He wants to talk to you. Then he said he'll leave peacefully."

Taesha pulled up to the house, driving so fast that slamming on her brakes caused her tiny compact car to jerk forward. She got out of the car holding a bat. Pam got out the other side, trying to be the voice of reason. Eva pulled up behind them and hastily got out of her vehicle ranting, in Spanish, about how Taesha had lost her mind and to give her the bat.

Marcus shook his head and looked at Nate. "I *really* don't need the ghetto fabulous version of Charlie's Angels here right now."

"Well, one of them belongs to you."

Marcus sighed as they approached. "You're worried about my safety, but you show up with sticks and shit, babe? Why are you here?"

"I had to tell Tae. She came over determined to check on Arianna because..." Pam paused.

"Because what?" Marcus asked.

"Because Taesha doesn't trust Anthony," Arianna said.

Taesha grabbed the photo from Arianna. "Oh, this shit is classic. Let's go bust some heads, Nate. I knew this micro-dick bitch was just trying to get Arianna alone."

Marcus put up his hand. "Just stop, Taesha, please. This shit is childish."

"I agree," Eva said. She tried to grab the bat. Taesha jerked away from her. They bickered over possession of the weapon. Nate grabbed it and threw it into the yard, clearly fed up. "You know what? I'm not doing this. Job or not." He opened the front door. Taesha ran after the bat.

"Nathan," Arianna said.

"I'm cool. Trust me." He stepped inside.

"Well, well, well," Anthony said. "The gang's all here."

"Get out of my house," Nate said to Anthony. Taesha tried handing him the bat. He rolled his eyes and backed her up.

"Or what? You gonna put your hands on me, oh so Special Agent Jackson? I *wish* you would."

"So much for keeping him calm, D.J," Marcus said.

"He's a dick. What do want me to say?" D.J. replied.

"You don't wanna tangle with me. I promise you that," Nate said to Anthony.

"Leave before I arrest you for trespassing," Marcus said.

Anthony dismissed Marcus and looked at Arianna. "You know what, pretty lady? Despite my malicious intent, you almost had me."

Arianna moved closer to Nate.

"Collar him for trespassing, Marcus. Now," Nate said.

"Right, pretty lady?"

"I'm gonna kill him, Marcus."

"I'm on it, Nate."

"You know what?" Anthony got in Arianna's face before Marcus could stop him. "It's not too late to consummate our relationship."

"That's it." Nate stepped forward. He raised his hand, grabbed Anthony by the neck, and shoved him straight into the front door, pinning him.

"Nathaniel!" Arianna screamed.

"Jack his shit up, Nate," Taesha said.

Aside from the clamoring of Anthony's body against the front door, the house went silent for an agonizing five seconds as Nate's grip, and his next move, dominated the moment. Nate had clenched his hand so tightly it seemed that his bicep, tricep, and every vein in his arm wanted to tear through his skin.

"This is what he wants, Nate," Marcus said.

Nate didn't take his eyes off Anthony. "A few years ago, I would have killed you, without a sound, without a flinch. I'm going to tell you—for the last time—get your tired, wanna-be-Nate-Jackson ass out of my home. And if you ever step within an inch of my wife again, I will smash your brain into your gallbladder."

Nate let go of Anthony. In doing so, he surprised all of them, even himself. He opened the door. "Bounce."

"I would be nice to me, if I were you. One call to the DEA, and you're done."

Arianna's stomach knotted. The threat was real. Her husband could lose his job.

"And one call to the APA and *you're* done," D.J. interjected, shocking everyone.

"Come again?" Anthony asked.

"Nate asked you to leave his home. Instead, you got in his wife's face. That's battery."

"Good luck making that stick."

"I'm Dominick Jeremiah Pratt. I can make anything stick."

Taesha smiled. "I knew you had a little bit of thug in you."

"Thug?" Anthony said. "You a thug, too, oh so Special Agent Jackson?"

Nate had had enough. "No...but I am my father's son." Nate's fist drilled Anthony straight into his jaw, and Anthony almost went down. He held on to the doorknob and anything else he could grasp to keep from falling.

"I'll be damned if you're gonna be all up in my house telling me what for." Nate instinctively grabbed Anthony by the shirt, got half throat, half collar, and threw him out the front door like trash. "I better not ever see you around here again."

Anthony shot Nate a look of contempt so powerful, it would have lingered around a lesser man. "You haven't won, Jackson."

Nate slammed the door and was done with it. Arianna ran to him. He gripped her tightly as he looked at his friends. "The American Psychological Association, D.J., really?"

Everyone laughed. Nate caught Taesha smiling at D.J. Maybe there was hope for her after all.

~~~

The Jackson home gave off a quiet, tranquil sense of conclusion, as if the last piece of a complicated jigsaw puzzle had been placed, and everybody could step back and marvel in the beauty. Nate had just locked the door after everyone else had departed to pizza night—D.J. finally getting a real date with Taesha—even though they ended up double-dating with Pam and a reluctant Marcus, plus Eva as a bonus tag-along.

"Our friends," Nate said.

"What would we do without them?"

"I can think of something." Nate embraced Arianna and kissed her like he'd just returned from battle. "Goddamnit to hell, I missed you." He backed Arianna to the wall and put his hand up her shirt. Her mouth reached for his neck.

She stopped suddenly and backed up. "Wait, baby, wait."

For a moment, Nate felt as if he'd just received a shot of deja vu from a big-ass syringe with a long-ass needle. Talk about panic. *Not again.*

"No, Nathan, it's not that. I promise you."

"What's wrong then?"

"We need to talk before we just rush to the bedroom."

"I really wasn't planning on making it that far actually."

"Can you just be serious for once?" She laughed. "Geeze."

"Okay, I guess you're right. I'm serious."

"Let's sit at the table." She grabbed his hand and led him.

"C'mon, Ani, not a table talk. I didn't say I was *that* serious."

"Just hush, silly."

"Fine."

They sat.

Arianna began by telling Nate she'd learned a lot on her visit to Knoxville. Then she told him she was flying back to Tennessee tomorrow morning, alone, and had already made the plans. "I need to see my father, Nathan."

"You sure about this, Ani? After what you just faced up there? Now, you wanna go see your racist-ass dad? Alone? Why?"

"I didn't make it this last trip."

"So, I'll take you."

"I love you... *so* much, Nathan. But as much as I want you to come with me, you can't. I need to do this for me. I took Taesha the last time because I felt I needed support. I need to be my own support this time. I should have gone alone last time."

Nate still couldn't comprehend why Arianna would want to leave the weekend he returned. Perhaps his angst over her leaving for just two days heightened his realization of how much he had missed her.

"I don't follow, Ani."

Arianna explained. "One day, when I was eighteen, I walked into a grocery store and there you were, and there I stayed. Seven months later, I married you. Ten months after that, I had your baby. The few trips I've made to Baltimore to check on my store have been with you. And I loved, and still love, every minute of it. Every second I get to explain to Darius that downloads aren't cheap. Every second I have to wipe Tre's hands and his entire body. Every time I walk past you and drink you in. I breathe my family, Nathan."

"So what's wrong?"

"I need some space, baby. Not a lot, just a pinch."

"What the hell is a pinch of space?"

"Just a couple days. I have to face things by myself without a man."

"I know I'm spontaneous when it comes to flights, but you? You sure this is what you want?"

Arianna told him she'd already booked the ticket and made childcare arrangements with Gloria, who had bought a finger-painting set and an Xbox controller. "I wasn't gonna tell a soul other than her."

"I don't like it."

"Nathan, I need your support."

"Let me finish."

Arianna stayed quiet.

"I *really* don't like it. But if this is what you need, then I'm on board, as long as you promise to stay away from that damn prison."

"I've had my fill, trust me."

"Okay, then. You have my support."

"Thank you, Nathan."

Nate leaned in for a kiss. She backed him up.

"You're killing me, Ani."

"I know it sounds crazy, but right now I don't need you as my husband. I need you as my best friend. I have to get this out. If not, I'll get lost in you and we won't get anywhere."

For the first time, Nate actually got *it*—where she was coming from, and the need to journey into another kind of closeness, a friendship they'd developed long before they'd ever become intimate. "Wow, I think I'm getting old, because I actually agree."

"I don't want to get into heavy detail tonight, Nathan. But it's important that you know why I was so cold."

"I get it. And I'm ready to listen. But not at this damn table." Nate led her to the foot of the stairs. He sat on the third step. Arianna sat on the second step directly in front of him. Nate leaned over, put his head on her shoulder, and wrapped his arms around her body. She held onto Nate's arms. They enjoyed, for the first time in a long time, friendship, the same way they'd done when they'd first moved into Stone Oak.

"You always know where to go, Nathan."

"It's my job."

"Oh, wait." Arianna went upstairs, and came back down holding her mother's letter. She handed it to her husband. He read; she talked.

"I was four when he started. It lasted for eight years and a lot happened. I had terrible dreams about it for a long time. That package my mother sent me contained this letter. It brought back so much pain. My bad dreams came back too. They triggered everything, reminded me of how I'd kept it all from you, and then it became a mountain from there. You don't know how many times I wanted to tell you. I couldn't even look at you without feeling guilty, without feeling afraid that I'd destroy you. I thought after our twelfth anniversary that I'd somehow licked it. I was just buying time. The aftermath of your affair made it worse, and I realized he'd completely overtaken my life."

Nate read every word of Helen Statton's words with the same seriousness he would read a warrant, arrest record, or otherwise. He folded it back up in decisive creases, tucked it back into the envelope, and waved it at Arianna. "Baby, this should have been in my hand the minute you got home that night."

"I know. God, I know. I just didn't want to put more pain on you."

"Arianna, my back is stronger than yours for a reason. Do you see what I mean by that?"

She nodded. "I do."

Nate put the letter beside them. "I won't turn this into a Q & A tonight, but I do need to know one thing."

"Sure."

"What made the dreams stop initially?"

"You."

"Me?"

"You came into my life and everything turned around."

Nate brought his arms in closer and tightened his hold on Arianna. "Do you want us to see a crisis counselor? For real this time. I mean in a real treatment program."

"Yeah, I think that's a good idea."

"What can I do right now? Please tell me what you need at this moment, and I'll do it."

"You can take me back to college."

Nate knew exactly what Arianna meant. She wanted him to take her back to before they'd ever had sex, back to when it was just them, back to when she had her own identity as a track and field athlete, back to when Nate was part of her world, but held her in his arms with no expectations. Back to the nights filled with pillow talk.

"Can I come over?" Nate asked. "You know, be a part of your world?"

"I didn't say you had to role-play."

"I just wanted to see if it still sounded as lame now as it did then."

"Yep, but it still works."

They went upstairs. Arianna put away the letter, then slipped into one of Nate's T-shirts.

"That's where that went," he said.

"I had to sleep in something."

"I can't believe I'm a grown-ass man about to spoon with my wife." He took off his shirt and pants, but the rules called for him to keep some type of barrier.

They crawled into bed.

"You feel good in your underwear."

"Can you at least turn around so I can look at you?"

Arianna turned to face him. Nate put his arm around her and held her to him. He commented that he was sick of hotel beds and mini-fridges. Then he went into a story involving Dave, Dave's mother, and the beaded curtains Dave had been forced to hang. She giggled, told him how much she missed his humor.

They talked about Nate's mentorship, how the kids were coming along. Arianna allowed Nate to unload his frustrations about how society has turned at-risk kids into the forgotten youth. She listened as he talked about the success of some, the recidivism of others. He mentioned the solid, as well as the dysfunctional, parenting he'd witnessed. Most of all, he talked about Jeremy.

She realized just how much noise Nate had been holding inside his head and his heart. She hadn't given him room to properly vent about much of anything these past couple of years.

He explained the pain he felt, and what was going through his head when he'd decided to have the affair. While not excusing his actions, he did give Arianna some much needed insight.

"You know, Nathan, with everything that's gone on, we never really talked about it. Whatever you need to say, whatever I need to say. I need to know things, and we both need to get this out, and really, *really* need to be done with it."

He rubbed her cheek with his thumb. "What do you wanna know?"

"Kind of everything."

Nate became her open book. He answered all her questions. He copped to the schedule, made it clear that he'd contained the fling to the motel and that no extra amenities had accompanied the room or the intercourse. No kissing, no oral, no music, no bond. He told Arianna she'd ended it, but he would have. He confessed that he needed Shawnee to climax because it allowed him to hold onto some shred of his manhood. He mentioned their limited positions, that he never undressed her and she never undressed him. Arianna asked about their topics of conversation. Nate admitted they were good in the beginning, but there was far less talk than action. In summary, the visits were short and to the point.

"She wasn't you, Ani. She never was and nobody ever will be."

"Could Shawnee, you know, good?"

"What? Perform?"

"Yeah. I guess she did something right. Obviously she made you come when I couldn't."

"When the time came, pardon the pun, I would close my eyes and picture you. Every single time."

Arianna got teary. "All those times you wanted me, and I just turned away."

"It's over. Let's not look back. The affair was a shot of heroin, Ani. You're my multi-vitamin."

She looked at him and shook her head. "Really, Supervisory Special Agent Jackson?"

"That was smooth. You gotta admit."

"How did your corny ass get somebody else to sleep with you?"

"Oh that's cold. I was just about to tell you that you're the glass to my Hennessy."

"Okay, I'm done. The struggle is real."

They laughed. That's when Nate knew that Arianna could get over what he'd done.

~~~

Some minutes passed. Nate had put his head down on Arianna's chest. It was a time of quiet and innocence, with Nate caressing her, the tips of his fingers making circular motions right below her collarbone. Arianna's fingers skated across Nate's shoulder blades in return.

She thought of ways to make their marriage stronger than ever—one with no secrets and no reasons to make any. Her heart exploded with feelings she wanted to express. She lay still, thinking of the words.

"The night Shawnee died. Remember the way we were that night?"

"A man can't forget something like that."

"I felt like, after that, I had to protect you more than ever. I didn't want you to hurt worse, especially not after Baltimore. And I didn't want to ruin your career or worse."

393

"I'm crazy at times, but I'm also smart, Ani. I wouldn't be where I am in the DEA if I were stupid. You have to understand that. And yes, what I saw in that basement was horrifying, but if I didn't know how to keep it in check, I'd be on a ward somewhere."

"When I stepped out onto that porch, thinking you wanted a divorce, I almost died. I was never so happy to see a lease in my life."

"I acted like a jerk to get you away from the house. You know I would never take the kids from you."

"I know that."

"Tre would drive me crazy anyway." Nate chuckled. Arianna didn't make a sound.

"What else is it, babe?"

"I never..." she began, but stopped.

Nate propped his head on his hand. "It's okay. Talk. We need to get this out."

"I never slept with him."

"I know that because I know you."

"I was confused. I wanted comfort." She rubbed his arm. "But..." Arianna hesitated, unsure of how Nate would react to how close Anthony had gotten to her. It was important to her for Nate to know that his words were what had stopped her from going all the way, that she'd remembered what he'd asked of her when Anthony had abruptly leaned over to kiss her. *Never forget I need you, even if you feel the need to.*

"Tell me."

"When Anthony leaned over to kiss me—"

"Whooaaaa. I never said tell me that." He hopped up.

Arianna created the moment, the same feeling as in the moment just after a head-on collision. That instant of hoping that maybe the wreck hadn't happened. That one second the at-fault driver wished she could turn back the clock, only briefly, to make a smarter choice.

"Did you have to give me that much of a visual, Ani? Jesus." Nate rubbed his forehead. "I already hate myself for it. Why did you make it worse?"

Nate slipped on sweatpants. He was angry, but remained calm. "I guess he tried to stick his tongue down your throat?"

"Nathan, let me explain it all, please." Arianna could not stop the cyclone she'd formed. She wanted to tell Nate that she'd backed away from Anthony and had kept her lips sealed. But with Nate's anger, she didn't want to keep rehashing the visual and end up telling him that she'd been that close to Anthony, in his vehicle, at three a.m.

"Guess so." Nate went into the bathroom and looked inside the medicine cabinet. He swallowed two ibuprofen tablets. "I should have choked his pasty ass when I had the chance."

"I'm gonna give you a minute." Arianna went downstairs to get water from the kitchen.

Nate followed. "Hold up. You drop this atomic bomb on my head about how you almost tongued this bastard, who just left my house, I might add, and then, just to be nice, you're gonna give me a minute to absorb it? Really?"

"I just wanted you to listen."

"Listen? News flash. You don't start a conversation by reminding me that another man got that goddamned close to you. You already know I can't take that. I carry enough guilt. Please stop." His voice cracked. He tossed up his hands and walked away.

Arianna saw the tears in his eyes before he turned away. She knew he was shouldering immense pain and had been for a very long time. She also figured out why he was so calm. Her husband wasn't pissed. He was, without a doubt, devastated.

"I'm sorry, Nathan. I didn't think."

Nate turned and walked back toward her. "Throughout this whole ordeal, the focus has been on you. What you went through, what I put you through. What you've suffered through. And I've taken all of it. I've shouldered every burden." Nate came in close to her face. "But do you know what it does to a man, to sleep with his wife for years knowing all she wants is for him to climax, and then bounce? And later learn that she shared with another guy her most intimate details about why she couldn't touch her husband?" Nate went around Arianna and grabbed a beer from the fridge.

"I didn't tell him *details*, Nathan."

"You told him enough. Damn sure more than you told me. From where I'm standing, I may have had the sex, but you had the affair."

Arianna stayed silent.

"Call me an asshole. Call it a double standard. Send me to the chair. Put the needle in my arm. I can't sit back and take hearing about how another man almost kissed the only woman, in this world, I have ever loved."

"You're the only man I've ever loved."

"Then why do I gotta hear from my best friend that my wife was ravaged by a *convicted* pedophile and murderer when she wasn't even old enough to ride a fucking bike!"

"I didn't know how to tell you."

Nate got louder. "I am your goddamned husband, Arianna Rae." Nate counted off with his fingers. "You have *stripped* in front of me. You have *pissed* in front of me, *bled* in front of me, *masturbated* in front of me, not to mention the freaky shit you've done *to* me, and you think you can't *talk* to me? You didn't even give me a chance." He slammed the counter. "I have my issues. But being closed off with you was never one of them. You made me the last to know. I should have been the first."

Arianna started to cry. "I didn't want to break your heart, Nathaniel. My father had already done enough. Baltimore had already done enough. You didn't need *this* on top of it. I didn't know how you'd handle it, or what you'd think of me."

"You honestly thought I'd look at you differently? Really? I'd slit my own throat if it'd keep you alive, but you thought I'd be that goddamned shallow?"

"No. Yes."

"No? Yes?"

"You don't get it. Surviving abuse makes you rethink, overthink, mis-think—if that's even a word—everything. You are my whole world, baby. I freaked out. I wanted to protect you."

"By dating another guy? You did a bang-up job."

~~~

Arianna and Nate sat safely in the hands of silence for an hour. No hurtful words, just a chance to regroup before either said something they couldn't take back. Arianna migrated all over the house. Nate followed suit. He sat on the kitchen floor with his head in his hands as she stood bent over the island. She got up and went to the den. He got up, sat on the counter, and then jumped off the counter and sat at the foot of the stairs. Arianna left the den, heading for the stairs.

She approached slowly. Nate had his head down and was cracking his knuckles.

Their beautiful reconciliation had turned into an ugly disembowelment, and she began to realize that what was worse than Nate's pain, and what paled in comparison to his guilt, was his shame.

As Taesha had done with her, it was now Arianna's turn to try to get a person she loved to love himself. "Never forget I need you, even if you feel the need to."

Nate kept his head down. "What?"

"You could say I followed through."

"Ani, what are you talking about?"

"You." Arianna took a seat next to him. Nate didn't fight her.

She explained it all, how she'd needed so badly to forget how much Nate loved her, because she'd needed so desperately to forget how much she loved him. But when Anthony had leaned in, she couldn't forget. Nate had spoken to her from miles away. "I knew from the moment I'd met him, he wanted more. And in the back of my mind, I knew he just wanted an excuse to take me away from Texas. He was too quick to set everything up." Her voice cracked. "Thank God, you intervened. I don't know how it would have turned out." Arianna waited for a response, an indication that she'd gotten through to him. Nate perked up, lifted his head. At least Arianna had gotten some movement out of him.

She continued. "And really, to be honest, during all that time, being manipulated felt a hell of a lot better than being without you." She noticed Nate's eyes starting to water. "You've been so good to me, Nathan, all these years, that being naïve was never a flaw until I didn't have you, a stand-up guy, anymore."

Nate immediately looked at her, as if what she'd just said was the capstone of her speech, as if she'd just gripped his soul. But he still didn't speak.

"I'm so sorry, Nathan." Arianna walked into the kitchen, not knowing any right direction. She faced the counter. To her relief, Nate followed and put his hands on the counter surrounding her. "I'm sorry too. I didn't give you a chance to explain. In my mind, I saw him getting close and I lost it."

"When he tried to kiss me, all I saw were your shoulders. Then I knew... I was only going through the motions."

"My shoulders?"

"Yeah. I didn't know where to put my arms when you leaned in. It just seemed so natural to wrap them around your shoulders. Then I remembered gripping you as you laid me back."

"You know how to get straight to my heart, don't you, woman?"

"I try."

Nate wrapped his arms around her. "Thank you, Ani. I swear I think it would have killed me more if you'd tongued him rather than screwed him."

"You sure about that, Agent Jackson?"

"Oh, don't make me analyze it, baby."

"You were right about so many things. I had no business with Anthony any more than you had with Shawnee. All I talked about the week leading up to her death was that flyer we'd gotten for Anthony's gym and maybe I needed to go, get stronger. She never mentioned him. I was setting up my own body to be used and didn't even realize it.

Hell, in her sick mind, she probably wanted him to hit on me." Nate didn't move his arms. Arianna was caged. She didn't try to move either. "Nightmare's in for murder."

"I know."

She laughed lightly. "I guess you would."

Nate guided her around to his face. He grabbed a paper towel and began wiping her eyes. "A man's biggest obligation is to protect his family. Above all that is holy. You have no right to rob me of that, baby."

"I felt so, so damaged, Nathan. Nightmare used pens, water guns, whatever he could find. The memories completely eclipsed me, and I couldn't let them do that to you, too, not after all you've been through."

"He doesn't define who you are and he shouldn't define what we become."

"I am so sorry," Arianna said over and over until she ended in the strength and security of Nate's clasp. He sandwiched her between his body and the counter. She cried harder, using all the muscles in her arms to cleave to him in his bodily shelter.

"Can I make a suggestion?" Nate asked.

"Of course, Nathan."

"Stop calling him Nightmare."

"Why?"

"By naming him, you give him an identity and control. He isn't," Nate reminded her, "a creepy crawly creature hiding under your bed. He's just a no-good bastard." Then he made a profound point. Nate could protect her body, all day long, but there wasn't a damn thing he could do to protect the thoughts that entered her mind. "Remember how you mentioned earlier about doing stuff for you, without me?"

"Yes."

"This is a prime example. *You* have to block him out. *You* have to tell yourself there is no place for him in your life," he said. "You have the strength. Use it.

You were a little white girl, with a dysfunctional father, who not only survived a housing project, you fit in, made friends, and held your own. You were assaulted for what, eight years? And then you turned around and became a track star with a Summa Cum Laude MBA and CEO credentials. And, if that's not enough, you married a military intelligence officer turned high-level federal agent. Who does that? You think I married you because you're fine? Don't get me wrong, you are fine, but no. I married you because you're amazing. I have the complete package. Why do you think I got so wrapped around the axle when you told me another man had touched you?"

She just stared at him. "It's ironic."

"What's ironic?"

"I made you the last to know, yet you've given me the best advice of all."

"I'm supposed to."

"That's your job?"

"Yup."

She put her hand on his cheek. "There's one more thing. I need you to be calm. Promise me."

"I'll try."

Arianna took off the T-shirt and bared her breasts. She stood in front of him naked except for her panties. "I didn't burn myself."

"HE BURNED YOU?"

She barely breathed the word, "Yeah," before continuing. "I told him, 'no more.' Then I fought like hell to get away. He wasn't having it."

Nate repeatedly pounded the counter with his fist. The small appliances on the counter rattled. "I'm gonna separate this guy from his spleen."

"I'm not done, baby." She paused. "It wasn't a curling iron. He threw drain cleaner on me."

"ACID?"

"I'm afraid so."

"I'll be back. I need something to hit." Nate moved swiftly toward the basement. Arianna reached for him. "Ani, let go, baby. I need to be alone for a minute."

The sounds were loud and obnoxious. Nate's screams and the sounds of pure rampage made it hard for Arianna to breathe.

She put Nate's T-shirt back on.

When the noises finally stopped, she crept downstairs. Nate had reduced the basement to almost rubble. He was sitting on one of their older couches in the middle of the aftermath of his tornado. He looked at Arianna as she came down the stairs. "I'm gonna kill this guy, I swear to God. But first, I'm gonna cram roaches down his fuckin' throat, and when he gasps for air, I'm going to force that bitch to swallow them with Drano."

Arianna walked around the books, remnants of shelves, and other storage obstacles on the ground to stand by Nate. He turned his leg, an indication he wanted her to sit on his lap. She sat with her side to him, and he rubbed her bare thigh. Then she expressed her biggest concerns—the scar and the lie. This was the one thing she'd directly deceived him about. The rest she'd withheld was bad too, but this was an outright lie she'd carried the entire marriage.

"You know, I never told the girls this, but deep down, I had a fear, as irrational as it might sound."

"What fear?"

"I thought you'd leave me, Nathan."

"Leave you? How can I leave a woman I can't live without? Hell, I stabbed my couch when *you* left *me*."

Arianna turned and gripped him tight. He responded by tilting his neck so their foreheads could touch. "I have taken down drug lords, collared countless criminals, kicked in a zillion doors, and punched a few thugs in the face that, professionally, I probably shouldn't have."

Nate raised her head, his voice cracking. "But you stand in front of me, and I melt like butter." He clung to her, almost depriving her of oxygen. "I'm the luckiest man alive, and your lie doesn't change how I see you. You're beautiful, inside and out. You have to trust me enough to know that so I don't have to hear from somebody else."

"I know."

"Is there anything else, Ani? Anything at all you're keeping from me."

"He said he'll always be my nightmare."

Nate motioned her off his lap, and they both stood up. "No, he won't." He gently placed his hand under her chin and raised her head. "Not if you don't let him."

She looked into Nate's eyes and didn't move. He grabbed the bottom of the T-shirt and lifted it up to Arianna's neck. She raised her arms and Nate took off the shirt. Then her eyes followed his hand.

Softly, Nate ran the back of his forefinger across her scar, so slowly and so meticulously that he touched every ridge. Then he placed his entire hand across the scar. "Does that frighten you?"

"No, not at all. Your touch never frightens me."

"Then he shouldn't either."

Arianna embraced him. "Thank you. Now you know the whole truth."

"We're done with this, understand? We're done."

"We're done."

Nate grabbed the T-shirt and slipped it back over Arianna's neck. She put her hands through the sleeves.

"Aren't we supposed to go spoon or some shit?" he asked.

"You've been so patient for so long. And you've given me so much." Arianna looked between his legs, then kissed his neck. "It's not fair to make you wait any longer. It's my turn to give you something."

"Not tonight, Ani."

"Why not?"

"You needed a friend, and that's exactly what I'm gonna be tonight. I have the rest of my life to feel you."

"It's been over two years since I've gotten down on my knees for you. Please let me do this, Nathan."

"Okay, but not here. And not on your knees, baby.

Nate led her upstairs. His back hit the bed. Arianna's lips hit his chest. She made her way down his body as Nate focused on the blur of the ceiling fan blades while enjoying the feeling of Arianna's petal-soft lips enveloping him, bringing him into another world.

~~~

Arianna lay asleep, cleansed of affairs and nightmares as Nate stroked her hair and stared at the ceiling, too full of emotion to sleep. He was home, in his own bed, finally. Every sound, from the low click of the ceiling fan chain, to the hum of the air-conditioner, to the sounds of insects in the Texas night, wrapped him in the comfort of the place where he knew he belonged—home.

The Bible on the dresser caught his eye. Arianna must have been reading Scripture. Nate's profound gratitude for his family made him realize that giving the Book a run couldn't hurt.

What the hell...heck...sorry, God.

Nate turned on Arianna's reading lamp, grabbed the Bible, and then fought a war with his memory. He could not recall enough about Sundays to know what to read. Random sampling would have to suffice. Proverbs 31:29 was the lucky Scripture.

Many women do noble things, but you surpass them all, he read.

"So You think You're slick." He whispered and looked up. "Let's see what else You got for me."

Nate flipped the pages while looking up at the ceiling. He stopped at an arbitrary page and pointed. He looked down at his forefinger, which marked Ephesians 5:25.

Husbands, love your wives, just as Christ loved the church and gave himself up for her.

Nate looked up at the ceiling again, giving props. "You're good. I'll give You that." He flipped back through the Good Book. "Let's see if You can do it a third time, shall we?" Nate looked down. Exodus 20:14.

Thou shalt not commit adultery.

"Okay, well, I won't try that again."

Nate listened to the pages rustle as he flipped, sometimes a few at a time, sometimes just one. He massaged the pages between his thumb and forefinger, almost mesmerized by the thin, fancy, gold-trimmed paper. He shut the Book, looked at the binding, then flipped the Bible to the back like a curious child looking for the sharpener on the crayon box. He ran his hands over the cover, realizing he hadn't placed them on a Bible in years, and that his boys needed a better example. *My kids.* Nate shut the Book, promising to return to it more often.

Nate grabbed Arianna's cellphone. He plugged in the old code, 1225 for his birthday. It worked. He smiled. She'd never changed it.

Nate scrolled through her contacts. *This has to be it.*

He grabbed his phone and entered the number. Then he walked out of the room.

"Gloria, this is Nate."

"Do you have a fever, dear?"

"Uh, no, listen, I'm home now."

"I saw your car."

"Of course you did."

"Are you being facetious, Nathaniel?"

"No, ma'am. Is Tre still up?"

"He dozed off hours ago."

"I know it's late. But would you mind— "

"Come get him, Nathaniel."

"Give me five minutes."

Nate texted Darius next. *You awake?*

Bout to die.

Nate laughed as he pictured Darius yelling through his Xbox microphone and trying to stay alive. *I'm home.*

For real?

Nah, I just like emotionally traumatizing you… yeah, I'm for real.

Cool.

Pick you up in the AM.

Nate got Tre from Gloria's and put him to bed. He was about to go to bed too when his cellphone went off. "What's up, Son?"

"Got killed. The party's lame."

"Text me the address."

Chapter 54

Arianna looked at the front entrance of the pale pink convalescent center. She approached the building, her arms folded in her black sweater. She switched her hands to the back pockets of her jeans, then crossed her arms again. Her indecision about how to handle her father made the sidewalk seem never-ending.

Plates clattered in the kitchen, and Arianna's hope for a pleasant smell washed away with the uneaten mashed potatoes. Some elders creaked along the halls, others sat in wheelchairs seemingly unaware of their surroundings. A man waved to Arianna. She smiled and waved back to the stranger who, according to the military hat he was wearing, had no idea World War II had ended a long time ago.

Funny pictures of black cats and witches covered the plain white walls, and rubber spiders dangled from the ceiling. Arianna thought it fitting. The place already seemed scary, and the orange and black garland fit right in.

Before reaching C3, the Alzheimer's hall, Arianna grabbed the railing to settle her stomach. Then she went up to the reception desk.

"Excuse me, I'm looking for Mr. Statton's room."

A nurse pointed behind her. "Right through there. Glad he's getting company. Maybe he'll be in a better mood."

Arianna grabbed the long silver handle and pushed the heaviest door she'd ever walked through. She wondered if he would remember her. In a way, she hoped he wouldn't. It would make for a quick visit.

She saw a sick old man left to his own bigotry and hatred. Blue-striped hospital pajamas and slippers made him appear far different from the dictator Arianna had known growing up.

She placed a framed picture of Darius and Tre on the counter next to the sink and bent down to her father's wheelchair to get his attention.

"Daddy... Daddy."

Her father looked up. "Arianna? Is that you?"

Arianna sighed. "So you remember me?"

"Why you never come see me?"

"You disowned me, remember?"

Her father didn't immediately respond. Arianna didn't know if she'd get hostility from him, or regret. "I'm sorry," he finally answered, his voice dropping. His apology seemed sincere, but she glossed over it anyway. She felt caught, not knowing which emotion to act upon, her anger or her need to forgive. "Here." Arianna handed photos to her father. "I brought pictures of your grandchildren."

He sounded surprised and interested. "Really?"

"Yes, really."

"Well, let me size 'em up." Her father reached for his glasses. "How they doin' in school?" he asked.

"Very well."

"Good boys? Do they listen?"

"For the most part."

"Wow. I got grandchildren."

"Yes, you do."

The skin on her father's shrinking neck moved like a rooster's as he gestured, holding up the pictures and then bringing them back down. Tears were in his eyes. His acceptance of her children was either remorse or the effects of his progressing disease. Arianna didn't care. She just wanted closure.

"You've missed out on a lot, Daddy."

He started crying. Arianna realized that, in all of her years, she'd never seen him cry. But did tears earn him sanctuary? Did remorse override his throwing Arianna to the wolves? Should a bloodline acknowledgement erase the hateful things he'd said about Nate?

"I'm sorry. I'm so sorry," he said. "Please forgive me."

"You hurt us so badly." Arianna's voice started to crack. "You took my mother from me."

"When life catches up with you, you realize things."

She contemplated bringing up Nightmare. Did her father already know? For years, she'd dreamt of this day, the day she could face Daddy Dearest and hit him with his wrongs, create some wounds, and then point out her good life to further insert the knife. But seeing him lonely and isolated, she realized she didn't have to prove anything. His hate had grown like mold. Telling him so now would serve no purpose other than to add to his guilt. She could see from his frailty, that guilt had already done a pretty good job of occupying his mind.

"Mom put you here because she couldn't take living with you anymore. Isn't that right?"

"I think so. She hated me, but I loved her. I wasn't the best man in the world. But I had feelings."

Arianna didn't know how to respond without increasing the tension.

"When can I see your family?" he asked.

The question was too much, too fast, too soon. "I need to go now."

Her father grabbed her arm. "Save me, Arianna. I don't want to go to hell."

"Only you can save you."

"You comin' back to see me? Maybe bring my grandchildren? Ya know, if you wait too long, I may not know you, with my mind the way it is."

"I'll try, Daddy."

Her father reached up to her. She stood steadfast and stared him down, but she realized he was right. This might be her last chance with him. Ralph Statton looked so broken.

"Can I hug you?" he asked.

She didn't move, unsure if she wanted his affection.

His voice cracked, a signal that he seemed about to crumble. "Please."

Arianna bent down and hugged her father. His vein-embossed arms smothered her and his hands wrapped around her neck. He started bawling like a colicky baby. "I know what he did. I know. I'm sorry."

Arianna's tears streamed. She let years of pain and bitterness fade away within the confines of that hug, cleansing her toward lucidity. But she still remembered every hateful word, every loathsome action of her father toward her, her mother, and her husband. She was hugging him, but not fully embracing him. While not ready to forgive him, at least now she wasn't riddled with rage against him. "Thank you for that. But there's nothing you can do now. It's my problem to deal with."

"But it's my cross to bear. I wanna help you."

Arianna stood up, breaking their connection, now feeling nothing but sorrow for this shattered man. "I have help, Dad. His name's Nathaniel."

"You guys still married?"

"Surprised?"

"Yes, honestly."

"He's an exceptional man. He's taken damn good care of me. You lost out on a good son-in-law because of your hate."

"My grandchildren too."

"I pray you make peace with yourself."

"I love you, Arianna."

She thought about her response. "You don't know what I would have given for you to have realized that a long time ago, Dad."

"Will you come back?"

"Yes. I will come back. You have my word. But that's as far as my promise extends." She left his room, left him with hope, and left him on her way to a cleansed life.

Chapter 55

Gucci pumps. Silk stockings. Black skirt three inches above the knee. Short blazer showing the world Arianna hated panty lines across her smooth behind. Frameless glasses. Black purse. Hair flipped up in a clip, with just enough hanging over to swish when she walked. Red lipstick. Matching nails.

Men lowered their sunglasses. Women struggled to find any flaw as Arianna strutted into the lobby like she owned the water that ran through the river.

Arianna was back, back from Knoxville, back from the bullshit, and back to a new and improved normal.

She nodded to everyone who passed her and hopped onto the elevator, heading to her office.

It was Monday morning, and she was heading to work straight from the airport. She had scoped out commercial real estate in Tennessee for a fourth coffee café. Her original plan had been to stop by the house after touching down, but she'd gone back to the cemetery one last time and then taken a later flight. She was already late at returning important calls. Plus she was eager to tell Taesha her ideas for a New Year's event she had thought of on the plane.

"Good morning, Jenna."

Arianna stepped into her office and got comfortable. She powered up her computer, kissed her finger, touched her picture of Nate, and smiled. *My baby.*

"Would you like some sugar to go with that attitude?" Jenna smirked.

"Did you make coffee?"

"Yeah. Somebody had to. You don't know how to make it right." She turned to get Arianna a cup. "Old people."

Taesha walked in and sat down. "You been home?"

"No. Came straight in."

"Could have called a sistah. I was gonna meet you at the airport."

"Why?"

"Because I love you."

"Okay, Tae."

"Why'd you take off hush-hush?"

"Had to be alone."

"I feel you. Talk to me, diva."

"I told him everything, Tae."

"And?"

"He annihilated the basement."

"I see."

"You don't seem surprised."

"It's Nate, dude."

Arianna smiled. "Yes, it is."

"He seemed happy."

"What?"

"I mean that night. He seemed happy to be home."

"He was even happier when he went to sleep."

"I'm sure he was. How was the trip?"

They discussed the weekend and Arianna wanting to take Taesha to Knoxville to check out some possible locations. Arianna mentioned her mother and how she'd almost fallen asleep sitting next to her at the cemetery. Then she talked about the visit to her father and how liberating it had been.

Jenna came in with some much needed coffee.

"Okay, damn," Taesha said.

"What?" Arianna asked.

"I can't pretend I don't know." She stood up. "C'mon."

"Where?"

"Let's just go."

"I can't. Things are changing. I'm a CEO and it's time I started acting like it."

"You're killing me. Jenna?"

"Yes?"

"Tell your boss to come on."

"Do I need to get my gun, Arianna?"

"Let's go, Tae."

Arianna walked into the house. The carpets had been shampooed and new furniture had replaced the outdated predecessors. A shiny new curio cabinet matching the rest of the wood stood in the corner holding her scrapbooks.

"This was just a bonus." Taesha led her downstairs. Arianna discovered the basement cleaned and repainted. Then Taesha led her upstairs.

The sink in the master bathroom was new, red marble. New bathmats added a touch of grey and pictures of roses in charcoal-colored frames hung on the walls. A hint of pink in the ceramic tile on the floor complemented the color of the tile behind the new whirlpool bathtub. At last, she had her spa tub.

"Open the cabinet."

Arianna did. She grabbed the white-chocolate rose and an envelope. Inside she found an Internet receipt with a note that read:

I know this can't wipe out any scars, or erase any burns, but I thought I would try to make it easier for you to look at them.

Love,

Your Nathan

P.S. If you don't stop making me spoon, then you owe me $11, 685.29. And by the way, since you wanted a pinch of space, I thought I'd give it to you.

Arianna looked at the receipt. Nate had slipped it inside the envelope in lieu of the certificate that had yet to arrive. "He bought me a *star*, Taesha?"

"It was Eva's idea. Nate thought it was stupid, but he knew you'd eat it up. Mumbled something about it could help him get laid. Eva punched him in the chest. I died laughing. I'm not supposed to tell you though."

Arianna giggled. "My practical man."

"Yeah. It was hilarious. Marcus told her that it didn't mean anything scientifically. Nate said women like that kind of shit. We actually debated for an hour about the differences in guys and girls. Marcus and Nate said we're too emotional, and then Pam hit both of them with the bathmat."

"Sounds like you guys had a blast."

"Mostly."

Taesha told Arianna that Nate had "strongly encouraged" them to be at the house that weekend to renovate. Pam set the groundwork for the decorating and pretty much led the whole endeavor, except for the carpentry work, which Nate orchestrated and carried out with help from Marcus, D.J, and a couple of contractors Gloria's husband knew.

Arianna smiled. "D.J.?"

Taesha smiled back and told her D.J. had taken her to the Del Rio carnival Sunday afternoon after they finished with the house. "He won me a teddy bear, like huge." Taesha stretched her arms out.

"Guess he's not shy anymore."

"He's sweet. Just because he didn't pin a dude by his neck with his bare hands doesn't mean he's not a man, you know?"

Arianna put her hands up and laughed. "Okay. Okay. Excuuuuse *me*."

"I almost slept with him, but I found myself not ready. Isn't that crazy?"

"I think it's the sanest thing you've ever said."

413

Taesha pointed out the nooks in the new bathroom as she went on and on about D.J. Arianna examined the work and noticed the meticulous care that had gone into it. The detail alone was enough for her to know that Nate knew her immensely well, and had taken the time over their years together to understand that the soap dish went on the left, the toothbrush holder went on the right, and the disposable cup dispenser went near the edge so Tre could grab one cup, or all of them, when he brushed his teeth. The primary color, red, was something she'd mentioned years ago, in passing, when she was cleaning the bathroom. He'd remembered all of it.

"He put the cups near the edge, Tae," Arianna whispered. "And it's so clean in here."

"Uh, okay," Taesha said.

Arianna ran downstairs. "I gotta find that man of mine."

Taesha ran behind her. "Hold on. You can't. You're not supposed to know about this yet. Nate's out planning something. He will choke my ass."

"Really, Tae?"

"Sorry, just popped into my head. Let's get you out of here and meet Pam and Eva for lunch."

"Let me run upstairs and look at my bathroom again right quick."

"Oh my Jesus, hurry before your husband pulls in and jacks me up."

Arianna raced to the stairs, then stopped abruptly and put up her hand. "Wait." She smirked. "I have an idea."

"I'm listening."

"I can't fake a reaction. He's gonna know that I already saw the house."

"So?"

"*So*, I'm gonna make Supervisory Special Agent Nathaniel Darius Jackson Jr. react—in a way he'll never forget."

Taesha laughed. "I'm all in."

Arianna called Nate and told him she was at work. She asked him if he could pick up the kids after school and take them to Taesha's place for the night. The traveling had exhausted her, she said, and she wanted a date night alone with him. He agreed with no argument and full compliance. It didn't take a genius to deduct that Nate had bigger plans after the reveal of the renovations.

Arianna hung up. "Let's go."

"Where?"

"Victoria's Secret. And we have to hurry, so you can get back home in time."

"You owe me."

Chapter 56

D.J. went for a lay-up. Marcus blocked his shot. D.J. called a foul. Marcus grabbed the basketball, said "check," then thrust the ball toward D.J.'s chest. "Only punk-ass white boys call fouls." D.J. threw back the ball, talked his own trash, and got into a defensive position. Marcus dribbled, stopped short of the goal, and performed a fadeaway.

"Luck," D.J. said.

"Skill," Marcus said. He tried again but missed the shot.

D.J. took the ball, ran around Marcus, and made a lay-up. "I used to play for UNLV, fool."

Marcus huffed. "Just play."

For a moment, no talk of blood spatters or body positions dominated the day. It was just Marcus pretending he was younger than his age. A few minutes into their game, they'd covered their clothes in sweat, D.J. was up by one and had the ball, and he was ready to make the winning shot.

Marcus blocked the ball.

D.J. objected. "Goaltending!"

Nate walked up to the court. "What's up, scrubs?"

"What are you doing here?" Marcus asked.

"I could ask you the same question." Nate took the ball and made a three-pointer.

"You want next?" D.J. asked.

"You don't want none of this." Nate nudged Marcus. "I need a minute."

They sat on the bench and watched D.J. practice. "He's kinda good. Not better than me, though."

"You're pathetic. What's up?"

"I'm gonna take the kids over to Taesha's when they get out of school so Arianna and I can have a night alone."

"You know, Nate, we talk about the women and the messed-up shit they do, but I gotta give it to them. They got each other's backs for real. At the drop of a hat."

"I know, right."

"So, what's up?"

"I need your help."

"The last time you said that I almost got divorced."

"Man, I'm past all that bullshit. I just need to take care of something."

"What?"

Nate fidgeted, seeming unsure of how to approach the issue. "One time. There was one time."

"One time, what?"

"One time with Shawnee, about six weeks before she died. When I was done I threw the condom in the trash instead of the toilet. Wasn't thinking. I went back and it was gone. She said she flushed it. Didn't question it at first, but now..."

"She may have been touched in the head, but to deliberately inject that shit? C'mon, Nate."

"It's been known to happen. I need to know if the baby was mine. I can't begin an honest marriage like this. If it comes back to bite me later, and I'm fired, Arianna will never forgive me if I've kept her in the dark."

"Assuming it can still be done, you probably won't find out the results today."

"Aren't you in good with the M.E.?"

"We're cool."

"Call her."

~~~

Nate and Marcus waited for Dr. Imani Barnette to return. The sign on the door said she'd be back in fifteen minutes. They sat outside her office. Nate tried to pretend he wasn't as scared as a woman walking alone in a dark alley.

Five minutes later, Imani strutted down the long hallway in a red suit and holding a file. She was slender, with porcelain, ebony skin and long black hair that draped her shoulders. Nate stared her down. "If I wasn't so on edge, I'd make a comment about how hot she is."

"Whatever, Nate."

"Does Pam know you guys are friends?"

"We're colleagues."

"Does Pam know you guys are colleagues?"

"Shut up, Nate."

"Just sayin'. A receipt would be the least of your worries."

"You got jokes, really?"

"You're gonna get your ass kicked if Pam ever sees her."

"It's the job."

"Of course."

Imani approached her door. "Let me guess, Marcus. This is Nate."

"Yeah, but don't look at him too hard, Imani, he'll try to nail you. Oh wait, he only likes white women."

Nate glared at his smart-ass best friend. "If this wasn't such a contentious situation..."

"Spell contentious."

"F.U.C.K. Y.O.U."

Imani rolled her eyes and unlocked the door. "Come in, guys, before I have to call the principal on you two."

They followed her in. Nate sat in a chair, but Marcus remained standing. Nate told her to get on with it before he might have to throw Marcus out of the window.

"There's no need to run a test," she said.

Imani opened the file she was holding and handed Marcus a printout with short lines in pairs, some straight, some squiggly. They were a perfect match to the fetus Shawnee had lost in the fall.

"Mr. Jackson, you're not the father. We ran a conclusive test on somebody else a little while ago."

Nate sighed with relief.

"How come you didn't tell me?" Marcus asked.

"He's a colleague. He came to me in confidence."

"First name Anthony?"

"How'd you know?"

"It doesn't matter. I'm investigating this case. You should've told me."

"I would have if I'd thought something wasn't right. But it works both ways, Marcus. You couldn't tell me you were personally involved in this? You couldn't trust me? I can do stuff on the D.L. for you, but nobody else?"

Nate crept out of the office to wait. He wondered about Marcus's and Imani's connection. He knew Marcus loved Pam, knew he would never jeopardize his good name or his good thing. But something lay between Marcus and Imani, fostered from something much bigger than forensic science.

A few minutes later, Marcus emerged.

"You were hard on her, Marcus."

"She had no business keeping DNA results from me. Said she's sure he didn't kill her and checked his alibi without telling me." Marcus beat his chest. "Without telling me, Nate."

"She was covering for her colleague, Marcus. Have you never done that?"

Marcus began walking off. "No. I was too busy covering for my stupid-ass best friend instead. Let's go."

Nate followed. "So...you've never pictured hittin' that?"

Marcus got loud. "Oh, God, really, dude?"

"Uh, yeah, really."

"Uh, no. I'm a married man. You oughta try it sometime."

"Struck a nerve."

"No, okay? I would never cross the line. You happy?"

"Didn't say you would cross the line. I just wonder why you're so pissed."

"I'm not pissed. What does that have to do with anything, anyway?"

"You're upset that Dr. Barnette didn't show you any loyalty. That implies a connection."

Marcus stopped walking. "Why are you doing this?"

"I saw how you looked at her, Marcus. And I know firsthand how it ends."

"I'm not you."

"All it takes is one crack." Nate stared him down and wouldn't relent. Marcus was feeling guilty about *something*. Nate could tell from his desperate attempt to avoid the head-on collision of eye contact.

"Okay," Marcus conceded, "for two months, Pam gave me the cold shoulder over driving you to that motel. She would barely talk to me, wouldn't allow me to say shit about why I helped you. She wouldn't even let me touch her. It got to me."

"Did you...?"

"No," Marcus answered defiantly. "But I was tempted."

Nate looked at the floor and looked back up, feeling an empathy he'd mastered all too well. "Almost doesn't count. Give yourself a break."

"I talked all that shit about *you* cheating, and I almost caved at two months. Now I realize how easy it is to affirm a stance against something when nothing at home needs affirming."

Nate quietly held Marcus's gaze for a moment. Then he said, "And you call *me* Aristotle."

Marcus stood unfaltering as Nate stared him down, until they couldn't help but chuckle. Then there was a moment of silence. They stood stoically, allowing the strings of their friendship to show, without revealing the softer side they both had when it came to what they were, the point Marcus had driven home months ago at a distant Memorial Day—family. "I am attracted to her. But Pam is everything to me, Nate. I would never cross that line."

420

"Hey, you don't have to explain it to me. Been there, done that." This time, Nate walked off and led the way. "But just remember, Pam's an attractive catch too."

"Excuse me?"

"Just sayin'. Somewhere in San Antonio, some guy is telling his best friend how attractive your wife is to him. He might even be white, named Connor or Tanner, or something."

"Oh, hell to the nah. Hold up."

Nate chuckled. "C'mon, I'll buy you a drink."

"I'm on the clock."

"In that case, I'll buy you two."

Chapter 57

Nate felt pressed for time. He had to go out of his way to pick up the boys and then visit the San Antonio Field Office for Agent Greene. Nate hadn't counted on every secretary in the building parading the boys around to every cubicle. Thankfully, he was now at his last stop.

Nate knocked on Taesha's door.

"Why we gotta come here?" Darius asked.

"I thought you liked coming here."

"I do. I just wondered why Tre can't stay home."

"Don't start," Nate said.

"Mommy needs to rest," Tre answered.

"I wasn't talkin' to you, idiot."

Nate laid down the law. "I know you've been through a lot, and I'm trying to understand that." Then he raised his voice. "But call your brother an idiot, one more time, and I'm gonna throw you down the stairs, understand?"

"He's irritating, Dad."

"He's your brother."

Taesha opened the door. "How did I know it was y'all?"

"Just let us in," Nate commanded. He put his keys on the counter. "You have something to drink? It's hot as hell outside."

Tre ran to the corner of the living room where Taesha had constructed the tent and put his sleeping bag inside. He sat Elmo down, poured out his plastic letters, and started spelling words with Elmo.

The Xbox was plugged in, two controllers waiting to do battle. Darius had connected to Xbox Live before anybody could blink.

"Wait until I get over there. You're goin' down," Taesha said.

"Bring it on," Darius said.

"Put up your book bags," Nate said. Then he shook his head.

"What's wrong?" Taesha asked.

"He's had an attitude about Tre for months now. I'm gettin' so frustrated."

"You feel guilty."

"Don't start, Taesha."

"I heard what he said outside. You can't let the fact that you feel bad stop you from disciplining him. Screaming at him isn't gonna work."

"I know that," he whispered quick and deep. "But lately I haven't known what else to do."

She put her hand on his shoulder. Nate continued to stare at Darius. "You've been through a lot and it's wearing on you. Calm down. Use the evening to reconnect with Arianna. Then you'll be better able to deal with Darius as a team," she said.

"We do need a good night alone without me choking folks, that's for sure."

"Let me put up the book bags and we'll talk. Leave them be."

"I gotta go."

"Hold on."

Taesha walked down the hall with the bags, slyly grabbing Nate's car keys along the way. She shut the bedroom door behind her and called Arianna. "How much time do you need?"

"Keep him busy until nightfall."

"That's like three hours. I can't hide his keys that long. He's already irritated."

"Why?"

"Nate's realizing he's raising a clone."

Arianna chuckled. "Thank you for watching the boys. Nate and I need this time. It's important to our marriage and the kids."

"That's what he said."

"Is my husband growing on you?"

"Maybe a little. But that doesn't mean I can stall him."

"You're resourceful. Think of something."

Oh, the things Taesha could do: breaking an appliance he could fix, perhaps having him wait at the apartment while she ran to the store. Then she thought of her icepick and it came to her, so perfectly.

"Oh yeah. This is gonna be fun." She came out of the bedroom, ready to play.

"Where are my keys?" Nate asked.

"I dunno. Did you look over there?"

"I've looked everywhere."

For an hour, Taesha "helped" Nate look for his keys, inside and outside her apartment. The more he cursed under his breath, and the more he tried to remain composed, the funnier the ordeal became. Nate threw her couch cushions, swearing the keys had been on the counter. Taesha fought like hell not to laugh.

"Where are they!" he screamed. "Damnit!"

She almost burst, but remained cool. "Oh, wow, here they are. By the toaster."

Nate grabbed the keys. "Bye."

Taesha waited for Nate to come back into the apartment, screaming loud enough to implode the building.

"This shit is not happening," he said when he returned.

"What's wrong?"

"I have a flat tire. Marcus is on his way. It's gonna be a minute because he's gotta get a spare."

"You don't have a spare?"

"It's flat too!"

424

Taesha grabbed the Xbox controller. "You're welcome to stay here."

"Gee, thanks." Nate plopped onto the sofa.

Taesha squeezed together her lips. Then, as seriously as she could, she gave advice. "You should probably call Arianna and tell her what's going on."

"Yeah, you're right. I was gonna meet her at the front door. Damnit."

Nate dialed. "Baby, I'm gonna be a little late. I had a surprise for you, but...yeah...I know that...I realize you wanted a date night, but...I'll be there...what?"

While holding the phone, Nate headed for the door.

Taesha put down the controller. "Hold on, Darius."

This shit is gonna get good. She peeked outside.

Nate was yelling. "You don't know what's goin' on, Ani...Why are you acting all insane?...How am *I* unfair?...You're going *where* with Gloria?...This isn't my fault...Excuse me?...*I* need to have more consideration?...You're the last one who needs to talk about somebody's driving."

Taesha felt a sudden urge to laugh the way a drunken person might have a sudden urge to vomit. She ran back into the house and doubled over.

"What's so funny?" Darius asked.

"Nothing." She composed herself and went back outside.

"Stop screaming at me, Ani. I lost my keys. It was an accident... You know what?" Nate sounded like he was about to lose it. He quickly clammed up, probably remembering how close he'd come to losing her. "I'll see you when I get home. And you're welcome in advance for the home improvements."

Taesha ran back inside and almost dove onto the controller.

"Adults are so weird," Darius said.

Nate came inside.

"You okay?" she asked.

"Peachy."

"Here, Daddy," Tre said. "We can play dinosaurs. I didn't know you were staying the night too."

Taesha pressed her lips together, trying her best to stay collected. Self-discipline almost failed her because she had to suffer through Marcus bickering about how delivering a tire hadn't been on his agenda. After he and Nate took off, Taesha settled Tre in his makeshift fort and put up the potato chips Darius had chomped on before he'd crashed.

The evening now consisted of a glass of wine and the spreadsheets she'd created showing Empowerment's projected profits. Taesha played with formulas and what-if scenarios until she heard a knock on the front door. She took off her glasses, the ones she barely wore and which most people knew nothing about. "Hi," she said to D.J.

"Can I come in?"

Taesha let D.J. into the apartment. He glanced at Tre knocked out in his fort and Darius, who'd fallen asleep on the couch. "Sleepover?"

"Guess so." She smiled and walked into the kitchen. Finding something to clean in a spotless kitchen proved pointless. Finding a way to process the fact that D.J. had found his way into her apartment and into her heart proved her vulnerability. No man had ever made a sincere effort.

He followed. "I don't care."

"What?"

"The men. The past. I don't care."

"You should."

"Why?"

"You don't wanna know."

"Try me."

"D.J, don't do this."

"Try. Me."

Taesha took a second to breathe. She knew D.J. wasn't gonna let up as much as she wanted him to. Her only choice was to tell him what had turned her beautiful black and white soul into the Scarlet Letter. She reluctantly spoke. "Sit down, D.J."

He did as she asked, and Taesha poured out her soul, flooding the room. "Okay, so, you're like eighteen and you

426

meet this guy, right? You marry him. He's loaded. He promises you the world, and you leave home. Nothing is ever good enough for him from that point on."

She started to pace, playing with her hands. "Then one day you turn thirty and realize you aren't the one with the problem. You tell him you're not gonna take it anymore. He tries to make up for it, apologizes for the heinous things he's called you, like, how, since you're mixed and have no money, you're poor white trash and a broke black bitch at the same time. So you live another empty year or so with the lie we call marriage.

You cheat, you know, to find completion, and you don't stop. You just don't stop. You get caught, you get beat, and you get ridiculed. You're labeled a slut, that's the best part, and then you're forced out of town...then you look forward to a new life in Texas and apply for an accountant position with a small coffee house. But you realize when you get there that bad habits die hard no matter how much you want them to."

Taesha had placed it all at D.J.'s feet. The silence seemed deafening as Taesha took a breath, wondering what D.J.'s next move would be. He got up and approached her. "Guess you got the job."

"Arianna and I clicked at the interview. She said she saw my eccentric side as an asset, along with my brain. I was the push to get her to incorporate all three of her coffee houses."

"I think she was right."

Her eyes welled. "D.J."

"And I'm gonna tell you what else I think." He grabbed either side of her face. "I think you want exactly what your friends have. That's why you defend their men so much. You might let on that you don't, but I know better."

"I don't deserve a guy like you, D.J."

"I know. You deserve better, but you're stuck with me. What a shame."

Taesha found D.J's touch too genuine to be complicated. She dropped her defenses and let go of her New York detriment as he leaned in, heading straight for her lips.

427

They kissed until their bodies met Taesha's bed, until D.J. introduced her to the difference between mindless sex and making love.

Chapter 58

By the time he made it home, Nate was burning hotter than a cast-iron skillet sitting on an open flame. Standing outside his house, key in the front door, he attempted to calm down.

"Try not to yell too loud, Jackson," he said to himself before opening the door. "She has the nerve to talk about *my* driving? Really?"

He walked inside.

One look around the house made the last few hours, and his anger, diminish with the twilight. The house was shadowy, illuminated with candles (of course). A wisp of perfume sweetened the air.

He called Taesha. "You're on my list."

Taesha laughed so hard, she couldn't respond.

Nate put his keys and a six-pack of beer down on the table. Then he picked up a note with his name on it. Crisp, with a sharp fold, and smelling like sweet jasmine, the paper widened along with Nate's eyes as he opened it. *We use it for formal occasions, and we almost broke it when you came home from your third interview.* The frustration of the past few hours vanished as Nate played Arianna's favorite game.

Oh yeah.

Briskly, he walked to the dining room table where two wine glasses and a basket of strawberries rested. Next to them, lay the second clue. *You tried to teach me how to play, but I never learned because I kept fouling you.* His body temperature spiked like the stock market during an unforeseen rally. He slid open the back door and noticed a jar of chocolate sundae topping next to the base of the basketball goal, with the third note peeking out from under the bottom of the goal. *If I were a bottle of Alize, where would I be?* Nate broke records rushing to the fridge.

Inside, their wedding photo wrapped a frosted red bottle. Nate moved the butter dish looking for the clue, only to realize it was written on the back of the photo. *Come make love to me already.*

He sprinted upstairs, forgetting the Alize and Arianna's fruit.

Candlelight covered the master bedroom. Sensual light and dancing shadows softened the ambience, complementing Robin Thicke singing about some well-needed Sex Therapy. "Ani?"

Noticing an envelope, Nate walked toward the dresser. He assumed it was another clue until he grabbed it. He almost collapsed as his wedding band fell out of the envelope. *I don't have 11,000 plus dollars, but I have this. And I couldn't buy you a star too because that would be lame. I did buy you some beer though.*

He stared down at the note. His watery eyes didn't see Arianna's reflection in the mirror. Her slim hand, the long nails painted translucent pink, came around his body and grabbed the hand that held the message.

Nate felt nothing but the allure of her, her scent dancing in the air.

She lifted his face, immobilizing him with her mirror image. "Find your keys?"

He broke another record turning around. "Good God Almighty, you are gorgeous."

The pearl and diamond earrings he'd given her for their second wedding anniversary dangled from her ears. The lingerie she wore emphasized her every curve, the long silk nightgown a little longer than she was tall. Her light makeup enhanced her smooth skin and made her eyes, cheeks, and mouth brighter. Long, loose versions of elegant spiral curls draped her face, neck, and shoulders. Her wavy, strawberry-blonde locks ebbed and flowed more smoothly than a well-written love story.

Nate soaked in her Amarige, which without fail, transported him to another world whenever she wore it.

"If you weren't so goddamned sexy, I'd strangle you," he said.

"I've been a bad girl."

"I see that."

"As you would say, 'You got got, fool.'"

"Yep." Nate nodded and licked his lips. "But now that you got me good, what are you planning to do to me?"

"Turn you out." Arianna felt her way between Nate's T-shirt and his button-down jersey. The jersey dropped to the floor.

Nate caved at her touch. No space remained between them after she put her head down onto his chest.

"I need to shower," he said.

"I like you dirty."

Nate raised her head. "I really, really need a shower. You'll thank me." He tried to kiss her.

"Not yet. And you don't need a shower." Arianna grabbed his hand and led him to the bathroom. She'd filled the tub with water, bubbles, and rose petals.

"A bubble bath? Really, Ani?"

"Yep. Strip." She placed her hands on the bottom of his T-shirt and lifted it. He did the rest and pulled the shirt over his head.

"Pants," she said. She unbuckled his jeans and shot them to the floor.

He looked at her.

"The rest," she said.

"Yes, ma'am."

Nate stepped into the hot water and sat down. Arianna sat on the edge of the tub, took a washcloth and squeezed the hot water over his back.

"Are you getting in?" Nate asked.

"No, this is all for you."

Nate felt that hot water and wanted to fall asleep. He put his head down and reveled in the heat. "Can I get my damn kiss?"

"Not yet. Stand up."

"You're killing me."

Arianna washed every part of Nate's body.

He looked down. "I think he's clean enough."

"Just making sure." Arianna took the washcloth and squeezed water onto Nate's shoulders. It trickled down the contours of his body. After a few rounds of rinsing him, she led him out of the tub, and dried him off with a plush towel and her gentle touch. Then she draped him in his thick, black robe and led him from the bathroom to the edge of the bed.

Arianna tried to speak, but Nate put his finger across her mouth, letting her know there was no more need for words. He glided his finger across her lips and in between them, opening her mouth just enough for her to stroke his finger with her tongue. Nate kissed her neck and then ran his palms down her arms. "Okay, I'm clean now, so I need to ask you an important question."

She looked up.

He closed in. "Can I please have my kiss now?"

Nate's mouth dominated the moment. He grabbed her face and kissed her once, profoundly. He backed off a touch, only to return to voraciously swallow her closed mouth a second time.

The sheer ecstasy of the kiss seemed too much for Arianna. She slid down, her knees buckling. Nate held her tight, letting his body tell her how badly he wanted her. He charmed her with his third kiss, slipping his tongue inside her mouth as she received him with hers. Then he brought both of his hands to her face. "One day, somebody's gonna tell me what I did, so right, the Lord allows me to wake up next to you every morning."

Arianna stepped back. "How can you stand in front of me, like you have a million times in my life, and paralyze me the way you do?"

"Because you make it so easy to want you."

"That's what I mean."

Nate whisked her up and gave her his version of sweet nothings. "I'm gonna tear your ass up, Mrs. Jackson."

Nate put his knee on the bed, laid Arianna down and softly separated her from her lingerie, with the diligence of a man who had not made love to his wife in months.

He now had to feel all of her against all of him, and he descended on her, leaving no space between them. Soon, they were entangled in each other, limb to limb and soul to soul, connected through the design of gender and the power of undeniable passion. Nate let out a low moan when he felt her warmth. He called out her name, leaving no doubt as to how grateful he was to be home. He worked strong, trying to make up for months of being without her, until they both set free their screams.

He lay on Arianna's chest. She rubbed his back, lightly. They smothered each other in their arms and fluids, without making a sound. Arianna kissed the top of his head. Nate closed his eyes with a feeling of comfort that could only come from being a satisfied man.

~~~

The Stone Oak Community Park provided a stark contrast to the crime-ridden areas on the other side of the city. The cool air, clear sky, and abundance of stars were the only entities surrounding Pam and Marcus that night.

He sat on a blanket with her and they shared jokes. She kicked her legs, laughed with an occasional painful scream, loud and with enough force to almost push the empty swings. Then she huffed, wiped her tears, looked at Marcus, and started the cycle over again with an occasional slap to his shoulder.

"I got one," she said. "If a plane crashes—"

"You don't bury survivors."

"Alrighty, then. There's a boy—"

"The old surgeon is his mother. Find some new jokes."

Still breathing heavily from her outbursts, she changed up. "Truth or dare."

"Now you wanna play something different."

Pam grinned slyly. "See, I'm in it to change the game." She got up and gyrated at what she thought was so comical.

Marcus lay back with his elbows propping him up, believing it *was* somewhat funny. "My jerseys are too big for you. Am I gonna have to pay seventy-five dollars a pop for you too?"

She ran out of breath and fell on him. "Maybe."

Marcus put his hands around her. The breeze soothed them, reinforcing their comfort as he rocked her. He couldn't remember the last time he'd looked at the stars, smelled the outdoor air, or even listened to the crickets chirping and the insects buzzing in the bushes.

Life hadn't spoken to Marcus in a long time.

He studied Pam's face, from her arched eyebrows to her defined cheekbones and full lips. "You are my angel," he said.

"What's wrong? There's something weighing on your mind. I can tell."

"I'm letting it all go, Pam. I'm letting Houston handle my mother's case. It's driven me crazy and I'm no better off than I was when I was a beat cop looking for clues. I hope they find something, but I can't drown in it anymore."

"I know."

"Same with Zach. I can't keep harboring these conspiracy theories. I know something happened in that house, but I can't do this. I can't do Kyle Ridgeland. I can't do these dirty cops who don't wanna see me succeed for whatever reason."

"But he's gone, right?"

"Yeah, but it's everything. I'm sick of seeing dead children, beaten wives, decapitated bodies in backyards. I'm just tired."

"You do what you need to do."

"There's an opening in Narcotics. I'm gonna take it. I just hate leaving D.J. behind."

"D.J. is going to be just fine. Taesha will see to that." Pam placed her hand on his cheek. "I'm here. Whatever you need."

"I need to see Zach."

They packed up and left for the cemetery.

Marcus called his boss and took the following day off. Then he grabbed his beloved wife's hand. "Pam?"

"Yeah?"

"Do you know a Conner, or a Tanner?"

Chapter 59

Buzzzzz. Buzzzzz. Buzzzzz.

"Marcus, your phone."

Buzzzzz. Buzzzzzz. Buzzzzzz.

"Damn, what time is it, baby?"

"Six-forty. I gotta get up."

Buzzzzz.

Marcus answered the phone and lay back in his bed with his eyes closed. "What part of the day-off memo didn't you read?"

Pam giggled, and went to take a shower.

"The Shawnee Redman case. We have a person of interest," D.J. said.

"I know it's important, but not today, Deeg."

"Marcus, listen to me."

"Was it another one of her nightly acquaintances?"

"It's Nate's son."

Marcus sat up. He looked over to the bathroom to make sure Pam was still in there. "What are you saying?"

"Get to the shop. Hurry, before we have an audience."

~~~

Forgive me, Father, for I have sinned.

436

Marcus threw down the suicide note. He wondered why he hadn't deciphered Darius's penmanship the first time he'd read the note back in March. Maybe he couldn't believe Darius would commit murder. Perhaps it was another version of depraved indifference. He had covered for Nate for so long, maybe he'd hidden the truth from himself.

Marcus tore out the page in the notebook that read: *Where were you, when Mom needed you? No doubt in her bed, with that bitch who's now dead. I'd give my life for my family, is what you once said. But you lied... made my mom cry... so I made sure that bitch knew she had nowhere to hide... I saw her tears fly... when I told her she was unwise... then I stood as close as I could to watch her fall... straight to her demise...*

"I'm sorry, partner," D.J. said.

"Where'd you find this?"

"At Taesha's house. Nate's son left the notebook this morning. Do you think he killed her?"

"Shhh."

Nate walked in. "What's up? Gettin' ready to hit the gym."

"You look tired."

"I earned it."

"Follow me." Marcus led Nate into a back room. Nate was walking different, lighter. Last night must have gone well—life-changing.

Now Marcus had to take away all the happiness Nate had just gotten back.

"We've been friends a long time," Marcus said.

"What's going on?"

"There's no easy way to say this." Marcus handed Nate the notebook page. "I think Darius killed Shawnee Redman."

"What?" Nate snatched the page from Marcus. He read the lyrics. Marcus could tell from Nate's deep breaths and the way he kept staring at the page that he didn't need to defend his position. The evidence was clear. "God, no, please, no."

Marcus handed him the suicide note. "He wrote this too."

Nate took the note. He compared Darius's musical chicken scratches with the words that had haunted Marcus since March of that year. Nate's eyes roved over three places: the note, the rap, and then Marcus, pinging each of them several times.

"There's more." Marcus took what looked like a small sandwich bag out of his desk. There was a small white piece of paper inside it. "We found this paper on the roof. I ran it for prints but didn't receive any hits because I wasn't looking for a kid."

~~~

Darius's dreams, though far-fetched, were still dreams, which meant the young man could see greatness for himself. He had compassion and the ability to defy the crowd for his principles. The time he'd spent in the basement, the moments Nate had been forced to listen, over and over, to stuff he couldn't decipher, the on-the-job training Nate was getting in learning how to give constructive criticism in a way that wouldn't make Darius give up, all led to one question: How could Nate lock up a son who'd taught him just as much about life as he had taught Darius?

Nate had to think objectively in the midst of a very subjective situation. Evidence demanded that he consider Darius a possible suspect, but as a father, he had to search far deeper to rationalize reasons for his innocence. Perhaps, even though it seemed unlikely, his son hadn't done it.

"Let me see that paper you found. The one in the bag." Nate took a good look at it before shaking his head. "No need to run prints. It's the receipt Darius tried to give me at the park the day Tre ran into the water. There's the logo. It's faint, but it's there." Nate picked up Darius's writings and reread them.

"We have to bring him in," Marcus said.

"Wait a minute." Nate held up his hand. Each word, each line, each rhyme processed through Nate's mind until he could read between the rap. "Take another look at this." He handed Marcus Darius's lyrics. "It doesn't say he made her fall. It says he watched her fall."

"C'mon, Nate. The tone in those words is hostile."

"No, look again. His word choice. Unwise? How was Shawnee unwise?"

Marcus read it again. "For sleeping with you. It's not verbatim, but it's enough, Nate. If this were somebody else, we would have collared him already."

"But he isn't just somebody."

Marcus stood there quietly. He seemed to soften his position after Nate reminded him of how he'd watched Darius grow up, about how Nate knew Marcus felt just as much like a father to Darius as Nate was. Besides, how could a kid help another kid out of a trashcan and then turn around and kill another human being?

Nate continued reading over the pages. "Unwise, unwise, unwise." He looked up, eyes big. "Darius isn't implying she was unwise to sleep with me. He saying she's unwise if she jumps."

"You sure?" Marcus grabbed the music.

"You ruled it a suicide for a reason. Because it was."

"Why would Darius even be there?"

"Let's go find out, quietly."

By the time Nate and Marcus made it to the school, Darius was long gone. Nate tried desperately to stay calm. Pam, Marcus, and Nate checked everywhere, the entire premises from classrooms to closets. Ronald told Nate Darius had run out the back after he discovered his notebook was missing, but didn't give any other details. Nate called Darius fourteen times. He never answered. Ronald was confined to Pam's office. He knew something he wasn't saying.

"We have to call it in, Nate. He's missing."

"Just a little bit longer. I haven't been the best father, but I know my son. He'll reach out to me...where the *hell* is he?"

Marcus agreed to give Nate some room, twenty more minutes.

Nate's phone rang.

"Sup, Dad?"

"Where are you?"

"I'll let you guess."

"Son, please."

"I'll tell you what, Dad. If you truly know me, you'll know where I'll be." He hung up.

Nate thought and processed and thought some more. "He's at the court. Let's go."

Chapter 60

The basketball court was quiet and empty. The only remnants of activity were the plastic soda bottles hugging the chain-link fence around the perimeter. The city hadn't gotten around to cleaning up. Napkins from concessions danced across the ground, giving a hint of the slight sway of a mild wind on a sunny September day.

Darius was sitting on a bench. Nate approached.

"You passed the test, Dad."

"How'd you get here, Son?"

"A cab."

"How'd you pay?"

"I stiffed him. Guess I learned to cheat from you."

"I deserve that."

"It's only down the street. It would have been a cheap ride anyway."

"I deserve that too." Nate sat next to Darius. "How did you find out I cheated on your mother?"

Darius didn't answer. "Dad, did you know that for the last year, I've known where you keep the key to your gun arsenal?"

"What? No."

"Yep. I thought about going into the basement, grabbing a weapon, and causing a scene."

"Maybe we should get you to talk to somebody."

"Believe me, Dad, if I was crazy, I would have killed myself. I'm fine. From where I'm standing, I'm the sanest person in the family."

"I never said you were crazy."

"You just implied it."

Nate looked around the court at the beautiful homes, thought about the beautiful life he had finally gotten back. For months, he'd obsessed over, and wallowed in, his guilt over the hurt he'd caused Arianna. Not once had he processed that not only had he cheated on his wife, he'd cheated on his kids too.

Nate saw Marcus flanked to his right, some distance away. "I've made some tremendous mistakes. I haven't been there for you," Nate said.

"Don't make me a victim, Dad. Trust me, I'm far from innocent."

"I'm just letting you know that I'm here now."

Marcus walked up to the bench. Nate nodded that it was okay that he join them. They sat on either side of Darius.

"You know, Dad, schools sit all of us students in a class, and they teach us all about sex and where babies come from. But they don't say a thing about how to control it or what it means. They leave that up to the parents. But how can you parents teach us, if you can't control it yourselves?"

"You're too smart for your own good. I wish I had the answer, Son."

"It's never gonna be the same." Darius shook his head.

"How so, Son?"

"You think Shawnee went to Heaven?"

Nate and Marcus stared at each other.

"Where did that come from?" Nate asked.

"She said she wanted to make sure she went to Heaven."

Nate was utterly confused and ill-prepared. He hadn't yet addressed the real issue of how Shawnee died because he'd wanted to lead in gently. Nate still had no clue how Darius had found out about the affair, and he was so flustered from trying to reconcile how Darius had known, that he barely noticed Marcus staring off into space as if he were contemplating the meaning of life.

"I told her to stop. I told her how stupid she was for doing it," Darius said. "As much as I hated her, I didn't want her to die."

"I know. You tried to stop her, right?"

"Apparently, I didn't try hard enough. If you'd kept it zipped, I wouldn't have had to."

"Excuse me?" Despite Nate's recklessness with his anatomy, he was still Darius's father and, in his mind, commanded authority, the way he'd learned as a little boy. Nate sat there, remembering his upbringing and sounding like Nate Sr. "Who do you think you're talkin' to?"

"The person who took my dad."

Nate had no comeback.

"Heaven," Marcus blurted out. "Ah, shit." He put his head down and then brought it back up. "It was in my face the whole damn time."

"What has you about to jump out of your damn seat?" Nate asked.

"It was all about her faith, not about evidence," Marcus said.

"I hate it when you think," Nate said.

"You don't get it. Darius didn't do it."

"Yeah, you're late."

Marcus looked at Darius. "She ran, didn't she?"

"Yeah. From back near the building. She took a piece of paper and a pen out of her purse. Asked me to grab them. She was acting so crazy I was scared not to."

Nate looked at Marcus, and then Darius, as if he were watching a tennis match. "Would you please clue me in, Marcus?"

"She wanted to hit the river to wash away the sin of suicide before dying. That's why she landed far from the building but still on the concrete. She missed," Marcus said.

"Okay, I've drummed up some ludicrous scenarios, but this?"

"She asked me to write her words," Darius interjected. "Forgive me Father for I have sinned. I did it because it sounded like she was having a panic attack. I didn't know what to do."

"So, you weren't writing that to me?" Nate asked.

"No, why would I do something stupid like that?"

"Guess you wouldn't."

"After she jumped, I was still holding the note. It kinda seemed fitting, because it was my fault and your side chick. I dropped it and ran as fast as I could down the back way before anybody could see me."

"Why do you think this was your fault?" Marcus asked.

"I could have stopped her. Tripped her or something. I let it happen." Darius looked at his dad. "No, you let it happen. If you hadn't been so selfish, none of this would have gone on, Dad. I hate you. I hate you. I hate you!"

Nate felt as if he'd just been stabbed in the heart with a steak knife. He looked at his son and saw his sadness, his guilt, his rage, and his hopelessness. Nate had to do something to remind Darius of the bond they'd once shared, the love they had between father and son. It had to be profound, something with a lot of power, something that might involve sacrificing Nate's life.

"Stay with him," Nate said to Marcus.

Nate walked to his car. He blocked himself behind the passenger door so they couldn't see what he was grabbing. He knew Marcus would be completely against this.

Nate walked back down to the court. "You hate me, young man?" he said, firmly, almost abusively. "Do you?"

"Yes."

"You want me dead?"

"Nate, c'mon, man," Marcus said.

"I know what I'm doing."

"I want to go back to before you cheated on my mom," Darius said.

444

"I can't do that. I can't take it back." Nate reached behind his back and pulled out a gun. "But you can rectify it."

"What are you doing?" Marcus asked.

"You shoot me, and you don't have to worry about me hurting your mom anymore." He walked up and put the gun in Darius's hand.

"Give me the gun," Marcus said.

"No," Nate said. "He keeps it."

Darius swung around and accidentally pointed the gun at Marcus.

"Whoa, shit, put your hands down, Darius. See what you've created?" Marcus yelled at Nate.

"Look at me, Darius. I'm the one you hate, remember? Shoot me, D. Right here, right in the heart. Go ahead. Cause that scene you wanted to so badly."

"Nate, you're an stupid moron," Marcus said. "No, D."

"Anger's your worst enemy, D. It'll eat you alive," Nate said. "So why don't you come closer and get rid of the main source of your pain? Aim for my head. You're sure to kill me then, at least give me brain damage."

"I'm not gonna kill you, you'll kill me."

"Your last rap was whack. And your girlfriend's ugly."

"It's not gonna work, Dad."

"No. It's *really* jacked up. And your girl, I don't know what planet she came from."

"You always gotta insult me."

"Here, let me get on my knees. You can shoot me execution style, that's cool. Take a shot. Shoot me, Darius. You won't have to deal with me anymore."

Darius raised the gun and placed his finger on the trigger. He aimed for Nate's head.

"No!" Marcus shouted. "Drop the gun, D!"

Nate shut his eyes. "*Lord, stay with me. Don't let him pull the trigger. I know You don't harbor hate, but after all I've done, and what I'm doing now, You're probably thinking about making me a test case. I'm sorry. I'm so sorry. I've tried to be a good father. I don't wanna fail. Maybe this isn't the best way, Lord. But it's all I know. It's all I know.*"

Nate heard what sounded like something dropping to the ground. His heart was pounding like a jackhammer to hardened tar. He opened his eyes. The gun lay on the ground. Darius ran to him and hugged him with what seemed like the strength of five men.

"Whoa. You're gonna knock me down if you're not careful, Son."

Darius soaked Nate's shirt in tears. "I love you, Dad."

Nate held tight to Darius. "I love you too, kid. Sometimes, we have to be faced with hurting someone before we can appreciate the love we have for them."

"I'm sorry," Darius whispered.

"I'm sorry too."

"That day Tre jumped into the river, remember that?"

Nate nodded and stood up.

"I had your phone. When I went to get the blanket I heard a text alert, but your phone was off. Then I heard it again coming from the glove box. I was nosy... and I looked. I saw another phone with a text that said: *I'm pregnant.* I knew it wasn't Mom. So, I texted her back. Told her to meet me, I mean you, someplace, anywhere. I made her think you were leaving Mom for her, so she'd say yes."

"What have I told you about grown folks' business? Damn, D." If Nate hadn't felt so relieved that Darius was innocent, Darius wouldn't have seen the outside of his room until graduation. "Go on."

"She texted back like within a few seconds and suggested the rooftop of the Gleason Building because the cameras were cut off due to construction and you guys could talk privately. She told me exactly how to get up there, without security seeing. Then she suggested other things you two could do I'd rather not say."

"That's why you were gone to the truck so long that day."

Darius nodded. "I had to make sure all the texts were erased too. I put the phone back under your registration and insurance papers. Then I planned the sleepover. All day I prayed she wouldn't text you again about it."

"How'd you get downtown?"

"Ronald's mom was out of town for her job and a friend was staying at their house. She dropped us off at Rivercenter Mall. We told her we were going to watch a midnight movie. We walked to the Gleason Building instead. Ronald waited for me downstairs. I snuck up the way she told me, or *you*, to go. I went all the back ways up the building, took a couple of service elevators. It was easy."

"This *friend* didn't care how young you were, or how late it was?"

"Dad," Darius sounded resolute. "Not everybody has Mom's friends."

"What did you have to gain?" Nate asked.

"All I wanted was for this chick to leave us alone. But when I showed up instead of you, she snapped, Dad. We argued about Mom. I told her that she wasn't half the woman Mom is. Then she began to pray for forgiveness or something. She was crazy, like horror movie crazy, Dad. She jumped just as I finished writing the note. I was so scared of getting in trouble."

"Do you have a purse somewhere I don't know about?"

"In my closet. Dad, you can have it. I'm tired of all of it."

Marcus nudged Nate to the side. He spoke low. "I've seen you do some stupid shit, but this takes the cake."

"Go touch the gun, Marcus," Nate said. "Take a good look at it."

Marcus picked up the gun and saw that it was a toy, an exact replica of a street revolver. "Where did you get this?"

"At work, we were given a training session about toy guns being sold that look like the real thing. We all got one to study. It has a real trigger."

"This doesn't make what you did right."

"Last May, Reuben Guerro put a gun to my head. I was three seconds from having my brains scattered all over a goddamned row house. If putting a toy gun in his hand will make him realize how precious I am to him, so he won't have to live knowing he hated me when I died, I'll do it again."

"I don't care how you spin it, it was wrong."

"I'm just glad it ended well."

"So, why were you praying so hard, if it was a phony-ass gun?"

"Because if he'd pulled the trigger, it would have let me know he hated me enough to want me dead. I wouldn't be able to take that."

"Still stupid."

"How is what I did any different from when that boy came to see Gwen?"

"No, no. I told that kid five times not to come around her anymore. He didn't listen and his parents didn't do anything about it."

"He was just fifteen years old."

"Exactly."

"You charged the poor kid with trespassing. You slapped cuffs on him, drove him to your job, and put him in an interrogation room for two hours. He was so scared he damn near pissed on himself. You almost lost your job over that."

"He doesn't come around her anymore, does he?"

"You have no room to talk about me, Marcus." Nate nudged Darius along. "C'mon, D."

The three of them walked off, Nate and Marcus continuing to bicker over who had won Father of the Century.

"Dad, you didn't get what I meant when I said you always gotta insult me, did you?"

"It was because I talked about your music and that girl you like."

"No. I can't believe you actually thought I didn't know what a fake gun feels like."

"You knew?"

"Not at first. When you put it in my hand I did. A kid at the court had one. He was showing everybody."

"You picked it up?"

"I was curious, but I wasn't amused like everybody else. I just wanted to play basketball. You're raising me well, Dad."

"Why, thank you. Don't ever pick one up again. Understand?"

"Yes, sir. It was funny watching Uncle Marcus duck though."

Marcus grimaced.

"So what was running up to me all about?" he asked.

"That was real. When you got on your knees like that, it just reminded me of all the crazy things you do to keep us happy. I like having a controversial father. It's kinda cool."

"That's the best thing I've heard in a long time, Son... assuming you know what controversial means."

"It means people don't always agree with you... and you don't care."

"I care when I should care."

"I don't wanna be a rapper anymore, Dad. I wanna be a cop, a fed like you."

"That's my boy."

"Just what the world needs. Another Agent Jackson," Marcus said.

"Can we keep all of this from Mom?"

"Nope. Just the gun part."

"So, I get to get in trouble, but you don't?"

"Yep. Perks of being the dad."

"Hey, Dad, what are those scratches on the back of your neck?"

"I ran into a rose bush."

Marcus shook his head.

"Backwards?" Darius asked.

"Yeah, sure, Son."

As they approached Nate's car, Nate noticed Anthony's vehicle parked on the other side of the lot. He must have just pulled in.

"You guys wait here for a second," Nate said. "Then we'll go eat... and just you and I'll come back," Nate said, referring to Marcus, who he hoped had caught on about coming back to his house and searching Darius's closet for the purse.

"You've already made one dumb decision today," Marcus said. "Don't make it two with this guy."

"I'm cool." Nate walked toward Anthony's SUV.

Anthony was sitting on a bench on a nearby patch of grass. "Using the fear factor. Heavily debated, but effective."

Nate's first instinct was to wrap his hands around Anthony's throat. Then he thought about Agent Greene's words, about modeling what Nate should want others to see. Darius was just a few feet away. Nate wasn't going to make the same mistake with his son that he had with the juveniles at the prison in Baltimore. He stayed cool. "What the hell do you want?"

Anthony stood up. "Need to talk to you."

"How'd you know I was here?"

"Went to the SAPD to spill everything I knew about Shawnee, now that I don't have to keep quiet to screw your wife, of course."

Nate looked back. *Stay cool, Jackson.* "Get to the point."

"Your friend's partner wrote up a police report about how I assaulted your wife. Said he would file it if I didn't back off."

"Did he now?"

"Good job corrupting him."

"He told you where I was?"

Anthony nodded. "Gave him my word that I would walk out of the precinct without a scene if he told me where you were."

Nate wasn't keen on what D.J. had done, but he was also grateful for his intention to quell the issue.

"Hear me out and you'll never hear from me again, Jackson."

"Make it quick."

"Did Shawnee call you to end it, and then a couple hours later, text you that she was pregnant and wanted to change her mind about ending it?"

"How'd you know that?"

"She did the same to me in reverse that morning, left me alone and confused as hell. I went home after working the gym. She'd left me the used pregnancy test proving she'd just found out. She even had the nerve to leave the receipt proving she'd just bought the damn thing that morning, like that was going to make me feel better. Then if that didn't hurt enough, she left me a note that she was taking you with her."

"I wasn't leaving my wife."

"She knew that. She was probably ready to let go of you until she found out she was pregnant and realized she couldn't have your child while you had somebody else."

"What are you implying?"

"What did you say to her on that roof?"

"I don't do question for question."

"She was going to end your life too. Probably push you and then follow. The sad thing? I just found out yesterday the baby was mine. She deliberately killed it."

"Why are you telling me this?"

Anthony's mood spoke of a man far different from the one Nate had thrown out by the throat. In the flesh, he was the same guy. But now his demeanor was far more defeated and far less cocky. "A few weeks before Shawnee died, she moved in with me. I knew what she was. Thought I could change her."

"Only God can change a person."

"No shit. That's what I told her. Talk about extreme. She wanted to change, I think. She tried, but she got obsessed with religion in the process and couldn't stop her promiscuous nature anyway. It was a cycle. I think the more she battled it, the more obsessed she got, until she almost went insane."

Nate nodded. Shawnee was starting to make sense, why she'd changed and demanded a ring from Nate. "What are you looking for here?"

"I've been so driven by anger for so long that I'd forgotten who I was. When I got home from your house, I wrecked mine. During my one-man riot, I found a Bible Shawnee had left. She'd highlighted Scriptures for granting and seeking forgiveness. Then, this morning, when I got the DNA results, I went home, looked in the mirror, and didn't recognize myself."

"You didn't recognize yourself."

"Just listen."

451

"Your time is running out."

"It hit me. What I did to your wife. She was so clearly devoted to you, and I almost destroyed her for payback. I was gonna walk away as soon I got her. When she walked into my gym that morning, I thought it was fate. Perfect opportunity."

"So you didn't plant that flyer?"

"What? No. But I did plant the seed when she came in. I need to make it right. I need your help."

"My help?"

"I want to personally apologize to your wife. You know, privately."

Nate stared him down. "Do you think I'm stupid?"

"I'm being sincere."

Nate stepped into his personal space. "When did you get the DNA results? Think really hard before you lie. Because I know you got them weeks ago. Trying to play on my sympathy to get to my wife one last time. I knew this was bullshit when I first walked over here. And don't think your whole Tennessee plan is lost on me, because it's not."

"What do you mean?"

"You didn't want my wife to get better. You wanted her to get worse, so she'd cling to you. Confrontations like that take weeks to set up properly." Nate wanted to punch him with everything he had. "You knew that bastard was in for murder and you wanted him to hurt her, so you didn't tell her. You wanted the confrontation to fail, you evil bitch."

"You assume a lot."

"I called your colleague in Tennessee the other day. He said you told him Arianna had been your patient for months."

Anthony suddenly changed up, chuckled, and flashed a sinister smile. "You're formidable. You caught me. Nice. I like that."

"Damn, you're a sick fuck."

Anthony frowned, then laughed deliberately, with a sound of pure evil. "Well, I guess you're smarter than I thought."

"This is your last warning. Mark my words, I am watching you." Nate walked off.

"No fight? You remember, oh so Special Agent Jackson, I will always have something hanging over your head. Special Agent with a history of infidelity who drove a vulnerable woman to kill herself."

Nate turned around. "Hey, fill me in on something. What happened in Arizona and California? Some women claimed you groped them in hypnotherapy and harassed them? Tried to sleep with one of them? And you paid them to keep quiet? Isn't that why you don't do family therapy anymore?"

Anthony froze, eyes big, mouth open.

"You left out one important detail about Shawnee. She was loose, and she wanted to change, but when she did, it drove *you* crazy because you couldn't control her anymore. You were the one who filled her head and drove her insane." Nate stepped off again. "I do agree with you on one thing, Dr. Carone, or whatever you call yourself. I am smarter than you thought. And I'm one hell of an agent. The prize goes to the wisest, not the strongest."

Nate walked back to Marcus and Darius, feeling satisfied, confident that he'd shut Anthony up for good. But he couldn't get the torment off his back. Anthony might have been setting Nate up, but he was doing it with the truth. Shawnee, out of desperation to change, had fallen off the deep end and ended up trying to hit her head in shallow water. Nate had escaped death, but Darius could easily have taken his place if Shawnee had been willing to drag him along.

This, Nate's premeditated murder, Nate knew for sure had been set in motion for one simple reason: condoms. Shawnee had been too certain the baby was Nate's child. That level of confidence when using condoms meant one thing—she was devious as hell and, when it went awry on her, she literally jumped off a cliff.

What the hell did I do?

Arianna had almost fallen into the hands of a psychopath, Darius had almost fallen to his death, and Marcus had almost fallen straight into divorce.

For months, Nate had felt enough remorse over the affair's fallout. Now he was drowning in its untapped potential.

He walked back to his car and let Darius inside.

"What's wrong with you?" Marcus asked. "You look whiter than your wife."

"I was right."

"About what?"

"She injected that shit."

Nate drove off knowing that all the bullets he'd dodged in Baltimore were miniscule compared to the one he'd dodged in a San Antonio motel room. He kept quiet the entire ride to Darius's favorite pizza joint, as he came to realize that he couldn't live with his actions anymore.

Nate told Darius to go inside and get them a table.

"What's up with you, Nate?"

Nate watched Darius walk into the restaurant. He looked at Marcus. "We've been best friends for years."

"You're weirding me out, Nate."'

Nate sounded defeated. "My son is hiding the purse of a suicide victim I had an affair with. How low did I go?"

"Nate."

"I need to fly to Baltimore. And I need you by my side. I'm gonna need the support."

"Why?"

"I don't deserve the shield."

"Oh, c'mon. That's stupid. It was a *mistake*, Nate."

"I'm resigning, Marcus. And I'm telling Agent Greene everything."

"And your family?"

"I'll make it work. At least I won't be living a lie."

"You're not living a lie."

"What would you call it?"

Chapter 61

The waves of the Atlantic Ocean crashed around the edges of Baltimore's Inner Harbor. A scattering of people walked the brick sidewalk in the brisk morning air. Nate and Marcus were attempting to get an early start on using their senses—the feel of the nautical wind, the smell of coffee, the sight of people getting ready to open their doors, or shut them, depending on the business, the taste of pastries, and the sounds of boats and waves. Nate absorbed the familiar environment, feeling like a local. Marcus cursed him out for not reminding him about the temperature difference.

They stopped at a unique lamppost, one with a square light shade. Looking across the water, over the ships and to the aquarium, Nate said nothing. Agent Greene was sitting on a nearby bench.

"Give me a minute, Marcus," Nate said. Then he sat next to his boss.

"I'm here," Agent Greene said. "What's so important you have me freezing my balls off?"

Nate handed him his gun, his badge, and the cellphone retrieved from the purse. Then he confessed all. "I've covered up so much shit. I don't deserve the badge."

Agent Greene looked at Nate's credentials and the weapon. He set them down on the bench beside him. Then he looked over to the water, and to the aquarium, still holding the cellphone.

Nate felt lighter. He was freed from his baggage, even though he'd just given up the one thing that made him who he was—the law.

"You ever wonder what those triangles are on top of the aquarium?" Agent Greene asked.

"Can't say I have." Nate shrugged.

"You ever watch the paddle boats go by?"

"Uh, no."

"Am I wasting your time, Agent Jackson?"

"Kinda."

"Good." Agent Greene got up. "Because you're wasting mine. Pick up your goddamned gun. Don't forget that shield you love to flash."

Stunned, Nate took back his gun, his badge, his soul.

Agent Greene walked over to a trash can. Violently, he threw down the phone and stepped on it, smashing it into bits. Nate stared, mortified by Agent Greene's reaction, yet relieved, because he knew what it meant.

"We're not perfect, Jackson," Agent Greene said as he put his final footprints on the phone. "We break rules. Shit, if we were perfect, or had superpowers, winning the war on drugs would be a slam-dunk. We're just men, trying to do what we can, while we can."

As Agent Greene preached, Nate knew this was coming from a personal point-of-view. It was obvious his boss had his own iniquities.

"I'm not gonna lose one of my best people because he gets a shot of morality and wants to confess his sins," Agent Greene said, before bending down and picking up the pieces of the cell phone. He threw them into the trash. Next, he pulled out his lighter, held the tiny SIM card between his fingers, and then burned Nate's secrets.

"Thanks," Nate said.

"Don't flatter yourself. I'm not doing it for you. I'm doing it for Baltimore."

Nate shook his head humbly in agreement and followed his boss's lead. He stood up. "See you in two weeks."

"Next week. Brick shot up a church last night trying to kill Reese's mother in retaliation for his thugs taking his corners. Killed four people."

"Did he get his mother?"

"Yep."

"Baltimore's about to get bloody as shit."

"At first, I thought you'd called me here to request a transfer to Texas because it was getting too rough up in these parts."

"Not a chance."

Agent Greene nodded. Nate felt as if his boss was leaving something unsaid. "Is that it?"

"You're not the only one who's made the mistake. You just got caught up worse than others. It doesn't make you a bad man. It makes you human."

"I'm trying to believe that. It's hard though, when somebody dies because of it."

"But you've learned from it, and you'll get through it."

"My family is everything."

"It always is and always should be," Agent Greene said. "Anything else you've imploded I need to know about?"

"No, but I do have one more trip to make. I need a huge favor."

"I'm afraid to ask."

Nate explained his situation. Agent Greene seemed hesitant to give him what he and Dave always referred to as the Greene light. "Again? Last time was different. Rollins helped you because it was Arianna, not you. I can't condone you going there. I may as well go to jail now for accessory."

"I'm not gonna kill him, I promise."

"Why do you have to do this?"

"I wasn't there for Arianna. She confronted the biggest pain of her life, and I was nowhere to be found."

"You're there now."

"Boss, c'mon, he burned her chest beyond recognition. He told her he would always be her nightmare.

457

You've always said you were just like me back in the day. Sure, I'm there now, but it's not the same."

"Not the same as thrashing him?"

"I am who I am. I'm not apologizing for it anymore."

"You're asking for a lot, Jackson."

"I haven't been fair to her. I've cheated, I've ignored her, hell, the day I told her about my affair I blamed her for holding me back because she was white, and then in the same minute I turned around and tore my goddamned house to pieces because she threw race back in my face."

"I'm not gonna lie. You can be an asshole."

"So can you. So can Graffiti. So can my best friend." Nate nodded at Marcus who stood freezing a few feet away. "I don't excuse it, but name one alpha male who isn't sometimes. The most I can do is rectify the situation the only way I know how, and grow into a better man."

"What else are you trying rectify, Jackson?"

"I don't know what you mean."

"Yeah, you do."

Nate quickly caught on—the bastard from the basement. He'd put a bullet in his brain, denying his victims any justice, and himself any closure. "I need this."

"You're gonna do it regardless of what I say, aren't you?"

Nate pleaded. "He sexually assaulted my *wife*, Agent Greene. That woman's never hurt anybody her whole life, and he terrorized her." Nate's voice cracked as he fought to stay hardcore and represent, as he would say, the alpha male. "That woman is my life. And now I have to look at her body, every day, and think about the pain she went through. I can't let it go, Agent Greene. I can't. Not this time."

"Eight years?"

"Yep."

Agent Greene took a second to think. "Okay, you have my backing. But if you kill him, you're done with the DEA along with your days as a free man. I don't care how elite you are."

"Ending his life would let him off too easy. You know that all too well."

"We finally agree on something. Now get your ass out of here before we start believing we actually had this conversation."

"I'll keep you posted." Nate walked off.

"Nate."

Nate stopped, hearing for the first time his boss use his first name. "Yeah?"

"You're right."

"About?"

"I would have done him."

"I know."

"When you're in that room, and you wanna kill this guy, you remember—there's a reason why you're the youngest agent to ever make six-figures in the DEA. That's a legacy you don't wanna mess with, my friend."

"Boss, I could cure cancer and still not get the respect you get."

"Why the hell do you think you're on my team?"

Agent Greene walked away and left Nate standing in the cold, harbor air.

Chapter 62

It had been a while since Nate had come back to the place his life began as a young man learning to live and love. A little farther north, and colder and more desolate than he'd experienced in college, but no less vital a place for Nate to end this chapter, this story of his life so far. He prayed for strength, prayed for restraint, and prayed for vindication and understanding from the Lord as to why he had to do this. Years of pain swirled in a nightmarish haze had come down to a day of reckoning a certain inmate would never forget.

Halloween had haunted its way out, making room for a hearty Thanksgiving and a peaceful Christmas, plus Black Friday in-between, the event where Pam kept his wife out of the house from pre-dawn to the black of night. The winter season was now ending and riding the coattails of late February, waiting for March to pick it up.

Nate stepped out of the rental car in Mountain City and smashed the snow under his feet. Certain parts of the country, it seemed, stayed at sub-zero despite the certainty of spring.

He analyzed the prison. "Finally," he said to himself.

Nate put his hand on his weapon, trying to decide whether it would serve as a liability to his freedom if he couldn't contain his anger during the confrontation. Then he shut the driver's-side door, leaving his weapon by his side as he read the sign calling for no weapons in the facility. *There is no way in hell I'm walking into a maximum security prison unarmed.*

The long concrete sidewalk seemed sinisterly welcoming as Nate readied himself for a retribution void of taking Nightmare's life. He remained composed, committed to staying that way, and prepared to walk down the path that had taken Agent Greene months to clear.

Nate strode down the sidewalk, to him, a journey of a thousand miles. He reflected on his long road to manhood with each step toward the door. He thought about pain wrapped up in growth, agony wrapped up in redemption. Counseling had been long overdue, and so far, it was going okay. He'd stormed out of the counselor's office a couple of times when Darius reminded him that he wasn't a perfect father, and when he couldn't stomach it as Arianna described Nightmare, and when she brought out that he still had to deal with things long ago involving tortured girls left to die in a filthy basement. That was the toughest to take. When the counselor would ask the kids to wait outside, Nate knew he was about to learn more about quarters, curling irons, and stolen childhoods wrapped up in chains.

But he always returned. "You don't have to say a word, as long as you return," Arianna would say.

To help him return, he returned to the Word. He didn't tote a Bible twenty-four-seven, he didn't cite Scripture every minute of the day, and he didn't attend service every week. He didn't listen to much gospel and remained loyal to his explicit lyrics. But, he did download a Bible app and attended service with his family when he could. He'd learned the power of prayer, and prayed daily. Nate continued to mentor, continued to check clothing, continued to walk the line, up and down. But he'd also begun telling the alternative students to pray for strength when things got tough, and pray for wisdom whenever Reese rolled up in all his luxury.

Nate reached the guard who was standing outside the door waiting on him. They nodded to each other. Then Nate walked alone into the facility. He took off his shades and placed them in the pocket of his leather jacket.

The warden was waiting for him.

"I appreciate you arranging this," Nate said.

"I've bent over backwards to accommodate the DEA. But this is the last time."

They briefly spoke about rules and regulations, policies and procedures. The warden asked Nate if he had any questions. Nate looked around the facility, picturing Arianna walking down the hall without him. "Was she scared? My wife?"

"I think so. She was shaking pretty badly when I met her."

Nate nodded, understanding how intimidated a woman could feel walking into a prison housing rapists and murderers.

"I don't mean to get personal," the warden said, "but does she call you *Nathan*?"

"The only one who does. I think she copyrighted that shit. Why?"

"Right after I walked into the room, she was standing near the window, close to the door. She whispered something that sounded like 'Nathan.' I think I was the only one who heard her. Didn't think anything of it at first. She clearly wanted you."

"I see." Nate was already on fire. The warden probably had no idea he'd just poured more gasoline onto Nate's need to avenge Arianna. "Take me to him *now*."

"I need your weapon," the warden said. "Not making this mistake again."

Nate put his hand on his gun, but didn't move any further. The weapon wasn't just a reflection of power, but also of perseverance and pride at beating the odds and not ending up in prison himself. Stripping Nate of that symbolism in order to protect the life of the inmate who'd shredded Arianna's body to shrapnel made Nate want to kick the warden in his teeth. But rules were rules, and Nate knew the warden had a boss and wanted to keep his job. Plus, Agent Greene had fought hard for Nate, and Nate wasn't about to disrespect *his* boss by arguing with the leader of a maximum security prison.

He reluctantly began to unhook his weapon as the warden stood there waiting.

"He keeps his gun," said a voice that hit every angle like a pool ball struck by a strong-armed, calculated cue stick.

The warden and Nate looked back. "Boss?"

Agent Greene was standing there, Dave at his side, his entire team in tow. "We're in this together, Jack," Dave said, as if he were ready to take Nightmare down himself.

"Always," Nate replied. Then he nodded to Agent Greene, a nonverbal thank you for showing up and standing by him.

"I'm taking his weapon, Fenton," the warden said.

Nate and Dave looked at each other; the use of first names indicated a personal relationship between the warden and their boss.

"I take full responsibility. It's a federal matter now," Agent Greene said.

"He shoots him, it's on you," the warden said.

They walked down the corridor to the meeting room. Nate looked through the glass, getting his *second* glimpse of the reason his life had spun out of control. He remembered a day back in college when he'd gone to Arianna's neighborhood. "I've seen this bastard before."

"Where, Jack?"

"Years ago, I saw a man peeking out through a curtain near Arianna's place. It creeped my ass out to no end. It was him."

"Now he gets a second look at you," Dave said.

"Yep."

"Where's his attorney?" Dave asked the warden. Nate continued to stare at Nightmare, picturing the years he'd tortured Arianna.

"Told the inmate he was getting another visit, said he didn't need representation." The warden looked through the glass.

"Did you say *visit*, or *visitor*?" Nate asked.

"Visit, I think."

"Cool."

"What does that mean, Jack?"

"It means this stupid bitch doesn't realize my big ass is the one standing behind this glass." Nate looked at the warden. "Uncuff him. I don't want, or need, protection."

"No." The warden stood defiantly. "And you're not to lay a hand on him. I can't have this in my prison. We made special arrangements for your wife, but this is different. You'll kill him."

"Uncuff him, Walter," Agent Greene said.

The warden and Agent Greene had a brief interaction, the warden staring at Agent Greene like he was crazy, Agent Greene looking back with authority, as if he was far from insane.

The warden shook this head, gave the order. "Uncuff the bastard." He looked at Agent Greene. "You've put a lot of faith in your agent, friend." He stared Nate down. "I sure hope it's not misplaced."

Nate glanced at Dave, then his team, and lastly at Agent Greene, the mentor, the father figure, and the only man who, at times, could calm Nate down and make him listen to reason.

Just remember, no matter how good you think you are, there is always somebody else thinking the same thing. The prize goes to the wisest, not the strongest.

"Remember what you stand to lose, Supervisory Special Agent," Agent Greene said to Nate. "What we *both* stand to lose."

Nate nodded and opened the door. Agent Greene held the door open, a nonverbal order implying that Nate wasn't to shut it.

Nightmare whispered something about how Arianna was back for more. Nate entered the room, took off his jacket, and placed it over a chair. His arms looked as if they were about to rip apart the short sleeves of his T-shirt. Nightmare stared at Nate as if he were the reaper coming to escort Nightmare's soul to hell.

"Expecting somebody a lot smaller without a dick?" Nate asked, receiving a blank stare in reply. "Surprise, motherfucker."

Nightmare looked as if he was about to piss on himself.

Nate attacked like a Rottweiler that hadn't been fed in weeks. "Eight years?" A minute for each year was Nate's plan, but after two minutes, the sounds of tables, chairs, and Nightmare violently toppling over ceased. Nate had to stop early because he was short of killing the man. Each blow, Nate was sure, brought with it a massive bruise, broken bone, or some other busted body part.

He bent down and grabbed Nightmare by the neck to give him one last word. "If I wasn't a self-respecting officer of the law, or an even better man, I would take a broomstick and jack your insides *up*." Nate threw him down and kicked him in the stomach. "That's for burning her."

Nate backed up. The anger he thought he could control went out of control, and he drew his weapon.

Dave jerked and moved to enter the room. Agent Greene stopped him. "He won't."

This moment, Nate's next choice, would be the culmination of all he'd learned these past couple of years. The pain, the lies, the tears, the love. Could he muster enough self-discipline to leave Nightmare alive, or would he take his kill shot on an unarmed man, and become a savage too? Would he be justified? Would losing everything he ever fought for be worth taking this scum's life?

Nate thought of his family and the promise he'd made to his boss about keeping this bastard alive, the faith Agent Greene had placed in a hand holding a loaded gun. Then he thought of spending his life, what would be left of it, locked up, his legacy destroyed, his kids growing up with a felon for a father, his wife, now in her second trimester, giving birth to their baby girl by herself.

Nate took in all his lessons. He thought about everything he had overcome and all he'd learned. Finally, Nate lowered his firearm and stood over Nightmare. "You will see my face at every hearing, every discussion, and everything else that has to do with your fate at this prison. If a piece of paper so much as gets filed with your name on it, I will hear about it, and you will see me. Hell, I might just drop by for no goddamned reason. Your stupid ass is gonna see me so much, you'll believe I never left this prison. You won't even be able to take a shit without thinking I'm there."

Nate got close to his ear. "And when they strap you down in Nashville and prep that needle, I'm gonna personally take control of that shit and push all that phenobarbital straight into your veins. Until then? Good luck going to sleep."

A few last painful grunts preceded Nate's departure. He looked back. "Who's the nightmare now, bitch?"

Nate walked out of the room. He looked at Agent Greene. Nate's boss in turn looked at the warden and thanked him on behalf of Nate and the DEA. Then he looked at his people. The air made it extremely clear. Nobody was to move, or ever move, unless Agent Greene said so. "Let's go."

They walked off, Agent Greene leading the pack. Nate and Dave flanked right behind him, on either side, with the rest of the team closely behind.

With each step, the barrage of DEA agents walking down the hall made every guard and employee stop and part. The group walked outside and down the cement steps, as if the stairs were servants to Agent Greene's and his agents' every move.

The team disbursed to their transportation and left. Nate thanked his boss and his battle buddy.

"Rayburn, go wait in the car," Agent Greene said.

"Again?"

"Trust me, one day it'll be Jackson's turn. Go."

Dave left, ranting like a little kid.

"Boss, thank you for showing up."

"I figured you'd get some resistance, Jackson. You know why I brought the team, right?"

"Ride or die?"

"Uh, no. Try again."

"To show them I can restrain myself?"

"Close."

"Help me out here."

"When I was coming up in the DEA, times were different. We could do whatever it took, to bring down anybody. Nowadays, it's all about following all these procedures in the name of humanity. The only way, I mean the *only* way, we can do our jobs successfully is to sometimes bend the rules just shy of breaking them. That's a skill you, and your crazy-ass riding partner over there, have mastered. The team needed to see you use your head before you crossed a line you could never reverse."

"You just spent a lot of taxpayer dollars for them to see me two seconds short of bashing in a guy's skull."

"It's called investing in human capital for the enhancement of organizational development in the new learning culture of a more empowering organization."

"Nice."

"You're not the only one married to an MBA, Jackson."

"I see that."

"One more thing." Agent Greene reached inside his jacket pocket and pulled out a yellow envelope. It appeared to be a card addressed to Nate, mailed to the Baltimore field office. "This came for you. Figured it couldn't wait."

Nate opened the envelope and read the card. A yellow rose decorated the front of the card, and it was blank inside except for the sender's words.

Agent Jackson,

You probably don't remember me, but I was the girl in that awful basement some years back. The one you picked up off the floor and carried upstairs. It seems like a lifetime ago, yet yesterday.

Anyway, I thought it was time to reach out.

I don't know how much you remember. But I still remember all of it, and you need to know why. I remember how everybody tried to get close to me and I freaked out. You looked so reluctant to try, like a rookie or something. But then you walked up after I bit one of the officers. You crouched down beside me and told me that you knew I had been through a lot, but if I didn't let you guys touch me, then I had to get up and walk out of there myself, and you didn't think I was ready to do that. Then you told me I had to be strong because I had to help you be strong, and that maybe we could be strong together. Then you looked up to the basement window and told me, "The sun is missing one of its survivors. What are we gonna do about that?" Then I let you carry me upstairs.

Because of you, I never considered myself a victim, even though others treated me like one. It's as if you set the tone for my recovery. I became that survivor, got married, and had a son. We named him Nathaniel Darius. I hope you don't mind.

I've kept up with you. I know you have a young son who suffers from articulation disorder. It's ironic because I became a speech pathologist after my ordeal. I didn't speak for a year after I was rescued. The trauma, I guess. As I got better, I became intrigued with the human voice. Isn't that strange? Now I never shut up.

Nate smiled and chuckled.

Anyway, I wanted to drop you a line and let you know you saved me, in more ways than one. I run a center in Annapolis now, for victims of sexual assault who have trouble speaking about their ordeal. Perhaps you could stop by and say hello one day.

Well, I guess I should go. I hope this letter finds you well. Take care, Agent Jackson.

Your friend,

Linda

Nate's feet felt stuck to the snow, his heart stuck in his throat, his tears stuck frozen to his face. He couldn't believe it. "She said I saved her."

"Not a bad way to go home, is it?"

Nate felt as if scores of doves we're flying off his shoulders. "Now I know how my wife felt when she learned she didn't have to hide her past from me anymore."

"Yep. Now, let it go. And let it be done, Jackson." Agent Greene nodded before walking off. He looked back. "By the way, tell Arianna I'm still waiting on my cream cheese pies to show up at her shop."

Nate smiled in his relief, chuckled at his boss's relentless need for sweets. "Will do."

"Don't forget."

"Won't. So, I guess I'm free to go?"

"For now... or until the next time you and Agent Rayburn do something incredibly stupid and very normal I have to answer for."

"That'll be next week then." Nate chuckled.

"Don't get smart. I'm not that guy you just waxed the floor with. Meeting next Thursday. Expect to see you, Jackson."

Nate pulled into the driveway late that night, having taken a connection from Mountain City, to Nashville, to San Antonio. The drive from the airport to Stone Oak took some time because of an accident on the outer loop. Thankfully, he was finally home and, by his standards, vindicated.

He went upstairs with a gallon of ice cream and a jar of sundae topping. Arianna was standing in the bedroom doorway, waiting for him, naked, belly and all, as she rubbed across their baby girl.

The ice cream met its fate, alone, melting on the dresser as Nate ate another sweet dessert, unaware that, in a city named Baltimore, a drug lord had just blown up a Mercedes parked in front of a DEA field office.

Epilogue

"Please, help me!"

Nate stood at the foot of the stairs. The building had a majestic feel, two gold-trimmed staircases coiled around either side of a beautiful table highlighting the foyer. Perhaps it was a castle, or a glimpse of what Heaven would look like. Nate wasn't sure why this woman in a white dress had run into the building from an open field. He wasn't sure why he'd been in that field in the first place. All he knew was that this lady needed saving—so he'd run after her.

Nate followed her up the stairs until they reached the top, where the staircases came together, connected by a loft. He reached out to touch this mysterious woman, to save her from whatever she'd escaped.

But Nightmare emerged and stabbed the woman in her stomach. Then he slit her throat. She fell into Nate's arms, blood coating her dress and Nate's badge as she gagged and gasped for air. Nate was helpless as she died in his grasp. Nightmare laughed. Nate still held the beautiful soul with the blurred face.

Nate looked up as Nightmare faded. The victim opened her eyes and asked Nate how come he hadn't saved her. She laughed with a sound that grew louder and louder until it echoed around the vacant mansion. Then Zach, body charred by the explosion that had killed him, emerged at the top of the furthest staircase. His skin was red, peeling in layers, turning jet-black; his face morphed into a skull held together with burnt tissue. Startled, Nate dropped the woman. In the deep voice of a demon, Zach told Nate he had failed to save yet another victim.

Nate backed up and fell down the stairs. The hum of a phone ringing jolted him awake.

He sat up, skin moist, heart racing, phone ringing. He looked over at Arianna, who lay still in her slumber. *Good God, what just happened?*

Marcus hung up and texted: *Urgent.*

Nate was so rattled he couldn't even process the text. He got up and peeked in on his sons before going downstairs. He checked the doors, made sure they were locked. Then he went into the basement, put in the code to unlock his arsenal (he'd upgraded it once he'd learned how close Darius had come to grabbing a weapon), counted his guns, and shut the safe. The house was eerily dark, except for the subtle light shining over the stove from the vent above.

Nate walked past the kitchen and looked outside. The neighborhood was quiet, dark, peaceful, with no activity at 2 a.m.

The safe upstairs lay behind Nate's suits, the ones he rarely wore except for court. He unlocked the safe and pulled out the loaded Glock before going back to bed armed and dangerously spooked.

Marcus called again.

Nate took a deep breath and answered. "What's wrong?"

"Meet me at the racetrack off I-10. And play it cool with Arianna."

"It's after midnight. How cool can I be?"

"You need to see this. Now."

Nate woke Arianna, made an excuse about Marcus having a flat, hopped into his car, and jumped onto the I-10 heading toward Houston until he reached the outskirts of San

Antonio. He pulled in and drove around to the back of the track. There, he saw Marcus's truck and a black sedan. Marcus was leaning against the sedan, arms folded, looking ready to kill anybody who stepped in front of him. "Before you say anything, I'm just as surprised as you." He opened the door, and Nate got into the backseat. Marcus entered next.

Nate looked at the disguised driver, who was wearing a baseball cap, glasses, and a black jacket collared up his entire neck. Then he looked at the man sitting next to him. Nate's heart raced and his breathing spiked, his joy trying desperately to break through his anger. He sat frozen inside the conflicting emotions that were stopping him from pulverizing his friend like a blender to ice. "Guess Eva wasn't crazy after all. I don't know if we should jump for joy, or fuck your lying ass up."

Zach leaned forward. "I missed your volatile ass too, Nate."

Nate contemplated punching Zach in the face. Then Dave called. *What now?* Before Nate could answer, a muffled voice came from the trunk, along with the bang of pounding feet.

Marcus looked toward the back. "You have somebody in the goddamned trunk, Zach?"

"*I* do," said the driver. Marcus zeroed in on his face after he recognized the voice. "D.J.?" He looked back at Zach. "You better start talking. Now!"

"We did this for you," Zach said. "For us."

The pounding continued. D.J. opened the door. "Hold on, Sanchez. Let me quiet his ass up."

"Who's in the trunk?" Marcus asked.

D.J. looked into the backseat. "Kyle Ridgeland...the man who killed your mother."

Nate restrained Marcus with all he had, as Dave attempted yet another call.

Acknowledgements

My manuscript passed through many hands to become what I consider a fine work of art. Beginning in the early millennium, until now, I need to thank many people.

To my sons, DeVante and Devin, a mother's love knows no boundaries. I am so proud of both of you.

To my family and friends, fourteen years is a long time. There are far too many of you to name. I would never be able to live with myself if I failed to mention one of you, so I think it is best if I thank you this way. As the journey continues, I will remember you.

And a special thank you to those who purchased *Understanding the Affair*, the original work with the original title before Misha and her crew gave it a much needed oil-change. All of you bought my book before it was cool, and I will never forget it.

This brings me to Misha, Amaya, and Cindy of Eliseon Marketing. Thank you for your editorial wisdom.

To Marti Kanna of New Leaf Editing, thank you for my first introduction into the world of revision and for continuing with me.

To the Drug Enforcement Administration, thank you for lending me a consultant and helping me to NOT look like a complete and total idiot while trying to describe a day in the life of a DEA special agent.

To Assistant Chief Billy Wusterhausen of the Round Rock, Texas, Fire and Emergency Services Department, thank you for helping me learn the intricacies of fires and burns.

To Nancy Gwin Walker, Executive Director of the Funeral Consumers Alliance of Central Texas, thank you for taking the time to point me in the right direction to learn about Texas funeral laws.

To Dr. Lamar Hankins, Attorney, President Emeritus, Funeral Consumers Alliance of Central Texas, thank you for the valuable insight into the legality of burials in Texas.

To Dr. Rochelle Hall-Schwarz, Ph.D., LPC-S., thank you for your education in victimology.

To Amina Cain, my thesis mentor for my Master of Fine Arts in creative writing, thank you for your guidance along the way.

To Tom Hyman, my guide through the Long Ridge Writers' Group's *Breaking Into Print* writing course, thank you for your feedback on my short works. They helped shape me into the writer I am.

To my focus group, Jeff, Fleur, Charlene, Chris, Leigh, and Lisa, thank you for your critiques.

To the editors at *WOW! Women on Writing* magazine, thank you for the critiques. They helped tighten my writing.

Most importantly, best for last, thank you, God, for the ability to channel my thoughts into something worth reading. I know it is by You that I have the talent to do what I do.

www.ingramcontent.com/pod-product-compliance
Lightning Source LLC
Chambersburg PA
CBHW021118260626
47169CB00005B/1335